MURDER MOST PUBLIC

A US Marshal Ward Wilkinson Murder Mystery Adventure

James T. Siburt

Cover design by Vila Design

Published by Van Rye Publishing, LLC
Ann Arbor, MI
www.vanryepublishing.com

ISBN: 978-1-957906-16-4 (paperback)
ISBN: 978-1-957906-17-1 (ebook)
Library of Congress Control Number: 2024949523

Dedication

In memory of my parents, Paul and Wilda Siburt.

For Diane, my wife, who suffers my hours in front of the computer with equanimity, critiques my initial efforts, and, on numerous occasions, employs her historical knowledge of women's clothing and fashions to save me from considerable embarrassment.

And in fond memory of my mentor and dear friend, Dr. Leland R. Johnson, who will always be remembered for his sage advice and boundless encouragement.

Contents

Prologue

UNBIDDEN, HIS EYES again turned to the grandfather clock that sat along the far wall, and he cursed in disgust. Two damned minutes since the last time he looked. With a sigh of exasperation or perhaps inevitability, he removed his work garment and donned a long-tailed black coat over his shirt. With his left hand, he grasped a small cloth bag, and with the right, a short-barreled revolver. He thrust the revolver into the right-hand pocket of the coat. The clock hand, inexorable and insensible to his inner torment, advanced once more as he shut the door and started up the street. For the hundredth time, he asked himself, "How the hell did I get entangled in such an appalling mess?"

From his first step into the street, the desire welled within him to go back inside and stay there. His feet felt like great blocks of wood, demanding all his strength to move ahead. Despite the coolness of the early spring day, he felt the sweat pop out on his back, roll from his armpits, and drip down his chest. He could feel the blood pounding in his ears, his heart hammering against his ribs, and a sour rising in his throat that made him gag. He was afraid, terrified even, that the clock in his shop, now ringing in the noon hour, heralded his death.

Today was unlike any other Saturday in his memory; the street was empty. Townspeople, none having any desire to be a bystander that got injured or worse, were remaining indoors until this business concluded. If things went horribly wrong, they could claim under later questioning that they'd seen or heard nothing. He passed the restaurant that flanked his business and reached the bricked storefront of the dry goods store when he saw the man he was to meet coming toward him. The man looked scared as well.

Beyond the dry goods store lay a vacant lot, and he slowed his pace to allow the man to close on the place they had designated to meet. Once more, the terrible need to flee enveloped him—a dread that required all his steadfastness not to waver. Should he backpedal, the people of the town would thereafter look upon him with disdain. A yellow coward, they'd proclaim him. He wouldn't blame them if they did. Chastened by the thought, his lips thinned into a grim, determined line, and he forged ahead. The two of them were now fifty feet apart.

He stared with a bleak expression at the approaching man, who had likewise dressed for the occasion in a long black coat. In the man's left hand was a cloth bag, and somewhere on his person was a concealed pistol. The man's face was red as a beet, and he walked in a bent-forward, crab-like fashion as if some invisible weight impeded his progress. He wondered what he would do if the man turned and ran.

The next building along the street, flanked by vacant lots on both sides, was the town saloon—a brick edifice that attracted more business than he thought fitting. All too many men in town, some near-hopeless drunkards, habituated themselves to the place, giving most of their earnings for strong drink. Usually well attended, often boisterous, the saloon now was eerily quiet. The realization that everyone in town must know what was occurring frightened him more than anything he'd yet contemplated.

Along the front corner of the saloon, a third man slumped carelessly against the bricks. Muscular and powerfully built, although not exceptionally tall, he had a handsome, if rather egotistical, face. His features, framed with flaming red hair and luxuriant sideburns, were fair and marked with many freckles. He had a firm, clean-shaven chin, cornflower blue eyes containing not the slightest hint of warmth, and full lips that he curved in an amused grin of unconcern.

Now a few feet apart, the two men stared at each other with deadly intensity. The man to their right disengaged from the wall of the saloon, and in unison, they turned toward him. The third man still had that impudent, self-assured smile plastered on his face, and his eyes retained their predatory look. It was the kind a hawk displays as it swoops down on a field mouse. He started toward them, his gaze focused on the cloth bags in their hands, when both frightened men hurled the bags to the ground and began clawing pistols from the pockets of their coats.

The amused expression on the red-haired man's face turned startled, then furious. The treacherous bastards had come to kill him. With a snarl, he backed away, tugging a pearl-handled .45-caliber Colt revolver from his waistband. As he yanked it free, he saw the man on his right fumble an attempt to cock his weapon, then drop it in the street. Clumsy sonofabitch. He flung himself to the ground just as the man on his left squeezed the trigger of his weapon.

The roar of the report drowned out the whine of the bullet as it ricocheted away. The red-haired man, his features flush with fury, vaulted onto his left knee, pulled back the hammer on the Colt, and leveled the gun at the man who'd fired at him. He'd show these two the errors of their ways, which would be a damn fine lesson to anyone else in this community that took a notion to defy him. He was taking careful aim when another violent detonation echoed off the walls of the adjacent buildings.

The bullet struck the red-haired man in the back, tearing through his lungs and throwing him forward into the dirt. In a reflex action, he pulled the trigger of the Colt, but the bullet thudded uselessly into the hard-packed earth. He fell on his side, struggled to right himself, then collapsed as a torrent of blood gurgled from his mouth. Another lead slug slammed into him, and then another. By this time, however, he was oblivious to their effect. Foreign hands rummaged through his pants pockets and then inside his coat, and having discovered what they were seeking, his killers sprinted behind the saloon and disappeared from sight.

Several minutes passed before anyone ventured forth from their homes or shops to investigate the commotion. Some shared glances of constrained elation, while others viewed the scene with worry and distaste. Regardless of their feelings, all of them agreed about the shooting. Some admitted to hearing firing, but none would say they had seen anyone on the street, seen anyone talking with the dead man, or seen anything at all. The killers, known to all of those present, had disappeared into the afternoon glare as swiftly and silently as they had come.

Chapter 1

A MONTH LATER, US Marshal Ward Wilkinson and his deputy, Tom Seibert, were spending the morning in their Broad Street, Nashville, Tennessee office performing the dull, administrative chores of file purging, file creation, and report writing. From a board on the wall, Ward stripped away several wanted posters of men now behind bars or interred in a cemetery, tossing them in the waste bin. "Glad to be done with Matheson here," he commented, "a double murderer and stagecoach bandit." Tom grunted an assent, but the nib of his pen never ceased scratching the paper laid before him. The monosyllabic reply drew a quick grin from Wilkinson. He and Tom had worked together for a long time and were the closest of friends.

When an hour had passed, the waste bin overflowed with ancient, dusty parchment, and some of the yellowed sheets lay scattered about the floor. Wilkinson replaced the discards with new folders and filed them in alphabetical order. Seibert—at last finished with a multitude of tasks related to paying fees and expenses of federal court clerks, the US Attorney, and recent jurors and witnesses—had likewise amassed an impressive pile of summonses, writs, warrants, and other orders of the court. The deputy proceeded briskly to collect the debris from the floor, then swept it; US Marshals had no budget for janitors. Tired of this labor and ready for lunch, Ward was about to call a halt when knuckles rapped against the office door, and a messenger, still a lad the lawman noted, entered the room with a small sheet of notepaper folded in half. Giving the boy a penny, Ward waited until he left the office, then unbent the crease in the note and straightened it. Lunch would have to wait.

"Judge Morton wants to see me right away, Tom. I was going to suggest we go down to Market Street and wash down this dust with a quart of cider. If you wish, go home and eat with Frances. Since I'm wanted at the courthouse, I'll go back downtown and see Charlotte after I'm done."

"Is she feeling alright today?"

"No more morning sickness if that's what you mean. Since me and Anna never had children and since this is Charlotte's first, neither of us expected it."

"When you see the judge, tell him I've hired his bailiff and other personnel for his upcoming trial. Also, I've paid Sheriff Culver for the past quarter's prisoner space and maintenance."

"I'll be sure and pass along all this good news. I'm grateful," Ward concluded with a frown of concern, "that we've been diligent these last couple of days getting all this donkey work out of the way. Judge Morton doesn't summon me without a particular reason in mind. Be prepared; we're about to receive a fresh case. See you this afternoon, Tom."

The early spring day felt unseasonably warm when Wilkinson stepped into the street, but it was nothing like it would become once the scorching heat of summer arrived. Yesterday's light rain showers were keeping down the choking clouds of limestone dust from the thoroughfares. Had it been a downpour, the roadbed would still be a muddy slime. Unavoidable, though, was the stench. The odor of the city center, swept along by a swirling, westerly breeze, caused Ward's nose to wrinkle in complaint. "Somehow, someway," he muttered to himself, "I've got to find a cool climate for Charlotte to spend the last weeks of her pregnancy and convince her not to be headstrong about going. I don't want her in town when the baby comes."

Wilkinson could see a multitude of reasons for concern. Dray vehicles, carriages, and other conveyances clogged the streets. Toward the river, east on Broad, a wagon carrying barrels approached while he trudged uphill toward the Customs House. The team, four large, dappled gray draft horses, strained against their black harness, and their ponderous hooves thudded against the pavement. Presently, one raised its tail and loosed an enormous mound of manure on the roadbed. The iron-rimmed wheels mashed the dung into the crushed stone, and before the wagon traveled ten feet, a party of flies descended on the fresh droppings. The flying insects, Wilkinson grimly determined, represented only an advance guard of the brigades that would later appear.

Further along the street, near a puddle of urine, lay the body of a dead dog. It, too, had attracted a swarm of flies, and the putrid, nauseating smell of decomposition was overpowering. To the north of Broad, up the cross streets to Ward's right, people pitched their garbage, kitchen offal, fireplace ashes, chamber pot effluent, and anything else they didn't damn well want to dispose of properly into the alleys or even the streets themselves. The runoff from rainstorms soon sluiced this muck downward from the higher ground to where he now passed. This resulted in the city scavenger laboring six days a week to load the waste, animal corpses, and other objectionable articles on his reeking cart and throw the contents into the Cumberland River. It was a common sight to see rotting carcasses bobbing on the surface of the waters.

Likewise common was Davidson County Sheriff Ross Culver rounding up every barfly, vagrant, and ne'er-do-well he could find, combining them with jail inmates, and setting them to work cleaning up the excess that the scavenger couldn't manage. In fact, Wilkinson noted, last evening there'd been such a crew down near the wharf removing a dead horse. In the main, he allowed, he liked Culver, although occasionally he thought the sheriff a mite needy.

The Customs House, completed the previous year, was a massive three-story, hipped-roof, ornate stone block, Victorian Gothic structure with a central clock tower, lancet windows, and a triple-arch entrance. Its newness gleamed in the midday sun. Once inside, Wilkinson proceeded to the office of the Clerk of the Court, Harvey Bryant. All visitors accessed Judge Morton through him.

Ward found the young man, spare and whipcord framed, with bright blue eyes and an untamed shock of reddish-blond hair, attacking a high breastwork of paper. Aware of his reading law and hoping to gain admittance to the profession, Bryant was, in Ward's view, one of the hardest-working people he'd met in this town. In a rather crotchety moment of reflection, he averred that the younger generation, overpopulated with slackers, would profit from emulating his example.

"Good morning, Marshal," Bryant said in cheerful greeting, his fingers never ceasing their motions as he sorted a stack of foolscap into a neat series of piles. "Judge Morton is in conference at the moment, but I expect he'll be free before long. In the meantime, would you like a cup of coffee?"

"I'll join you, Harve, if you're having some," Wilkinson replied. "Any idea what this summons is about?"

Bryant poured their coffee, a black, bitter brew, little different from what Ward had drank many times in the West. "Not a clue why the Judge wants to see you," he told Wilkinson. "However, the man in with him is from Governor Bate's office. My hunch is that it has something to do with him."

They finished their coffee, and Bryant returned to his mound of paperwork. After several minutes, Wilkinson, impatient to be getting on, arose and paced around the room. As he started another turn, the door to Judge Morton's chambers opened, and a rotund, middle-aged man with a balding pate and thick beard emerged. Well-dressed, carrying an ornate walking stick, he had a stiff bearing and strode with what the marshal recognized as a military swagger.

The man had a grim expression with hard, cold eyes and a rosy, even choleric hue to his cheeks. He favored the marshal with an imperceptible, if not particularly friendly, nod and continued on through the door, ignoring Harvey Bryant as if he failed to remember his existence. A moment later, the magistrate appeared and waved Ward back to his office. "Your ears must be burning," he chuckled, but the marshal detected little mirth in the laughter. "Here," he pointed at an armchair with an expansive gesture, "sit yourself down. We've got a serious matter to discuss."

Morton's chambers contained dark walnut furniture, the wood perfectly harmonizing with his funeral parlor black suit. When his grandfather clock chimed noon, the jurist glanced at a well-polished cabinet that held an excellent Kentucky bourbon. For a moment, he hesitated, then decided it wasn't too early in the day for a drink after all. He retrieved the bottle and a couple of glasses, poured a generous measure of the amber liquid in each, then passed one to Wilkinson before taking an appreciative sip. "That man with the ramrod trailing out of his ass is Barton Miller, an aide to Governor William Bate. They served in the war together. He's been here the last hour asking, no demanding, that you and Tom drop what you're doing and investigate a killing. Arrogant little prick if I've ever seen one!"

Wilkinson betrayed the hint of a smile. "Your Honor, did he tell you where this is supposed to have happened and why the governor wants us involved?"

Morton settled back in his chair, his long mane of white hair spilling over the dark wood. "I asked him those questions and some others as well. The alleged killing occurred in Buckland Station a little over a month ago. The widow of the man slain has appealed to Bate, saying local authorities have failed to take proper action to apprehend her husband's murderers. If they *have* taken measures, she's complaining they're inept. Whatever the reality of the matter is, she's got the ear of the governor. He wants the federal government to step in and do something about it."

Wilkinson emitted a grunt of derision. "That's in Bedford County, I believe. If the sheriff over in Shelbyville is anything like the one we dealt with in Giles County last fall, it isn't any wonder there's been no arrest. If not for his death, I'd have made it my business to see him removed from office. That man was neither honest nor competent. If you hadn't appointed him a temporary US Marshal and put him under my authority, I believe he'd have contrived to get me and Tom killed."

"I remember," the judge agreed. "Fortunately, this fellow, a man named Albert Parslow, seems to be composed of sterner stuff. Mr. Miller is aware of no other complaints against him; the state representative and senator from Bedford County vouch for him. However, he seems to have encountered a conspiracy of silence in the town when he attempted to investigate the killing. Nobody there will admit to knowing, seeing, or hearing anything. Given the killers shot the victim multiple times, on a Saturday at noontime, on a principal city street, that's damn hard to believe."

"Hmm. There's no question that the deceased was downright unpopular," Wilkinson replied. "Anyone disliked so much that none will identify his murderer must have a history with the person or persons who shot him."

"And in a small town like Buckland Station, almost everyone knows the quarrel and the people involved."

"That means the refusal to cooperate is organized. A conspiracy, as you said, Your Honor, to protect the killers."

"Agreed, but the reason for protecting them is unclear. Maybe town folks despised the dead man—hated him for a variety of real or perceived offenses. Maybe the killers are so well-liked that no one will identify them."

"It just might be, too," Wilkinson rejoined, "that the killers hatched an organized plot, and the residents agreed to keep their silence. If so, it means they loathed the dead man, and it will be extremely difficult to get anyone to talk."

The judge poured one more finger of whiskey into Wilkinson's glass and passed him a thick envelope that he removed from a pigeonhole in his old-fashioned rolltop desk. "This is the sheriff's statement on his investigation. There's a coroner's report attached. I doubt it will be anywhere near as thorough as Obadiah Howell's would be, but it may be of some value. Governor Bate," Morton concluded, "I suspect owes a favor to the dead man's family or some friend of theirs that has political pull. You'll need to get down there within a week and smoke these people out, fast!"

Wilkinson scoffed openly. "I doubt if it happens quickly. From what you've told me, we'll be lucky to smoke them out in a month."

"Nevertheless," Judge Morton cajoled with a note of warning, "urgency with care is required on your part. Any group sufficiently galvanized to carry out a planned execution might do others to escape detection. Give me a list of what you'll need in the way of funds or authorizations, and I'll grant them." Then, his mood lightening, he picked up a sheet of paper from his office desk and waved it in the air with a merry flourish. "The state of Tennessee is paying!"

Chapter 2

WILKINSON EXITED JUDGE MORTON'S office and returned to the street. Briefly retracing his earlier steps, he crossed Broad, carefully avoiding the animal excretions, and headed north along Vine until he neared the State Capitol. From there, he turned east, toward the Cumberland River, and walked down Cedar Street, past St. Mary's Cathedral, until it intersected with Cherry Street. Moments later, he arrived at the house he shared with his wife, the former Charlotte Marks.

Those who encountered Wilkinson on his walk saw a broad-shouldered man, nearly six feet tall, with brownish blond hair and light blue eyes. At forty-five years old, he displayed the beginnings of a battle with his waistline, which he partly fought by engaging daily in an exhausting twenty-minute exercise routine with his old officer's sword. The precise maneuvers of the West Point Manual of Arms, which he usually carried out right after dawn, left him dripping with sweat and produced, he believed, a disciplined start to every day.

By birth, Ward was neither Nashvillian nor Southern, a fact noted with disapproval in some quarters. Born and raised in Wisconsin, he was twenty-two years old, working for an accountant in Madison, when the Civil War began. Commissioned into the Quartermaster Corps as a lieutenant, his work as an inspector of accounts soon saw him promoted to captain and then major. He had an ability to uncover deviousness and graft, as several dishonest officers whose careers ended in the disgrace of a court martial could attest. During this time, a young captain from Ohio named Tom Seibert joined him. They were working on a routine audit of a Reserve Cavalry Regiment of the Army of the Cumberland when an unexplained death of one of its troopers changed their lives.

The unit, raised and mustered in Iowa, had spent the winter of 1862–63 at the Cedar Run Plantation in rural Triune, Tennessee, a small community south of Nashville. During the audit process, one of its night sentries died at his post, the third to do so in a short period. Given the job of investigating the killing by his mentor, Major General David Stanley, Wilkinson exposed the regimental adjutant as an avaricious murderer and the disloyal daughter of the plantation owner as his romantic accomplice. Together, they were stealing caches of family valuables that her father had buried at the base of various trees on the property. The officer, acting at night, disabled or killed the unsuspecting sentries and retrieved the items, and the daughter secreted them in a trunk in her bedroom. He'd promised her marriage while already wed to another.

Wilkinson had found the new experience exhilarating—much more satisfying than examining endless ledgers and numbers. When he petitioned Stanley for a transfer to the Provost Marshal's Department, the general, reluctant to lose him, demurred for a time. Eventually, though, he relented and granted the request. Wilkinson reported to Nashville and took Seibert with him.

For the next three years, from August of '63 to the summer of '66, the two young men served together. Soldiers of the occupying garrison, disgruntled Confederates, opportunistic smugglers, spies, pimps and prostitutes, plus criminals of all stripes, kept them regularly employed. Wilkinson became known as the top investigator in the department, with Seibert his constant and able assistant. Over time, they forged an uneasy alliance and eventually friendship with Colonel Obadiah Howell, the brilliant but prickly supervising surgeon of the garrison. After the war ended, they remained in town for a year to assist in the process of Tennessee's reconstruction. Then, new orders came that split up their partnership and sent them their separate ways. The Army severed another thing as well: Wilkinson's marriage.

Wilkinson's first wife, Anna, hated the war, all those who brought it about, the army, and the South. A lifelong Wisconsin native, she found Nashville's summer heat a hellish cauldron, the city filthy, and the people as cold as her beloved Madison in January. Never welcomed in society, snubbed at church, cut dead on the street for being a Union officer's spouse, and frequently ignored in stores unless Ward accompanied her, she spent more and more time away from Tennessee. During those absences, always spent at her mother's home, she frequently fired off letters begging him to resign his commission and return to the dreary existence—from his point of view—of his old pre-war employment.

For Ward, that could never be. The war, as it had done for countless men, brought about an irrevocable change in him. He found himself a different person, too driven, too curious, too interested, and too restless to sit behind a desk for the rest of his life. One day, finally realizing that he would never abandon what Anna considered an erratic, undependable, disorderly way of life, she left him and returned to Wisconsin, never to be seen again. While posted in the West, her brother, a Madison attorney, got the marriage annulled.

Wilkinson recalled the fifteen years following the war with no fondness. While some postings were interesting, particularly a year in Europe observing the Franco-Prussian War, he found many of them drab and dull, mostly composed of sitting on court-martial boards that prosecuted the myriad petty offenses that occurred at frontier forts. These included brawling, drunkenness, dereliction of duty, and loss or destruction of equipment; the boredom could be stupefying. Also, being married yet deserted by one's spouse made him neither fish nor fowl—approachable, perhaps even reachable, yet unobtainable. The ultimate result was loneliness.

Even after learning his marriage no longer entangled him, Wilkinson made no effort to obtain female companionship. He didn't even bother to advertise he was free. Hurt by the experience and determined not to be wounded in that manner again, his fellow officers could regularly find him during most post celebrations and dances reading in his quarters, sitting on the porch, or smoking a cigar. He had a voracious appetite for books, devouring anything related to military history, classical literature, and even modern authors such as Edgar Allan Poe. He enjoyed music, could sing quite well, and was a delightful conversationalist in the right circumstances. Mostly, though, people marked him down as an odd duck, a quiet recluse.

In 1880, after bitterly disagreeing with a court martial verdict that sent an officer to Ft. Leavenworth for five years, Ward had had enough. Disillusioned, he resigned from the army, and at loose ends for the first time in twenty years, joined the Pinkerton Detective Agency. During that summer, while pursuing a pair of stagecoach-robbing brothers in Oklahoma, he'd had an unexpected reunion with Seibert and his wife, Frances, who were traveling to Tom's next posting. From them, he learned Tom planned to resign his commission in the next couple of months and return to Nashville to work for Frances's father. Knowing that Dr. Howell had secured an appointment for him to be the US Marshal in Nashville, he offered his friend a job as his deputy. Seibert happily accepted.

The next morning, Ward's old friend saved his life when the bandit duo got the drop on him. In the gunfight that followed, one brother died in a hail of bullets, and afterward, he conveyed the survivor to Texas. Just before leaving Austin, a letter from a cousin informed him that his ex-wife had died of cancer. Unexpectedly overwhelmed by old, dormant feelings of love and affection, Ward still felt the grief of her demise when he returned to Nashville.

Days later, Wilkinson had met Charlotte at a party—an encounter cleverly orchestrated by the Howells. Widow and widower, finding much in common with each other, were before long nearly inseparable in their free time. Attraction rapidly blossomed into love, and barely a year after their introduction, much to the shock and consternation—both real and counterfeit—of the town's legion of tongue-waggers and busybodies, they were married. Their union and the love Ward felt for Charlotte far eclipsed any happiness he'd ever known. Now, seven months later, she was pregnant with their first child.

* * *

The housekeeper, Jenny Wadsworth, greeted Ward when he entered their home, and she informed him that Charlotte was resting in the parlor. Charlotte had made an early return from the dry goods store she owned and operated on nearby Market Street—a business inherited from her late husband. Wilkinson didn't betray his feelings at this news, but inwardly, he worried. His wife, normally an endless bundle of energy, was finding pregnancy more taxing than she'd expected. At first, the complaint was morning sickness. Now, nearing the end of the sixth month, the problem was fatigue.

Charlotte was reclining on a well-padded settee when Ward entered the room, her distended stomach plainly visible. She gave him a radiant smile, yet her green eyes lacked their usual sparkle. Ward bent and gave her an affectionate kiss, which she enthusiastically returned. "I didn't expect to see you until supper time," she said. "What's going on?"

The corners of Wilkinson's mouth crinkled. His wife was perceptive, often able to discern the existence of problems or a changed situation by observing his actions or demeanor. It reminded him of how she and her father had taken part in a wartime spy ring that successfully operated under the nose of the Provost Marshal's Service. Occasionally, she would playfully tease Ward about this, and his faux pouting in reply was often a precursor to passionate lovemaking. For the time being, though, that activity was being paused.

"I've just come from seeing Judge Morton," Ward replied, pulling over an ottoman so he could sit beside his wife. "The governor has requested that Tom and I go to Bedford County to investigate an unsolved murder. Seems it is a matter of some urgency. I haven't had time to read the brief, but it appears there is a town-wide plot to not cooperate with authorities, to cover it up. We're wanted down there as soon as possible."

"You don't have to worry about me, Ward," Charlotte replied, having noted the furrows in his brow. "When I got tired today, and my back started hurting, I came home; that's better than my breakfast coming up faster than I can eat it. Mr. Warren can run things when I'm not there. If he couldn't, I'd get someone in there who could.

"Obadiah came by this morning," Charlotte continued. "I understand the two of you have been scheming to get me out of town before the baby is born."

"We've talked about it," Ward admitted with a rueful grin. "I sure hope you'll consider doing so. As you may have noticed, it is rather warm today. That's nothing like it's going to be when August comes around. I think you'll be much more comfortable where there is less humidity, and almost anywhere away from here in the summer has to be healthier than Nashville."

With a hearty laugh, Charlotte relented. "Very well, husband, I shall do as you ask. For now, though, shouldn't you be getting back to the office? Tom will need to know where the two of you are going. If you haven't eaten, I'll join you at the table once Jenny has it ready."

"Just stay put," Ward softly admonished, giving Charlotte a peck on the lips. "I'll ask her for some bread and cheese, maybe an apple. Then, I'll bring it in here on a tray. Knowing Tom, he's already packed his saddlebags and valise. Other than matters of court administration, the judge seldom asks to see me unless he's sending us out of town."

Chapter 3

SEIBERT, SHORTER AND THICKER than Wilkinson, with dark hair and a heavy mustache, was sitting at the worktable when Ward returned to the office, grinding away at another of the endless reports that civil servants were required to generate. Tom had a squarish but not unattractive face, with gray-green eyes that sparkled with delight when something amused him. When he wasn't amused, the orbs turned frosty. "Where are we heading, Ward?" he asked without preamble. "I'm trying to catch up before we leave so we can fall behind again."

Wilkinson guffawed loudly. "South, to Buckland Station."

"Isn't that in Bedford County, pretty near to Shelbyville?"

"Go to the head of the class. Fortunately, there is a new sheriff in Shelbyville, and he is, according to reports, far more competent and ethical than his predecessor."

"Thank God for small favors," Tom muttered as his pen scratched across the paper. "I thought we might have to kill the one from Giles County last year. Just what is going on down in Buckland Station, anyway?"

"That's what I'm about to find out," Wilkinson said, holding up the report provided by Judge Morton. "A killing took place there a little over a month ago, and it remains unsolved. The circumstances are suspicious, and the local populace is unwilling to assist law enforcement in discovering the culprits.

"The deceased must have friends or relatives with political influence," Ward continued, "because the judge received a direct request for our involvement from Governor Bate's office. When you're done with what you're doing, draft up requisitions for train tickets, transportation for our horses, livery, room and board in Buckland Station for at least a week, and fifty dollars more for miscellaneous expenses. His Honor says he'll allow any amounts we need and that the state of Tennessee is footing the bill."

Ward sat down at his desk and unfolded the report, which blessedly was written in a fair hand. "Tomorrow morning, I'll take those drafts up to the courthouse for the judge's signature. From there, I'll get our tickets on the Nashville & Chattanooga. Meanwhile, I'd like for you to make sure our mounts are ready. I want us to be done with all preparations by noon so we can go home and be with our families for a little while." Then, sighing heavily, he concluded, "Let's see what's in this statement."

Seibert gave Wilkinson a grateful smile, but the marshal already had his eyes focused on the report. Tom had experienced many forced absences from his family while in the army; a few extra hours at home before heading out of town was welcome. He'd long considered his friend and colleague the older brother he'd never had.

Born in rural Ohio, his childhood scarred by the early loss of his mother and the upbringing of his gruff, often uncommunicative father—a man who gave liberal discipline and tightfisted affection—Tom grew up an emotionally-starved boy, eventually finding more liking for animals than people. He studied to become a veterinarian and began his practice mere months before the war came. The eruption of civil conflict seemed to galvanize him as nothing before had done. Mentally estranged from his father, and perhaps even more so from his sour, meddlesome younger sister, he enlisted in the Union Army while at the same time engaging in a whirlwind romance with a young woman that culminated in marriage during the final days before he departed to join his unit. Soon thereafter, he'd met Ward Wilkinson.

For the next two years, Seibert and Wilkinson followed in the wake of the advancing bluecoat armies, through Kentucky, Missouri, and Tennessee, performing the various tasks of the Quartermaster Department. Then, the April '63 events at Cedar Run Plantation altered the course of Tom's life. Like Wilkinson, he'd felt the excitement and adrenaline surge of solving the mystery of the sentinels who'd died in the shadows of green trees that lined the banks of a small watercourse that gurgled in back of the main house. When Ward determined to transfer to the Provost Marshal Service and asked him to join as his adjutant, Seibert, overjoyed, accepted with alacrity.

Within days of their arrival, during a treacherous attempt to murder Ward and himself, Tom had had to kill a man. It'd been his first time to pull a weapon and fire it at another human being. He still remembered the emotional trauma from the fear he'd experienced that day and could clearly see in his mind's eye the sight of his antagonist's bloodied corpse. By the narrowest of margins, he'd avoided spewing his recently consumed meal. That reaction no longer occurred, and that fact vaguely troubled him. Such violent encounters were a rare, unfortunate part of his job—something he never enjoyed—and the knowledge that some admired him for his skill with weapons left him cold.

By war's end, Seibert was involved in three more shootings, the final one during the pursuit of a maniacal killer who had attempted to murder his fiancé. With his first wife lost to a typhoid epidemic in the late summer of '63, Tom had met Frances Parsons, the daughter of a local business owner, at a church service that fall. Over the next few months, a romance kindled between them.

Tom and Frances were married in May 1865, shortly after the war's end. He had remained in Nashville with Wilkinson during the initial stages of Reconstruction, but scarcely a year later, with state readmission a forgone conclusion, both men received new assignments. Tom and Frances departed the city with their infant son in tow. It would be fifteen years before they returned.

In 1881, worn out with the army and its stagnant pay and promotions, Seibert accepted the offer of Frances's father to join his firm and prepared his resignation from the army. In a short time, however, Wilkinson, through the influence of their mutual friend Dr. Obadiah Howell, received an appointment as the new United States Marshal for the District of Middle Tennessee and Southern Kentucky. When his old friend offered him the position of deputy, and despite the grumblings of Mr. Parsons, he accepted, preferring work like his former duty as a

Provost Marshal.

Within hours of being sworn in, the marshals found themselves investigating the mystery of a corpse found in a barrel of whiskey. A decade and a half suddenly evaporated, and each man assumed the familiar roles of their past association. Wilkinson, having a talent for taking what seemed to be unrelated facts and formulating a shrewd hypothesis from them, relied on Seibert, an incisive investigator in his own right, to poke holes in his analysis and find the flaws in his reasoning. Sometimes, that could be trying, but he never complained, except in a good-natured fashion. And although his friend was quite capable with weapons, he wasn't in Tom's class; few men were.

Whether Tom liked it or not, he had a reputation. Thankfully, for the most part, it was within the fraternity of his fellow US Marshals. Perhaps unknown to anyone, even Wilkinson, who had taken part in many of his fights, Tom had killed nine or ten men in gun battles. After being dissatisfied with his marksmanship during a stagecoach robbery—one in which he and Frances were passengers—he'd begun a single-minded effort to improve his ability. Now a crack shot with a rifle and a very fast man with a pistol, Ward felt he was as good as any of the western gunslingers that had their exploits glamorized in newspapers and dime novels. Notoriety, though, he could do without.

* * *

Silence reigned for the next thirty minutes. The only noise came from the nib of Tom's pen scraping on the vellum and from an occasional creak of Wilkinson's chair as he absorbed the report on the Buckland Station slaying. At three o'clock, Ward asked him how the paperwork was coming—a question the deputy answered with a careless toss of the quill and a stoppering of the inkwell. "The report that is due next week is ready for your signature," Tom informed him. "And the requisitions are complete. What's in the report?"

Wilkinson rose from his chair and laid the document in Seibert's in box. "You can read all about it tomorrow. In brief, the county sheriff has a dead man—someone he didn't like and who he believes many of the local townspeople hated. He's provided an exhaustive list of names, including everyone from the mayor to the local saloonkeeper, and none of them have provided a clue or the slightest bit of information concerning the act or who might have committed it. I might add that it occurred near midday, on a Saturday, and close to the saloon."

Tom emitted a derisive snort. "With no evidence to support my suspicion, I'll bet you we'll find a man who well deserved what happened to him. Sounds like the twin brother of Ebeneezer Scrooge—not a friend in life and only a few people who stood to inherit to mourn his passing."

"Hmm, you might be right," Ward agreed. "Says in the report that he has a widow. My guess is she's bereaved. If so, it's likely a male member of her family who has asked for assistance from his representative. We'll have to factor in the possibility that politics is involved."

"At least until we learn it's not," said Tom, finishing Ward's sentence for him. "Could be that someone did him in because they owed him money and couldn't pay up."

"That's a definite possibility. In fact, the report notes that his wife stated he was meeting some men in town on the day of his death. Unfortunately, he didn't tell her their names. Pretty extreme manner to adopt in avoiding a debt, don't you think?"

"Depends on the terms and maybe how the agreement originally came to be. It doesn't seem that his neighbors thought this fellow a pillar of the community or an honorable man who they would want to do business with. So, why did they?"

"That's one of the many things we're going to have to learn. In the morning, I'll take all these requests up to the courthouse. While I'm there, I want to ask Judge Morton about arranging for some blanket search warrants for us. We're going to need to search for evidence as we learn of its existence, and we can't be contacting Nashville for authority every time we need it."

"Since the state is pushing this matter," Tom expressed with a shrug, "see if he can get Bate's office to prevail on the county judge in Shelbyville to supply what we need. I imagine the Attorney General could be quite persuasive if he wants to be."

"Damn fine idea. On that note, let's close this place up. There's a place on Cherry Street that has new barrels of an excellent apple cider on tap. I was going to suggest we go there just before Judge Morton's message arrived. On the way, we'll drop in on Sheriff Culver and tell him we'll be away for a while."

Chapter 4

THE NEXT MORNING, Wilkinson marched up Broad Street to the courthouse while Seibert made certain their mounts were ready to travel. Finding them so, he returned to the office somewhat before Ward, who continued on from the Clerk of Court's office a few more blocks to the train depot. There, he purchased their coach tickets and boxcar passage for the horses. Meanwhile, Tom made a painstaking review of the sheriff's statement and began composing lists of people to interview. Some were obvious: the sheriff himself, the dead man's widow, and anyone who lived nearby or had a place of business near the killing. A secondary list included all others named by the sheriff who had refused to cooperate. Of course, the most interesting list, he mused, would be a later one, of people who drew attention to themselves because of their actions or as a result of an unguarded comment made by another.

Wilkinson returned at ten-thirty, and the two men huddled around their worktable to discuss the next day's trip. "Our train leaves at eight," Ward declared, "so it will be an early morning."

"I'll be at your house at six-thirty with the horses," Tom replied. "All we'll have to do is put your saddle on the bay."

"Good. That will give us time to get the horses up the ramps and in the car without hurrying them. I've seen them get balky if they think you're agitated."

"I have, too. Neither of our mounts is the nervous or fractious type, but you worry a horse, and it can exhibit like behavior. I've seen plenty of them chew on a bit and foam at the mouth if they don't want to go where you have in mind, especially if it's an enclosed space where they'll feel hemmed in."

"If you want to come at six, our new housekeeper, Jenny Wadsworth, is an excellent cook. Frances will have something for you, but save a little room for her biscuits, pear preserves, and an extra cup of coffee."

Seibert smiled. "That sounds mighty good. While you were gone, I made lists of people we'll need to interview. Sheriff Parslow heads the list, and I reckon we need to talk to that deputy of his, Simon Garrett. It looks like he conducted a few of their interviews."

Wilkinson nodded in affirmation. "Who else did you have in mind?"

"Denise Harper, the widow of the late Theodore 'Ted' Harper—the man with no friends, at least none that aren't deaf, dumb, and blind."

Ward laughed in good humor. "Indeed. Maybe she'll reveal who influenced Governor Bate to request our presence. Even better, although the sheriff doesn't mention it in his report, maybe she'll enlighten us on who she believes had a grudge against her husband."

"Yes, a question I had when I read through this report. Is it possible they didn't ask, or did she say he hadn't an enemy in the world?"

"Wouldn't surprise me," Wilkinson replied. "It's one thing for no one to aid the law in finding a criminal; it's something else when officers of the law can't come up with even a single suspect on their own. Who else did you put on our 'do first' list?"

"I eliminated the mayor, Alexander Wiley. Parslow interviewed him and learned nothing. If we find that was due to connivance instead of ignorance, we can go see him later on. I've included Dr. Henry Morris, the Bedford County coroner, and anyone who lives or works close by the shooting site.

"One more thing, Ward," Tom continued. "How do you want to handle Sheriff Parslow? Are we going to telegraph and say we're coming or just show up at his door unannounced?"

"I've decided we're going to show up and catch him unawares. He may be a fine fellow, but we don't know that for a fact. If he's in league with those who killed Harper, we don't want him warning them ahead of time about our arrival. Like as not, he could also be a bucket-mouth that can't keep anything to himself."

At that, the old friends shared a good-natured chuckle, and Ward, seeing the clock hands closing on the twelve, told Seibert to go home to his family. "I'll see you in the morning, Tom. After I close up, I'm going to see Obadiah. Your mention of the county coroner reminded me he may have met him or at least heard something about him. You noticed there isn't a comprehensive coroner's report attached to Parslow's statement."

"Well," Tom rejoined with another bark of mirth, "unlike the citizens of Buckland Station, you won't have any trouble getting him to speak. He's been at the forefront of trying to establish a state medical association and licensing board. I'll bet he has information on every physician in Tennessee."

"I'll make you another bet," Ward grinned, waving Seibert toward the door. "The viewpoint won't be positive. His failing to prepare a thorough report in a murder case won't satisfy Obadiah's standards."

Chapter 5

DR. OBADIAH HOWELL'S RESIDENCE was a brick and timbered structure, clad in vine and wreathed in rose bushes that were the pride of his wife, Helen. In the house's rear, he'd put on an addition, and there, the former army colonel, his years betrayed by his silver hair and goatee, operated his own surgery. He treated patients, performed minor operations, and even found time to serve as county coroner. It was a testament to his medical skills and his care for the people of the city that he, a New England Yankee, could run a successful practice. Not only that, but society accepted him as well. He was a member of several prominent clubs and social fraternities, a church elder, and a member of the Board of Directors of a nearby bank.

Helen Howell had pulled off an amazing feat, Wilkinson reckoned, by rounding off the rougher edges of his old friend and comrade. He'd first encountered Obadiah during their wartime service, and the man's tetchy, irascible temperament had often been on display. Chief Surgeon of the occupying garrison, his aloof, superior attitude rubbed fellow officers the wrong way—a fact that nearly caused him to be transferred out on one occasion. The commanding general, however, recognizing that the brilliant, meticulous, and exacting man was an asset not to discard casually, refused to accept the recommendation. He might be a "miserable sonofabitch," as some called him behind his back, but he was the best physician in a blue uniform.

From uneasy coexistence, to grudging accommodation, at last succeeded by earned respect, Ward and Tom had forged an alliance with the crotchety doctor. One day, near the end of the war, Howell had invited Wilkinson to lunch, an extraordinary occasion at which he'd let down his guard and expressed what demons drove and consumed him. It was a heartbreaking tale of betrayal by the husband of his late sister, who had strayed into the arms of a prostitute and brought home venereal disease to his unsuspecting wife. The complications of the disease weakened her body, and the knowledge of what caused her condition sapped her will as well. After her death, Howell had begun a personal, one-man crusade against "fallen women" of every stripe, from high-class madams to bedraggled street whores. Like all crusaders, his triumphs had been altogether brief and, in the end, illusory.

After the war, Howell had resigned from the army and, having no desire to return to Connecticut, stayed in Nashville. Within eighteen months, military duty disrupted his friendships with Wilkinson and Seibert as both men left town for new assignments. Over the years, even as they trooped about the country, the officers stayed in touch. On occasion, they met for brief reunions. Most of the time, though, news from his colleagues arrived in the mail. During the two years following their departure, he grew his practice, and one day—one amazing, joyous, magical day—he'd met Helen.

Helen was, at that time, serving as a volunteer nurse at a hospital overflowing with victims of the grim Nashville cholera epidemic of 1867. In the beginning, she'd found Obadiah a seemingly inexhaustible bundle of energy that sped through the wards, hurling orders, ministering to the afflicted, then adding to his twelve-hour days by spending more time writing instructions for the oncoming shift and drafting letters begging for supplies, intimidating. Occasionally, he would display a tyrannical temper, yet Helen noticed that brief expression of profound sadness that crossed his face every time he pulled the sheet over the head of a victim. She was stunned when he asked her to attend church with him—an invitation that was extended with charming bashfulness. The following morning, he escorted her to services at the Presbyterian Church, and despite the scornful opinion of some friends that he was a "carpetbagger" and a "damned Yankee," they'd been inseparable ever since.

Over the succeeding months, Helen learned that a far different Obadiah Howell revealed himself when he wasn't on duty. A graduate of Yale, he was well-read in literature and history and could discuss politics, religious theory, and philosophy. He liked art and music and seemed to have an interest in almost anything. On New Year's Day, 1868, she accepted his ring and proposal of marriage, telling her dubious, disapproving confidantes it was the best decision she'd ever made. Fifteen years of wedded bliss confirmed her pronouncement.

* * *

Wilkinson was heading up the steps when the front door opened. An older man stood on the stoop for a moment, then he shook the doctor's hand and bade him goodbye. In a daze, the man plunged past the marshal without a word. Ward noted a streak of sadness in Howell's expression, and his eyes followed his patient until he reached the street. "Tough consultation, Obadiah?" Ward asked as he joined his friend.

"Not particularly, no," came the gruff reply.

"You don't fool me," Ward said in sympathy. "I've seen that look before. Someone you can't save?"

"If they remain your patient long enough," Howell said in exasperation, "you can't save any of them; hell, you can't even save yourself."

"Doctor, doctor, will I die?" Wilkinson intoned, remembering a snatch of an old nursery rhyme.

"Yes, you will, and so will I," Obadiah answered back in a voice no longer wistful. "Come on in, and we'll have some coffee. What brings you by today?"

"Mostly to ask you about the coroner of Bedford County, a certain Dr. Henry Morris."

Howell produced a non-committal grunt that revealed nothing of his feelings. A few moments later, as if by magic, Helen entered the room with a tray containing a pot with two cups and spoons, a sugar bowl, and a cream pitcher. She made some small talk with Ward for a few moments, then exited to placate Obadiah's next patient; he'd have to wait a little while. Once she'd left the room, he cleared his throat and spoke.

"Dr. Morris isn't a bad sort," Obadiah began, "but he's not qualified to be a coroner. Nearly twenty years my senior, he is, and he hasn't kept up his knowledge of new medical discoveries. The reason for that might be," his voice turning impatient, "that he has terrible cataracts. The poor bastard's close to blind. At a medical association meeting, a fellow physician informed me that Morris went out on a moonless night, during a rainstorm, to see the corpse of a man who had died several days before being discovered. He couldn't see much of anything in the flickering light of a lamp and asked his escort, who was making sure the old fellow didn't fall and break his neck, what had caused the man's death. The escort opined a heart attack, and you guessed it, that's what ended up on the death certificate. If you're having to rely on a judgment he's made, don't do it. That gentleman couldn't confirm whether someone died from lead perforation or from a perforated ulcer!"

"I'm not," Wilkinson replied with a smile. "Tom and I head to Buckland Station tomorrow to investigate the suspicious death of a local man, shot outside of a saloon at midday, on a Saturday, a little over a month ago. The county sheriff's report states that no one he interviewed would reveal anything about the killing. It's quite a list he's made, and one could easily determine that a conspiracy to cover up what occurred is ongoing. Dr. Morris never completed a thorough coroner's report nor issued a death certificate."

"Since he lives in Shelbyville," Howell snorted, "it's unlikely he ever heard about the man being shot. On a different subject, why is the federal government involved in a state matter?"

"Good question. All we know is that Governor Bate's office requested our help via Judge Morton. He suspects someone from the dead man's family has political influence, but who knows? If I have to have the corpse exhumed, will you do the examination for me?"

"If you can get me authority to work there, sure. There will be some difficulties because of the degrading of the body, and if an undertaker embalmed him, there may be little to tell. Hopefully, though, I'll at least be able to figure out the caliber of the bullets, whether they came from the front or back, the distance, and at what angle the weapons were aimed."

"I'll see if Judge Morton can prevail on the attorney general to get that approval. He's already working to get us streamlined access to search warrants." Wilkinson paused, emitting a troubled sigh. "Any new ideas where I can take Charlotte for the last part of her pregnancy? It already feels like summer outside."

"I'm looking at a place called Moffat Station. It's a little village near Monteagle Mountain, maybe two thousand feet in elevation. There's not too many people around, and the air will be much cooler there in August."

Wilkinson replied with enthusiasm. "How soon should she go?"

"During the last month, maybe six weeks. That would be around the beginning of July. I'll learn more about the place, and we'll talk again when your investigation is over." Obadiah looked at his watch and rose to his feet. "I'm sorry, but I've got a patient waiting, and I need to get him in here. You and Tom watch yourself down there," he warned with a steely stare. "What you described from that sheriff's report doesn't smell right. Those responsible deliberately targeted the dead man, and they won't want to be found out. If shooting you in the back preserves their life and liberty, they'll do it without hesitation."

Chapter 6

GLOAM STILL SHROUDED the streets when Seibert pulled rein at the Wilkinson house. Mounted on a small gray gelding, a sturdy animal with a stubborn personality that seemed to render it tireless, he was leading a tall bay horse Ward had owned for many years. He was carrying a pair of saddlebags, a bedroll with a waterproof poncho attached, and a well-oiled, 1876 model Winchester, which he stowed in a rifle scabbard. Strapped around his hips was a gun belt, the holster holding a .45-caliber Colt revolver.

Jenny Wadsworth answered Seibert's knock. With a friendly smile, she led him into the dining room where the Wilkinsons were having breakfast—at least, Ward was. Charlotte was nursing a cup of coffee but seemed little interested in food. Tom took a chair, then accepted coffee and biscuits and consumed both with appreciation. His friend's compliments on the young housekeeper's cooking skills were no exaggeration.

While Seibert finished his coffee, Ward saddled his horse. The time for going was mere minutes away. Having said little, Tom held his cup and stared off into an empty corner of the room, an action that didn't escape Charlotte's astute notice. "You've been rather quiet," she said. "Is anything wrong this morning?"

Tom turned toward her, rubbed his chin in a vexed manner, then spoke in a subdued voice. "It's nothing, really," he deflected, "just Ruth doing her usual sulking and moping whenever I go out of town. She's been doing it for some time now, at least since she entered her teen years. It's never got too irksome, but she sure put on a show last night."

Tom swallowed the rest of his cup, continuing his remarks without being coaxed. "Last night at dinner, Paul was all ears, wanting to hear about where we were going and what the case was about, and he all but asked me if he could come along. She sat there and pouted, stuck out her lower lip, and then, with a great deal of huffing, asked to be excused. On her way out of the room, she told her brother—you're aware he's going off to military college in the fall?—that he would become just like me: become an Army officer, then marry some poor, deluded woman and haul her off around the country to one godforsaken place after the other. It's pretty clear," he concluded in a despairing tone, "that she has a grudge about all those absences the army required of me over the years."

"What did Frances have to say?"

"She thought Ruth's behavior was appalling. After a moment, she got up, followed her out of the room, and forced her to return and apologize to me and Paul. It didn't seem all that sincere, but Frances was livid. That put a damper on the rest of the evening."

Charlotte started to speak again, but the sound of Ward returning reduced her reply to a sympathetic smile. "It's lightening up pretty well, Tom," he said. "I reckon we best be getting along."

Seibert stood, thanked them for the hospitality, and then walked outside to give the couple a moment of privacy. As he headed through the door, Jenny Wadsworth favored him with an admiring glance. Less than a minute later, Wilkinson joined him. They mounted up and rode away as Charlotte stood at the door, waving them goodbye.

Ward was using his elegant, high-backed, square-skirted California saddle, Tom noticed with a sardonic grin. Its long tapaderos and elaborately tooled carvings, all set in a rich, russet color, would surely attract the eye of any passerby. Initially, at least, this would throw observers off the scent of them being local lawmen. Such saddles were seldom seen in this part of the country.

The saddlebags were ornate. On the left side was a rifle scabbard, and this held Wilkinson's beloved seven-shot Spencer repeating rifle. Under his coat, secured in a shoulder holster beneath his left arm, nestled a Colt revolver. He'd observed colleagues in the Pinkerton Detective Agency employing such a method and had adopted it for himself.

In the gray light of dawn, a few people began leaving their homes and started to move about. As the marshals neared the depot, that number increased, with the usual hurly-burly of arriving and departing trains, passengers stepping down from the cars as others waited to go aboard, and porters scurrying in every direction, manhandling carts heaped with luggage. Above the din of simultaneously competing voices was the noise of grinding wheels, chugging engines, and hissing steam. "There's our train, Tom," Wilkinson motioned. "The stationmaster told me what track it would be on when I got our tickets. Let's get the horses squared away, and then we'll see if we can board early. I want to talk some more about how we'll proceed when we get to Shelbyville."

The men dismounted near a garishly painted boxcar, presented their tickets, and soon led their mounts up an inclined plank and into the semi-darkness within. They took their rifles, made sure their mounts were secure, and then exited the compartment to find the sky turning dark to the west. "Hope it's just rain and not a thunderstorm," Tom opined, his brow suddenly creased with concern. "You want me to stay with the animals in case they get spooked?"

"Might be a good idea. If the weather clears at some point, you can join me at one of the stops. It's a twenty-five-mile ride from Murfreesboro to Shelbyville, and we're going to interview the sheriff, his deputy, and Dr. Morris while we're in town. I'm thinking we may not go to Buckland Station until the day after tomorrow."

"We had talked about going to the courthouse to check on Harper's property transactions," Seibert replied. "That might take a while. I'll get us a hotel room as soon as we arrive. When is it we get there?"

"It's likely to be mid-afternoon, at least. While we're there, I'm thinking we might go visit the county newspaper. The editor must cover happenings in Buckland Station. It would be very interesting to see if he's ever printed a photograph that shows the town on a holiday, market day, a Saturday, anything like that."

Tom grinned. "Good thinking. You're way ahead of me this morning, Ward. The sheriff's report would make you think Buckland Station was a ghost town where not much ever happens. That will be hard to explain if we can show citizens pack the streets on such days. Go on to your car and give me my ticket. Hopefully, I won't be riding in here all the way there."

Even as Wilkinson headed forward to his car, a spatter of fat raindrops fell. He reached the steps and turned just in time to see a jagged pitchfork bolt of lightning descend from a dark bank of clouds that clustered above the cupola of the state capitol. A deafening peal of thunder immediately followed, and he hastened aboard to find his seat. Less than a minute later, the storm, blowing in from the southwest, began in earnest.

Wind-driven rain beat against the windows and sluiced down the glass as the locomotive made a mighty heave and chugged away from the station. Wilkinson, as he sat alone, ignored the pelting torrent pounding on the roof and gave more thought to the facts and information he and Tom would most like to learn from the new sheriff of Bedford County. Almost certainly, he was a local man—very few outsiders ever found their way into a political position such as that. If so, he had to have knowledge of some Buckland Station residents, perhaps even the dead man and his family. Part of that might come from his own investigation, other insight, and, if lucky, from records left by the useless predecessor he'd replaced. That wasn't too likely, he reminded himself, but the man had to have had occasional contact with the citizenry of the place. Could a previous complaint or investigation provide a clue as to who had reason to kill this Harper fellow? It would help a lot if that was true.

For the first thirty minutes, the rain fell in a relentless downpour, and then it slackened. The view through the window lightened, and minutes later, the train emerged from the gloom into brilliant sunshine. The tilled fields and pastures glistened as the moisture reflected the rays of light, giving the landscape a fresh, cleansed appearance. At a whistle-stop, Seibert had just enough time to sprint from the boxcar and join Wilkinson in the passenger compartment. "Horses are fine," he said as he dropped onto the cushions, "and the conductor tells me that reports from down the line show no bad weather at all. What have you been doing while I bounced around back there?"

"A couple of things. First, I convinced the conductor to allow us to remain onboard until we reach Cynthiana. That will take eight or nine miles off our ride. The rest of the time, I've been going over in my mind what we need to ask Sheriff Parslow. I know nothing about the former sheriff, other than he seems to have been less than desirable. However, there may be something in his files that might clue us to any trouble this Harper was ever in and who, if anybody, in Buckland Station was a part of it. My instinct tells me there is a history behind this killing; it wasn't an impulsive act."

"My instinct tells me that man was a shit," Tom replied in a decisive tone. "There's a history, all right, and his odor will be all over it."

Chapter 7

DESPITE THE HEAVY thunderstorm, the engineer chugged his locomotive to a halt at the Murfreesboro passenger terminal at its scheduled arrival time, nine-thirty. Forty-five minutes later, at the little hamlet of Cynthiana, Wilkinson and Seibert detrained and swiftly retrieved their mounts from the boxcar. Then, donning long linen dusters to protect their clothes from the clouds of grime produced by their horses' hooves, they rode southward on a well-maintained turnpike to the town of Shelbyville.

It was early afternoon when the weary lawmen stepped down from their mounts in front of the Bedford County jail. Next to that structure stood the office of the county sheriff. Stepping onto the boardwalk, Wilkinson rapped a perfunctory knock at the door, then turned the knob and went inside. Facing the opening, sitting at a desk, was a young man with a sunburned face, his shirt sleeves rolled up to the elbows. His dark eyes, reflecting intelligence, gave them a quizzical expression, and he asked, "Something I can do for you, gentlemen?"

"Yes, I believe you can," Wilkinson replied. "Sheriff Parslow?"

"I am."

"Sheriff, I'm Ward Wilkinson, United States Marshal from Nashville. This is my Deputy, Tom Seibert. The Office of Governor Bate has requested us and the US District Court to investigate the killing of Theodore Harper."

Parslow gave an astonished blink, arose, then stepped out from behind the desk and extended his hand. "I can't say I'm surprised to see you here, although I've received no word of your coming. Have you seen my report on this case?"

"It's a very interesting document. As you might imagine, we have questions. As to you not being informed, that's my fault. We didn't know what reception we might receive, and there was some concern expressed about the man you replaced. We had no evidence to suspect you being in league with anyone in Buckland Station to sabotage your investigation, quite the opposite. Still, with the extraordinary nature of the opposition you've encountered down there, we didn't want to take the risk of everyone in town knowing of our arrival before we left home."

Parslow frowned, considered the statement for a moment, and then shrugged in agreement. "I reckon that makes sense. Have a seat," he gestured, "coffee's on. Hey, Simon," he called back to the cells, "put down that broom and mop and come out here. Two US Marshals are here from Nashville to see if they can find out who killed Harper. Since you did some interviews, they'll be wanting to talk with you as well."

The marshals took a seat, and Wilkinson had a silent sigh of relief. Parslow, who appeared to be a local farmer when he wasn't wearing the county star, gave every indication that he was going to be cooperative. Local lawmen sometimes resented outside officers and could be quite jealous of their prerogatives. That didn't appear to be a problem here.

Further, the marshal noted, the office appeared neat and orderly, with floors scrubbed and papers filed. Remembering the quarters of the former Giles County sheriff, a place reeking with old sweat, stale smoke, and the rancid odors of spoiled food and chamber pot effluent, he was favorably impressed. As Simon Garrett—a small, balding man with sandy hair and a drooping mustache—poured the coffee, Wilkinson asked an initial question. "What was your predecessor dismissed for, Sheriff? If he's still around, I may have a question or two for him."

"The sheriff had a bit of a problem explaining his expenditure of county funds," Parslow said while Garrett passed around the cups. "I believe he expected to be taken up for embezzlement and cleared out before being indicted. After being dismissed, he packed up what he could carry and lit out. He didn't tell anyone about his leaving, but the prevailing opinion is that he's gone to Texas. He has family there, so I'm told."

"That's unfortunate. I hoped to learn from him whether he'd had any official contact with Harper while he was a lawman."

Parslow brought the cup to his lips, and the searing heat emanating from the steam caused him to put it back on the desk. "I'd advise leaving that awhile, would take the hair off a hog. As to your question, yes, he knew Harper; last year, although he didn't do so, he had every reason to arrest him for attempted murder."

"Why was that?" Tom chimed in, speaking for the first time other than the obligatory, "Pleased to meet you," when he shook hands with Parslow.

"The sheriff figured Harper would kill him, and I'd have to say that hunch was right. Mr. Harper was pretty good with a pistol, and the sheriff, he wasn't much of a hand at all."

"Harper would have resisted arrest?"

"Yes. He might have taken a more cautious approach with you, Deputy. He wouldn't have known your ability, but he would have noticed you're wearing a tied-down gun. There isn't a single person I can think of in this entire county that does that."

Wilkinson spoke again. "Sheriff, I'm getting a powerful impression that Theodore Harper wasn't a solid citizen."

Parslow laughed unpleasantly. "That's an understatement. I didn't find a single person in Buckland Station who had a good word to say about him." Wilkinson looked at Garrett, who nodded in agreement. "As long as the story they're telling doesn't involve them, they're willing to tell you what a sonofabitch he was and who he'd threatened, intimidated, assaulted, cheated, you name it. When you asked if they'd witnessed anything, heard anything, or who had the most reason to kill Harper, none of them had anything to say."

"Do you want to get some dinner, gentlemen?" Wilkinson asked. "I feel this may take a little while. Sheriff, is there a decent hotel in this town?"

Chapter 8

THE DINER WAS a middling place, with even more forgettable food. During the meal, by design, the men talked of other things: news of Shelbyville, yet of more interest, Buckland Station. "The railroad has done a world of good for that place," Garrett declared, "as it has for other places it's gone through. Population has doubled in the last ten to fifteen years. More than a thousand folks living there now."

Parslow concurred in his deputy's remarks. "Simon's correct. Place has grown like a bad weed. The train tracks run through the center of town. On the north side are a lot of fancy homes and churches. Supposedly, a new school is going to be built in the next year or two. Down near the rail right away there is a street lined with businesses, with another like it south of the tracks. The passenger depot is on the north side, and nearby is the hotel; that's where you'll be staying. Only fit place to board in town.

"All the commercial area," the sheriff continued, "is called the Railroad Square. On the south side, the freight depot is there, along with a stockyard. Further on, but still close to the tracks, is a cornmeal mill, a forge, and a sawmill. At the bottom of the square, intersected by Shelby and Chapel Streets, is the other business row. In there is a smithy, livery stable, some stores, a couple of restaurants, and" he noted with a deliberate pause, "the town saloon. South of that, there are some houses, and down Chapel Street aways is the Standard Oil Company building."

Seibert smiled. "Sounds a good deal like towns I saw in the West: families with nice homes and churches on one side of the railroad, the saloons and red-light district on the other. That's where the terms 'the other side of the tracks' and 'south of the line' came from."

"You were a lawman out west?" Garrett inquired.

"In a manner of speaking," Tom replied. "Marshal Wilkinson and I served in the army together as Provost Marshal officers."

"During the war?" Parslow asked.

"Then and later. Most of the time after the war we served in different places around the country. During the war, we spent several years in Nashville."

"Your accents give you away," the sheriff said with an affable grin. "People will spot you as Yankees in a heartbeat, although you'll stump some with the twangs and drawls you produce from time to time. Ever visit anyplace interesting out there? Denver? San Francisco?"

Both men replied in the affirmative. "The Army briefly posted me to Fort Dodge," Tom recalled. "Visited Dodge City while I was there, met the Masterson brothers and Wyatt Earp."

"The one involved in that OK Corral shootout a couple of years back?" Garrett asked in awe.

"That's the one, but don't spend time admiring him. He was a gambler, confidence man, and associated with ladies of the evening; I could never decide about him. To me, he seemed as much a criminal as he ever was a lawman."

The men finished the last of their beer—a weak, watery brew that was far better than the food—and returned to the office. Resuming their seats, Parslow took up the conversation. "Theodore Harper's a complicated story, but you'll need to know it in order to make any sense of what happened there. When I'm finished, you'll understand that he was due to be shot for a long time.

"The Harper family," Parslow began, "have lived in Bedford County for several generations, most of them farmers. They've been quite successful at it. Ted, as I'll occasionally refer to him, was born in 1849 and had just turned twelve years old when the war started. Old Man Harper, though, joined up and went off to serve in the Confederate Army. He had started a business here in Shelbyville but had his wife operate it while he was gone.

"In October of '63, Confederate cavalry, who were being pursued by superior numbers, came through town and looted their own countrymen as thoroughly as they would have people in Ohio or Pennsylvania. They were a damn disgrace," the sheriff grumped in indignation.

"We're acquainted with this incident, Sheriff," Wilkinson said, sharing a glance with Tom. "It came up in a case we investigated last year. I'm presuming this ruined the Harper's financially?"

"You presume correctly. They came out of the war without a pot to piss in or a window to throw it out of. The missus and her Ted, now fifteen, returned to the old farmstead, which was in a state of dilapidation; it was a long while before they made it a going concern again. Old Man Harper took a severe wound at Franklin. He recovered but was never quite the same again. Better than that, a conscription detail came by in December of '64 and grabbed the boy for a soldier in the Confederate army. He ended up fighting in a couple of serious battles in North Carolina before the declaration of peace."

"Did young Harper come back home after being paroled?" Wilkinson asked.

"I believe so. He stayed for three or four years, helping his father build back the farm, then one day up and lit out for parts unknown. At least, that's the way the story is told," Parslow said skeptically. "For the next couple of years, the parents held on, often by the skin of their teeth, during which Old Man Harper became very bitter, a person you tried to avoid. They owed damn near everyone in Buckland Station and were facing foreclosure. Then, one day, wonder of wonders, the miserable bastard became the happiest man in town. He had renewed pep in his step, smiled, and had a good word for everyone, yet there didn't seem to be the slightest reason for it. A week or two later, Ted returned home, rolling in greenbacks."

"Anyone ever ask or find out where he got them?" Seibert wondered.

"If anyone knows, they aren't telling. I'd say his parents were the most likely to have known, but both of them are dead now. Ted, to my knowledge, told no one where he spent those two years. It wouldn't surprise me if a bank or train robbery attributed to the James boys might have been his doing. At any rate, the boy trooped around town and paid off every cent the family owed. It wasn't until later that the townspeople slowly realized what they were dealing with."

"About what time did that occur?"

"1873, maybe a little earlier. Ted remained quiet for a time, continued to work on the farm. But some people told us he'd already developed a mean streak. That may be a remembrance that is faulty. About that time, he started courting and had several relationships before marrying Denise Flynn in '78. It's during that five-year period, '73 to '78, that things changed."

"How so? It looks like he was at last over the hump, you might say, getting ahead in life."

Parslow nodded. "I agree, but I'm not at all sure Ted ever saw it that way. As you remember, there was the financial panic in '73. Within a year or two, that problem moved from big cities to everywhere in the country. Banks failed or just hung on, and people around here who needed a loan couldn't get one at any rate of interest. Ted, though, had money, and for the right collateral, he was the only resort for borrowers."

"I'm guessing land was the collateral he wanted," Wilkinson conjectured.

"Correct. He told people that only had a place of business and their inventory to go piss up a rope. Also, he was an excellent judge of who wouldn't be able to pay up. If he thought someone might stay current on payments, he didn't lend to them either. A couple of people surprised him, yet they were in the minority. Them that didn't, he foreclosed on and took their collateral in payment."

"Any of these unfortunates among the people you questioned in Buckland Station?" Seibert inquired.

"Two or three. With a couple of exceptions, the people Ted took advantage of in his money lending scheme didn't live in town. They were farmers. He took their property and then sharecropped it. He was among the largest landlords in the county for tenant farmers when he died, and some of those in tenure were people he had working the land they once owned. Think about that for a minute."

Parslow paused for a moment, chewed at his lower lip, and weighed what he said next. "It's my view, based upon a stray comment or two here in town, that later on, Ted took fiendish delight in bankrupting small business owners when he got the chance. I wondered if personal bitterness over the fact that his father's place failed during the war could be the problem and that he wanted to see others like it go under. Could be that Old Man Harper urged him on, for all I could discover. However, one person pointed out to me that a couple of his victims happened to be ex-Confederate cavalrymen, and it occurred to me he might believe he recognized them as soldiers who plundered his father's shop. I can't say that I buy that, and the two of us didn't have time and resources to see if it had merit. Given Ted's disposition, I'd say if he thought that way, he decided that anyone resembling those looters could suffer for the rest."

Tom uttered an exclamation of disgust at the statement, and Ward felt the corners of his mouth slant downward as he considered the level of malice involved. "I suspect," Wilkinson remarked, "you're not even close to finishing your tale of Mr. Harper's misdeeds, and I suspect they're only going to become worse."

"Right again. Ted's mother began to fail in 1875—galloping consumption, they called it. She passed away in late '77, just a few months before Ted got hitched with Denise Flynn. The loss of his wife must have weighed heavily on Old Man Harper because he died about this time three years ago. When he passed, there wasn't anyone left to rein Ted in; perhaps there never was."

"His wife had no calming influence?"

"Denise?" Parslow asked incredulously. "Hell, no! In fact, I suspect he may have chosen her because he thought he could dominate her while at the same time receive her undying devotion."

The comment kindled Wilkinson's curiosity. "What makes you think that?" he questioned.

"Several things. For one, I guess you'd say Ted was a handsome enough feller. He was a desirable catch in that he was successful and could provide a comfortable home—the things, you know, that women consider important. Some men might have refused to allow their daughters any relationship with a man who had the repute Ted had, but his interest no doubt flattered Denise's family.

"Denise is a nice enough looking woman but nowhere near the most attractive one in these parts. Has curly red hair, lots of freckles.

The things I believe attracted Ted were that she was considerably younger than himself, probably a full decade, was naïve about men, and perhaps best of all is illiterate. She can neither read nor write. This allowed him to pursue his activities just like before he married, with her none the wiser."

"Denise Harper doesn't come from a prominent family?" Seibert asked. "We had the idea she's well connected politically."

"She is well connected. She has a brother over in Giles County who is a member of the General Assembly. I've read that he's a member of the House committee that oversees the courts. It has to be him that got the ear of the governor. However, not all families in the Flynn clan are created equal."

"So, you're saying Ted Harper stepped down in class in order to marry Denise?"

"That'd be about the long and the short of it, yes."

"They were happy together?"

"You'd have to ask her to find out for sure, but I'd say she looked at it that way. Since they wed, she's reveled in being Mrs. Harper, having more money to spend than many of the so-called 'well-bred women' in town and being catered to in shops and stores and so on. Behind her back, she's viciously despised. They had a son, who's three years old now, and I'd venture she's more than happy with him."

"Nevertheless," Wilkinson said, reentering the conversation, "many others hated him for his business practices and ethics. I imagine there are several other things. Let's move on to what else he got up to."

"By the time Old Man Harper passed," Parslow briskly resumed, "Ted was a known quantity. People understood how he operated and avoided involvement with him. Not that he fell on hard times, you understand; it just became difficult for him to get any bigger with his money loan and foreclosure strategy. From about 1879 on, anyone who did business with him on the terms he demanded had only themselves to blame. As a result, he entered the insurance business."

The sheriff favored the marshals with a conspiratorial grin. "No, Ted didn't begin offering policies—not in the normal sense. Further, what I'm telling you hasn't a shred of evidence to back it up; it's all hearsay. Simon and I got an earful about him targeting a carefully selected number of small shop owners. Apparently, he uttered threats as to what might happen to them or their businesses if they didn't turn over a certain amount of money to him every month."

"A damned extortionist," Seibert snarled. "I wonder if he got to San Francisco while he was absent from home. It's a popular crime among gangs that infest that city."

"We couldn't get a soul to identify a victim of this scheme, and no one would admit it had happened to them. There's nothing in the files to show anyone had complained to my predecessor, either. If they did, he did nothing about it."

"Might have shared in the collections," Wilkinson remarked.

"That sounds about like him," Parslow confirmed. "If so, it was a straightforward bribe. From what I can tell, those two had no friendship at all, and if they did, it fell apart later. Ted's continuing outrageous conduct affected that."

In an abrupt change of mood, the sheriff shifted his position and ceased to smile. Unlocking a desk drawer, he reached within and withdrew a yellowed envelope. "The sheriff's office received this in April 1881. It's an unsigned letter contending that Ted, finding one of his victims couldn't pay up, figured having relations with the man's wife would do just as well. Have a look," he said, passing it over to Wilkinson.

Ward read the brief communication and handed it to Seibert. He was aware of the icy glare in his friend's eyes; his irises turned gray whenever he became incensed. After a moment, he handed it back to Parslow. "Presuming this was true," Tom grated, "I'd return to Nashville and claim nothing could be determined. From the first, I've believed this man got what he deserved, and nothing you've related today changes that. If anything, it's reinforced it."

"Well," the sheriff said, "there's a bit more. August of last year, Ted got into some kind of dustup with Fred Reichert—he's a blacksmith and livery stable owner in Buckland Station. Mr. Reichert had done some farrier work on Ted's champion stallion, and Ted claimed to not like the results. I don't have any idea if the work was shoddy or if he had another reason for his refusal to pay. One word led to another, and gunplay ensued."

"Who drew first?" Wilkinson demanded.

"Depends on who you ask. Witnesses differed in their accounts. Most stated Ted did, and the result was the wounding of Reichert. Those same witnesses also stated that there wasn't a damn thing wrong with the work. Given my knowledge of Fred's expertise, I'd agree with their judgment.

"Of course, Ted contended Reichert drew on him, and one or two witnesses agreed or stated it was too close to tell. Thing was, though, the sheriff rode down there to arrest Harper for attempted murder, and he told him he would not surrender to him. It seems to me, based on a report he left behind, that Ted told him he'd turn himself in when he was damned good and ready, and if the sheriff tried to take him, he'd kill him."

Parslow produced another document and handed it over. "Check the note on the back. See if you agree with my conclusion."

Wilkinson scanned the one-page report, which was short on detail, then turned it over. At the bottom of the page, he read, "Harper refused to surrender when I asked him to turn over his weapon and come back to Shelbyville with me. Instead, he brushed back his coat, moved his hand to the butt of his pistol, and told me I wasn't taking him any damn where. Had I attempted to force him, I'm certain he would have shot me in my tracks. I'm no hand with a weapon, haven't had to use a gun in all my time in office; he is good with a gun and won't hesitate to use it."

"Did Harper ever surrender?" Wilkinson asked.

"About a week later. Turned up with Denise's brother, the General Assembly member; he's a real slick attorney as well. He got Ted unsecured bail and a delay in the meeting of the grand jury, and by the time it convened, no one would appear to testify about what they'd seen. The obvious implication is that Ted had spent his time intimidating everyone who might say he shot Reichert in an unprovoked attack. The prosecutor dropped the charge, and the entire populace got the idea Ted was a law unto himself."

"Which is precisely the reason the sonofabitch got shot," Seibert declared.

The four men grunted in agreement, and Wilkinson consulted his watch with concern. It was already past three o'clock, and they still had many names on Parslow's report to review. "Sheriff," he asked, "is there any chance we might catch Dr. Morris at home this afternoon? I still want to hear about the other names on your report, but my understanding is he's elderly. If he has an early bedtime, that will mean we'd have to wait until morning. I want to be in Buckland Station tomorrow."

Parslow laughed. "Your information is correct. He's eighty, at least, and can't see worth shit. It's a long walk to his house, so give me a minute to fetch my horse. We'll pick up with this when we get back. Simon, go to the restaurant and get us set up for some supper at six o'clock."

Chapter 9

THE MORRIS HOUSE badly needed repair, with the white paint blistering and peeling on the framed boards. The grass required mowing, and a rose bush, although in early bloom, looked bedraggled and in need of pruning. "Appears like it's been a spell since anyone performed maintenance," Wilkinson observed.

"Could use a lick and a promise for sure," Parslow agreed. "I don't know if Doc is at the age where he figures he won't live long enough for it to become an issue for him or if his eyesight is so damn poor that he can't see the problems."

"Hell of an impairment to have for a coroner's job," Ward noted in reply. "With his vision problems, does he still have many patients?"

"I doubt he does. He might have resigned this job if he wasn't afraid of falling into destitution. That's how things are, Marshal; society isn't very forgiving when you get too old to work and support yourself. When you do, most people that I observe figure you ought to go on and die and get the hell out of the way. There's not much human kindness in most folks," he declared. "They don't think they'll ever be among those that'll need it."

Seibert started to swing down from the saddle, but Parslow's comments brought him up short. He stared at the sheriff for a long moment, then nodded in sober acknowledgment. "In this kind of work, I can see how you might feel that way."

"I do," Parslow averred in an exasperated tone. "Let me tell you both something. There in the Good Book where Jesus tells the parable of the Good Samaritan? That fellow who went up from Jericho and fell among thieves, got robbed and beaten? Well, he was one lucky sonofabitch that one of the three people that passed by took pity upon him. There aren't any in Buckland Station, either; leastwise, not where Ted Harper is concerned!"

A gray-haired woman answered their knock, who the marshals at first presumed was Morris's wife. "I'm his housekeeper," she explained. "His missus passed away several years ago. I'm about to give him his afternoon tea. Let me ask if he'll see you."

After a moment, the woman returned, motioning them back through the house. The interior, Wilkinson noted, had a drab appearance, containing furniture and carpets that would now be antiquarian. Dr. Morris, hearing the footfalls, peered at the men as they entered the parlor, but it was apparent that he couldn't see them well. "Doc," Sheriff Parslow announced, "I've brought US Marshals Ward Wilkinson and Tom Seibert over to talk to you. They're from Nashville. They're ordered to look into Theodore Harper's death."

The older man sat silent for a moment as if his mind was going through a catalog, trying to find the proper page. Then, he abruptly straightened and spoke in a surprisingly firm voice. "Oh, yes," he enthused, "shot over at Buckland Station. Terrible business that, and nobody ever arrested for the crime."

"Doctor, I'm Marshal Wilkinson," Ward said, noting the opaque look from Morris's cataract-ravaged orbs. "With me is my Deputy, Tom Seibert. I'd like to ask you a few questions about your report on the Harper killing before we go over to Buckland Station tomorrow. Is that alright with you?"

"Don't see why not; there isn't much to tell. By the time I saw him, he'd been on ice for a couple of days, and I had nothing to rely on as to the time of death and where it occurred except from what I was told. What can I tell you about it?"

"It's our understanding it was murder and that the killers used firearms; would that be correct?"

"Yes, it would. Three bullets struck him. One came from the back. He wouldn't have survived that one but may have been conscious when the other two shots struck him. Both of them came from the front. Since the killer or killers shot him multiple times, and one was from behind, I figured that to be murder. Otherwise, his clothes were gone to where God only knows, rigor mortis was altered by laying him on a slab of ice, and as I'm sure you're aware, there wasn't a soul who'd admit they saw anything or did anything. Some people there are lying like hell, but I can't disprove what they've said."

"Had you ever met Mr. Harper?"

"Never heard tell of him, and never laid eyes on him until I saw him in that icehouse," Morris harrumphed. "I don't get to Buckland Station very often. Town has its own doctor, a fellow named Demarest. I had a talk with him while I was there, and he told me he was out in the country helping a farmwife with a difficult pregnancy when it happened. Wouldn't have mattered a hoot in hell if he had been nearby. The only help for Ted Harper, given his wounds, was a skillful undertaker."

Wilkinson arose, and the others followed suit. "Thanks for seeing us, Doctor," he said, "we appreciate your help."

"You're welcome, Marshal," Morris replied. "Come by anytime and let me know how it turns out."

"I'll be sure to do that, sir."

Moments later, the visitors were back at the street, and they shared a knowing look. "Neat coincidence that the local doctor was unavailable when Harper got shot," Seibert proclaimed. "Maybe *too* neat."

"That's what I was thinking," Wilkinson agreed. "We need to find out if a new baby came into the world while Mr. Harper left it."

Chapter 10

AT FIVE O'CLOCK, the men resumed their discussion at Parslow's office. Wilkinson, weary after a twelve-hour day that showed no signs of ending, plus a seventeen-mile ride, asked Parslow to focus on the most likely suspects that he'd mentioned in his report. "These will be the ones," the sheriff stated, "that Simon and I consider having motive and opportunity. Most everyone in town has the means or the means to get it. The ones we got around to were ones we determined the likeliest to be leaned on for money: small business owners who had their shops near where Ted got killed. Other ones, we discovered, had a quarrel with him."

"What about the rape victim or her husband?" Wilkinson asked.

"They're definitely possibilities, but we have no evidence, not even hearsay, to determine who they are."

"We'll take what we can get right now. Go ahead with your most likely suspect."

"The obvious choice," Parslow said, "is Fred Reichert. If someone put a bullet in me, I'd be a liar if I said I didn't want to return the favor. We questioned him closely, but he steadfastly claimed that he didn't have a thing to do with it. His wife swore and be damned that he was up at the wheelwrights when the shooting occurred, and we couldn't get anyone to say otherwise. I believe both of them feared Ted and were very glad he was dead."

"Reichert any good with a gun?" Seibert asked.

"Knows one end from the other, but he's clumsy as a quick draw artist."

"Doubt if it's him then," Tom declared. "Who's next?"

"Elijah 'Lige' Guthrie, the saloonkeeper. I don't believe a bit of that bullshit story of his that neither he nor any of his customers saw anything or ventured outside until well after the shooting stopped. He claims to have come from out west—Ellsworth, Wichita, Kansas, someplace like that. Told us he'd been in the saloon business most of his life. He's tough as nails, I'd say, and a prime target for Ted's 'insurance' scam. Lots of cash flows over that bar, and I doubt Guthrie intended to part with any of it."

"Did you learn the names of the saloon customers?"

"Guthrie claims not to remember a single one of his customers that morning. I can't prove he had any when it comes down to it, even though he'd been open for an hour by that time. Just part of the web of lies.

"Ronald Whipple is a noteworthy character," the sheriff continued, waving his finger in the air for emphasis. "He owns one of the general stores and is as mild-mannered and inoffensive as anyone in town. His wife, Edna, is not. You could make the case that she shot Ted herself or coerced her husband into doing it. Here again, their residence and place of business is near the scene, and that type of business is an attractive target."

"Anybody that's likely north of the tracks?" Wilkinson asked.

"I questioned those people," Simon Garrett replied. "We got no hint of their direct involvement, but it's almost certain some knew of a plan to kill Harper if it existed. Buckland Station isn't that big."

"A couple of neighbors of Ted's are far more interesting," Sheriff Parslow interjected. "He didn't get along with them, perhaps because they were successful and didn't need his money. I suspect he wanted to enlarge his farm by snapping up the adjacent properties, and they declined. One is a man named Perry Jessup. It might be one thing to intimidate him, but Del Orange is another matter."

"What's special about Orange?"

"Fought in the war, some elite sharpshooter unit. He may be the best marksman in the county and nobody to fool around with."

"Could he have shot Harper in the back?" Tom blurted.

"It's possible, not anything he hadn't done before. Also, he might have done so at a distance while someone else distracted Ted."

Wilkinson nodded. The scenario Parslow offered was one he'd been mulling ever since he'd read the report. "Sheriff," he asked, "what was this about some small book missing from Harper's clothing?"

"We don't know for certain. Someone turned Ted's pockets inside out to make it look like a robbery. However, I don't believe they intended to take his money. The book Denise told us was missing contained, I expect, all of Ted's transactions and the amounts owed to him. Since she can't read, she hasn't any idea what was in there unless he told her at some point, which I very much doubt. She claims those that owed him money aren't paying these days, but she couldn't or wouldn't tell me a single name of the delinquents."

"Odds are that the book burned to ashes in a fireplace grate minutes after they removed it from Harper's pocket," Tom conjectured. "What would be the purpose of keeping it around once they had possession?"

"Wouldn't be surprised," Wilkinson agreed. "Of course, whoever took it may not have considered that Ted had a duplicate copy somewhere. I wonder if he has a safe at home?"

"He could have, but if so, Denise said nothing about it," Parslow said with a coughing spasm. "There's a vague rumor that Denise has hired a new foreman for the farm. If there is a copy of Ted's tally book about, it will be interesting to see if this new fellow makes inquiries. What I *can* tell you is that it's six o'clock. Our supper is waiting over at the restaurant, and I'm starved."

Chapter 11

ALTHOUGH THE MEAL was once again pedestrian, Wilkinson, very impressed with the young sheriff, didn't notice the blandness of the food. Over coffee, he effusively praised the sheriff's work, attention to details, and hospitality. "I hope you won't mind," Ward concluded prior to their parting, "if I call on you for help, should we require it. Will you be in Shelbyville the next few days?"

"Unless there's an emergency, yes. Simon and I have quite a few warrants to serve, most of them being in and around the town. Send me a telegraph wire, and we'll come a running."

The marshals returned to their room, where they sat up for a while discussing what they'd learned from Sheriff Parslow and his deputy. "This list of prime suspects is helpful," Tom said, "yet I'm of the opinion there are one or more people involved who they never questioned."

"Quite possible," Ward replied from his precarious perch on the corner of the bed. "Unlike what one might believe, it isn't a matter of too few culprits. Instead, it's too damn many. Do you still think Reichert's not involved?"

"Hard for me to conclude otherwise. By Parslow's statement, he lacked skill with a gun, and he must have known that any second confrontation with Harper meant a killing matter. I'm surprised he risked it the first time, unless he suspected Ted intended to provoke a gun battle and went armed just in case. It doesn't seem logical to me he'd chance it."

"Unless," Ward said with a thoughtful look, "he was desperate or could count on help."

"That might put this Orange fellow into the picture."

"Could indeed. We need to find out from him and Jessup what Harper was trying to coerce them into doing. Old Ted may have found too late that leaning on a combat veteran was a dangerous thing. His body's going to be exhumed, and we'll have to get Obadiah down here to perform a thorough autopsy. Should he find the bullet that struck him in the back came from a hunting rifle or other large caliber, Mr. Orange will be at the top of the list."

"Agreed. Snipers, I'd say, develop a way to turn off their emotions and remain utterly calm. Shooting someone at a distance almost farther than you can see can become impersonal, especially if you repeat it often enough. Even if it was entirely personal, he would have been just as deadly."

Seibert scanned some of his voluminous notes and asked another question. "What do you think about Whipple, the store owner? You don't suppose it was his wife that Harper allegedly abused?"

"From the way Parslow described her, I doubt it. She sounds like the type to tear it loose from his body and beat him to death with it."

Tom threw his head back and laughed uproariously. "I think you may be right, and if so, richly deserved. I'll let you interview her. Wouldn't astonish me at all, though, to find out she helped organize the murder scheme."

"Who else do we have?"

"Several, but none strike me as very possible. They talked to the mayor, a banker, hotel proprietor, minister, and schoolmaster; none of these seem likely to interest Harper, given his goals. Seems to me they would be short on farmland and worked in occupations he would find difficult to exploit."

Ward gave Tom a thoughtful nod, acknowledging the logic of his statement. "If Harper was a certain type, money and success might not be what his motivations were. It's possible those things were merely a means to an end."

"Lust for power?"

"That's what I'm beginning to believe. Remember what the sheriff said about Harper? He took delight in bankrupting small entrepreneurs here in Shelbyville. I don't buy the theory that he recognized some of them as Confederate cavalrymen who looted his father's store. I'd say he did it to make himself appear fearsome, having dominion over others. If true, that doesn't reflect so much a desire to be rich as it does to be important."

"Think his wife might have had him killed?" Tom conjectured. "If she got wind of him warming the sheets with some poor woman who couldn't pay what Ted demanded, maybe she didn't stay as adoring as some thought her to be. I'd be afraid if Frances found out something like that about me."

"Doubtful," Ward chuckled in reply. "I don't want to think about such a thing in my home, either. We'll get a better idea soon, as I want to talk to her before we question anyone else. From what Sheriff Parslow told us, I got the impression she came from humble origins to marry one of the wealthiest men in the county. Given that he made her a home and provided enough money, regardless of where he got it, to allow her a comfortable lifestyle, she might not want to give up those trappings regardless of his infidelities."

Seibert emitted an expansive yawn. "Well, this day has had no quit in it. Let's get ready to turn out the lamp and take this up again in the morning."

"Fine by me," Ward agreed, unable to shake his own cloak of weariness. "As I'd mentioned earlier, before we leave, I want to drop by the *Shelbyville Gazette*, then visit the courthouse. If the paper has a photograph from a Saturday showing the sidewalks clogged with shoppers, we're going to take a dim view of people trying to feed us a line of shit about the streets being deserted when Harper was shot. We don't have to stand for election like the sheriff, and we don't live there. It's time to rattle some chains."

Chapter 12

WHEN WILKINSON AWAKENED, the first thing his bleary eyes beheld in the faint light in the room was the sight of Tom shaving at the mirror. Seibert, noticing his friend swing his legs to the floor, paused his scraping and voiced his disdain for the quality of the bed. "I've not slept on a more uncomfortable mattress since I served on a board of inquiry at Fort Concho. Damn thing is stuffed full of cornstalks or God knows what. It sure isn't down."

Ward, giving his shoulders and neck an uncomfortable stretch, added a grumble of his own. "The pillows are even worse. Let's get around and check out of this place before we're invalided by the accommodations."

"I won't miss that diner either," Tom declaimed. "How the Sheriff stands eating there as often as he does is more of a mystery than how Ted Harper died." That comment produced peals of laughter from both men, their grousing now forgotten.

After breakfast, a meal the marshals limited to toast and coffee, the men retrieved their mounts and rode the short distance to the newspaper office. "Are you certain you want to do this, Ward?" Tom asked. "If he knows who we are, he could turn right around and wire someone in Buckland Station about our coming."

"I thought about that. Still, unless he's a friend of Harper's—and we haven't found one yet—or is knowledgeable about who killed him, I can't see what benefit he'd accrue from doing so. If he cooperates with us, I'm going to promise him the earliest notification when we make an arrest and make clear he'll be the last to find out if he doesn't." They dismounted and stepped inside.

A thin, balding, and bespectacled man with ink-stained fingers greeted them, and both men noted the missing tip of the middle finger on his right hand, likely caused by an unfortunate smashing by the printing plate. Wilkinson asked to see the owner, and the man motioned to a figure with his back turned toward them who was leaning over a page of typescript. So intense was his concentration that he appeared not to discern their approach until they stood next to him. "Mr. Billings, I'm Ward Wilkinson, United States Marshal from Nashville. This is my Deputy, Tom Seibert. We're here to ask for a little information about Buckland Station."

Timothy Billings was in his mid-forties, Wilkinson determined, with curly brown hair, dark eyes, and a face framed with a mustache and extravagant sideburns. It mirrored the style favored by President Chester Arthur. His features reddened in irritation at the interruption, then assumed a shrewd, knowing look. "You're here about Theodore Harper, aren't you? Got to be."

"What if we are?" Wilkinson replied in a rather chilly voice. "What's it to you?"

"Don't be devious, Marshal," Billings rejoined in a faintly mocking tone. "It's obvious why I'm interested. It's news, sir. And more than that, it's local, sensational, and involves an unsolved murder. So, when federal marshals arrive to investigate, I'm definitely interested."

"Point taken," Wilkinson replied, "but I'm going to ask you not to make our presence known to your readers—not yet, anyway."

"I don't believe I can honor that request, Marshal. It would be a disservice to our readers to keep that quiet."

"A disservice to yourself and your bottom line, you mean." Billings made a spluttering noise, and Wilkinson cut him off. "Let me make myself clear, sir. You assist us with what we need to the best of your ability and keep our arrival here quiet until I say it's alright to publicize it, and I'll assure that you'll be the first person I notify when we make an arrest. I'll also make a statement or two for attribution that you can use in your front-page story. However, you inform someone there that we're coming, splatter it all over your next edition, or let it slip, inadvertently or not, and you'll be the last sonofabitch to get the word. I'll wire the Nashville papers and every county or regional journal in this area.

You'll get to read all about it in their special editions. Understand?"

Billings's face paled in fury, and his hand clenched the corner of the table until it turned white. Then, reading the determination in Wilkinson's face, he sagged in capitulation. "Very well, Marshal," he said in a thick tone, "what do you want from me?"

"Just one thing. Have you ever published a photo in your paper that shows the streets of Buckland Station on a market day, Saturday, or day of celebration?"

The newspaperman blinked in amazement. "Is that all? Well, yes, we have, twice at least. I'm not sure how they will help with your investigation. One was on the Centennial, July 4th, 1876. The other, though, occurred two years ago. We did a story on the economic effect of the railroad coming to Buckland Station. Along with that, we ran a photo showing the 'Railroad Square.' It's surrounded by the main commercial area in town. That was market day, and the streets were full of people."

"That's the one we want to see," Ward said with a smile.

Billings disappeared into a small office, the newspaper's library, for several minutes. When he returned, his hand held a yellowing sheet of paper. "Here," he said in a flinty voice. "Will there be anything else?"

Ward took the page, which was dated as a Saturday, studied the photo, then carefully passed it over to Tom. The image showed a street scene with many people, young and old, strolling past a row of commercial buildings. At a distance, in the upper half of the image, stood a large building with some type of structure to its front. "What is the structure at the top of this photograph?" he asked.

"That's the NC & STL freight terminal. In front of it is the stockyard. I took this on a market day; the enclosure was full of animals waiting for shipment."

"Thank you," Ward said as Seibert returned the sheet to Billings. "We've taken quite enough of your time this morning, sir, and we appreciate your help. You'll be hearing from us."

Billings uttered no words of acknowledgment or farewell. Wilkinson felt no great desire to pass civilities with the man. He and Tom headed for the door, and when they looked back, they saw Billings berating the man who'd first greeted them about a typesetting error. From an adjacent desk, a reporter tried to compete for the man's attention concerning some news copy, and along the rear of the building, another employee draped a freshly printed page to dry across a line that stretched from one wall to the other. The owner, alarmed at his carelessness, paused his chastisement of the typesetter long enough to caution the man against leaving wrinkles in the paper. "Remember, we print the other side once it dries," he scolded.

"How'd you like to have Billings's job?" Ward asked Tom as they mounted their horses.

"Hell, no," came the rejoinder. "I'd be afraid of what Obadiah would prescribe as a cure for ulcers."

* * *

The marshals retraced their steps to the Public Square and ascended the steps of the three-story, buff-colored brick and concrete courthouse. Built a decade earlier, it sported stately columns on all sides of the building between the second and third floors, with six on the north and south sides, topped by a pediment at the entrances, and four on the east and west sides, with a header above the roofline. In the center of the roof, a square tower, painted white, with a cupola and clock completed the impressive structure. Ward and Tom, seeing a clerk come out of an office, asked directions to the records and following the man's finger, entered a small room and set to work.

The lawmen started with the tax records, which revealed Ted Harper had owned numerous tracts of land throughout the county. Most of it, though, lay in and around Buckland Station. They traced his acquisitions back through the deed transfers and the grantors index and got a knowledge of the empire he'd amassed and the residents who'd done business with him. The number ran into the dozens, as did the pages Seibert scribbled in his notebook.

Most victims came from rural areas outside the town and didn't appear on Sheriff Parslow's list of potential suspects. Both lawmen agreed that this had little to do with whether they were involved in the crime.

"Some of these transactions, as hard as it may be to believe," Wilkinson said, "might have been straightforward, even boring."

To their amazement, Old Man Harper had transferred ownership of his farm to his son several years prior to his death. "Why in blazes would he do that?" Seibert asked in bewilderment as he ineffectually attempted to clear the dirt from the dusty tomes off his clothes. "He inherited; one would presume."

"If you could threaten to put someone out in the cold if they didn't do what you told them, it would impose your will on that person," Ward replied.

Tom gave his friend an incredulous look, then became wrathful. "If we discover he did that for the reason you suggest, I'm going to make a point of pissing on that sonofabitch's grave before we leave Buckland Station!"

Chapter 13

THE TEDIOUS NATURE of tracking Harper's real estate holdings required most of the forenoon, and Wilkinson, a sour timbre in his voice, opined that the diner they both abhorred would, of necessity, be the source of the midday meal. "We can only hope," he said with no small amount of sarcasm, "that Buckland Station has a place or two that has a halfway competent cook."

"If not, Obadiah will be happy," Seibert joked. "He's constantly on my ass about losing weight, and by damn, I believe I could around here. It's barely plausible," he contended in a withering tone, "but this outfit fucks up bacon and eggs."

Once more, the marshals were very selective in their menu choices. Neither trusted what might be in the day's soup, and they confined themselves to a slice of salted ham, some vegetables that looked as if the last rites had been uttered over them, and a hunk of semi-stale bread. Near the end of the meal, Sheriff Parslow came in, and Ward and Tom passed along what they'd discovered at the courthouse and newspaper. Then, taking their leave, they mounted up and began the dozen-mile ride to Buckland Station.

The lawmen's route lay to the northeast, at first through gently undulating terrain. Beyond, steeper slopes arose, and these escarpments, topped with narrow ridges, gave way to plunging ravines. Where the land remained undisturbed, oaks, hickory, red cedar, hackberry, and locust abounded. Among the smaller vegetation was trumpet vine, redbud, sassafras, dogwood, and honeysuckle, its heady aroma being pushed along by a prevailing southwest wind. On the cleared gradients, beef cattle and flocks of sheep grazed on broom sedge and similar grasses. Hogs roamed the woods, fattening on acorns.

The most often observed crop was corn, the now emerged greenery rippling in the breeze. There were wheat fields, and Tom pointed out the occasional tillage of cotton, tobacco, and rye. Some farms had significant numbers of dairy cattle; others were breeding horses and mules. "I wouldn't say these folks are getting rich," Ward noted, "but it doesn't appear they're in poverty either."

"Unless, of course," Seibert said, "some people we see laboring in these fields are sharecropping for the likes of Ted Harper. I can't see how anyone having to do that ever comes out ahead."

"Best part of this that I can see," Wilkinson replied, his tone thoughtful and somber, "is there isn't anyone riding about the field with a whip or club, barking orders and threats or laying into someone whenever he feels like it. Such things are going on today that don't pass muster, but I don't detect those practices here."

Tom swept his eyes across the distant expanse of an adjoining farm and nodded in agreement. Ward, he mused, with his nearly unquenchable optimism, saw a positive aspect in most matters, no matter how grim. For himself, though, he no longer ascribed to such views. The turmoil at home with his daughter, his father-in-law's damned endless carping about his choice of employment, and the growing cynicism he felt about whether their efforts produced any lasting value, even deterrence, weighed heavily on Tom's soul. If not for his ironclad friendship with Wilkinson, he would have resigned months ago.

For a time, Ward lapsed into silence, the quiet only broken by the clip-clop of iron shoes thudding on the hard roadbed. It wasn't until the lawmen stopped to rest their horses and stepped into a thicket to relieve their bladders that he spoke again. "I want us to keep our badges out of sight when we go into town. We'll reveal our identity and purpose soon enough. In particular, let's remain mysterious until we've interviewed Mrs. Harper. A couple of strangers in town might cause someone to make an impulsive move. If they do, it just might lead to a mistake."

At two-thirty, after observing that houses along the Shelbyville road were becoming more plentiful, the men paused at the western edge of the community and had their first look at Buckland Station. At a distance, it seemed picturesque, yet rather languid for this hour of the day. Commercial buildings of brick and stone flanked the central street, with the cross streets occupied by substantial houses, some of brick but most of wood shingles and clapboards clad in white paint. Through the middle of town, its two depots on opposite sides of the tracks, lay the rails of the Nashville, Chattanooga & St. Louis Railroad.

Neither man took the torpor for granted. In their experience, especially in western towns they'd known, a misinterpreted look, a wrong word, or an imagined slight often resulted in a sudden explosion of violence. There wasn't anything subtle about Theodore Harper if the information they possessed had any accuracy. He'd been an ogre who made plain his motives in as blatant and brazen a manner as possible. For those accumulated transgressions, he'd paid with his life.

Wilkinson pointed north, and he and Seibert steered their mounts along the edges of the settlement, then walked them west until they reached Independence Street. On this side of the tracks stood frame houses, well dispersed, most with backyard gardens. At a distance, they glimpsed a structure they would later learn was a private educational building. Turning southward and back to the east, the lawmen passed a sprawling complex comprising a large brick livery stable with shops for a blacksmith, wheelwright, wagon maker, and carpenter. Veering left, they headed toward the south side of the Railroad Square and became cognizant of interested stares for the first time.

The marshals passed the intersection of Shelby Street, and Seibert became aware of a face peering at them from the upper story of a large-frame house that stood near the corner. Further was a stone blacksmith shop with a frame livery stable and feed store. On their left lay the stockyard and freight depot. "In this next block," Ward said to Tom in a quiet voice, "if I'm not mistaken, is where Ted Harper met his end."

The first storefront was a grocery, followed by a restaurant, a pair of grocery and dry goods establishments, and then another restaurant. Both men felt eyes boring into their backs as they rode past. Beyond, across the space of a vacant lot, was a one-story red brick building with a sign emblazoned with large letters advertising itself as a saloon. A man sitting on a chair tipped back against the wall turned his head toward the doors and spoke to someone unseen when he detected the approach of the unknown riders. Ward and Tom made a close study of him as they went by, but the man buried his chin in his chest, refusing to meet their gaze. The marshals shared a knowing grin; there was at least one worried man in town.

The rest of the commercial street comprised a mélange of vacant lots and buildings, a bedspring factory, and a confectionary shop. "Let's go to the other side of the tracks, see what's there, and then go to the hotel and check in," Ward suggested. "I hope it has a dining room; the second restaurant we saw doesn't give me confidence."

Back to the north, they passed a large complex containing a cornmeal mill and sawmill, then recrossed the tracks to the right of the passenger terminal. Buttressed by the hotel on the right, the businesses north of the square included several professional and governmental offices. Among the other enterprises were furniture, drug, and clothing stores. The town bank was there, along with the post office. Nearby, along the southern border of Main Street, a thoroughfare that slanted diagonally away to the northeast, small shops were located: millenary, the butcher, barber, and cobbler. Ward, a voracious reader, noted a bookshop. "We've got our bearings now," he said. "After we check in, we'll take the horses to a livery stable, get them cared for, then get something to eat."

The marshals rode the short distance back to the hotel and tied their tired mounts to a hitching rail. Retrieving their travel valises, blanket rolls, and long guns, they entered the lobby and went to the reception desk, where a slight, smallish man with sallow features observed their approach with a look of manifest unease. "Something I can do for you gentlemen?" he asked, his tone hesitant.

Wilkinson regarded the man for several cool moments before making a reply. The wall receptacle behind the desk showed a room key in nearly all the slots, so it was likely the hotel had several vacancies. To support that view, the register lay open to his gaze, and only a half-dozen signatures occupied the dates reflected on the current page. "Room," he snapped in a peremptory tone, "top floor, facing the street."

The man's face became even more unhappy, and he fiddled idly with the pair of snappy-looking suspenders that held up his trousers. "I'm afraid those are all spoken for, sir," he replied, refusing to return Wilkinson's glare. "One of them would have to be displaced."

Given the level of occupancy, Wilkinson felt certain the man was lying. Even if he wasn't, he determined to carry this charade through to the end. "Then displace them," he said in an even harsher tone. "We haven't got all day to stand around here quibbling with you. This place have a dining room?"

The desk clerk produced a defeated sigh, and with a couple of fearful glances, he turned and pulled a key from the cabinet. "Room 302," he said in a subdued voice.

"Thank you," Ward replied in an amused manner—one that conveyed that he knew the man hadn't been telling the truth. "I'm glad to see you didn't have to vacate a guest from his room. Now, how about that dining room?" he reiterated as he signed his own name to the register.

"Through there to your left. We won't be serving until five-thirty. Will you be staying long?" the clerk inquired in a fretful tone that expressed tomorrow would be an eternity.

"Until we conclude our business here," Seibert replied, revealing nothing.

Wilkinson produced a twenty-dollar gold piece, demanded a receipt for the prepayment, and pitched the room key to Tom. "Go on up," he said, "I'll be along in a minute."

Seibert grabbed his gear and headed up the stairs. When he got to the room, he unlocked the door, placed his things in a corner, and proceeded to the window. From the inside pocket of his duster, he retrieved a small brass spyglass and ranged it on the street below. Several minutes later, Ward entered the room, and Tom, never turning his head, chuckled in admiration. "It's just as you figured might happen," he confirmed, "he's on the move."

Seibert stood motionless for a time, then swung the glass to the right. "He disappeared around the front of the passenger depot," he announced. "If we weren't on the top floor, I'd have no chance at all. Let's see if I can find him again." Tom extended the glass to its full focal length, and a moment later, he became rigid, focusing on a single spot. "I'll have to confirm when we take the horses to the livery, but I believe he headed into that saloon we passed. It's brick, and I recall there are vacant lots on each side."

"Wait for him to come out. Once it's clear he's coming back, we'll go on to the livery. I'm just hoping he doesn't go further down the street where we can't see him. It didn't look like he had anyone to cover for him on the desk, so I don't believe he'll tarry. I doubt if the owner, his name's Cochran if I recall correctly, would approve."

Moments later, the clerk reappeared on the square. "He's out of view," Seibert said, shifting his position. After a few tense seconds, Tom relaxed, and he peered over his shoulder. "He's coming back across the tracks and heading this way."

"Excellent," Ward replied, taking a notebook out of his saddlebags and jotting some observations. "We need to get that man's name. Either he's directly involved in this matter or is acting as a lookout for somebody that is. Let's give him a few minutes to get back behind his desk, and then we'll head out. This," he said with a broad smile, "is already getting interesting."

Chapter 14

IT WAS LESS THAN a quarter-mile back to the livery stable and feed store owned by Fred Reichert. As the marshals passed Elijah Guthrie's saloon, both men noted that the man they'd observed sitting outside had disappeared. They looked over the batwing doors, but the gloomy interior revealed nothing.

By now, it was late afternoon. More people were on the street, some heading home from work, others heading for the shops and stores before closing time. The people scanned the strangers with interest, some with evident apprehension. While not unusual for locals to be suspicious of strangers, Wilkinson thought, usually it wasn't this overt.

The doors of the stable gaped open wide, and a young man, no more than twenty years old, clad in faded dungarees, a sweat-stained shirt, and an ancient hat, stepped forward to take the reins. "Howdy, gentlemen," he called in cheerful greeting. "Water and feed for your horses?"

"Cleaned up, too," Wilkinson replied. "We want them saddled and ready by eight o'clock in the morning."

"They'll be ready. You come far?"

"A piece," Seibert answered in a noncommittal tone. "What's going on around the town?"

"The usual, I guess. Most of what happens centers on the railroad. Buckland Station is the major stockyard between Nashville and Chattanooga," the young man announced with a note of pride. "And all the herds and flocks move on freight trains. Oh, forgot to mention, it'll be two bits a day per animal."

Wilkinson dug into his pocket and handed over fifty cents. "Fair enough. We'll be here at least another day, likely longer."

"Anything else I can help you with?"

"Will you be here in the morning? If so, we might need help with some directions."

"Sure, mister. I'm here most of the time. Mr. Reichert, my uncle, owns this place and the blacksmith shop next door. He does the smithing, my aunt keeps the feed store, and me, I'm Dick Reichert, I run the livery."

"Well, Mr. Reichert, I'm Ward," Wilkinson volunteered. "And this is my partner, Tom. We're staying at the hotel. If you need to contact us, you'll find us there or can leave a message with the desk clerk. What's his name?"

"That'd be Andy McCormick," Dick supplied. "He's been there since the place opened."

"Thanks."

The marshals headed back to the hotel. The dining room wouldn't open for a half-hour, and both men wanted to wash off some of the trail dust they'd accumulated over the miles since leaving Shelbyville. After cleaning up, the men stepped into the hall, where Tom kept watch while Ward checked out the access to the fire escape. In a short while, he returned, a confident look on his face. "The lock will be easy to pick, and only the worst luck would have anyone seeing us coming and going once it's dark. Let's hope Mr. McCormick leads us to some more people we need to talk to."

"And if he just goes home?"

"We go see Denise Harper in the morning, see what she has to say about Ted's enemies, then go from there."

* * *

The dining room was functional instead of opulent, but the food made up for the lack of trappings. Its bill of fare featured fresh fish an angler had brought in that afternoon, boiled potatoes, and salad greens. The coffee was better than any they'd drank since leaving home, and the marshals determined that an apple dumpling to go with it seemed a capital idea. When finished, they loafed outside for a long time, enjoying cigars.

At dusk, Tom clumped upstairs, past the anxious desk clerk, while Ward remained behind. At seven, with the night clerk now behind the desk, McCormick plunged through the door, taking a furtive glance toward the lawman as he passed. When he was fifty yards along, he looked back, and Wilkinson, still lounging in a chair on the hotel's veranda, touched his hat in salute.

The man hustled away, and the darkness swallowed him up. Less than a minute later, a sudden flare of light blossomed at the rear of the passenger depot, and Ward made for the front corner of the building where Seibert would be waiting. A frisson of excitement sparked within him, and he was certain his hunch was correct.

The pale, waning moon hadn't risen, and the marshals stuck to the shadows as they followed in McCormick's wake. They kept near to the freight depot, scuttled onward toward the stockyard, then dashed across the square to where a forty-foot gap existed between the darkened blacksmith shop and the Reichert livery stable, the structure where the desk clerk had gone. Directly ahead of them stood an attached shed with a half-raised window from which faint lamplight was visible. Reaching the wall, they knelt beneath the opening. Within came the sounds of a heated conversation.

"I'm telling you," McCormick hissed, his voice cracking with angst, "those two are gunmen. Came in this afternoon, and that tall one acted like he owned the place the way he talked to me. Disgraceful. But when you got one with you, the one wearing the tied-down gun, just like that sonofabitch who's gone to work for Mrs. Harper, I reckon you can treat people any way you please."

"Did they tell what their business was in Buckland Station?" asked an unseen voice, sounding cold and imperturbable.

"No," the clerk answered with impatience, "but unless you're telling me they're outlaws come to rob the bank, why else would they be here other than . . ."

McCormick's voice trailed off, and the second man spoke again. "I thought I told you, Andy—I thought I told all of you—to keep your damn mouths shut about that. I don't give a shit what situation or conversation topic calls it to mind. You all agreed that this was going to be a forbidden subject. If any one of you loose-lipped fools spills this by betrayal or by accident, I swear I'll see to you myself."

"That's easy for you to say," a third man rejoined. "But then, you were in the war, seen things like this before; we're just shopkeepers and farmers. We never figured anything like this would happen. What if it turns out they're gunmen she's hired to get the answers she wants by any means necessary?"

"If that's what they truly are, we'll do as we did before; we'll make a plan and deal with the threat. However, suppose they're something else?"

"And I say, what else can they be?" McCormick asked with asperity.

"Could be lots of things, Andy. You said they brought long guns; maybe they intend to do some hunting."

"You don't believe that, do you?"

"I don't know what to believe; I've not met them yet. Maybe they are as you say. Yet if they are, it doesn't necessarily mean that the person you think has hired them actually has. They could be worse than freelance gunhands."

"Such as?"

"Pinkerton's, for example. Given their ruthless reputation, can you imagine what would happen if someone killed a couple of their agents in this town? Don't any of you be going off half-cocked until we find out who we're dealing with.

"Something else," the man with the chilly, unruffled tone continued, "we have to consider is the possibility that they're the law." At this, Ward and Tom's eyes locked, and they shared a frown of concern.

"The law!" McCormick squeaked, his voice sounding like a mouse in extremis. "Sheriff Parslow and his damnable deputy already investigated . . ."

This time, the calm voice vanished. "Andy, if you don't shut your fucking mouth, I'm going to shut it for you. Sheriff Parslow, for your information, isn't the only law officer with authority in this part of the country. There are US Marshals stationed around the region, and for all we know, the state could have appointed some special investigators to come down here. You kill one of them, and someone will get the noose. So, for right now, keep doing as you've been doing, eyes and ears open, mouth shut. You don't have to go seeking them out, talking among yourselves, or anything. If they are any of the things we've discussed, they'll come to us."

For a moment, complete silence reigned, and the marshals willed themselves to remain motionless lest they give themselves away. "The rest of you, any questions?" the man who was obviously the leader of the group asked. A fourth man replied in the negative, but a fifth asked if they'd be meeting again. "That depends on what Andy and your nephew learn when they're talking with these men. It needs to be important, though. We take a chance every time we get together like this. For now, let's get the hell out of here and go home."

There was a shuffling noise, with the sound of footfalls rapidly receding. Ward saw Tom reach back and loosen the rawhide thong that held his six-gun in place. If anyone came around the corner of the shed, they would find themselves staring down the muzzle of a .45. Once it was quiet for several minutes, they arose, carefully looked about, and then headed westward, through a pair of backyards, until they arrived at Shelby Street. Still finding themselves alone, the marshals made their way north, skirted the stockyard, and crossed the rails. From there, they made a beeline back to the hotel, crept up the fire escape, and returned to their room. They had much to discuss.

Chapter 15

THE MARSHALS REMAINED awake for a long time, speaking in muted whispers. Whatever slim doubts they harbored had evaporated. Their eavesdropping confirmed that the five men gathered were involved in some illegality, although both conceded they had heard nothing that would justify immediate arrests in the killing of Ted Harper. The leader of the group had seen to that. Whoever he was, that person intended to stamp out any mention of the act committed and to emphasize his determination by threats of violence. They needed to identify him and his fellow conspirators as soon as possible.

As the marshals discussed what they'd heard, both men realized they knew two of the five. One was the bucket-mouthed Andy McCormick, and the unknown group leader had revealed a second man. By referring to "your nephew" as someone who could provide information concerning the marshals meant the man must be Fred Reichert, the blacksmith and livery owner. "Five will get you ten that the leader is Elijah Guthrie," Wilkinson conjectured. "The third man referred to him as someone who'd been in the war. We know via Sheriff Parslow that he was in the thick of it."

"I'd say that's right," Tom agreed. "I'm wondering if those five make up all that are a part of this. If they arranged this meeting in haste, perhaps it wasn't possible for everyone to attend."

"I think you're right," said Wilkinson after a moment's consideration. "McCormick is nothing but an errand boy, a glorified spy in a job that's ideal for keeping an eye on visitors. Also, I'd say there's a good chance one of those who didn't speak until spoken to has developed a great deal of misgiving about his involvement. It's going to be difficult to establish the identities of the fourth and fifth men."

"Something else," Tom remembered. "The same man who was referring to the leader also mentioned 'she' when he said a gunslinger was working here. He's referring to Denise Harper. As you recall, McCormick mentioned her by name in association with this fellow."

"Yes," Ward affirmed. "Let's reduce this to writing and get to bed. I'd sure like to discover who this man is that the locals now defer to so much."

* * *

Breakfast was eggs, country ham, biscuits, and more excellent coffee. The lawmen dropped off their key with the cagy-eyed McCormick and, with their long guns and a satchel containing all their documents in hand, headed down to the livery stable to get their mounts. Wilkinson didn't care for the possibility that Dick Reichert might be a part of this murderous cabal, yet he couldn't discount the possibility since the conspirators had uttered his name during their clandestine council. He, too, was now under suspicion.

The horses, both brushed and curried, were ready, saddled, and tied to the hitching rail when the marshals arrived. One of them gave a soft nicker, and the young stableman, hearing the sound, appeared at the door and looked up and down the street. When he saw the men, he flashed a friendly smile that lacked the slightest hint of guile and walked over to where Ward and Tom were stowing their rifles in the saddle scabbards. "Been a couple of people in looking over your rigs," he remarked. "Yours particularly. Reckon they've seen nothing like it."

"And who might these curious folks be?" Ward asked, his grin equally easy.

"My uncle, for one. I think the saddle intrigued him. Said it didn't come from around here. I think he hoped I'd learn where y'all are from, but I will not ask such a question," he declared with an impatient shake of his head. "It's your own business."

The comment pleased Wilkinson. "Who else besides your uncle?"

"Mayor Wiley, of all people. I think he's afraid you're here because of that Harper business a few weeks ago. Wouldn't surprise me if he hurried up to the telegraph and wired the sheriff."

"Really?" Ward chuckled. "Do you know anything about the Harper business?"

The younger Reichert gave Wilkinson an inquiring glance. "Not a thing," he shrugged. "When it occurred, I was back in the barn currying the Reverend Hoffberger's mare. My uncle had replaced the shoes on the animal, and he brought her down here and told me to clean her up good. The gunshots spooked her, and she began rearing and plunging. By the time I got her quieted down, it was all over. I figured there were enough people to look about it, so I stayed with the mare in case she acted up again. Come to think of it, I couldn't have left. My aunt's sister in Wartrace is doing poorly; she was up there looking after her. We had a sign on the door telling people to come back to the livery if they wanted to buy feed."

"How about your uncle?"

"He was up on Independence Street, at the wheelwright. One of our wagons had a problem with its rim, and they were talking about how to repair it. He said he and Mr. Martin never heard a thing, only learned about it when somebody told them."

Wilkinson looked at Seibert and could tell he was sharing his thoughts. Reichert might be telling the truth, yet based on Sheriff Parslow's experience, it was also likely that this story was one of dozens they would soon receive: a well-crafted tale, difficult to refute, like as not a complete lie. "Well, Dick," he said, "it's ironic you should mention Harper. We need directions out to his widow's farm. Can you tell us how to get there?"

Surprise radiated from Dick Reichert's eyes, but Wilkinson was mindful that the expression wasn't wary or disturbed. "It's not far. Just go through the square, back to Main Street, then head past the Baptist Church about four miles, and it'll be on your left. It's an old, rambling farmhouse; Mr. Harper's father added on to it several times during his life. Awful big place for just Mrs. Harper and her son, but with her new ramrod and a couple of hands living there now, perhaps it isn't as empty anymore."

"There are rumors about this man," Tom said. "Have you met him?"

"Once. He came in here while my aunt was out of town to have his horse shod and had it trotting along behind a wagon. While my uncle changed its shoes, I helped him load grain sacks."

"What did he look like?"

"About six feet tall, slim build, dark black hair and eyes. Wears a gun belt slung low, just like you do, and ties down the holster. He isn't unfriendly but has a way he looks at you that makes a man right uncomfortable. I hope I never get on his bad side."

"Ever tell you his name?"

The young man made a disparaging noise that snorted from his nostrils. "Yeah. Told me he was called Slim Smith. Have you ever listened to such a load of horseshit in your life?"

Chapter 16

THE MARSHALS TROTTED their mounts along Railroad Square, then steered them left, over the railroad tracks, and headed for Main Street. As they made their turn, they passed in view of Whipple's General Store. The owner, Ronald Whipple, busy stocking shelves behind the counter, was oblivious to their presence, but his wife, Edna, whose views usually held sway in the marriage, studied them with interest. She'd heard gossip from customers that there were a pair of formidable-looking strangers in town. What she saw caused her lip to curl in distaste.

For a moment, she glanced toward her husband, a middle-aged man with graying hair that now only grew on the sides of his head, and determined it wasn't worth the effort to call his attention to them. Most men, she'd long ago decided, wanted three things: someone to cook for them, alcohol, and a woman when they wanted one. When it came to using their brains, they had to be disengaged from another part of their body first.

Edna had warned her husband about involving himself with the group plotting to do away with Ted Harper, that there would be consequences. Yet had he listened? Hell, no, he hadn't. Like everyone else, he'd dismissed her as a modern-day Cassandra—an alarmist. This was more than ironic, she considered, since most people in town thought her domineering. She was aware of her whispered nickname, the "Iron Butterfly."

Even more contradictory, Edna mused, was that Ronald, malleable and suggestible, had defied her. No, he hadn't taken part in the ambush, but he'd known all about it. "Come help with the inventory," he'd said right before the shooting, a request she'd agreed to since the store was unaccustomedly empty. She now wondered if he'd done it so she wouldn't see one of the shooters go by. When the gunfire began, he'd told her to stay in the back with him for five more minutes and it would all be over. She'd done as he asked without argument, and thereafter, he'd reverted to allowing her to boss him around. He'd been quite calm that day, but that was before all these outsiders appeared.

As Edna had expected, the outcome hadn't cured all their woes. The townspeople had success in rebuffing the new sheriff in his efforts to find the killers, but within weeks, that pistol-toting character—Smith, he called himself—started working for Denise Harper. Not only did he wear a gun, but rumor said that he was going about collecting rent and enforcing agreements that most thought would be null and void because of Ted's death. Thus far, there weren't any plots Edna had learned of to kill him.

These new strangers represented a danger unlike that of Slim Smith. He was a known quantity; they were yet to reveal their intentions. The man on the bay horse had a distinguished look about him, but his grim-faced partner made her unsettled, even frightened. It was a shame he hadn't been around in the past. He wouldn't have taken any bullshit from that bastard, Ted Harper, or anyone else. Such a presence in the community might have caused Ted to rein in his ambitions or at least think twice before running roughshod over people. That muse brought forth an awful thought: had the Harper's widow brought them here to do just that?

Edna realized suddenly that her husband had drawn near and was staring at the two men as they urged their mounts over the tracks. His color turned ashen, and he had a tormented expression on his face. Trying to convey a confidence she didn't possess, Edna reached back, squeezed his hand, and smiled.

Chapter 17

THE RIDE WAS an easy one. Wilkinson and Seibert soon found themselves at the entrance to a well-worn path adorned with a signpost that proclaimed ***Harper Farm*** in bold lettering. The lane led to a rambling, single-story, white frame house, one augmented several times over the years, with a fenced-in backyard. A substantial barn loomed in the distance with several smaller structures—one, a ramshackle dwelling that likely served as a bunkhouse for hired hands. It was a bright yet chilly morning, and a lazy curl of grayish smoke rose from the chimney. Someone was home.

"At least for now," Wilkinson said, reaching into his pocket, "we better pin these badges on. We don't know if Mrs. Harper knows that someone is coming, so we best be transparent as to who and what we are. I'm very curious to see if she's anything like Sheriff Parslow described her. My hunch is that while she may be illiterate, she's not as helpless as he thinks. Let's go."

The men rode up to the house in an easy gait, got down, and tied their horses to a hitching rail. Both mounts gratefully dipped their muzzles in the water trough and drank. A flagstone walkway led to the back, and they were about to follow it when a gate, its hinges grating in protest, opened at the far corner of the structure directly behind them. Both men turned to see a figure coming through the opening that fit the description of the mysterious foreman who called himself Slim Smith.

The man, glimpsing the marshals' badges, flinched, his mouth opening in startled surprise. His hand started down for his gun, then pulled away as he saw Seibert's pistol already drawn and ready. "If you'd gone just a bit further, mister," Tom declared, his voice tinged with menace, "you'd be at a different gate about now, talking with Saint Peter."

"Jeff Broughten, isn't it?" Wilkinson asked. "We'd recognize you anywhere from the 'wanted' circular in our office. Sought in Indiana for robbery and suspicion of murder. Thought to have ridden in the past with the Reno brothers. Wanted in Iowa for train robbery and in Nebraska and Illinois for safecracking. What brings you down here?"

The man peered at them, thunderstruck at being recognized. Then, realizing the stars on Wilkinson's and Seibert's coats were those of US Marshals, he became truculent. "You two are federals; you got no call to be hunting me."

"We aren't," Ward informed him. "We're here to see Mrs. Harper as part of our investigation into her husband's murder. Because of who you are, you're now part of that investigation. What are you doing down here?"

Broughten hesitated for a moment, deciding whether to answer. He looked at Seibert, saw the muzzle of the pistol still aimed at him, unwavering, then shrugged in resignation. "Ted offered me a job. Wrote and told me his operation was getting too big for him to handle alone and asked me to come down and manage some of the sharecropping farm property for him. I didn't find out he'd died until I got here."

"Where'd you know him from?"

The reply was evasive and accompanied by a cunning grin: "Here and there."

"Hmm. I'll bet," Wilkinson scoffed. "You know, Harper showed up at home back in the seventies, after several years' absence, with a large amount of cash in hand. It's what fueled the empire he built. Could be you partnered with him in one or more robberies, like that train hold-up. Got forty thousand dollars from that one. Or maybe it was the safecracking job at the Bank of Omaha. You and Ted? Or was it some job that people claimed the James brothers committed?"

"You don't have a shred of proof, Marshal, for any of that. Also, you've no authority to arrest me. So, just forget you saw me, and let me get on with my work."

"There's where you're wrong, Jeff," Seibert corrected. "We can arrest you on suspicion in the murder of Ted Harper as it's damn peculiar you show up here right after his death and almost immediately become foreman. You and the widow becoming cozy? You figuring to take over his holdings once you're wed? Even if that isn't the case, we can have the Bedford County sheriff come for you and hold you until Indiana extradites you back there. You'll be looking at least ten years for that bank job, and if the state prosecutes for murder, you understand what that means."

The outlaw's eyes bugged, and then his face became contorted with rage. "You don't know what the hell you're talking about," he seethed. "There isn't any property for me to get my hands on. Mrs. Harper has signed all of it over to her brother."

Wilkinson turned toward Seibert, but his friend's gaze never left the outlaw. "You'd better explain that, Mr. Broughten," he urged.

The man sighed in exasperation. "Mr. Flynn isn't some hero riding to the rescue of his sister, despite what she might tell you. He's pulled the wool over her eyes, and someday, it wouldn't surprise me if he boots her ass to the road. He's promised her he'll take care of all these people who aren't living up to their contracts with Ted, and he's using me to make sure they do. His price for doing all that is to have his name on the deeds."

"We didn't see that when we stopped by the Shelbyville courthouse," Tom challenged. "What are these contracts you speak of?"

"I don't know anything about the courthouse records," Broughten averred. "I'm telling you what Mrs. Harper told me. This spring, now that Ted is dead, people he had on sharecropping contracts decided not to work on his plots, rent tools, buy seed, you name it. It's spelled out in every damn agreement, but the missus, she can't read hardly at all. That's where her brother comes in."

"What did he do?"

"He come over here a few weeks ago, right after I got here. I hadn't decided if I was going to stay, but he convinced Mrs. Harper to hire me and bring on a couple of people to work the farm in place of Ted. Then, he paid a visit to these people Ted had contracts with and told them to honor them or else. He threatened some of them with prison. And others, the black ones that is, he warned them he'd have them prosecuted under the vagrancy laws and leased as convicts, put to work on his land at hard labor. He's not a man to be trifled with, let me tell you."

Wilkinson spat in disgust. This was a post-war practice that he and Seibert abhorred.

"Does Flynn give a damn about what happened to his brother-in-law?" Seibert asked.

"Doubt it. I'd say he sees his death as an opportunity not to be missed. Wouldn't surprise me if he had a hand in it himself."

Wilkinson considered the astonishing statement for a moment but decided it lacked plausibility unless the man was a fool. All he had to do was to assure his sister that beyond the sheriff's investigation, nothing could be done. That would have been the end of the matter. It made little sense that he would use political influence to provoke an investigation into a murder that he'd taken part in. "I'm doubtful if that's true," he said, "but I'd advise you to consider his ruthlessness. He may betray you when you least expect it."

"What about you?" Broughten replied.

"Us," Wilkinson said. "For the time being, we won't be bothering about you. However, once we're finished with our investigation, you ought to be gone from here. We'll be bound to inform the attorney general of your presence when we return to Nashville. He may inform the state of Indiana or other places where you're wanted. For now, as you mentioned you wanted to do, you can get back to your work."

Broughten turned away, but Seibert's voice, tinged with obvious enmity, stopped him in his tracks. "One more thing. We've been told that your friend employed other methods of bringing in the sheaves besides his agricultural holdings; to be specific, shaking down local business owners for money. Further, there was an allegation that he took payment in kind from one person in a manner that required being in the horizontal position. Ever been told that?"

The outlaw pivoted, taking care to be very deliberate in his movements. "I wouldn't know anything about that," he said, speaking to Wilkinson and avoiding eye contact with Tom. "I reckon you'd have to ask Mrs. Harper."

"We'll be sure to do that," Seibert replied. "Just remember, if we find you're doing the same, we will arrest you. Should you coerce some poor woman into bed with you in lieu of money, the charge will be rape. You might like to consider that in this state, a conviction on that charge can mean the rope."

Broughten started to bellow an angry retort, then thought better of it and stood in a bristling silence. Wilkinson waved him away, with Seibert delivering a parting admonishment. "Keep your hand well away from that Colt when you're around us."

The marshals watched as the foreman mounted his horse and rode away, heading to some distant field where men were sweating in the now-warming sun of a cloudless day. Not until he was out of range did Tom see fit to holster his weapon. "We need to be wary of that sonofabitch," he cautioned Ward. "He might be tempted to dry gulch us if he has the chance."

Wilkinson nodded in agreement. "Finding someone like that around here is a hell of a surprise. It's a pity we have nothing to hold him on. I doubt he figured out how difficult it would be for us to have him detained, but a good bluff, nonetheless. If he has attorney Flynn on his side, a writ of habeus corpus would be forthcoming in no time. Well," he said, flailing some of the dust from his coat, "let's go on around back and see what Denise Harper has to say for herself."

Chapter 18

THE LADY OF the house answered the knock, took in the stars pinned to the men's coats, and asked them inside. After they introduced themselves, she made a pair of brusque observations. "I was thinking my dear brother wasn't as well acquainted with the governor as he bragged. Nevertheless, I'm glad you're here. The new sheriff, I'm quite certain, couldn't pour piss out of a boot even if the instructions were written on the heel."

She led them back through the kitchen, down a center hall, past the dining room, and then to a parlor on their right. Wilkinson arched an eyebrow at Seibert as they followed her diminutive form, barely five feet tall, with a flowing mane of scarlet curls bouncing as she walked. "Sarah," she bellowed to an unseen maid, "US Marshals have come to see me; bring some coffee in here, please."

The widow motioned the men to a pair of armless chairs, then situated herself in an opulently upholstered Queen Anne that appeared far more comfortable than what Wilkinson and Seibert would sit on. A few moments later, a harried young woman hustled into the room with a silver tray bearing a coffee pot, cups, sugar bowl, and cream pitcher. Once the maid observed the niceties, she sat back, looked expectantly over the rim of her steaming cup, and addressed them in a direct manner. "What can I do to help you gentlemen find my husband's murderers?"

From across the room, Wilkinson examined Denise Harper with care. She was, he decided, far more estimable than the opinions of Sheriff Parslow and Jeff Broughten led one to imagine. There was a cool shrewdness in her expression, and her eyes, the color of emeralds, had the sparkle of intelligence and discernment. This was no ignorant, backwoods country girl, despite what others might say.

Seibert thought Sheriff Parslow's faint praise about Denise's looks showed he was mighty damn choosy or had seen a lot of women in the county that he as yet hadn't had the good fortune to encounter. A shaft of morning sun came through the window behind her, which set her hair ablaze and highlighted the creamy whiteness of her skin, daubed though it was with freckles. She had those magnificent eyes, an attractive mouth with full lips, and a set of gleaming white teeth. Very pretty, he thought, although she still wore her drab widow's weeds.

Wilkinson began with a simple question, something to break the ice. "Were you in town the day your husband died?" he asked. "We saw nothing in the report we received that indicated one way or the other."

"Unfortunately, no," Denise spat, her features now livid with anger. "If I had been, your presence wouldn't be required today. Those who did it would be dead, or I would be."

"You were home, I gather?"

"Yes," Denise replied, the vehemence in her tone evaporated. "My son and me. Ted had gone into town to meet with some men; he didn't always tell me who he was going to see. The undertaker, Mr. Crump, came out and gave me the news. Told me Ted was dead, shot by some unknown killer outside Guthrie's saloon, and that he'd had the body put on ice until the sheriff could get down from Shelbyville to investigate. Damn lot of good that did!"

"We've been told that your husband wasn't a very popular man. Do you have any idea who his enemies were?"

Denise made a disparaging noise. "It could be anyone who felt they came out on the short end when doing business with him. Look," she declared, the index finger of her right hand jabbing the air, "he didn't force a single one of those bellyachers to take his money. They came hat in hand, asking for help. They understood the terms of the agreement and had no reason to kick up the dirt when he foreclosed on them, same way with those who signed long-term leases to sharecrop his acreage and were nowhere to be found this spring when word got out that he was dead. If it wasn't for my brother taking a hand, me and my son would soon be destitute."

"Do you have copies of his land tenure agreements here at the house?"

"Back in the safe. I couldn't figure out how to get in it after Ted died, but his friend, Mr. Smith, got it open after he showed up looking for work. He's been a godsend to me."

Wilkinson cleared his throat, not sure of what to say. "Mrs. Harper," he finally said in a hesitant voice, "I'm sorry to tell you that the man you know as Smith is a wanted outlaw named Jeff Broughten. It's his good fortune that he's only wanted on state warrants, as we have no cause to arrest him at present. The crimes he's wanted for are serious, a couple of them for safecracking. I doubt he had much trouble getting into your husband's safe."

The color drained from Denise's face, and she looked almost ghostly in her black mourning garb. "You're not going to take him away, are you?"

"Not unless he commits a crime down here. He's wanted in four states, with robbery and suspicion of murder being the most serious charges. However, and we've told him this, once our work here is complete, we'll be duty bound to inform the attorney general's office of his presence in Buckland Station. Whether they relay that information to Indiana or the other states is up to them."

Denise Harper frowned, and Wilkinson feared for a moment that she might no longer be willing to cooperate with his questioning. Then, Tom spoke up and got things back on track. "Mam," he said in a deferential tone, "besides those that had business with your husband, do you know of any enemies he had in town?"

"Oh, there are plenty of them, too. I only had to see which of those old biddies was looking down their nose at me when I was in the stores to figure the men who didn't like Ted. That Reverend Hoffberger and his wife couldn't have made it clearer that we weren't welcome in their benighted congregation. And 'Lige' Guthrie, the saloonkeeper, was willing to take Ted's money but never uttered a welcoming word or thank you on the rare times when he bought a drink in there. The Whipples, the store owners there on the square, I got so sick of their attitude that I started going to the dry goods store next to them and to the grocer there on the corner of Chapel Street. If I didn't know better, I'd say Whipple wears a dress and his wife wears the trousers."

The widow, her temper up, scarcely paused to breathe. "Harry Colborne, the banker, despised Ted because he would loan money that he was too cowardly to risk. I don't believe he killed Ted, though. That man's got three feet of lace sewn on his drawers. Fred Reichert, the blacksmith, tried, and I'd have to say he's the one I suspect most. He did some shoddy work on Ted's horse and then got rough about it when Ted rightfully refused to pay. Fred pulled a gun on my husband and got shot for his trouble. Then, the damnable district attorney tried to have Ted prosecuted for attempted murder! When that scheme failed, I believe Reichert conspired with some others to kill him."

"Were there any others?" Tom inquired.

"Isn't that enough? It's probable there are some I don't know about. Ted didn't get along with Perry Jessup. He's a farmer whose property abuts mine and Mr. Orange's."

"What can you tell us about this Orange fellow?"

"Not much. He keeps to himself most of the time, was in the war, people say."

"Mrs. Harper," Wilkinson said, rejoining the conversation, "was there anything else of interest in the safe when Mr. Broughten opened it? I ask because the report stated someone turned his pockets inside out after the shooting. We assume that person took something."

"The missing item was a little book that Ted took with him everywhere, even to the privy. Once, I told him there was newspaper and old catalogs out there, so he didn't need to take it along. He didn't find that very funny. He never shared what was in it." The thought tickled Denise, and she giggled like a little girl for a moment, bringing a hint of a smile to the faces of both men. "Yes," she continued, "there was a small book in the safe that's written in some sort of shorthand. I sat up after midnight one evening trying to figure out what it meant but got nowhere."

"I don't mean any disrespect, but we were told that you aren't able to read or write."

A slow, coy grin spread across Denise's face, ending in an expression of cunning. "From the sheriff and Mr. Smith, no doubt. That feeds their assumptions that I'm like a lot of women, helpless. Even my brother believes me to be almost illiterate, but I assure you I can read and understand every word of those agreements. I beg you not to enlighten anyone on this subject. As long as people underestimate me, it's to my benefit."

"Broughten, I can't think of him as Smith, told us you'd signed over all your interests in Mr. Harper's properties to your brother. We found no evidence of that in courthouse records."

"It's a falsehood I told him to keep him from getting any ideas about courting me. If he thinks I'm existing at the benevolence of my brother, the better I like it. I've never had the slightest romantic interest in him, and even less now that I find he's a wanted criminal. Now, before we go on, let me refresh your cups, and I'll retrieve the documents for you."

The lawmen accepted the coffee with appreciation, for it was of fine quality and expertly brewed. Mrs. Harper disappeared into another room and returned moments later with a file of documents. She handed them to Tom, and he recorded the sharecroppers' names in his notebook. "These agreements are word-for-word copies of each other, Marshal," she declared. "I've studied all of them. As for this book, I've done much study and understand nothing."

As Seibert worked through the stack of contracts, Wilkinson examined the book. He found himself nearly as puzzled as Mrs. Harper. "I don't enjoy speaking of this, Ma'am, but allegations have been made to the sheriff that your husband was extorting money from certain business owners in Buckland Station, maybe Shelbyville as well. Is it possible these entries reflect such activity?"

"That is a viscous slander, Marshal!" Denise exclaimed, rising to her feet. "Ted owned two buildings in Shelbyville. The first has two or three storefronts under lease, and the second is an office building that's on the north side of the square, next to a hardware and paint store. It was the intransigence of those tenants, all of whom were behind in their rent, that made it necessary for me to employ a man like this Broughten. With him going around to collect in person, they are all up to date. Those leases are in the papers Marshal Seibert is reviewing."

"I'm sure they are. Have a look at this with me; I think it's a ledger." Denise pulled a chair next to Ward's and looked at the last page where Ted Harper had written entries. "The entry at the top," Ward said, "is four, which likely means the month of the year: April. On the preceding page, it's three, then two, one, and twelve. It looks like these columns go back to 1880, no further."

"What do these numbers and letters mean?" Denise asked.

"I'm not absolutely certain, but I have an idea. Let's look at this first one, '83BL2$.' You could conclude that refers to an 1883 payment from someone whose initials are BL and that they paid two dollars. This entry goes back to May 1881 and appears twice a month. The next one is '83CN2$.' It goes back to the beginning, January 1880, yet only appears once a month. As you can see, there are other line items that are similar. If I'm adding this up right, it looks like the amount is fifty dollars a month; that's a lot of money these days. Did you have that kind of money in the bank?"

"Ted didn't much cotton to banks. He dealt strictly in cash and kept it in his safe until after we were married. In time, my brother persuaded him to open an account at his bank in Giles County and one in town. Still, I found over five thousand dollars in the safe when we got it open. I have a feeling that Broughten, if he didn't have a friendship with Ted, might have killed me and took off with it all. To answer your question, I'm well off and can expect to continue to be so long as my brother can keep contract workers on my property. Whatever this is, though, I'm not collecting it. I wouldn't know where to start."

"Do any of these initials correspond to names of people that your husband did business with?"

"Not a single one," Denise said after studying the page. "I still don't believe my husband was coercing people to give him money because he was threatening them. This by itself proves nothing, and I'm guessing that nobody has come forward to make this charge. All the sheriff has got is rumor. Isn't that the truth of it?"

"You are correct," Ward confirmed. "No one disclosed names, and those that raised the subject claimed only that they'd heard it happened to others; that makes it all hearsay. The sheriff has a letter claiming such actions by your late husband go back to 1881, but while it's precise in allegation, it's vague in other ways and has no signature. Regardless, all these questions we're asking are to get as clear a picture as possible of who your husband's enemies were and what motive they would have to kill him. At the moment, my concern is that we have too many potential suspects."

By the time Tom finished recording the names on the labor contracts and made notations of the peculiar cipher left behind by Ted Harper, it was nearing the noon hour. The widow surprised the lawmen by inviting them to stay for dinner, and they accepted; neither man could figure a gracious way to decline. Wilkinson asked her opinion of various people around the town, and she rewarded him with several biting comments. Stuart Redmond, the confectioner, she proclaimed a "Nancy Boy." Coming off no better was Peter Taylor, the tailor, whose shop stood next to the hotel. "For certain, he's Redmond's special friend," she disparaged. Leroy Stafford, a restaurant owner next to Whipple's store, she described as "the most dangerous man in town." Demarest, the town doctor, she stated, "was only a smidgin less deadly than Stafford."

Denise saved her most damning language for Faye Sillinger, the seamstress on Main Street, just below the Baptist Church. "She's so uptight every time I go in there that you'd think she had a corncob stuck up her ass. I feel so ill-treated that I've started going to the shop between the barber and the shoe cobbler."

At a quarter of one, well fed, and fortified with more of Mrs. Harper's superb coffee, the marshals took their leave. She walked around the house with them, and in a respectful gesture, they doffed their hats in salute before turning their mounts away.

Back on the road, troubled by what he'd heard, Ward rode in silence. Denise Harper was playing a deep game here, but to what purpose? If she was telling the truth, her dealings with her brother and with new foreman Jeff Broughten were deceptions. Perhaps after her husband's death, she'd become paranoid, unable to trust anyone.

Ward looked over at Seibert and saw his friend's furrowed brow and compressed lips. "Do you suppose," Tom asked, "that she discovered he was bedding other women and found someone, like her brother, for example, to arrange his killing?"

"Possible. Or maybe she tired of him, and her brother saw an opportunity to cash in on him being dead. Perhaps he thought him worth more dead than alive. If her brother is involved, this assignment was a fool's errand from the beginning. Still, based upon what we found out last night in the livery stable, I don't think that's likely."

"How about the sharecroppers and the property owners Harper foreclosed?"

"It could be there is a motive for a person he fleeced that wanted revenge," Wilkinson concurred. "Seems unlikely they'd wait so long. As for the sharecroppers, it makes little sense. They all signed their contracts well before the murder. Granted, there were some who believed they could walk off his acreage with tools and seed in tow. As we've seen, though, Mr. Flynn thoroughly disabused them of that notion."

Tom chewed that logic over for a minute, then nodded in agreement. "Is it possible Broughten is responsible? Could be he arrived down here much earlier than anyone knows and did it for the widow."

"Not from what we heard in the barn. Even if we hadn't, it's hard to remain hidden for that long, and even harder as a complete stranger to insert yourself into a conspiracy to kill a local citizen. I mean, think about it, what is his motivation? What does he hope to gain? Also, he'd be a perfect patsy to stick it on as a wanted man and a complete stranger. It wouldn't take any time to arrest, convict, and hang him."

"Primary motivation is money," Seibert replied, ignoring Ward's reasoning for the moment, "and the delights of the widow herself. It's hard for me to contemplate he killed Ted for a foreman's job. That's all he's realized. It doesn't appear he's got any money out of it he hasn't earned, and he isn't getting into her undergarments either. If he agreed to kill him, he's received a piss-poor reward."

Wilkinson laughed in a harsh, sarcastic bark. "My view still is that people in town did it, given the way they closed ranks and stiff-armed the sheriff. In fact, I suspect we'll identify the ringleaders in the gibberish Ted wrote in that damned little book of his, provided we ever figure it out. I'd like to know who took the original off his corpse. One man we need to interview is that Perry Jessup fellow. Mrs. Harper said he and Ted didn't like each other, and the sheriff confirmed as much. We need to get a copy of the town directory, if there is one, and start putting names to these businesses on the square and elsewhere. After that, we'll split up and start knocking on doors."

"What about our badges?"

"Now that we've displayed them, they stay on."

Chapter 19

WHEN THE MARSHALS rode back into town, the stars on their coats brought gasps of astonishment from many who bothered enough to watch them go by. At the corner of Main, they turned right, trotted halfway up the block of businesses on the north side of the square, and stepped down in front of the Buckland Station Bank and post office, which adjoined each other. Seibert entered the post office to see if it had a town directory, and Wilkinson stepped into the bank to talk with Harry Colborne.

The banker, a fortyish man with wavy persimmon-colored hair and chin whiskers, noted the marshal's badge and greeted him in a friendly manner. He invited Wilkinson back to his office, and as he preceded him, Ward noticed the man wore a black suit with wide lapels, an ascot tie, and a dark waistcoat that were more in keeping with the fashion of the past decade. Could that indicate the bank wasn't in a sound financial position? "A customer informed me there were a couple of visitors in town," Colborne said, "but not that you were lawmen."

"We're here at the behest of Governor Bate's office to find out who murdered Theodore Harper," Wilkinson informed him. "I might add that he died outside of Guthrie's saloon on a Saturday midday, in broad daylight, yet the county sheriff found no one who would admit to seeing or hearing anything."

"That's pretty much what I've heard," the banker admitted. "The deceased didn't enjoy a good reputation in this community; you'll find it difficult, I should think, to get anyone, if there were any that saw it, to identify the killers."

"Do you know who they were?"

"Not a single one. I can't say I'd tell you if I did, though. I thoroughly disliked Harper; he was a scum who preyed on vulnerable people when they were their weakest. He knew full well that many of the people he lent to wouldn't be able to repay him. If they were likely to, he wouldn't give them the time of day."

"His widow referred to you as 'cowardly,' saying you wouldn't take risks to help people who badly needed money. She referred to her late husband as a lender of last resort."

"He sure as hell was," Colborne snorted in disdain. "I can tell you for a fact that after he lent them money, they could never get a dollar from anyone else. Also, his goals didn't, and never would, align with the bank's. He wanted to acquire land to farm it or sharecrop it. If the bank has to foreclose, it's an anchor on our bottom line. The property has to be maintained until we can auction it. Usually, they sell for considerably less than they're worth, often less than the amount owed.

"I want to lend to people who will pay the amount back with interest," the banker explained patiently. "I want more deposits so that the bank is in a better posture to lend to more borrowers, and I want to pay a small percentage rate to depositors for showing faith in our ability to safeguard their funds. Lending to those who can't pay up leaves a nonperforming asset on my books, and, ultimately, a problem I don't need."

"I presume you and Mr. Harper didn't do business together."

"Never. Surprisingly, given what you told me, Denise came in here a couple of weeks ago and deposited a considerable sum. There are rumors she made a similar deposit at the bank in Pulaski."

Wilkinson nodded. "One last question. Where were you on the day Harper was killed, and who did you see that day?"

"I was right where I am now when the shooting occurred. You can ask my teller, Mr. Gordon, to verify if you need to. We heard the shots but didn't know where they were coming from. I think a westbound freight train that was pulling out from the depot somewhat muffled the sound, and it prevented anyone east and north of the square from seeing anything. I understand they asked the man in the caboose if he witnessed the shooting, but he claimed he had duties to attend to and was giving his attention to them."

"Who did you see that day?"

"We close at one on Saturday, and I don't recall a soul coming in after eleven-thirty. Most of them were clerks for the larger businesses like the mills, the bedspring factory, and the hotel. A few had deposits, but most picked up payroll money. Mr. Gordon and I accounted for what we had in the till, locked up the safe, and headed home. We both live in the same part of town, and we walked together. Neither of us knew a thing until we heard about it at church the next morning."

Wilkinson thanked Colborne, stopped to speak with Gordon for a minute, then went outside, where he found Seibert sitting on a bench poring over his notes. "I hope you accomplished something more immediate than I have," Tom grumbled in a cross tone. "The postmaster had a town directory, and from it, I have the name of every business in town, the address, and the owner's name; there are forty-one of them." The number brought a groan of despair from Wilkinson.

"If you really want to have something to moan about," Tom continued, "Mrs. Harper wasn't lying to us. There isn't a single sonofabitch whose initials correspond with the letters in the cipher. It's too bad Obadiah isn't with us. He cuts his teeth on things like this, and, speaking of him, I noticed you didn't bring up the subject of exhuming Ted when we were at her house this morning."

"I'm still hoping we can avoid it. However," Ward ended in a dark tone, "it's becoming more likely every minute."

Chapter 20

WHILE THE MARSHALS conferred outside the bank, twelve miles away in Shelbyville, Jeff Broughten headed down the boardwalk of the main street to where he'd stabled his horse. He was in a surly mood after hearing all the begging, pleading, bitching, and moaning from Mrs. Harper's tenants. He'd had to threaten two lying bastards with an eviction notice before, magically, they coughed up the rent they owed. All he wanted now was to get back to Buckland Station, have a cold beer at Guthrie's, and get out to the farm for supper.

Broughten was passing an alley when the sound of a familiar voice, one he'd hoped never to hear again, called to him. "I'll be a suck egg mule if it isn't Jeff Broughten." He peered into the shadows, expecting to see a gun barrel pointed in his direction. "Come on in here, Jeff," the man continued in a gregarious manner that dripped with falsity. "I don't want to shoot you. We've got a lot to discuss, you and I. Such as, where the hell is my damn money?"

The man appeared older than Jeff remembered—thinner, grayer, even more greasy and unwashed, if that was possible. His clothes looked threadbare and didn't fit him well, and the leather of his vest and boots was spider-webbed with cracks. The only thing that seemed to be newer was the Starr revolver he had thrust into his waistband.

Broughten chanced a look down the street, but there was no way to escape. His horse was fifty feet away, and he had no illusions that the man he knew as Braxton wouldn't shoot him in the back. The outlaw's sallow features creased in a smile, revealing browned teeth, at least where there still were some. "You weren't going to be stupid and try running, were you, Jeff?"

Broughten eased into the lane, keeping his hands in plain sight. This was the second damn time he'd been threatened with a gun today, and he didn't like it. "What are you doing out of prison, Charlie?" he demanded, a surge of anger running through him. "Last I knew, you weren't due to be released for another five years."

"That's what you and Harper counted on," the man replied with an evil cackle. "I got early release on good behavior."

"See you're honoring your parole."

"I don't give a shit about no damn parole," Braxton snarled. "What I care about is my share of that train job, about five thousand dollars if memory serves. Kept your identities secret, yes I did, and you haven't any idea what they did to me in the Iowa state prison trying to get your names. I'm due more than my share," he said with an accusing sneer. "Where is it?"

Knowing there was no money, at least none he wanted to talk about, Broughten tried to keep the conversation going. He knew that Braxton's hand was now on the pistol butt, and any attempt by him to draw would be foolish. "How did you find me, Charlie?"

There was another cackle, even more diabolical than the first. "Easy. When I got out, I headed for a town in Colorado you talked about as a hangout when we worked together. Only when I got there, you'd hightailed. Took me a little while, had to tickle the postmaster with this persuader of mine." To demonstrate, he withdrew a wicked-looking hawkbill knife from a sheath on his belt.

"Well?"

"He told me soon enough," Braxton said with malicious relish, punctuating the declaration with a spasm of laughter. "General Delivery, Buckland Station, Tennessee. I started out for here that very day and got into this place just an hour ago. Couldn't believe it when I saw you walking down the street. What the hell ever made you decide to come *here*?"

"I got a letter from Harper. He knew I was down on my luck and offered me a job as foreman on his farm. I agreed, but when I arrived here, he was dead. Someone murdered him. The widow kept his bargain, and I'm working for her."

Braxton sniggered. “How many duties do you perform after dark?”

“There isn’t any money, Charlie,” Broughten said with a resigned sigh, “and shooting me won’t get you any of it. When I showed up for our split after the job, Ted gave me my share, and I lit out. He held onto yours. It wasn’t until two weeks later that I saw in a newspaper that you were in jail.”

“Maybe his widow knows where it is,” Braxton sputtered, his face purple with rage. “When she gets on the sharp end of this blade, she’ll talk as quick as that postmaster.”

“I don’t doubt it, yet it won’t help you,” Broughten informed him in a fatalistic tone. “My money’s gone, Charlie, some pissed away, some paid to people to hide me when the law got too close. Why do you think I’m working? Ted put all his money, including yours, I figure, into farmland. The people he bought it from have burned through what he paid them; times are hard down here.”

“Then she can damn well get off her sweet ass, sell some of it, and pay what he owed me.”

Broughten shook his head. “No, she can’t. She’s illiterate—can’t read or write at all. Here a few weeks ago, her brother—he’s a big-time lawyer and state politician from the next county over—convinced her to sign over all of Ted’s property into his name and he’d manage it for her. She doesn’t control a cent. Some of the money he put in a bank over in Pulaski, his hometown, and some more in the Buckland Station Bank. There’s very little cash around the house except on payday.”

Braxton, his color not improved, squeezed the handle of the knife until his fingers turned white. “I ought to shove this sonofabitch in your guts right now. It wouldn’t get me my money, but I’d get a lot of personal satisfaction. It’s too bad Harper couldn’t have stayed above ground for a few more weeks.” He maneuvered the blade toward Broughten, the tip glistening as it dove in and out of the shadows. Then, without warning, the man began laughing uproariously. “It just occurred to me that if my money is in that Buckland Station Bank, I’ve got an experienced man to help me withdraw it. You stay put while I get my horse.”

Braxton walked back a few steps and untied his animal from some old scrap lumber. Stepping into the leather, he motioned Broughten ahead, walking his horse parallel to him as he fetched his gelding from the stableman. As they rode out of town, Deputy Sheriff Simon Garrett watched them with curiosity.

When the two men reached the outskirts, Broughten spoke again. "You'd be wise, Charlie, to forget all about this and go back where you came from."

"And you'd be wise, you dishonorable sonofabitch, to do what I tell you. If so, I might not kill you!"

"I'm not worried about you, Charlie," Jeff replied. "There are two US Marshals in town investigating Harper's death. The only reason I'm not in jail right now is there aren't any federal warrants out on me. One of them is greased lightning on the draw. He threw down on me this morning, and if I'd been any faster, I'd be dead. His partner didn't pull his weapon; he didn't need to. You try to take that bank with that man around, and he'll kill you dead as a doornail. I'm not fooling!"

"I'm not fooling, either, Jeff," Braxton growled. "I'm owed five thousand dollars, and I don't give a fuck if his name is Wild Bill Hickok. You and I are going to get it."

Chapter 21

WILKINSON AND SEIBERT sat for a half hour to divide up the interviews. "For now, what do you think of the idea of eliminating the larger businesses from our inquiry?" Ward asked.

"Which ones do you have in mind?"

"I'm thinking the mill, the bedspring factory, the Standard Oil place, and that larger livery operation over on Independence Street. Those places strike me as too big with too many employees for Harper to isolate someone or make them feel vulnerable. It's the local shops, one or two persons, the family businesses, where he'd feel emboldened to lean on people. I know the oil place only has a couple of employees, but I doubt he'd have tried that with them. If he had, they could have contracted for a couple of Pinkertons to come down here and teach him a lesson. It's probable Ted was aware of that."

"How about the hotel?"

"It stays on our list. We haven't met the owner, Mr. Cochran. For now, we'll give him the benefit of the doubt, yet any place employing a weasel like McCormick bears scrutiny."

"That reduces the number to thirty-seven. No . . . make that thirty-six," Tom corrected. "You just talked to the banker; he provide anything useful?"

"A little. Like everyone else, he claims not to have heard a thing. Said he and his teller, a Mr. Gordon, only learned of it the next day when they attended church." Tom rolled his eyes at the perceived mendacity, but Wilkinson motioned for him to wait for the rest. "Both men noted the bank emptied by eleven-thirty. Most of the customers that did come by were representatives from the larger businesses picking up payroll money at week's end. Also, Mr. Colborne stated there was a long, westbound freight train, maybe forty cars or more, leaving the depot at the approximate time the shooting occurred. If so, that means anyone north of the square and back to the east couldn't see what happened."

"The whistle, all that chugging, clattering of the cars, and the like might have muffled the gunshots as well," Tom added. "Train crew saw nothing?"

"Not according to Colborne. He stated that they questioned the brakeman to no avail. We need to confirm that with the stationmaster."

Seibert looked up from his scribbling and looked Wilkinson in the eye. "Are you seeing the pattern I'm seeing? This is the second or third place we've been told that there were few customers inside a business during the thirty minutes to an hour before the shooting."

Ward considered that, sifted through what they'd heard, and nodded with emphasis. "Makes you think there were a lot of folks that knew what was coming and planned accordingly. For a moment, though, let's forget all that," he said, getting to his feet. "I want to go over to the scene of the crime and have a look around. After that, I'll buy us a beer, and we'll have a little talk with 'Lige' Guthrie."

Ward and Tom swung back into their saddles and trotted their mounts over the tracks to the saloon. After tying the horses to a hitching rail, they walked to the east side of the building, a long wall of continuous red brick unbroken by neither window nor door. To the rear of the structure, fifty feet away, was a large building that looked to be abandoned, its grounds unkempt, paint peeling, the interior dark and silent. Nearby was a smaller edifice, also empty, that stood a story and a half in height. Further in the distance, partially obscured by the closer construction, were dwellings.

"Without a doubt," Ward fumed to Tom, "every mother's son in those houses will claim his family was visiting his twenty-third illegitimate son or had taken everyone to the country for a picnic."

Seibert, despite his friend's obvious rancor, could not squelch a snort of laughter.

* * *

The saloon stood alone, with undeveloped lots on both sides. The corner where the marshals stood was within a few feet of where Ted Harper had been gunned down. In a deliberate manner, Wilkinson turned about, a complete three hundred and sixty degrees, taking in everything there was to see. To his right lay the mill complex, but it was a considerable distance away. Next, almost directly in front of him, the passenger depot. Further left was the freight depot, and he reminded himself that Colborne had related there was a long freight train pulling out of the station at the time of the shooting. Afterward, there was nothing but the stockyard until his gaze fell on Leroy Stafford's restaurant, operated by, according to Denise Harper, the town's most dangerous man.

"It will be interesting to hear what the restaurant owner has to say," Tom said. "At the noon hour on a Saturday, you'd think he'd have a few customers. Mind you, I'm not eating his food. Have a look along the sidewall here, I'll check out back."

The grass, near a foot high, wafted lazily in the gentle breeze. Guthrie, presumably seeing no importance in the matter, was neglecting to mow. The turf, trampled in many places, showed that locals routinely used it for a cut-through. In addition, there were tracks of a wagon and the shoe prints of a pair of large draft animals. None of Harper's blood remained, either removed by Guthrie or washed away by a spring rain. Wilkinson scoured the narrow lot and found nothing useful.

The first thing Seibert discovered when he turned the corner was empty beer barrels stacked one upon another by the rear door. The wagon tracks continued, and it seemed likely that whoever put them there delivered Guthrie's beer and took away the empties. Little else attracted his notice, and he turned back to rejoin Wilkinson when he noticed a small object that winked brightly in the late afternoon sun. Bending over it, he found a half-buried yet identifiable spent .44-45-caliber shell casing.

Tom dislodged the casing from the tamped-down earth, then motioned Ward over with a slight twist of his head. Wilkinson studied it for a moment, then looked back toward the thoroughfare. From here, it was a simple shot for someone with a rifle. The killer would have walked out into the open ground, away from the corner of the building, in plain sight to anyone behind him and, to a more limited extent, possibly from his right and left. He thought it also possible that the casing might now be in a different place from where the gun's lever had ejected it.

"Most back shooters would use the corner of the building as cover," Seibert observed. "He could be inexperienced at this type of work."

"He might also not have given a damn in that he knew nobody was going to identify him. How many times did Parslow's report say Ted was shot?"

"Three or four, I believe."

"This almost guarantees there was more than one shooter. Further, it's my current view that whoever drives that barrel wagon is the shooter, a getaway driver, or both. Let's go in and see what this Guthrie has to say. I look forward to hearing his voice."

They walked back toward the front, observed by Leroy Stafford from a grimy window in the storeroom of his restaurant. The man's features bore a distrustful aspect. "I wonder if those two nosy bastards found anything out there," he muttered to himself.

Chapter 22

MURKY LIGHT BATHED the interior of Guthrie's, and it took time for the marshals' eyes to adjust. The place was functional, Wilkinson thought, yet utterly lacking in ostentation. There was a planked floor, which was cleaner than many he'd seen out west, and on its boards were four battered tables, each adorned with several decrepit, mismatched chairs. The bar, despite being highly polished, had a variety of pits and scars. Behind and above it hung a large painting of a scantily clad female, who, in Tom's view, should have done everyone a favor and kept her clothes on. The only person in sight, other than a single customer sitting in a corner, busied himself drying glasses with dexterous, practiced hands.

In the process of gradually going bald, Elijah Guthrie slicked his remaining black hair and combed it back. He had one of those faces that seemed ageless, and his eyes were cold and measuring. Watching the lawmen approach, he forced the smile with which he greeted all patrons and said, "What'll it be, gents?"

"Two beers," Wilkinson said. "If you have a few minutes, pour one for yourself; we have some questions for you about the shooting last month."

Guthrie sighed, tossed his towel under the bar, and nodded. "I could use the break," he said with a poker face. "You the marshals who came to town yesterday?"

"I'm Ward Wilkinson, and this is my deputy, Tom Seibert."

The beer, golden in appearance with a fine sheen of foam on top, was quite good. It was a bit malty for Wilkinson's preference, but it had a smooth taste. Seibert, taking a healthy swallow, smacked his lips and informed the publican that he had a friend back home who he believed would be interested in purchasing some of his beer to serve in his own establishment. "Do you brew here on site?" he asked.

"No. I have a friend out in the county who does it for me. There isn't enough room on the premises. He brings me fresh barrels twice a week and picks up the empties."

"I can tell you this would sell very well in Nashville. If you'd give me your friend's name and address, my friend back home would write to him, I'm sure of it. He might travel down here and see him."

Guthrie seemed caught off guard by the inquiry. "I don't know if Blackwell, Jimmy he's called, would be interested or not. He does this for me because we're friends. Don't know if I want him supplying anyone else; frankly, he doesn't like to work that much."

"He'd be in line for some decent coin if he did."

Guthrie quaffed his beer while considering how to answer. "Jimmy doesn't have a proper address," he said at last. "There are some springs east of here, and he lives nearby to them. That's where he gets the water. Your friend might be better off coming down and visiting him in person."

"Spring water," Wilkinson exclaimed. "I was wondering how it was so crisp. That explains it. This brew is like some I've drunk out west, in Colorado. Say, that reminds me, we understand you're from out west."

"Yes," Guthrie affirmed, almost preening. "I was born in St. Louis, so not that far west. My father moved us to Kansas in the 1850s, and I've lived most of my life there. I was in the Union Army during the war, and after that, I worked in saloons and gambling houses before running my own places in Wichita and Ellsworth. About five years ago, I decided the cattle drives were ending and got out while the getting was good. I sold my saloons, moved back to St. Louis, and discovered this place when the train I was taking to Atlanta broke down right across the way there. While we were waiting for a new locomotive, I put down a deposit on this building, moved here a month later, and opened this establishment. Other than being bothered by the busybody temperance creatures, it's been the smartest thing I've ever done. Like another of these?"

"Don't mind if we do," Ward replied. "I gather you never had problems with Ted Harper?"

"Can't say I knew him except by reputation."

"Which was?"

"As a dirty sonofabitch. He came in here maybe two or three times altogether after I opened, and I was glad of it. Whenever he showed up, most people paid up and left. Sometimes, it was a week or more before they showed up again. He was bad for business."

"Ever try to lean on you for money?"

Guthrie chuckled. "I've got a twelve-gauge, double-barreled stagecoach gun behind the counter. I believe Ted determined that bothering me with his bullshit was an unhealthy thing to do. It's too bad, I guess, that he misjudged someone that wasn't any more tolerant than I am."

"Hear tell of anyone he was pestering?"

The saloonkeeper looked around to determine if anyone could overhear. "What you mean is," he said in a near whisper, "do I know who killed him. The answer is no, nor do I want to find out. There was gossip from time to time, in here and other places, that rumored he was gouging money out of people. I never knew but always figured it was from some of the small business owners in town. Like I said earlier, I wasn't one of them. I'd have blown that smart-alecky sonofabitch in half if he'd tried that with me."

"Fair enough," Seibert said, enjoying his second glass as much as the first. "On the day of the shooting, were you here?"

"I was. Opened at eleven o'clock. Business was slow, though. Most of my regulars don't come until the workday ends, and there were only two or three people in here."

"Remember who they were?"

"Vaguely," Guthrie replied with a shake of his head. "Two of them were staying at the hotel and were just killing time until their train arrived. Never saw them before or since. The other was a railroad employee waiting to catch a ride to Chattanooga. I've seen him occasionally, but he doesn't live here. It scared the hell out of all of them."

"Did you go outside to investigate the cause?"

"Not hardly. You learn fast out west not to center yourself at the batwing doors when a cowboy, likely drunk as hell, starts shooting up the street. I warned my customers to get on the floor, and I grabbed my shotgun and waited to see if someone was going to bring the show inside. After a few minutes, five or so, I guess, there were running feet on the boardwalk, and I walked out to see what was happening. At least two-dozen people were standing over Harper's body. They weren't doing anything, just gawking. I told them to send someone for Doc Demarest and to send a wire to the sheriff."

"What did you do then?"

"Headed back inside, provided a free drink to my shook-up customers, and went back to work. Ted Harper was no friend of mine, and there were plenty of people about to look after what remained of him. He wasn't much account, and I figured he'd received his just due. It was long delayed but very appropriate."

"Do you remember any of those people who were in the street?"

"My fellow shop owners along the street. In fact," he mused, "I'd say almost all of them. The others, I figured, were store customers or people from the two restaurants up the street. By the time I was back behind the bar, there were more people, flocking like buzzards, coming to have a look."

The marshals finished their beer, praised its quality once more, and then bade Guthrie good day. "Thank you," Ward said. "We may have some further questions, but we'll definitely be back for your beer. A last question for now: we were told that Mr. Stafford was the most dangerous man in town, even more so than Dr. Demarest. Is his food that bad?"

Guthrie erupted with a deep belly laugh. "Well, they weren't far wrong. Leroy's the best cure for constipation in town, better than anything you'd get from Demarest. The best meals in town are at the hotel and at Gardner's, which is back up the street from here. Ask for the pot roast; it's always good."

The marshals walked out to the street and fetched their mounts. Wilkinson's features creased with disappointment. "An informative conversation," he stated, "but one thing is sure, Guthrie's voice isn't one of those we heard in the stable last night."

Chapter 23

WILKINSON CHECKED HIS pocket watch and frowned. Three-thirty-five, the workday was nearing its end. "Let's see if we can find Dr. Demarest. I want to get his perspective on Ted Harper's wounds. Any thoughts on what the saloonkeeper said in there?"

"Yes," Seibert replied, "but you will not like them. 'Lige' Guthrie may be an accomplished liar who had the means and opportunity to sneak out the back of his saloon for a minute, dry gulch Harper, and go back inside as innocent as you please. As he tells it, none of his customers at the time were regulars; they wouldn't have noticed anything out of the ordinary until they heard firing. Second, his brewer, Jimmy Blackwell, may never have brought his wagon to the saloon except for the purpose Guthrie cited. Those that killed Harper may have taken off behind his place, knowing there weren't many people around, or they may have walked up the street knowing that nobody was going to give them away."

"Still plausible that Blackwell was waiting with his wagon and hauled the shooters away under a tarp or something," Ward rejoined.

"True," said Tom. "I notice you continue to use the word shooters, not shooter. Isn't it possible one man killed Harper?"

"I reckon so, yet I doubt it. Mrs. Harper said Ted came into town to meet someone, or perhaps more than one person. I can likewise conjecture that whoever met him was in league with the one who left that shell casing behind. They distracted Harper, a man who wasn't the kind to let someone get behind him, and he took a bullet in the back. Also, I can't see why Ted would hang around outside the saloon at midday unless he was waiting for someone."

* * *

Wilkinson and Seibert stepped down in front of a small brick structure that was on the north side of Railroad Square, sandwiched between a grocery and a hardware store. A knock brought a gray-haired woman, the physician's wife, who gawped in amazement at the marshals' badges on their coats. She left them in the anteroom for a moment, tapped at a closed door, exchanged a few hushed words, and then Demarest stepped from his examining room. He motioned them to a tiny cubbyhole of an office that obliged Wilkinson to jam his knees against the front of the desk and Seibert to stand for the entire interview. "Now, gentlemen, if you please," he said in a clipped tone, "let's keep this short, I've a patient waiting in there. What is it you want to know?"

Wayne Demarest looked to be near seventy, with thinning white hair, a neatly trimmed Van Dyke beard, and piercing blue eyes that sparkled with intelligence. It would be hard for a sufferer to tell him some cock and bull story, Wilkinson determined. "What we're here about, Doctor, is what you observed when you examined Ted Harper's body. However, before that, I have another question. We've been told that you were called out into the countryside to deliver a baby the morning of his killing. Is that true?"

"It is. Had to go to the McBain place. It's about seven miles northwest of here. I didn't have a clue there'd been a shooting in town until I got back. Some fast-thinking sort, I never knew who, got him to the general store down at the end of the block. They've got an ice business, and they stashed him in the building out back. If need be, you can check the Shelbyville paper for the McBain birth announcement. Little Timothy came into the world about one in the afternoon at six pounds and five ounces. As to Harper's body," Demarest continued without pause, "his death was by gunshot wounds; there were several of them."

"Where was he hit?" Ward asked. "How many times?"

"I counted four holes: two in the front, one in the back, and a fourth that struck him in the groin. From the angle of that one, I'd say it was a coup de gras."

"Delivered after death?"

"I hope so, for his sake. It was straight down while he lay on his back. Destroyed his testicles."

"Any idea how many shooters were involved or calibers of the weapons?"

"I'd say at least two shooters," Demarest replied after a few moments. "The bullet in the back would have been fatal regardless of the others, and I'd say it was from the largest weapon involved, most likely a .44. The others were smaller, from a pistol, and possibly fired after Harper was already dead. There was a bit of powder residue on the front of his shirt."

"Did you retrieve the bullets?"

"No. It was obvious what he'd died of, and I did a small report for the Coroner because, bless his heart, he's going blind. I can tell you this, though, they're still in his body. There weren't any exit wounds. Once the sheriff got down here and released the body, his widow had a wagon take it home for burial."

"Last question: was he embalmed?"

"Mr. Crump is the undertaker in town. If it was done, I'd say he carried it out."

The marshals thanked Demarest for his time and left. "We're going to have to get Obadiah down here," Ward grated, his demeanor unhappy. "We have damn near nothing in the way of physical evidence, and Denise buried a major part of it with Ted. Let's go down here and send a wire to Judge Morton. We're going to need an exhumation order and an authorization for Obadiah to perform the autopsy. If we can have any luck at all, one of those bullets is going to be from an unusual weapon, something to match with the killer."

* * *

More vexation confronted the marshals when they returned their mounts to the livery stable. Dick Reichert, a strained frown on his face, met them as they stepped down, informing them that his uncle no longer wanted any business with them. "He told me to inform you it would be better if you took your horses up to Bill Martin's on Independence." After the day they'd had, it was the wrong thing to say to Ward and Tom.

Wilkinson, his patience considerably frayed, now snapped. "Is your uncle in his shop?" he demanded, his voice crackling with anger. The young man, alarmed by the tone, nodded in the affirmative, and the marshal responded with an ultimatum. "You go get him and tell him he better come over here and speak to me. If he doesn't, he'll be in the county jail before the sun comes up."

As Reichert hustled away, Wilkinson's eyes bore a hole into his back. "I'm going to put the fear of God in this man," Ward told Tom, "and by damn, I hope word of it spreads like wildfire before we start questioning these people tomorrow morning. Watch him closely while I'm reaming him out."

A couple of minutes later, an irate Fred Reichert came through the space between the buildings and swept down on the lawmen almost at a run. Mid-forties, powerfully built, with a thick neck set on massive shoulders, he had a barrel chest and long, muscular arms, which he waved in agitation as he approached. His face was beet red, and a bellowing roar erupted from his mouth when he spoke. "Who the hell do you think you are coming around here bullying my nephew and threatening me? You get back on those nags of yours and get the fuck off my property!"

"If we do that, Reichert," Wilkinson answered with absolute certainty, "you'll be joining us for a ride to Shelbyville, in handcuffs. In fact, if you utter one more word at me, that's what will happen. And we'll still be using your stable for our animals. I've got a requisition here that allows me to call on businesses for services while we're in the field at a fair rate of compensation. You will honor this requisition, one way or another."

Ward bit off the sentences, almost starting the next before the last ended. "You may refuse to look after our animals," he continued. "If you do, we'll do it ourselves. Then, after we've finished our investigation, you'll receive a form to make a claim against the government for what we procured. Experience tells me you'll be waiting a couple of years to get compensated if you're lucky. In addition, you'll be liable for any loss or injury to our horses and loss or damage to our saddles or other equipment. If you have to make good on my saddle, you just might go bankrupt."

By now, Reichert's face was white with indignation. "You can't do that! I've got rights! My congressional representative will hear about this!"

"When this is over, you can tell whoever you damn well please. For right now, though, I'm ordering you not to leave town. We have enough evidence to have you held as a material witness in the Shelbyville jail concerning the murder of Ted Harper and may soon develop other proof leading to your indictment in a conspiracy to take his life."

"What evidence? Who says I've done anything?" Reichert yelled, the tenor of his voice belligerent.

"I'm not obliged to tell you anything, Mr. Reichert," Wilkinson said coldly. "I'm making you aware of my admonition not to leave town. Now, are you going to take care of our animals or not?"

"You can go to . . ." Fred Reichert began, then stuttered to a stop. "Take care of them, Dick," he said in subdued resignation. "I don't know what you're talking about," he said to Wilkinson as he turned to go. "I didn't kill Harper, and you can't prove I did."

"We'll see about that. From what we understand, you pulled a gun on him and tried to kill him last year. Why shouldn't we believe you'd do it a second time?"

"Wrong! He pulled a gun on *me*, and I defended myself. The sonofabitch refused to pay me for shoeing his horse, claiming it was defective. Ask anybody in town who's come to me, and they'll tell you they've never had a problem with my work. When he found out I was planning to sue him, he decided he was going to force me to back down or goad me into a gunfight and kill me. He damn near succeeded, too."

"Why wasn't he tried?"

"Intimidated the witnesses, of course. First, he stared down the sheriff—the former one—and avoided any jail time thanks to that snake oil salesman of a brother-in-law of his. By the time the grand jury met, no witnesses would testify against him. He either threatened them harm or bought them off."

"Who were these witnesses?"

"The local schoolmaster, Jordan Delaney, was one; he's a weak sister. I can't blame him, though. Harper frightened him out of his wits. I thought Reverend Hoffberger would help, but he told the sheriff it happened so fast that he couldn't tell who drew first. The other one was Perry Jessup," Reichert said bitterly. "He's a local farmer who lives next door to the Harper's. He failed to answer his summons, and instead of adjourning until he appeared, the grand jury voted not to indict. Ted Harper either threatened to kill him or gave him money not to be found at home for a few days. Some on the grand jury might have had their palms greased as well."

"Where were you on the day Harper was shot?"

The blacksmith sighed as if he'd answered the question a hundred times. "Up on Independence, talking to Bill Martin, the wheelwright. I had a wagon at his shop with a cracked rim. Walked up there about eleven-thirty and stayed at least forty-five minutes once I got there. By the time I got back, it was all over."

"Did you go down there?"

"I had work to do and wasn't interested in what was happening down the street. Dick came in sometime later and told me."

"What did you think about that?"

"Told him it was better him than us and returned to my forge. The sonofabitch got his comeuppances, and it was damned long overdue. Whoever did it deserves the Congressional Medal of Honor."

"Who is that deserving person?" Seibert asked.

Reichert turned on his heel and walked away. "If I knew," he called over his shoulder as he disappeared from sight, "nobody would ever find out from me."

"There's no doubt he's lying like hell," Seibert observed as they headed back to the hotel. "He knows damn well who did the killing. His voice is identifiable as one of those we heard in the barn."

"He told one truth," Wilkinson replied. "He told us he wouldn't reveal the killers. Until we get some hard evidence, that's irrefutable; we'll get nowhere. We need to talk to that undertaker."

* * *

Ward and Tom returned to the hotel, where they found McCormick, sour as ever, behind the front desk. He refused to meet their eyes, retrieved the key, slapped it on the counter, and turned away. "I know nothing, and I got nothing to say," he said in a truculent voice, "so don't even ask."

Tom started up to the room, but Wilkinson lingered for a moment. "We never stated we had an interest in you, Mr. McCormick, but now, we'll be talking to you soon enough," he advised in an amused tone. "For your information, we have enough evidence to have you held at the Bedford County jail, should we choose to do so, as a material witness. While you're in there, we'll be developing further information that might incriminate you in a conspiracy to murder Ted Harper. When that time comes, I reckon you'll become a total blabbermouth."

The desk clerk's face turned sickly, and he reeled backward in fear. "I told you, I know nothing," his voice panicked. "You got no right to be coming in here bullyragging me. Go about your business, leave me be," he pleaded.

"Tomorrow," Ward continued, pressing the man's terror to new heights, "we're going to interview every business owner around the square and may call on a few houses as well. Someone's going to tell us what we want to know, and I'm betting your name is mentioned." The clerk gulped audibly, and Wilkinson continued, his tone now gentle and conciliatory. "You know, someone always talks because they don't want to hang with the rest; you should think it over. Good evening, Mr. McCormick."

Wilkinson clomped up the stairs, leaving the clerk to wipe beads of sweat from his brow. When he entered the room, Seibert was at the window with his spyglass. "He's as reliable as Big Ben over in London," Tom said, his voice tinged with disgust. "He's heading for the saloon as fast as his little legs will carry him."

Minutes later, McCormick reemerged, trudging, his head bent, a chagrined slump in his shoulders. "He doesn't look thrilled," Wilkinson noted. "I sure wish we knew who he was talking to down there."

"Wouldn't it be Guthrie?"

"I don't know," Ward replied with a tinge of anxiousness. "I wish I'd got a better look at the gent who was sitting out front when we rode in yesterday. He spoke to someone inside, and it almost certainly wasn't him. It had to be a man sitting at that first table near the door. If he'd needed his voice to reach the bar, we'd have heard what he said as well."

"Logical," Tom agreed. "You know, this is the second straight evening he's gone down there at the same hour. That suggests to me his contact is there every day at precisely the same time. It's the meeting place for McCormick, or anyone else in on this plot, to pass on news and information. I've continued to watch down there and have seen no one come out or leave from around back. Want to go back and see who's inside?"

"Not now. It might give away the fact we've got McCormick spotted. The saloon as a meeting place makes sense. Out of sight of wives and children and people that might overhear. Keep up the surveillance for another ten minutes, and then we'll go eat. We'll make it our business to be there at five tomorrow and see who else appears."

Five minutes later, Seibert motioned Wilkinson over to the window. "There's someone walking away from the back of the saloon, black hat and coat. See him going down the hill there? He hasn't turned his head, so I can't get a look at him. Could be our man."

"Yeah, might be at that. Very peculiar that he exited the back instead of the front. Could that be Guthrie himself?"

"Only one way to find out, but you said you didn't want to risk giving ourselves away."

Ward gave Tom a look that conveyed he was a real pain in the ass when he wanted to be, then produced a wry smile. "I don't. Let's go down and get some of that fried chicken before the place runs out. Did you see the size of the walrus that ate across from us this morning?"

Chapter 24

SLEEP CAME HARD that night for Ward Wilkinson. And in that, he wasn't alone. From every corner of town, residents bedded down in an atmosphere of dread, vexed by what the morning might bring. Word had spread that these outside marshals were claiming the discovery of additional evidence that pointed to their neighbors. Soon, it was rumored, they would question many of them and even make arrests. Apprehension gave way to suspicion that someone would squeal.

When supper was over, the marshals sat on the hotel veranda and enjoyed a cigar while waiting for McCormick's relief to show. When he disappeared inside, Tom evaporated into the shadows, then followed the man when he departed. Fifteen minutes later, the lawman was back, his face reflecting his frustration. "Headed straight to the house he shares with his widowed mother and stayed there," he reported to Ward. "I got close enough to see them sitting down to eat, and then I came back. Looks like he's in for the night."

"Figures. Let's go on to the room and make our plan for tomorrow," Ward suggested. "These damnable mosquitos are getting aggressive."

Upstairs, the men began work on their last task of the day. "Let's start with those businesses off the square," Ward decided, "the ones near the hotel and along the south end of Main Street. We want to be sure to ask everyone who they saw that morning and, if they volunteer anyone, where and when. We're going to need some kind of map or drawing to document the sightings."

"There's a large map on the wall in the post office," Tom said. "Don't have any idea what kind, but it might be a map of the town. I didn't pay any mind to it, as that wasn't what I was there for. We could check it first thing."

"Soon as they open. If we can't get a copy, we'll get that photographer to come and take an image for us."

After they extinguished the lamp, Seibert fell asleep right away. That didn't surprise Wilkinson. His friend's problem wasn't getting to sleep, it was remaining that way. Many the time, he'd awakened in the wee hours of the morning to find him up and readying for the dawn. Tonight, however, it was his turn.

Ward moved a small table to the window, lit a candle, and took a book from his saddlebag. Tired as he was, he was wide awake. What, he pondered, compelled a large group or an entire community to connive together to murder one of its members? None of the usual motivations seemed to apply here. Most times, there was a deep-seated hatred, thirst for revenge, greed, envy, or lust. Here, the most likely motivation appeared to be fear and loathing of a man who, if the things said of him were true, was more than worthy of trepidation. Presenting such a case to a jury might well cause misgivings among the deliberators to render a guilty verdict.

The meditation brought no answers, nor did it narrow Wilkinson's focus. He lost himself in a new book, *A History of the Zulu War and its Origin*, staying with it until his eyelids began an uncontrolled slide. When he crawled into bed, the hands on his watch stood at midnight.

* * *

Earlier, as the marshals savored the hotel's mouthwatering fried chicken, a figure in a dark coat and hat rapped on a door that a man with a calm exterior answered. "Two nights in a row?" he asked, a pointed edge in his tone. "I told you people not to be coming around unless it was urgent. It's too dangerous for us to be seen together this often."

"Those marshals got around today. By the end of it, they threatened both Reichert and McCormick with arrest, said they had enough evidence to hold them as material witnesses in Harper's death. McCormick told me they intend to question everyone, starting tomorrow. What the hell do you think they know?"

"When it comes to knowing, we're all equal. We know nothing; they may know nothing."

"Running a bluff, you mean?"

"Might be. Look how unnerved you all are. Even if they have discovered something, it isn't enough to charge anyone. Also, and we discussed this possibility from the beginning, they might figure us out and make arrests. If we're convicted, some of us may hang or go to prison. This was the chance we all agreed to take. Just remember, though, even if we go to trial, the life story of Ted Harper is going to be presented to the jury in all its ugliness. A jury might agree he deserved killing."

The thought of standing over a trapdoor did little to mollify the man. Still, his host's unfailing calm settled his nerves. "McCormick," he said dismissively, "has not the slightest bit of backbone. That man must piss his pants at least once a day. His information isn't worth the concern he'll betray us. However, I want to make it clear that no one's to harm him. That would be an unmistakable signal to those marshals that they're onto something. On your way home, stop and see everyone who attended the meeting the other night and remind them of my instruction to remain close-mouthed. For the rest, there isn't time, and it's too hazardous for us to be running around town like a chicken with its head cut off, talking to people."

"Anything else?"

"No, that's all. Say, are you sure nobody followed you out here this evening?"

"Positive. I rode out past your place and waited in that turnaround for five minutes to see if anyone would come by. It was too dark to see by then unless they were right on top of me.

"Why?"

"Something McCormick said them marshals told him. That part about holding them as material witnesses concerns me. Those two are the only ones in the group they've talked with who were in our meeting last night. Other than that, they haven't been together so far as I know. It will be interesting if they give us that same threat when they talk to us. Remember now," he reminded his caller with a wintry smile, "it's likely they're running a bluff."

The messenger made his appointed rounds, adding several more stops than commanded. From his viewpoint, the message did not mollify its recipients, and his sense of well-being vanished by the time he crossed his own threshold. There were too many skittish people who knew all or part of the plot, and those who knew nothing couldn't be clueless about Ted Harper and what had happened to him. Jittery, his stomach a bundle of knots, he hardly touched his supper. A couple of slugs from a whiskey bottle did better, and he soon collapsed in bed.

Chapter 25

"WHAT'S THIS THING?" Wilkinson asked in a puzzled tone as he peered at the map behind the post office counter.

"Check out the emblem at the top," the postmaster replied. "It's a fire insurance map put out by the Sanborn Company. They've got them for places all over creation, I expect," he said with a relaxed smile. "It depicts the principal streets, the square, all businesses, and many personal dwellings. I can't give it to you, though; it's the only one I've got. The mayor's office may have one, but I don't know of any spare ones available. You'd have to order one from the company."

"We don't have time for that," Wilkinson averred. "Would it be alright with you if we get the photographer to come over here and make a copy for us?"

The postmaster shrugged. "Makes no never mind to me. He can set up back of the counter here as long as he doesn't get in my way when customers come by."

Wilkinson thanked him, and they hurried to Ross's Photography, which sat on the western edge of the square. The young man told them he'd head over there right away and would have a print ready for them later that afternoon. Seibert asked where he was on the day Ted Harper was shot, and, unsurprisingly, Ross answered that he was not in town. "Over in Shelbyville, photographing a wedding," he said. "Found out about what happened when I got back home on Sunday."

"Just like clockwork," Tom grumped once they'd returned to the street. "Everyone has a readymade, unshakeable alibi. Let's take our lists and start knocking on doors. I'll start with the confectioners and meet you in the middle."

"Right," Ward agreed. "Looks like I get to begin with the seamstress. She's a single proprietor."

* * *

Faye Sillinger saw Wilkinson and Seibert part company, and she cringed in revulsion when Ward moved her way. She'd noticed him earlier, as he had a distinguished air, but his deputy, with his stern expression, ever-roving eyes, and his hand never more than a hairsbreadth away from his pistol, filled her with disgust. Virtually all men, in her experience, were about the devil's work. That was a certainty if they were here on behalf of Ted Harper and his wife.

Faye'd never had a positive relationship with a man, not even her father, who was an austere, distant figure who seldom acknowledged her existence. With her plain, too-long face, too-large nose, too-small mouth, and wispy brown hair, she knew she wasn't pretty, and men confirmed that fact by looking toward the far horizon when they encountered her on the street. That had helped her business, as her looks didn't threaten female customers; she wasn't going to steal their husbands.

The thought of Ted Harper brought a sour rising in Faye's throat, and anger—a runaway, unquenchable rage—followed it. If this man had wanted to do something worthwhile, he ought to have come years ago, when it still might have mattered. The only useful thing he could do now was go back to where he'd come from.

Faye's memory of Harper coming to her shop at closing that long ago day and what followed ruined what miniscule illusions she still harbored about life and people. Admitting him without concern, she presumed he'd come by to pick up a jacket she'd sown for Denise. Once inside, though, he made plain there was a different purpose. "You and some of your neighbors are in a sad lack of protection for your business," he informed her in a smooth, honeyed tone. "Why anyone could come around here at night, set the place on fire, loot the merchandise, shoot your dog. Therefore, for a small monthly fee that you'll pay me, I'll make certain that none of that happens." An insincere, toothy smile, knowing and simultaneously threatening, climaxed the statement.

The assumption Faye would surrender to Ted's extortion, an act as shameless as it was brazen, made her blood boil, and in a voice thick with emotion, she'd ordered him to get the hell out of her shop and never return. When he swung about, she thought he was leaving; however, that had been only to lock the door. It hadn't occurred to her that he would respond with instant violence.

The simpering smile on Ted's face dissolved into a menacing scowl, and in two swift strides, he crossed the room and stepped behind the counter. He shoved Faye against the wall, clamped his left hand over her mouth, and murmured softly into her left ear. "Since you aren't aware of the danger you're in, I reckon I'll have to show you."

Ted's hand clamped over Faye's mouth even harder. She felt like her face was in a vise. Then, to her shock and horror, he reached down with his right hand, pulled up the hem of her dress, and began probing, searching for a way beneath her undergarments. Within moments, it seemed, he was touching her most private area and then, with a determined thrust of his fingers, was inside her. At that moment, she later reflected, her brain seemed to shut down, and she recalled little of what followed.

The assault seemed endless, yet how long it continued, she could never determine. Harper intensified his motions from time to time, using all of his digits, brutalizing her. His breath became hoarse as he nuzzled against her, and his exertions seemed to excite him as much as they revolted her. At last, though, he pulled his hand away. "If you scream," he warned, "I'll break your neck."

Harper had taken his left hand away from Faye's mouth, and after seeming to have not drawn a breath for several minutes, she hyperventilated. As she gulped for air, he grasped her by the shoulders and forced her down into her chair. "If you decide to be stupid," he emphasized, "and complain to the sheriff or someone here in town, not a soul will believe your story, especially my wife. Further, on some moonless night, I'll burn this damn place to the ground, perhaps with you in it. So, if you know what's good for you, you'll fork over a dollar every two weeks. If you don't, I'll figure you want more of what you got here tonight. Pay it now!"

Dazed and frightened, Faye paid and continued to pay. Ted was right; nobody would believe her if she revealed what he'd done. She found it impossible to be civil to his wife and felt immense relief when Denise began going to the other shop in town. Was it possible she never knew what a bastard he was?

Then came the day when a man, someone Faye'd never seen before, entered her shop and invited her to a secret meeting concerning the problem with Ted Harper. While at least half of the business owners wanted nothing to do with the group, and half of those who attended the first meeting dropped away when eliminating him was adopted, she continued to the end. Her task was to secret the firearms used in the shooting, the determination being that she'd be about the last person in town to be suspected as the killer. After the excitement died down, she was supposed to dispose of the weapons, but the appearance of that wretch hired by Denise Harper caused the group to wait and see if they might be needed again. Faye'd hidden them well. Maybe they'd be useful in getting rid of this marshal and his deputy.

* * *

Wilkinson walked up to the porch where Faye sat drinking her coffee, and he gave her a genuine moment of surprise by removing his hat. "Ma'am," he said formally, "I'm Ward Wilkinson, US Marshal from Nashville. My deputy and I are here by order of the federal court to investigate the murder of Ted Harper. Would you be Miss Sillinger?"

After coolly regarding him for several moments, Faye acknowledged his statement with a nod. Her expression remained neutral, yet Wilkinson was aware of the muted hostility. He felt certain this lady loathed him or at least what he represented. "I have a few questions," he began, "some that we're asking every person who was nearby when the killing occurred. Were you here that day?"

The reply was blunt. "Marshal, you can ask whatever you want to, but it won't do you any good. I know nothing, saw nothing, heard nothing. The only thing I can tell you is that it was a great day in this town, the best in many years. Whoever shot him should receive sainthood."

"What makes you say that?"

Whatever self-control Faye Sillinger possessed evaporated at his question. She rose to her feet, and Wilkinson saw her features were now taut with suppressed fury, that her eyes glittered with hatred. "Ted Harper was vermin," she spat, "the lowest form of life. All these years when he was riding high, wide, and handsome around here, swindling and cheating folks, bullying and stealing, not a lawman of any kind could be bothered to come here and put a stop to it. But just as soon as someone did your work for you, then you appear. I've never had much use for people of your stripe," she concluded with vehemence, "especially that spineless former sheriff!"

"If it wasn't for the governor requesting our involvement via the Federal District Court in Nashville, we wouldn't be here," Ward said with a shrug. "Did *you* shoot Harper?"

The laugh was bitter and incredulous. "You think *I* killed him? It's only a pity I didn't. After that business where he shot poor Mr. Reichert last year and that lily-livered sheriff wouldn't lift a finger to arrest him, somebody had enough. I figure he got killed while trying to take something that didn't belong to him."

"Were you one of the people from whom he was extorting money? We've been told about that filthy scheme of his."

Faye's lips turned white, yet her defiance didn't falter. "You're either forgetful, Marshal, or hard of hearing. I told you the moment you walked up here that I know nothing about it. If there's nothing further, I need to get to work."

Faye turned away, and Wilkinson frantically searched his memory for something to extend the conversation. He thought to ask her if she was the anonymous letter writer but then remembered the woman identified was said to have a husband. Awkwardly, he asked, "Are you married?"

The query, completely unexpected, stopped Faye in her tracks. She turned back to face him and responded in a jeering manner. "Why do you want to know? Interested?"

"Just curious," Ward replied gruffly, by now irritated with her truculent attitude. "You still haven't answered my initial question. Were you here that day?"

Faye Sillinger shot him a scornful look. "Yes, I was here. Spent the morning working on a rush job for Reverend Hoffberger's wife. When I'm sewing, I don't take notice of much of anything. Like I told you, I know nothing about the shooting other than it was a public service. You can ask Mrs. Hoffberger if I was here; she was by just before noon to pick it up."

"Hmm. Last question. Did you see anyone out and about that morning?"

Faye's expression turned crafty, and she exhibited a trace of a knowing smile. "I'm sure there were people about, as there are on any Saturday," she replied. "If I'd known you were going to ask, I might have made a list. The only person I remember seeing that morning was the reverend's wife; she surely wasn't the shooter. It was a slow day."

"Others have told me that." Ward was ready to bid Faye good day when an idea sparked in his brain. "My wife is going to have a baby in a couple of months. Would you have anything that would work alright for either a boy or girl?"

"You're one of the most confounding people I've ever met. Come inside," Faye said with a jerk of her head, "I think I've got just the thing."

Minutes later, Wilkinson emerged with a wrapped garment he believed Charlotte would find darling. What he most valued, though, was the receipt. He had a hunch it might match the handwriting on the letter he and Tom had viewed in Shelbyville.

Behind her counter, Faye Sillinger sighed in relief, glad to be rid of Ward at last. He was intelligent, too knowing, and far more adept than that greenhorn sheriff. After she'd thanked him for the sale, she'd told him, rather tauntingly, that he was no more informed than he was when he said hello. To her astonishment and discomfort, he told her she'd been most enlightening. She wasn't sure how that could be; almost every answer she'd given him was untruthful.

Some of Faye's lies made her uneasy. The one about seeing no one but the reverend's wife that day was of particular concern. She'd been out that midday, and people had seen her. Most would keep her confidence, yet betrayal took only one.

Chapter 26

WILKINSON STOOD IN the street for a couple of minutes, made an entry in his notebook, and then watched people go by. There was a steady, if slow procession of foot traffic going in and out of the shops, an occasional solitary rider, and here and there buckboards or wagons. Hard to believe this was a ghost town that Saturday. That blasted freight train was going to give everyone up here a plausible reason to claim ignorance if they so desired. He made another note to confirm that departure time with the stationmaster. Not seeing Tom, he turned to the next business, a small grocery run by an Al Bluhm, and stepped inside.

Ward received a friendlier welcome but left no more the wiser. Bluhm was barrel-chested, with legs like tree trunks. Incredibly hirsute, the bristles cascading from the rounded collar of his already sweaty shirt, he was hefting a barrel of pickles into a position where it might tempt a customer's eye. When he was done, his blue eyes favored Ward with an expectant look. "You're that marshal that's staying at the hotel, aren't you?"

Wilkinson told him his name and why he was there. Bluhm, ostensibly ignoring what Ward had said, asked if he'd like a pickle. "Too early after breakfast, but they look good. Got a few minutes to talk to me?"

"Only that. I operate this place alone. Do you know someone came in here a few days back and asked me if they could have one of these barrels to make a chicken coop for his dog?"

Despite himself, Ward laughed heartily. When the merriment subsided, Bluhm imparted much the same story as everyone else the marshals had questioned. He'd been busy that day, at least up to eleven or thereabouts; after that, customers were few. "I was out back unloading a wagon when they say it happened. Didn't hear a thing and still can't figure out how I didn't. People in the store that day were my regulars, ones who live north of the tracks and the square. Folks on the south side don't come in that often."

"Did you know Harper?"

"Not really. I had no use for the sonofabitch, and he and his wife did me the honor of keeping out of here. I'm pretty sure my neighbor, Miss Sillinger, hated his guts. Can't say why, but you could sort of tell at the mention of his name. Still, all I know is rumor. Some, all, or none of it may be true."

Next was the bookshop proprietor, Arthur Ryan. "He never bothered me, Marshal," Arthur said, his face impassive. "I think it might be because he didn't have the slightest understanding of my business. I believe he was putting the arm on some merchants along here. I'd see him in the street once in a while, near the end of the month, mostly."

"Interesting," Wilkinson responded, "yet why do I feel you aren't telling me all you know?"

"Because nobody is going to do any favors for Ted Harper or that wife of his. We don't owe them anything. Our duty is to the people he bedeviled and persecuted."

"Meaning you and many others know what happened here?"

Ryan gave Wilkinson a furious scowl, then spoke in a grudging voice. "I'm going out on a limb telling you this much. Listen, then don't ask me anything more. Not a single soul is apt to tell you anything about Ted Harper's death. If you run a business, and it's discovered you talked, you may as well close up and move away. You'll face ostracism just like the Puritans did to Hester Prynne in *The Scarlet Letter*. That man was an objectionable, contemptible person who earned his fate through the accumulation of despicable acts over many years."

The frank, dispassionate comments of Arthur Ryan left Ward discouraged, and the results of his conversation with Ray Alston, another grocer, were just as depressing. According to the man, Mrs. Harper came into his store on infrequent occasions, yet he claimed to never have met her husband. "Never heard a good word said about him," he said. "And don't be asking who blasphemed against him; I won't tell you."

The next shop belonged to the town barber, James Finchum. For a moment, Wilkinson sat on an old, battered chair outside the door and wrote more notations in his book. He was getting nowhere fast, he concluded, save for the unsupported fact that Ted Harper was the victim of a well-orchestrated plot to murder him and that a considerable number of residents knew of it yet refused to come forward. A customer left the shop, leaving the owner by himself, and Ward arose to go inside. At that moment, Seibert exited the adjacent milliner's shop. He had an exasperated look on his face and spoke with asperity. "I'm having a hell of a time with these interviews, Ward. How are you getting along?"

Wilkinson motioned Tom to the opposite side of the street where no structures stood. "Much the same," he confessed. "I haven't discovered a thing we can offer a grand jury, yet I can now say, unequivocally, that Harper was a victim of an organized plot, of which many residents are well aware. When the time comes, unless someone comes clean, we're going to execute a search warrant on the property of every suspect we believe we have. Otherwise, we'll develop no tangible evidence."

"What did you learn?"

"The Sillinger woman, who's the seamstress, is involved. I can't imagine anyone in town who hated Harper more than she did. My notion is that she sent that anonymous letter to the sheriff, alleging Harper was abusing someone's wife. I now believe he was doing it to her. To test that, I bought some baby clothes from her. It'll be interesting to compare the writing on the receipt with the letter Parslow has."

"Very clever. Anything else?"

"Mr. Ryan, the bookseller, as much as admitted to me that the circumstances of Ted's death are common knowledge. He knows himself. It's his other remarks that concern me. He said that nobody in town owed the Harper's anything and that anybody who snitched would become a pariah in the community. Said they might as well pack up and leave town."

Seibert nodded in understanding. "Very similar to what I was told. I had the idea that the confectioner, Mary Bosworth, might have been the woman referred to in that letter. Once I saw her husband, Charles, that thought dissolved. He works at the depot and came up for a few minutes while I was there. Man's a full head taller than me and weighs at least two hundred pounds. He'd have kicked Ted's ass up between his ears.

"Mike McDonald, the butcher," Seibert continued, "isn't a man to fool around with, and I doubt Harper did. He handles a meat cleaver way too well for that. Has nothing good to say about him, either. Despite Ted taking three bullets, one in the back, he told me it was the worst case of suicide ever."

Wilkinson made a disparaging noise. "A real funny guy, isn't he? How about the rest?"

"Couldn't get a word out of the cobbler, Will Sharp. Told me he didn't have a damn thing to say and said he'd be obliged if I got the hell out of his shop. When I reminded him we could subpoena him before a grand jury, he said to go ahead and be damned. 'I'll tell them the same thing I'm telling you,' he told me; 'they're wasting their time. I know nothing about it.'"

"He may get on our search warrant list for nothing more than being a horse's ass."

"I just finished with Miss Clarke. She runs the millinery shop. Likeable lady, I'd guess you'd say. She confirms that Denise Harper is one of her clients, and from what she said, I gather they get along. If so, it doesn't seem likely Ted was extorting money from her."

"You wouldn't think so. How did they answer the questions we're posing to everyone?"

"All claim they were at work, and all say they were unaware of Harper being killed until well after the fact. I don't buy that answer any more than you do. Whether they saw anyone out and about, all gave the same vague answer that it was their usual clientele and that few people, if anyone, came by their place after eleven. Miss Clarke said that she thought she saw Faye Sillinger coming back to her place from somewhere on the square between twelve and twelve-thirty."

"Did she now," Ward said contemplatively. He stared up the street, wondering where she'd been that morning and why she'd felt compelled to lie about it.

Chapter 27

JAMES FINCHUM WAS a slight, sallow-faced man of fifty years with a nervous disposition that caused Wilkinson to decide that he didn't want him anywhere around his face and neck with a razor. Sweat glistened on his thin features, and when he learned who his visitors were, he swayed from one foot to the other. He found a need to do something with his hands and jammed them into his pockets. The smell of his fear was palpable.

Both lawmen detected James's discomfort. Wilkinson, determining that the man was an ideal target for a bully like Ted Harper, wasted no time getting to the point. "Tom, I get the sense Mr. Finchum here is exactly the type of person we've been seeking, someone who can give us information about the recent murder here in town."

The barber was so startled by the statement that he visibly shook. "Wha . . . what do you mean?" he protested. "Who told you such a thing?"

"You did, sir. It's written all over you. Ted Harper was taking money from you by force, wasn't he? He was doing so for a long time before someone killed him, wasn't he? Marshal Seibert and I aren't necessarily of the opinion that you were one of those who shot him, but we are very much of the suspicion that you know who did."

Finchum's rheumy brown eyes bulged in their sockets, and he noisily sucked his upper teeth. "I got no idea what you're talking about!" he blustered. "Honest, I don't."

"Sure you do," Tom replied in a calm tone. "We know from the county sheriff and from some records of Mr. Harper's that he was extorting money from you, and Miss Sillinger up the way as well. So why don't you quit bullshitting us and tell what you know."

What color the man's face possessed drained away, leaving him pale and wan. Wilkinson, studying him, realized that Tom's shrewd ploy had struck home. Finchum, his forehead trenched with furrows, was struggling to decide what to say. After a long silence, he dropped into his barber chair, buried his face in his hands, and wept.

The sobs were wracking, and the man's shoulders shook violently as he tried to throw off his distress. Seibert, uncomfortable at hearing a grown man cry, looked at Ward with a questioning expression, but Ward held up his hand and signaled patience. They already had one answer: Finchum was a former victim of Ted Harper.

At length, the sobs subsided to snuffles, then ended altogether. The barber dried his reddened eyes with a towel, then spoke in such a quiet whisper that the lawmen strained to hear. "Harper took me for four dollars every month for over four years. Came in here one night in 1880 and choked me in that corner over there until my face turned blue. Said if I didn't pay up, somebody, probably a customer, would find me with my throat cut. I've slept with a pistol under my pillow and a small bureau pushed up against the bedroom door since. Even though the no-good bastard is dead, I still do."

"Did you take part in killing him or planning it?"

"No. I was afraid it'd fail, and he'd find out. And then where would I be? Someone, a person I'd never seen before, never has sat in this chair, came by one night just as I was closing up. He told me Harper was going to be dealt with and asked if I wanted to join the group. I declined and never saw him again."

"What did he look like?"

"Can't help you much there. He stood in the shadows where I couldn't make him out. He wasn't a real big man, wirier and more rawboned I'd say. The only distinctive thing was his voice. It was very calm and determined. My guess is that he organized the whole business. Fortunately, I don't know him, and I'd refuse to tell you if I did. That man did me the biggest favor anyone ever has."

Wilkinson and Seibert shared a look of realization, then thanked Finchum and left. At the door, the man called to them, asking if they would mention what he'd said around town. "Not if we can help it, sir," Ward replied. "Not if we can help it."

Out on the boardwalk, Wilkinson asked, "What do we have on people observed on the streets that morning?"

"Besides Miss Sillinger, the butcher told me that Bill Gardner and Leroy Stafford, the restaurant owners, were in that morning but claimed he didn't remember when. Said he was quite busy and didn't recall his other customers. When I asked if he had accounts, his answer was that he didn't extend credit. He's a member of the 'trust in God, and all others pay cash' brigade. Nothing from anyone else."

"Most forgetful bunch we've ever encountered," Ward grumped. "You have two; I got one. My instinct says that sighting of Faye Sillinger is significant."

The men continued to compare notes for a few minutes, with Seibert asking Wilkinson how he wanted to work through the rest of the morning. "It's now ten o'clock," Ward replied. "How about you go down to the freight depot and find out about the train that was leaving the station when the shooting occurred. Meanwhile, I'll go talk to the druggist and tailor who are next door to the hotel. We'll meet back there and have lunch. After that, we'll divide the places on the north side of the square and knock them out so that we can be at Guthrie's saloon by five. I'll see you in about an hour."

Chapter 28

TEN MINUTES LATER, Seibert sat in the map-and-document-strewn office of the stationmaster, an impatient, ill-tempered man named Dunlap, who didn't conceal that the marshal was intruding on time he couldn't spare. "It's amazing that dumbass sheriff didn't ask this question when he came here last month," he griped in clipped tones. "This ledger shows it departed right at noon, and it was a good-sized train, with forty-five cars. Between the whistle, the grinding of the wheels, and the chugging of the engine, all I heard was a muted sound that might have been anything."

"When did you realize there had been a shooting?"

"Don't remember for sure. Fifteen to twenty minutes, perhaps. Someone with nothing better to do rushed in and announced Harper's shooting. Nobody cared, and those that did only hoped someone had shot him more than once."

"Has anyone working here mentioned seeing or hearing anything?"

Dunlap shook his head. "By the time the cars passed the platform, everyone was already back inside, preparing for the next arrival. It's that way around here. Speaking of, are we done?"

"Yes," Tom grated, finding himself irked yet again. "If there's anything more we need to know, we'll be back." As he headed back toward the hotel, a morose thought crossed his mind. If Dunlap wasn't lying like hell, those north of the square were truthful about failing to hear the shooting. That would include those they'd be interviewing in the afternoon.

* * *

The interior of Black's Drug Store was a homage to the owner, Wilkinson thought. The counter, plus a table and chairs, all sported a sable color. Even the wallpaper was an intricate pattern of black and cream. When Ward realized the cash register was likewise of a dark color, his eyes sparkled with amusement.

Harvey Black was sixtyish, with silver hair and luxuriant sideburns. He had a ruddy complexion, wore gold spectacles, and exhibited a cherubic grin. "I expect you're here to ask me about Ted Harper," he said once the store emptied. He made the observation with relaxed unconcern. "Can't imagine I can tell you much."

"Did you know the Harpers?"

"The missus comes in from time to time. Never saw him but on the street once or twice. Had he come in," Harvey said with a mischievous grin, "I'd have likely prescribed strychnine."

Ward tried to suppress a chuckle but was unsuccessful. "A popular opinion in town. Did you see or hear anything that day?"

"The store was closed; my apprentice was sick with quinsy, and the wife and I were in Shelbyville. Learned of it when I opened up on Monday. Can't say I'm surprised. His reputation was all bad."

"Was he leaning on you for money?"

The eyes, a brilliant blue, never blinked. "Even he wasn't that much of a damn fool. Marshal, my family and my wife's family have been around here for over fifty years. Had he attempted that, he'd have had more people down on him than he could have handled. While he left me alone, I can't say the same for my neighbor, Mr. Taylor."

* * *

Peter Taylor was a fastidious man, Ward thought—persnickety even. But Taylor gave no evidence of being the "Nancy Boy" that Denise Harper termed him to be. That view, Ward surmised, probably resulted from him being unmarried, of a somewhat delicate build, and looking as if he'd never shaved in his life. His shop was immaculate, not a speck of dust to be seen.

Taylor was nervous, though; that much was clear. The same apprehensive, unhappy expression, one Ward had seen multiple times since arriving in town, was on the tailor's face, and it became even more alarmed when Seibert, done with the stationmaster, came in from the street. His gaze whipped back and forth between the two lawmen.

"There's no need to worry, Mr. Taylor," Wilkinson assured him. "We're not here to threaten or abuse you the way Mr. Harper did. We know from others that he bothered you, and we also know that he was shaking down merchants in this community for money. You were one of them, weren't you?"

If the floor could have opened beneath him, Taylor would gladly have dropped through it. Fretful, he shuffled his feet from one to the other, trying to think of a plausible way to answer the question in the negative. Finding none, he looked at the marshals and spoke with as much determination as he could muster. "Don't ask that question," he said, "there's nothing but trouble in it."

"We must, sir," Ward replied. He was weary of the organized evasion they were encountering, yet he respected the man's fortitude. "At any rate, you've already admitted you were a victim. You're the third we've found, so if you didn't know, you weren't alone. Since we know you were a victim, I have to ask, did you take part in killing him?"

"I had nothing to do with it and made it my business not to know," Peter said mulishly. "I wasn't aware of anything going on when it happened, either."

"See anyone about the street that morning?"

"Saw people from the hotel coming and going, a few customers came in to pick up alterations, and Mrs. Wiley, the mayor's wife, came in to be measured for a new gown. Otherwise, I didn't spend my time staring out the window."

The conversation was at an impasse, and Ward decided it was best to curtail it. "When we've learned more, Mr. Taylor, we'll be back to see you," he warned. The words seemed to jar the young man, and he made no reply when the lawmen turned to leave. At the door, Wilkinson looked back and saw his shoulders sag. His head shook in dismay.

Chapter 29

"I'VE HAD ABOUT enough of this for right now," Ward said with a grimace of distaste. "I know it's a bit early, but I'd much rather sit down with you to beef stew and a loaf of fresh bread than talk to another living soul."

"Amen to that," Tom concurred. "By the way, your hunch about the freight train was correct."

"Fear, you mean," Ward chuckled.

"Whatever the inspiration, it was right. The stationmaster, a regular fountainhead of gloom, confirmed it. Minus the ones we've talked with already, we can expect the same song and dance from the shop owners on the north side of the square."

"I may order a bottle of wine with our meal," Wilkinson said with an attitude of resignation.

The men entered the hotel and were about to head to the dining room when Seibert espied an envelope sprouting from their room's key slot. Behind the desk, McCormick, looking as if he was a dray driver with a boil on his ass that needed lancing, obdurately refused to meet the marshals' gaze or to speak. The man's continued recalcitrance caused Tom's anger to boil over. "I see there is a message for us, Mr. McCormick," he said in a lashing voice that was loud enough to be overheard by the hotel owner, Wilbur Cochran. "When were you planning to inform us of its arrival? Hand it over, now, sir!"

The clerk cringed at the verbal assault, no doubt fearing that Cochran would appear to add his displeasure. He passed the packet across the counter as if it was on fire. Wilkinson had got them a table, and when Seibert joined him, both men discerned muted snickering from the wait staff.

The men placed their order, and Wilkinson, once the waiter departed, studied the envelope closely. There were no signs of tampering, so he tore it open and withdrew several items. Whatever they were, Seibert could tell they met with his approval.

"Obadiah will be here Sunday evening," Ward murmured from across the table. "Judge Morton has provided everything we've requested."

All the documents were from the Tennessee Attorney General, yet it was obvious that Morton had instigated each of them. The top sheet was an order signed by the AG to exhume Ted Harper's body, and it designated Dr. Howell to perform the postmortem. Next was a letter agreeing to issue search warrants for the property of any resident that the marshals would request. Last was a blanket proclamation informing those to whom the marshals would present it that the lawmen were there on behalf of Governor Bate's office. The state expected cooperation with their investigation. Violators would be subject to such penalties as the state criminal code might specify. "We'll have to serve that exhumation order tomorrow," Seibert said matter-of-factly. "It will take several people and several hours to do all that work."

Wilkinson nodded. "We'll do that right after breakfast and get back to town. All the business owners on the south square will still have to be interviewed, and I want to get a good look at what a normal Saturday looks like, if there is such a thing around here. Ah, here comes our waiter."

The noon meal was excellent, and both men had a full stomach when they headed out to visit the small shops and stores on the north side of railroad square. Ward gave Tom a copy of the document that extolled citizens to cooperate with them and opined it wasn't likely to impress anyone who was determined to be evasive. That prediction proved prescient.

Nine establishments, all bricked buildings with awnings that extended over the boardwalk, aligned along the base of a "V" that was formed by Main and Independence Streets. Further down, to the left, lay the NC & STL passenger depot, then a dual set of tracks that ran parallel to the front of the buildings, and almost directly before these structures, below the rails, were the freight depot and stockyards. Wilkinson began at the furniture store on the far end of the line, following that with hardware, grocery, and clothing establishments. That left Tom with a druggist, two dry goods stores, and another hardware place. "I can't figure how all these duplicate places remain open," Seibert declared. "When we meet up, it will be at a general store. I suspect it has little sections that carry a bit of everything that the rest have in abundance."

Wilkinson, who, like most men, detested window shopping, an activity that left him weary and footsore, exhibited a wry smile. "You know, I believe you're onto something there. If you could convince Charlotte of that fact, I'd be forever grateful."

* * *

David Franklin, the furniture store owner, was more forthright than the people Wilkinson had previously encountered. "Ted Harper was a pissant," he declared, "far too cheap to spend money in here. I think his brother-in-law has an interest in a Nashville factory. My guess is that they got their furniture at cost, maybe less for all I know. Just as well, I didn't want his damn trade anyhow."

"Did you hear the shooting that day?"

"The sound of the train going past muted it. However, I was in the war. I knew what it was."

"Go out and see what caused the excitement?"

"No. Whoever it was, they weren't shooting at me. Before you ask, I'll tell you that Harper would have been my number one choice as a person in this area most likely to be shot. After that scrape where he wounded Mr. Reichert and got away scot-free, it was just a matter of time."

"Did you take part in the plot against him?"

"Wasn't aware that there was one."

"You weren't aware he was extorting money from small businesspeople like yourself? We've identified three so far."

"Knew of a rumor or two. He stayed away from me, though. He was a mite careful to steer clear of anyone who's seen combat. He preyed on the weak and vulnerable instead. I'd say you've got more to discover when it comes to Harper's targets."

"See anyone out and about before the shooting?"

Franklin scratched his scalp and thought for a minute. "Well, Seth Rowland, the Standard Oil man down on Chapel Street. He and his wife came into the store that morning. I saw Mr. Reichert at some point, but it wasn't near to noon. Things got quiet after eleven, and I was doing paperwork when the shooting broke out."

Wilkinson thanked him and moved on to Fred Gorman's hardware store. The owner was a stocky, square-built man who exuded his prosperity by sporting a pair of fancy new boots that he was wearing on the job. Like many of the more prosperous merchants, he wasn't especially forthcoming. "Harper was a first-class prick," he informed the marshal. "Whenever he came in here to purchase tools for his sharecroppers to rent, he always was trying to haggle with me on price. One day, I got fed up with it and told him if he didn't like what I charged, he could take his business to Larry Everhart down the way here. Never saw the sonofabitch again. Me and Larry don't see eye to eye, so I can't say to what degree he was selling to Harper; they did some business together. Don't know how much and don't give a shit. When I lost his trade, it was addition by subtraction."

"Do you know who killed him or planned the act?"

"Don't know and wouldn't say if I did. A stack of those proclamations from the attorney general would be more useful out in the privy. He and the governor don't have to deal with people like Ted Harper. I'd buy a barrel of bourbon for the man who pulled the trigger if I knew who he was."

The conversation, having turned belligerent, was at an end. Wilkinson entered Ted Young's grocery, a few steps distant, and heard a familiar tale. Harper was nearly a stranger, but his wife came in from time to time. Young's usual customers appeared that day, customer traffic dissipated as the morning advanced, and he hadn't heard the shooting. The deceased was a hated man, he allowed, but he had had nothing to do with his death. Ward figured some of his statements were false and, perhaps worst of all, useless. With considerable ill grace, he returned to the street.

There was an old, cane-bottomed chair on the dusty boardwalk, and Wilkinson sat for a moment to make notes from the previous interviews. When he finished, he looked down the row of buildings and saw Tom emerge from one of them and go into the next. He then noticed a man who lounged at the corner of a vacant structure that was situated across from the bank. He wasn't a familiar figure and looked down at the heel. His attire consisted of old, worn-out clothing and scuffed boots. It was too far to be certain, but Ward suspicioned the man was concealing a pistol.

Wilkinson continued to surveil the man discreetly, watching as his eyes darted back and forth, noting passerbys and where they were going. He decided the stranger was lining up the bank for a holdup, shifted his position, and loosened the top buttons of his coat to give instant access to his six-gun. He was debating whether to go confront the man when the stranger spun about and disappeared out back of the abandoned building. Moments later, Ward observed him on horseback, riding away to the west.

The stranger's actions left Ward uneasy. It was possible, of course, given his disheveled appearance, that the man was an idler whiling away the afternoon. "You know better than that," he muttered to himself. "Sometime soon, unless he loses his nerve, he's going to use that hideout gun to make a withdrawal." On a separate page, he made notes about the man, then turned down its corner so he'd remember to tell Tom. With that done, he turned to the clothing store and, for the moment, dismissed the incident from his mind.

Chapter 30

THE VICTIMS OF Ted Harper, at least the ones Wilkinson and Seibert were sure of, fell into two categories: angry and vengeful or subdued and reticent. Frank Bunting, the clothing store owner, was in the second group. When Wilkinson introduced himself, the man interrupted in a restrained manner, "I know who you are. Word travels fast in a small place like this."

"Therefore, you know I'm here about Ted Harper. Were you acquainted with him?"

"Unfortunately." The word escaped Frank's mouth in a regretful, melancholy tone.

"Shaking you down for money like some other folks? My deputy and I are aware of several by now."

Bunting, a diminutive man with curly black hair and bushy eyebrows that had the consistency of wire, rubbed his chin for several seconds, then looked about his store. It had a neat appearance, with clothing for both men and women on offer. "Yes, Marshal," he said with reluctance, "but perhaps not in the way you imagine."

The answer surprised Ward. "I think you're going to have to explain that to me."

"Technically, Harper never took a cent off me. Nevertheless, he made clear that if I failed to do his bidding, I'd arrive here some morning to a smoking ruin. This storefront is too small to live in, so I'm not here at night. He said I'd be bankrupt, and that'd be about the size of it. I'm certain he wasn't running a bluff; everyone around here believed, rightly or wrongly, that the county sheriff was in his hip pocket or was deathly afraid of him."

"That would be correct on both counts," Ward agreed, "but if he didn't take money out of the till, what did he do?"

"Funded his wife's wardrobe out of my pocket. Twice a year, spring and fall, she'd come in here with a catalog from Marshall & Field's, point to what she wanted, and I ordered it for her. The dresses were always expensive, for which I never received payment."

"Was Mrs. Harper aware of what was going on?"

"If she was, she always had the absolute gall to tell me to put it on Ted's account. I doubt she did, but who can say? Most people around here despise her, figuring that she must have been aware of his shenanigans. If she did know, you'll never see a more artless performance in your life."

"There was a plot to kill him, you know," Wilkinson said with a direct stare. "Did you take part, or do you know who did?"

Bunting didn't meet Ward's look, preferring instead to gaze past him and direct his answer to the front window. "No, I didn't take part in a plot to kill Harper, and what I know of it will remain my business. Why would I imprison those who freed me from his persecution? I'd rather serve the time myself than implicate anyone."

"And so you might before all's done," Ward rejoined. "Tell me this, though, did you see anyone out and about the morning of the shooting?"

"Lots of people from about nine to eleven; I made a few sales that morning. With the grocery next door and the druggist on the other side of me, there's normally a lot of foot traffic on Saturday. Then, you've got the other stores and the bank. I didn't keep track of anyone."

Wilkinson bade him a good day, scratched a few notes in his book, including a need for a search warrant for Bunting's home and shop, then headed down the street, toward the end of the row, to a general store. It was there he was to meet Tom. As he passed the bank, he glanced across the street and again considered what the unknown man had been doing there.

* * *

Seibert was just leaving a dry goods store owned by a man named Kenneth Paul as Wilkinson neared the last of the buildings. "Can't say I've got much to report," Ward called out. But when they were side by side, he whispered, "Found another one: Frank Bunting at the clothing store."

"I've got two," Tom announced, "and we've surely missed someone by now. The one in there—the one with two first names—is talking out of both sides of his mouth, or maybe it's his ass. He claims Ted wasn't bothering him, and I'm inclined to agree, given the number of crimes we already know he was committing along this row. Even at that, you'd think his actions were obvious to everyone who works along here. Mr. Paul, though, says he knew nothing about any plot, heard no shooting, and didn't see anyone about that morning. I came close to asking him how he prevented someone like Harper from robbing him when he's blind and deaf."

"Deliberately dumb," Ward said with a contemptuous note.

The marshals walked across the access road and took a load off at a bench provided for tired shoppers. At this hour, there weren't many of those, and the lawmen had it to themselves. Several dray wagons were making deliveries, the sweating drivers paying them little attention. "Before you tell me about your interviews, I want to mention something I saw earlier. I was about to go into the clothing store when I saw a disreputable-looking character hanging around the corner of that vacant building across from the bank. I'm of the opinion he was casing the place for a holdup."

"Recognize him?"

"Isn't from one of the wanted circulars we have. Whoever it is, he isn't doing well—unwashed, unshaved, shabby clothes, and worn boots."

"Sounds like someone who'd be wanting money."

"I believe he had a pistol stuck in the waistband of his pants," Ward concluded. "I was ready to go over there and confront him when he took off behind the building, got on his horse, and rode away. That's not normal behavior."

"Perhaps not," Tom replied, "but it isn't our elephant and not our circus. We've got enough on our plate as it is."

The crotchety tone in Tom's voice surprised Ward, but in principle, he agreed with his viewpoint. "What did you find out?"

"I started with the drugstore," Seibert said after making a scan of their surrounding for eavesdroppers. "Lou Johnson's the owner, and he's one of Ted's victims."

"That's pretty brazen on Harper's part," Wilkinson interrupted. "First time we've found he was preying on businesses next to each other. He was forcing the clothing store owner to order expensive apparel for his wife twice a year and eat the cost. I don't believe Mr. Bunting knows his neighbor was paying as well."

"Nothing about the sonofabitch surprises me anymore," Tom said crossly. "Johnson claims Harper ambushed him one winter night, forced him inside at gunpoint, and then rummaged through his records for several hours. Since the owner's a bachelor, no one was going to miss him at home. It seems the randomness of a druggist's business, the unexpected ebbs and flows, was too damn challenging for Ted, so he told Johnson to cough up four dollars a month or else. Johnson says he was told that if four dollars was too much, given his volume, that was too damn bad. Conversely, if things were so good that he didn't miss it, he should be glad. What a piece of shit that man was!"

Seibert paused his diatribe for a moment, combed through his notes, and added one last fact about Lou Johnson. "You know what made him the maddest? It was when I told him that Harvey Black hadn't paid Ted anything. I thought he was going to have apoplexy."

"Provide any useful information about the day of the shooting?" Wilkinson inquired without hope.

"Not sure about the usefulness, but yes. He confirms you can't hear much of anything when a train passes by, but after observing a few go through, I'm not at all sure it's that loud. I'm thinking this was an agreed-upon strategy if anyone ever asked. If you're down there at the depot platforms, it's noisy enough, I guess. But up here? He also passed along that he saw Faye Sillinger walking back to her shop from the direction of the hotel around twelve-thirty that day."

"That's two witnesses that independently say they saw her that day when she told me she never left the shop. I'm even more convinced she was involved in the killing and am wondering if she might have taken part in the shooting itself."

"Possible, I suppose," Tom said. "Ted might have been too arrogant to believe she would try to kill him and failed to react quick enough. Then again, he ought to have been wary to see her approach him on the public street near the saloon, a place I can't imagine her frequenting. She'd have been out of place there, and he'd have been suspicious."

Ward's forehead wrinkled in thought, and his lips puckered into a frown. His friend's logic frequently confounded his presumptions, and he was grateful for it. A matter well thought out saved a lot of time and boot leather in the end. There wasn't enough evidence to prove his conjecture, and he moved on. "You mentioned you found two victims," he said. "Who was the other?"

"Well, it wasn't the other dry goods purveyor, Mr. Hess. That fellow has damn near anything you'd want in there that isn't liquid: clothes, other textiles, tobacco, sugar, coffee, and tea. Told me that Ted left him be because he's the Bedford County prosecuting attorney's brother-in-law. Said the bastard stayed as far away from him as he could get."

That statement severely tickled Wilkinson's funny bone. "Guess that shows that while Harper was a bastard, he wasn't necessarily a stupid one." An all too infrequent grin spread across his face, and he started laughing. When Tom joined in, the mirth became uproarious, causing midafternoon shoppers to shake their head in wonderment or disapproval. One incautiously raised her voice and expressed the opinion the men had been drinking. That made their glee even more raucous.

By the time they were done, Ward was wiping tears from his eyes with his handkerchief, and both men, although they didn't verbalize it, felt much better. "Now," Tom stated, "about Larry Everhart, the other hardware store owner; Ted had him by the balls. He discovered old Larry was having it on with a widow here in town and forced him to pay up to keep it quiet."

"Yet another form of extortion. Did Mr. Everhart explain how

Harper got onto him?"

"Yep, Ted was only too willing to tell him. One night, while Ted was making one of his clandestine visits to Lou Johnson, he spied Larry leaving his shop and heading away from where he lived, keeping to the shadows and trying not to be seen. He followed and watched him go to this woman's door and be received enthusiastically. Ted waited until the lamps were extinguished, which proved his suspicion. It wasn't long before he had his hand entrenched in Larry's cashbox."

"Is Everhart married?"

"No, but he says Ted still had him by the short hairs. He was gallant to the degree that he refused to reveal the lady's name, but he admitted they attend the same church and that there would be a scandal if news of their relationship leaked out. With all the prosperity the railroad's brought here, the hardware business is quite lucrative. Ted was taking him for one hundred a year, and Larry could afford it. Told me he was afraid his business would suffer if people knew."

"If he likes her that much," Ward snorted, "why hasn't the damn fool married her? That would have ended Ted's leverage. After all, he had no reputation to boast of, and if he'd given out that story, most people would have marked it down as another of his endless lies. Mr. Everhart needs to get his brains out of his crotch."

Seibert emitted a snicker but made no comment on Ward's judgment. "Larry denies any involvement in killing Ted, despite his hatred for him. He considered the money paid for his silence as well spent and hoped, rather naively, that he wouldn't ever ask for more. Given his secret, I'd say he kept as far from the plot as he could."

"Did he do business with Ted?"

"To some extent, although I couldn't persuade him to tell me how much. From what he said, I got the impression what he sold brought him little or no profit. As we know from others, the man was a cheeseparing sonofabitch."

Ward pulled his pocket watch and scanned its face. "It's two-thirty. Let's go back to the hotel and get a cup of coffee; I'm dry as dust." He jerked his thumb toward Rodney Gregg's general store and grumped that the man wasn't likely to tell them anything worth knowing. "I'll come back and see him while you check with that photographer about our map. Oh, I almost forgot; I took a few minutes and sent a wire to Parslow, asking if he'd send Garrett down here with that letter so we can compare the handwriting with Faye Sillinger's. I'm hoping he'll have him here tomorrow."

"That should put us pretty close to five o'clock and time to see who's hanging out at Guthrie's."

Wilkinson nodded. "I want us to take a long walk beyond the depots and go south until we hit Chapel Street. From there, I'll return to the square and walk down the boardwalk to the saloon. It can't be over sixty to seventy yards along there. What I want you to do is to keep going behind those buildings to the backdoor of Guthrie's. I'm thinking there'll be someone leaving in a hurry, and you'll be in place to apprehend them."

Chapter 31

AT THREE O'CLOCK, the marshals descended the hotel steps and departed in opposite directions. They'd enjoyed the break, with the coffee being excellent. During their respite, McCormick appeared with a telegram, exiting the dining room as if a strong wind was pushing him. "Sheriff Parslow will be here around noon tomorrow," Ward informed Tom as they swallowed the last of their java. "Let's get back to it."

When Seibert entered Ross's photography shop, no one was visible. A bell over the door announced his arrival. From the back, he heard a raised voice call, "I'll be with you in a minute," and presently, the photographer appeared, drying his hands with a towel. "It's you, Marshal," he said with a note of surprise. "I wasn't expecting you until around five. Your photograph is drying in the darkroom, but it will be about an hour before it's ready. Would you like me to deliver it to the hotel when I close up?"

The timing was going to interfere with the marshals' visit to Guthrie's, yet Tom agreed. "Can you wrap it in something?" he asked.

"I can. I can also slip it under your door for you if you like."

"That will work fine," Seibert confirmed. "Marshal Wilkinson and I are in Room 302. Put your invoice inside the wrapper."

It surprised Tom to find Ward standing outside Gregg's store. "The owner's wife has had some sort of family emergency, and he's gone to Manchester with her," Wilkinson stated. "Might not be back for a week. However, his brother is working the place, and he was quite helpful. The second Mr. Gregg says Harper never darkened the doors, and neither has Denise. An unsigned note appeared under their door one morning, inviting them to a clandestine meeting to discuss dealing with Ted, but he contends they didn't go."

"Did he keep the letter?"

"First thing I asked, and no. Told me he used it that morning to light the fireplace. I'd say they are a dead end."

Tom told Ward about the arrangements he'd made for the map photograph, and after considering it for a moment, Ward decided it would be all right. Even if that nosy bastard McCormick let himself into their room, he'd have to tear the wrapping off it, and then he wouldn't have the slightest idea why they wanted it. Afterward, he or the hotel proprietor would have a lot of explaining to do.

* * *

The lawmen ambled along the boardwalk as the sun slid toward the western horizon. Passing the bank, Wilkinson had that knowing feeling in the pit of his stomach. He looked at the vacant building where the stranger lurked and saw an empty corner now cast in shadow. Sidling north, they reached the bottom of Independence Street and paid a brief call on the carpentry business. Ward had little belief that the owners, the farthest removed from the shooting site, were going to be much help, and Henry Dillon didn't disappoint.

Mere mention of Ted Harper's name seemed to strike a raw nerve in the middle-aged carpenter, and over the next few minutes, he told them why. "The man was a sorry sack of shit," he harangued, "who'd long overstayed his time on earth. The sheriff has already investigated this matter, and your presence isn't needed nor welcomed. Harper was due to be shot the day he was born," he raged, "and it would have been better if his grandmother had died in infancy."

It was all Seibert could muster to keep from laughing and might have done so if Ward wasn't present. He found nothing objectionable in what Dillon said, sharing the same opinion of Ted Harper.

Dillon, his face red as a beet, abruptly rocked his head and asked, "What was it you came to see me about?"

"We came to ask if you knew anything about Ted Harper's murder,"

Tom said drily. "To hear you, sir, one would think you were a principal player in his destruction."

Dillon's features rapidly altered as the blood drained from his face. "Are you accusing *me* of killing him? I tell you, I didn't. Mr. Martin and his people next door will tell you I didn't do it, and Mr. Reichert was up here that morning and saw me as well. None of us had anything to do with it."

"How about telling us who did?"

The carpenter took several deep breaths and stared in defiance. No longer threatened with the noose, his anger flared again. "I'll never point a finger at anyone in this town for killing Harper," he declared. "As far as I'm concerned, he fell in with evil company down there around that saloon, spouted off to the wrong person, like as not a lodger at that hotel, and got the shit shot out of him. That's all you'll ever get out of me."

The marshals proceeded to the sprawling Martin Livery Stable & Blacksmith Shop, an enterprise that encompassed several buildings and had numerous employees. This was a place too large for Harper's petty scheme, yet Wilkinson wanted verification that Dillon, and especially Fred Reichert, were here at the time of the shooting. Inside the livery, they asked for the owner. The harried stableman, who was busy forking straw, motioned them next door without a word.

They found Bill Martin in the blacksmith shop, wielding a hammer as if it was a goose feather. When satisfied with the piece of iron he was shaping, he thrust the heated object into a tub of water, where it steamed and sputtered. Only then did he turn in the marshals' direction and ask their business.

The smithy was going bald except for tufts of black hair along the sides of his head. He sported a thick mustache under a prominent Roman nose, and his dark eyes flashed with intensity. Yet it was the man's physique that Wilkinson found impressive. Martin was six feet tall and at least two hundred pounds, without a spare inch of flesh on his frame. His biceps bulged beneath the rolled-up sleeves of his sweat-stained shirt, and his pectorals threatened to pop the buttons. Bill Martin looked like a man who might be hard to get along with if he decided to be.

"If you're here to ask after Ted Harper," he said in a voice that brooked no argument, "I can't help you. He did all his shoeing trade with Reichert, probably because he knew I wouldn't tolerate any of his foolishness. If he'd tried that here, he might have departed his life a mite sooner than he did."

"Actually," Ward said, "I wanted to confirm that Reichert and Henry Dillon were up here when Harper got shot. Were they here?"

"Yeah, they were here. Reichert had some wheelwork he needed done and came up to see Dillon. They visited me for a few minutes. While we were talking, he got plugged."

Wilkinson thanked Bill and then headed on with Tom. At the livery door, he called to Martin, who brandished his hammer anew. "I never figured you for one of Harper's victims," he declared, "at least not once I'd laid eyes on you."

The smith smiled in reply, a frosty, malevolent grin that told Ward all he needed to know. He would have squashed Ted like the pissant he was.

Chapter 32

THERE WAS STILL time before heading to Guthrie's. The lawmen used it to recross the tracks, continue south for a short distance, and then head over to Chapel Street and The Standard Oil Building. There, they waited for the manager, Seth Rowland, to finish with a customer from the large grist and sawmill company that lay almost due south of the hotel. He confirmed for them that he and his wife had visited the furniture store on the morning Harper was killed and was proud to tell them they were seeking a cradle for the baby his wife would have in a couple of months. The statement caused Wilkinson to feel a certain comradeship with the man, and he smiled. "Mine is having our first, and at about the same time," he replied. "Best wishes to both of you."

Ward and Tom stepped out of the building a few minutes before five and looked around with caution. In the distance, the rear doors of the livery stable stood wide open. There was no one in sight, although that might change in an instant. It was still light and would be for more than an hour. Should any of the Reichert family step out back, they'd easily spot them.

Tom motioned to the right, where there was a scattering of dwellings, telling Ward he'd use them to shield his approach to the rear of the saloon. Wilkinson nodded and said to go ahead. "I'm going straight up the street until I get to the square, then I'll walk down to Guthrie's. If anyone comes out of Reichert's and starts heading in that direction, I'll follow them."

Seibert stepped off and was quickly behind a large building. When he reached the far corner, a few more strides brought him behind a pair of frame dwellings that were at a diagonal from the rear of Reichert's. Once he reached the front corner of the second, he removed his hat and peered around the corner. With the livery yard still deserted, he sprinted across the clearing and, a few seconds later, was standing by the back of the saloon. As he caught his breath, he wondered how long Ward wanted him to wait before going inside.

Wilkinson walked up Chapel Street at an unhurried pace. He wasn't worried about someone seeing him and trying to run off to Guthrie's and give warning. If they headed down the boardwalk, he would reach the square and see where they went prior to them getting there. Anyone going out the back way would run head-on into Tom. As he passed Reichert's, he thought he detected someone in the building's front—the owner's wife, most likely. It didn't matter now if anybody saw him or not. In the distance, now in plain sight, were the batwing doors of "Lige" Guthrie's saloon.

A light breeze freshened, and it stirred up the dust of the square and scattered it along the boardwalk as Ward strolled forward, his spurs jingling at each footfall. Shopkeepers were closing, except, of course, for the two restaurants, and smells of cooked food wafted from each. Ahead was Guthrie's, and Ward realized that the man sitting out front was wearing a hat identical to the one they'd observed in the same place two days earlier—a man who again had his head inclined toward the batwing doors. Closing on him, Wilkinson acted as if he would pass by, then pivoted. "I'm the federal marshal from Nashville," he said in introduction. "I've got a few questions for you."

The watcher, who'd dropped his eyes to the planks, jerked so violently that the sweat-darkened brown hat fell from his head, revealing a tangle of greasy hair. "Don't give a damn who you are," he blared in irritation. "Go on about your business and leave me be."

"If you don't answer, you'll be taking a moonlight ride to the county jail in Shelbyville."

The man rose, spilling over his chair as he did so. "You're not taking me anywhere," he snarled. "Get the hell away from me while you still can!" The ominous click of a revolver being cocked immediately followed his threat. The sound froze the man in his tracks, and he raised his hands.

"I think you'll find we can," Seibert replied. "Get your ass inside and keep your hands up."

The muzzle of the .45 Colt didn't waver, and, quailing visibly, the man scuttled through the doors. Seibert motioned him to an empty table, and he sat down heavily. "This fellow over here," Tom said, "appeared right where you predicted he'd be. After I asked if he was going somewhere, he tried to feed me a line of bullshit about going to the privy. His eyes and feet were all heading southeast when he came through the door. Asked me if I wanted to come along with him and hold it for him."

The interior of the saloon lay quiet as death. Guthrie had a pained expression on his face, yet wisely kept his palms face down on the bar and well away from his shotgun. Patrons were hanging on every word, but after hearing the commotion out front and Seibert's lightning response to it, none of them had the slightest idea of interfering. All realized they had a seat at an unexpected drama and were eagerly awaiting the next scene.

"Anybody recognize this fellow in the brown hat?" Wilkinson asked.

"His name's Ezra White," Guthrie said.

"You live around here, Ezra?"

The man ignored the question, and Guthrie answered again. "Lives on a little farm. Spends a lot of his time, though, doing odd jobs for people here in town. In the evenings, he comes down here, sits outside, and tries to decide whether he's going to take his money home or drink it here. Drinking it is his usual decision."

Wilkinson considered that for a moment, and Guthrie interrupted the silence by asking if he could start serving people again. "It's alright," Tom affirmed, "as long as you keep your hands above the bar. You put them where I can't see them, and I'll have to shoot you. I don't want to, so don't push your luck."

The saloonkeeper looked at Seibert, who continued to level his pistol, and nodded in assent. "Mr. White, here," Wilkinson said, his voice crackling with anger, "has a damn bad habit of calling to someone in this saloon every single time we come by here. Any of you overhear who his friend is? This fellow who was trying to escape out the back, perhaps?"

Silence met the questions. Ward recognized several people from the hotel dining room, travelers who had no reason to involve themselves in any trouble. The others, he reckoned, including Guthrie, were locals who weren't likely to help outsiders like him and Tom. White sat motionless, staring at the tabletop, refusing to meet Ward's gaze. "You better get ready to ride, mister," Ward grated. "That jail cell in Shelbyville awaits you. I'll have you remanded as a material witness in the death of Ted Harper, which means you might be there a long time."

White twisted his hat in nervous desperation. In Wilkinson's opinion, he looked as if he hadn't any idea of what to do and was afraid if he began answering questions, he'd give himself away. Finally, White decided to bluff it out. "You'll have to get me a horse; I don't own one. As for jail, won't be anything I haven't done before. It'll be three squares and a roof over my head."

"He has convictions for petty theft, being drunk and disorderly, and vagrancy," Guthrie said, trying to move the conversation along and get the lawmen out of his place. "Spent half of last winter in the hoosegow."

"Did you now?" Ward said to White with a sardonic smile. "You know, sir, I've decided not to do you the favor of putting you in jail. If you ever go, it'll be to the state prison in Nashville, a place you can be sure is no hotel. Go on, get the hell out of here. Once you're gone, I may have better luck with your shy friend."

White disappeared through the batwings, and the pounding of his boots on the walk died away. By now, some people were becoming bored with the proceedings and had gone back to their personal conversations, drinks, and card games. The marshals walked to the opposite side of the barroom where the second man sat in a disconsolate slump, and Wilkinson addressed him in a lashing tone. "Alright, funny man, who has a bad back, and his doctor doesn't want him to lift anything heavy. Who are you, what are you, and where do you live?"

Witnessing White's success with the obstinate strategy, the unknown man adopted it as well. Guthrie, however, no longer tolerant of the disturbance, answered for him. "He's Stuart Redmond. Lives down near the end of the square. Has a confectioner's shop and lives in the upstairs." Redmond glared at Guthrie but said nothing.

"Mr. Redmond come by here often?" Ward asked Guthrie.

"Comes by for a beer two or three evenings a week, right after he closes his shop; never is any trouble."

"Leaves through the back, does he?"

"Sometimes. The privy is back there, and I don't mind if customers go out that way to use it."

Getting nothing more that was useful from Guthrie, Wilkinson sat down at the table while Seibert, still clasping the gun butt in his fist, flattened himself against the wall and kept his gaze on the crowd. "Now, Redmond," Ward said with quiet intensity, "we know damn well you weren't going out to take a piss; you were trying to get away from here so we wouldn't see you. In a few minutes, I'm going to buy me and Deputy Seibert a beer, and while we drink it, I'm going to ask Mr. Guthrie if you were in here two nights ago. If he says yes, we'll know that Mr. White tipped you off when we came to town on Wednesday. What's the arrangement, a nickel an evening for keeping a lookout for him?"

Redmond gasped involuntarily, and the unexpected reaction caused a few puzzle pieces to find their places in Wilkinson's mind. "Do you know McCormick, the clerk up at the hotel?"

"It's a small town," Redmond finally answered.

"It sure is! Everybody knows almost everything about their fellow townsmen, unless it comes to knowing who murdered Ted Harper. You were one of his victims, weren't you? He was extorting money from you, wasn't he? Maybe you were one of them that pulled triggers on him? If you weren't, you knew all about it and are involved as an accessory after the fact to keep the truth from being discovered. Isn't that about it?"

Redmond's face reflected multiple emotions as Wilkinson's accusations rained down on him. First was anxiety, followed by bewilderment, then horror. When he spoke, he could only stutter that the marshal was insane, a raving maniac. The questions that followed—who were his accomplices, what had he done that day, where had he gone, who had he seen—were all ignored. Ward ordered him not to leave town and motioned him to the rear of the building with a dismissive wave. "My deputy is going to escort you out back, and from there, you can go where you were in such a hurry to get to. You can even go to the privy."

Seibert prodded Redmond with the muzzle of his pistol, and the man got to his feet. As he did so, Wilkinson stood, drawing his pistol. "I've got you covered," he said, then stepped into the open so his weapon was visible to all.

Tom marched the man through the rear door and directed him to the left. Redmond started off, but after fifty feet, he turned at right angles and plodded southward without looking back. Seibert watched him as his form receded, and, at last, he vanished in the dying light of day.

When Tom returned, Ward was at the bar but positioned so nobody was behind him. "A couple of beers, Mr. Guthrie," he ordered. "I'm sorry for having to use your place for interrogations. Without a sheriff's office here, I couldn't avoid it."

"Ah, it's alright, I suppose," Guthrie grumbled. "Might be good for business once word gets around. Some folks might come in to see if something sensational, like another shooting, might happen."

Wilkinson leaned across the bar and spoke to the keeper in hushed tones. "Was Redmond in here Wednesday evening?"

"Hmm. He's in here often enough now that I'm not sure. Used to be he seldom darkened the door. If I had to give an answer, I'd say he was."

"McCormick ever show up?"

"Yeah!" Guthrie said in disparagement. "Man's a damn gossip-monger. He sneaks in here from time to time, while he's on duty, to wet his whistle. One of these days, I expect old man Cochran's going to catch him and fire his ass."

"Ever talk to Redmond?"

"Yes to that, too. However, he talks to about anyone who'll listen. Like I said, he's a tale carrier and a nosy bastard. I wouldn't have him working for me."

"They were together in here recently?"

Guthrie deliberated the question for a minute, then smiled. "I remember now," he said confidently. "It was Wednesday evening, just like you asked me."

Ward drained his glass and thanked Guthrie for his candor. "Two more of these, sir," he proclaimed.

Chapter 33

SUPPER WAS THICK venison steaks in a rich onion gravy with boiled potatoes and carrots. During the meal, the hotel's owner, Wilbur Cochran, came by the marshals' table and beamed with pleasure as the lawmen praised the talents of his cook. "I've admonished McCormick about his dawdling in delivering your messages," he confided in a conspiratorial whisper. "If you have any more problems in that regard, come and see me."

After the meal, the marshals took a leisurely stroll, most of which was spent in companionable silence. Wilkinson continued to mull over the earlier events of the evening and developed several hypotheses. That no one would cooperate with Sheriff Parslow showed significant planning. Still, Ted Harper being hated by all had something to do with that. Regardless, the organizer of this plan remained nervous, or at least some of his co-conspirators were. Why else were they having an unlikely character, such as the town drunk, sitting outside of the saloon watching for strangers and lawmen? Also, why was another man, presumably one involved in the killing, sitting in the saloon at a predetermined location? Reason said he was there to receive information from McCormick, a man strategically placed to pick up news of anyone who asked about the matter.

If Guthrie wasn't lying, and that was a big if, Redmond was only visiting the saloon two or three times a week. That suggested that someone else, perchance one of the shooters, was taking his place on the alternate days. Given that these establishments were far more than places to drink, were ideal locations to exchange news and information, no one was likely to take particular notice of a local man being joined for a beer by another local man. Redmond clearly didn't wish to be found there by anyone investigating the crime, and his uneasiness showed that fear lingered among the perpetrators. These facts led Wilkinson to the deduction that long-term confidence, if it ever existed, in people maintaining their silence was waning. Also, if concern existed about having overlooked a critical fact, that was wearing on some people's fortitude.

Wilkinson shared these thoughts when he and Tom returned to their room, but he learned that Tom's dour mood had resurfaced. "What the hell are we doing here?" Tom questioned. "There isn't a solitary soul in this town who wants this solved other than Ted's widow, who may have been in cahoots with him on his crimes," he said with asperity. "You ought to be at home with Charlotte, and I ought to be with Frances so I can help her sort out what's rattling around in the mind of our daughter. Based on what we've heard, and must surely discover, I don't want to find his killers. When you consider the number of victims he's wronged, he might just be the dirtiest sonofabitch we've ever encountered!"

Ward sighed inwardly; this wasn't a conversation he wanted to have. "I don't like it any better than you. Nevertheless, I'll have to stick it out to the end. If you insist, I'll detail you back to Nashville and give Parslow a temporary appointment in your stead. I know you're troubled by Rachel's behavior, and we can mark this down as a family emergency."

Seibert blinked in astonishment, then exhibited a contrite expression. "Hell, Ward, don't do that. I've built up a loathing for Ted Harper that I can't escape. If he'd been a son of mine, they'd have had to amputate my leg to get it out of his ass."

"If he'd been your son, he would have turned into a fine man instead of a turd."

"I guess what I'm saying," Tom continued, "is that these people haven't done differently than those western vigilantes who turned the tables on rustlers, horse thieves, claim jumpers, and robbers. That happened when there wasn't any law, or what passed for it was corrupt or weak."

"You also know," Ward replied, "that those groups often lost control and started hanging innocent people. Frequently enough, they let power overcome their judgment, and some settled scores with those they didn't like. Reminds me of Robespierre and that crowd in France during their revolution. After a time, as Charles Dickens wrote about it, they started guillotining shopkeepers and parlor maids, people who hadn't the slightest taint of aristocratic blood. One of these folks may take the notion to shut someone up if there's a fear they might decide to talk."

"As I remember it, Robespierre and the rest of the revolutionary leaders got their own comeuppance. What followed was Napoleon and a quarter century of war. Do you suppose the result of killing Ted will be worse for this community than if he remained alive?"

Wilkinson considered the weighty question and waved his hand in surrender. "That's much too difficult a question for this late at night. I've marked our map where people state they saw Faye Sillinger, and I intend to leave it there. Let's blow out this lamp and get some sleep. Tomorrow is shaping up to be as joyful as the last several have been."

Chapter 34

THE EXHAUSTED LAWMEN fell into a deep slumber that was invaded by vivid dreams. Ward, awakened by a most peculiar reverie, had again drifted off when a thunderous knocking at the door jarred him into consciousness. From the darkness of the room and the absence of light through the window shades, he knew it was not yet dawn.

Another round of thuds brought Ward alert, and he felt the blood coursing through his veins. A glance to his left revealed that Tom, who'd slung his gun belt around the bedpost, was already in the room's corner, weapon in hand. He motioned for Ward to get off the mattress, and Ward tumbled to the floor, grasping his own pistol from the adjacent table as he scrambled aside. When he was in the opposite corner and had the muzzle of his gun trained at the door, Seibert called out a challenge. "Whoever you are," he commanded, "identify yourselves and be damn quick about it!"

There was a pause, and then, to their amazement, both marshals heard a familiar voice. "Marshal Seibert, this is Jeff Broughten, don't shoot. I'm here with Mrs. Harper's brother, Delbert Flynn."

"Well, Mr. Broughten, we know you, but we've never met Mr. Flynn. You'd better have a damned good reason for waking us at this hour. There are two pistols trained on this door, and you're going to turn the knob, raise your hands, and nudge the door open with your foot. Once we can see you, I'll invite you inside. If you have anything in your hands, it better be your cocks."

There was no reply other than the knob beginning to rotate. A moment later, the door swung toward the marshals in a lazy sweep, the opening revealing the men with their arms raised. Broughten, Wilkinson noted, wasn't wearing a gun. "Get in here," Seibert barked, "and let us in on why in hell you can't wait for the sun to rise."

Broughten and Flynn entered the room with care, and after lighting the lamp, Tom checked them for weapons while Wilkinson covered them with his pistol. Flynn, Ward could see, resembled his sister, having the same hair and eye color—even the body build was similar. He stood uneasily and not a little angrily as Seibert patted him down, yet he remained composed enough to keep his mouth shut. "Mr. Broughten is a wanted man in several states, Mr. Flynn, in case you aren't aware. And he came close to getting himself killed the day before yesterday when we confronted him. I hope you'll understand why we can't take chances. Now, what is this all about?"

Flynn didn't seem especially surprised by the announcement. Still, he peered at the foreman with disdain. "It's your pile of shit, Broughten," he stated without compromise. "Let's see if you can put any sweet cream on it."

Jeff Broughten had his reasons. The previous morning, soon after riding away from the farmhouse, Charlie Braxton had brought him up short with his revolver. "Tomorrow is the day, Jeff," he said with a sneer, "and you'd better not fuck this up. There's a bench across from the bank, and no later than eleven, I want your mangy ass to be sitting on it. When I'm satisfied you haven't bollocksed things, I'll be along. When it's done, I'll be riding away and you'll get nothing, understand? Your share is that you'll still be alive."

"Just how are you and this Braxton acquainted?" Ward demanded.

There was an uncomfortable pause, but Flynn clearing his throat finally prompted Broughten to speak. "We took part in a train robbery with Ted Harper up in Iowa some years back. Ted and I got away, but Charlie got captured and sent to prison. I received my split and took off. Ted kept all of Charlie's share: five thousand dollars. When Braxton got out, he tracked me down by my forwarding address in Colorado and came down here. Since none of the money remains, he's going to force me to help him rob the bank today and get it for him."

"When is this supposed to be?" Seibert asked.

"He wants me on a bench across from the bank at eleven. Told me he'd join me when he thought it was safe for him."

"Is this man scruffy looking, old clothes and boots?"

"That's him; how did you know?"

"He was casing the bank yesterday afternoon, right near where that bench is," Wilkinson interjected. "Did Braxton say anything else?"

"Only that he was going to take it out of Mrs. Harper's hide if he didn't get what he wanted."

Those words brought a venomous glare from Flynn, who stated that Broughten had revealed to his sister that her husband was a former outlaw. "If you had the merest smidgin of brains," he fumed, "you'd have figured someway not to mention that. She may never get over this."

Wilkinson, given his brief association with the widow, thought the statement was overly dramatic. Denise Harper wasn't a shrinking violet. "Since you are your sister's lawyer," he informed Flynn, "I have a state exhumation order here for your brother-in-law. You need to have gravediggers at the site on Monday to bring up his casket. The Davidson County coroner will arrive tomorrow to conduct an autopsy."

"Why do you need to do that?" Flynn asked with extreme annoyance. "They shot him; everybody knows that!"

"Because the bullets remain in his body," came the reply, its tone likewise provoked. "Had they been removed, this wouldn't be necessary. Identification of the calibers may tell us the number of shooters and could lead us to them. If you don't like it, Mr. Flynn," Ward said pointedly, "you shouldn't have got us involved. Take it up with the attorney general; he signed the order."

Flynn gave him a black stare but said nothing. Wilkinson, his curiosity not satisfied, had another question for the man. "How is it, sir, that you appear here this morning with Mr. Broughten?"

"It's my sister's good fortune the legislature is in recess and I'm back home in Pulaski. When he came clean and confessed what was occurring, she drove into town and telegraphed me. I'm surprised you didn't see her. By the time I got here last night, it was late, and by the time I got out of him what had happened, it was too late to bother you.

That's why I'm here at this early hour."

"Very well," Ward declared, accepting the reply. "Understand this, Broughten, you stay the hell away from that bank until Braxton wants you there. In the meantime, once Mr. Colborne opens up, we'll visit him and make arrangements for your friend. If he shows up ahead of time, we'll take him, but my guess is that won't occur. The closer it gets to time, the further removed we'll have to be; we don't want him to spot us. You're likely going to be on your own for a bit."

The outlaw objected, but Seibert cut him off. "You're not calling the tune here; you are the one who's made Braxton our problem. He's going to expect you to be carrying a gun, and you're going to be wearing that belt. I can assure you, though, if I find any bullets in your pistol after this is over, we'll arrest you for bank robbery."

Broughten looked to Wilkinson but found no surcease. "This discussion is at an end. Get the hell out of our room and keep away from us until this trouble is over. If you'd come when you first knew about this, we might have managed things differently. Good morning, gentlemen."

The visitors departed in a state of chagrin, with Wilkinson seething in their wake. "I intended we spend our morning watching what people do on Saturday, paying attention to certain individuals, and conducting some more interviews. With a lot of these businesses only staying open until two o'clock, we're going to get damn little of that done." Then, he noticed Seibert's features, which were rapt with suspicion. "Alright, Tom," he said, "what else is bothering you?"

"What's bothering me is how many ways this could go wrong. First, maybe Broughten and this Braxton character are in cahoots with each other. They agree to rob the bank, and Jeff gets an idea to lure us there, kill us from ambush, and likely eliminate any immediate pursuit. Once they're away, he shoots Braxton in the back and escapes with all the bank's money."

Wilkinson whistled. "That's a hell of a hypothesis. Any other ideas?"

"Second, let's say Broughten is telling the truth. What's keeping Braxton from showing up with some extra gunmen he's recruited on his own? Third, maybe Braxton intends to use Jeff as a mark to dupe us. Suppose he figures Broughten will do as he tells him, to be on that bench at eleven when he intends to pull the holdup at eight-thirty. If he figures lawmen won't stake out the bank until around the time he's told Jeff to be there, then he'd catch everyone flatfooted and be long gone."

There were no holes in Tom's logic, and Ward made a two-word reply: "Well, shit!"

The marshals, their bleary eyes reddened from lack of sleep, splashed water on their faces, shaved, dug fresh shirts from their valises, and hurried down to breakfast. The dining room opened when they reached the door, and once the meal of eggs, country ham, and biscuits was complete, they ventured out to the lobby where the night clerk was preparing to hand over his duties to the still unarrived McCormick. "Marshal," he called, "a wire arrived for you a few minutes ago, sir."

Wilkinson tore it open, read it, then handed it to Tom as they stepped out onto the deserted veranda of the hotel. "The sheriff's on his way. If he makes decent time, he ought to arrive prior to this holdup attempt. First piece of good news today."

"Let's hope so," Tom cautioned. "If Braxton's hiding out along the Shelbyville Road, Parslow could run right into him. Do one of us need to ride out that way and keep watch for him?"

"Damn, damn and hell!" Wilkinson exploded in consternation. "Broughten's a damned idiot for not informing us as soon as possible, and Flynn is a double-damned idiot for getting you and I involved in this in the first place." Then, his anger abated, and he refocused his mind on the problem. Cursing and fulminating solved nothing.

"He left an hour ago, if he departed as intended," Ward said in a deliberative tone, "and it'll be at least a half-hour before a wire would reach Deputy Garrett informing him of the trouble. By that time, he'll be over halfway here, and we have too much to do to go out there in search of him, especially if Braxton pulls the trick you theorized about robbing the bank early. My hunch is that he wants as brief contact with people as possible. Despite that, the sheriff's going to have to look out for himself. I don't like this worth a damn, yet that's the way it is."

Tom frowned but offered no complaint; he liked the young sheriff and wanted nothing to happen to him. "Where do you think we'll surveil the bank?"

"The structure across the street, according to the map, is vacant. I've an idea we'll monitor it from there. Let's go there now and see if we can find a way in."

They walked around the back of the hotel, detoured up to Main Street, crossed over between Faye Sillinger's shop and the Baptist Church, then proceeded down the rear of the buildings that populated the lower reaches of the street. From there, they strolled nonchalantly down to the corner of Gregg's store. None of the businesses along the row of commercial buildings were open as yet, but soon, their owners would stir, and customers would move about the square and its nearby thoroughfares. Time was of the essence.

A small structure stood where the corner of Main met the square, and from it, the lawmen studied the vacant building where Wilkinson had observed Braxton casing the bank. It was less than fifty feet distant, and they studied it for several minutes before they advanced to it. "If Braxton doesn't make his attempt until eleven, I'm going to have my Spencer with me," Ward said, his features grim. He turned a full circle, seeking any sign of trouble but seeing none. "Damn if it doesn't look like the rear door's got a padlock on it."

The lock on the door was sturdy, and while Wilkinson examined it, Seibert kept watch, his hand resting on the butt of his pistol. "Let's go around front," Ward said. "Can't do anything here." To their relief, the street that fronted the row of business structures still lay empty, but down below, both men could see wagon activity beginning to appear around the square. Soon, the banker, Harry Colborne, would arrive; it was going to be a far more exciting day than he and his teller could imagine.

The front door likewise had a lock, yet it also bore a sign that advised anyone interested in the building to inquire at the bank. "I'm presuming that this was a foreclosure and Colborne is looking to sell it off," Tom said. "If so, we can get a key and see if it's suitable for us."

They moved away from the building, crossed the narrow service road, then sat down in front of the post office to wait for the banker to arrive. "Ward, we stick out like a sore thumb," Tom said with concern. "A convict like Braxton will spot us for lawmen as soon as he lays eyes on us."

"Chance we'll have to take. At least we have the advantage that I've seen him—a fact that he doesn't know. He shows up, and we'll take him before he gets started. Hey, here comes Colborne now."

The marshals rose to their feet, and Colborne, noticing them, raised his hand in greeting and started to speak. Wilkinson put his finger to his lips in warning, and the banker, a confused and worried look upon his face, unlocked the door and beckoned them inside. It wasn't quite eight o'clock.

Colborne sat heavily behind his desk and asked Wilkinson why he was so secretive. The answer shocked him to his core. "Most likely, sometime between now and eleven," Ward informed him, "a man who has a previous connection to Denise Harper's foreman is planning to rob your bank. He's using this fellow, whose real name is Jeff Broughten, as an unwilling partner in the crime. Broughten has informed us of this plot, and yesterday, I observed a man fitting his description watching your bank from the corner of that empty building over there."

"Can't you stop him before he starts?"

Wilkinson shook his head. "He's not wanted in Tennessee. Until he makes an attempt, we can't arrest him. Broughten states that this fellow, Charlie Braxton he's called, has threatened to rob Mrs. Harper and inflict harm upon her if Broughten fails to assist him. Braxton doesn't trust him to follow through and has ordered him to have a seat on that bench across the way at eleven o'clock. When he's satisfied that he hasn't been double-crossed, he'll show up."

Colborne mopped his brow with his handkerchief and fidgeted with some papers on his desk. "How do you plan to stop him if he tries to rob us?"

"We'll stop him," Ward said. "My primary concern is that you and Mr. Gordon, or one of your customers, don't get hurt. When will Mr. Gordon be here?"

"In a few minutes. We've got our normal chores to perform before opening, which will be at nine o'clock sharp."

"Very well. Item one: don't resist, don't reach for a weapon; we'll take care of the gunplay. Follow their directions and give them what they want. When they leave, don't follow them. In fact, duck behind your desk and get to the floor. Item two: do you have a key to that vacant building across the way?"

"Yes. We own it by a default judgment and want to sell it. Why do you wish to know?"

"We want to go over there, go inside, and see what kind of vantage we have. If it's good enough—if we've got a line of sight—we'll be waiting in there when they make the attempt."

Colborne detached the key from a ring and handed it across the desk. "I'll tell Gordon all about it. Is there anything else we need to know?"

"I don't believe so. We'll hold on to the key until this is over. Unless we come back, it means we've found the place suitable. Also, the sheriff's on the way here with some information pertaining to our investigation. He'll be some more help. Good luck, Mr. Colborne."

Ward and Tom walked across the street and let themselves inside. The interior was murky. What little light penetrated the windows showed a thick curtain of dust standing in the air. The middle of the room lay empty, the furnishings cleared out, with only scrap lumber and other detritus piled near the back. A pair of windows flanked the front door, and Seibert peered through each of them for several minutes, checking the angles and line of sight. When he was done, he grunted in satisfaction, pronouncing them sufficient for what they needed, albeit rather grimy. "There aren't any side windows," he told Ward, "which isn't ideal, but it'll keep us from taking any flanking fire that might come if he spots us in here. We'll leave that rear door locked."

They departed, locking the front door behind them. "Let's go back to the hotel," Ward said. "The sheriff should be along and will look for us there. Once he arrives, we'll let him know what's going on and finalize what we're going to do. I think we need to be in place by ten."

In minutes, they were back in the room, and Wilkinson retrieved his seven-shot Spencer repeating rifle from under the bed. Seibert, after considering how the action might occur, stuck with his .45. He did, however, add to his firepower by thrusting a second Colt into his waistband. Having armed themselves, they hurried downstairs and took a couple of chairs on the hotel veranda.

At nine-thirty, a dust-covered Sheriff Parslow rode up to where the Ward and Tom sat and climbed down. "Morning, gentlemen," he called in a cheerful tone. "I've brought what you were asking about. Anywhere around here to cut this dirt?"

"Come on up," Ward said. "I've got my comparison document with me. As for the other matter, I'm afraid that will have to wait. It's likely there's going to be a robbery attempt at the bank around eleven."

The affable grin vanished from Parslow's face. "*Robbery?* What the hell are you getting at?"

"I'll tell you in a minute. First, let's compare these documents; I suspect they'll match."

Parslow withdrew the letter from his pocket, and Wilkinson took the receipt from his satchel. With great anticipation, the three men looked at them side by side, and all nodded in agreement. "It was Miss Sillinger, for certain," the sheriff said with an audible exhale. "I doubt you'd find two people in this town who write an 'S' the same way she does. Now, about this bank robbery?"

The marshals explained what they'd been told and how they intended to foil it. "You might want to take a vantage point out back of the bank in case they decide to escape that direction," Ward suggested. "I don't think that's likely due to there being nowhere to tie their mounts. We don't know when Braxton is going to appear, only that Broughten's been told to be sitting out front at eleven o'clock. He may appear from any direction, and given that he's been a holdup man in the past, it's reasonable to assume he's planned out an escape route. When it gets to be ten, which won't be that long now, we're going up to wait inside that vacant building I mentioned and see what happens."

"It's a pity Jeff Broughten won't be heading to prison," Parslow said, his voice thick with disappointment. "He's leaning on those renters that Ted Harper has on the hook in Shelbyville, and there's nothing I can do about it. Maybe I'll be lucky, and he'll do something stupid and get himself killed."

Chapter 35

THE LAWMEN PARTED, each going a different direction. Wilkinson walked down to the passenger depot, studied the street scene along the south square for a frustrating couple of minutes, then headed back to the lair they'd selected. Seibert took a long look on the backside of the abandoned building and scanned the approaches from Independence and State streets but saw nothing suspicious. He edged to his right, rejoined the row of north square shops at its eastern end, then walked back toward the bank when he saw Ward reappear. Parslow, presuming he'd taken their suggestion, was now somewhere behind the bank.

When Seibert neared, Wilkinson unlocked the door, and they disappeared inside. Shoppers and delivery drays passed their filthy window, yet Broughten and his shabbily dressed associate remained absent. Neither of the marshals was content with the circumstances, especially that the outlaw held the initiative. He would determine the time of the robbery, how it was attempted, and whether there were any changes to the plan that he didn't want to reveal to his reluctant partner. That meant the marshals' response had to be reactive, a condition they found dangerous. The only advantage they possessed was Broughten's betrayal of the scheme.

The hour drug interminably. To his annoyance, Wilkinson found he was checking his watch every three or four minutes. At five minutes of eleven, Jeff Broughten, wearing his gun in plain sight, strolled by the building and seated himself on the bench opposite the bank. Seibert motioned to Ward and pulled the pistol from his belt. "He's in position," Tom said. "No sign of Braxton."

Wilkinson nodded, picked up his Spencer, and moved to the door. "Figures he'll be along soon. Are there many people on the street?"

"A few," Tom replied, his voice calm. "There's more than I care to see. At the moment, there aren't any customers in the bank; wish the sonofabitch would come along now." The words barely escaped his mouth when he spoke again, the tone intense. "Braxton just appeared," he whispered, "and he's got a third man with him."

Wilkinson's head came up sharply, and he levered a shell into the chamber of his rifle. "Keep an eye on them," he said. "If they pull weapons, we're going out there."

Seibert watched as Broughten engaged in an animated argument with Braxton. He gestured angrily with his hands toward the unknown third person, but the untidy man, his back to the window, gave no sign of backing down. Tom watched him point toward the door of the bank, and Broughten, his unhappiness evident, walked away, the unknown man following behind him. Braxton, a supercilious sneer creasing his face, sauntered over to the bench and sat down.

As he headed for the door of the bank, Broughten could feel perspiration spring from every pore in his body. "I don't care if you like it, Jeff," Braxton had said, "I've brought another man into this operation. You know what I want, and he's going to help you get it. Meanwhile, I'll keep watch out front."

By the time Broughten's hand turned the knob, his heart was pounding, his palm slick with the sweat of fear. It was never a good thing to have an unknown person introduced to a gang of outlaws before a job, and in this instance, far worse. The man remained behind him, and the danger of this position was obvious. After they had the money, this fellow was likely going to shoot him in the back.

Once inside, with a bandana covering his face, Jeff pulled his unloaded pistol, an impotent act he reminded himself, and pointed it at the teller. Behind him, he could hear the man clearing leather with his own pistol, a .44-caliber percussion cap and ball Starr revolver. As he tossed a grain sack at the teller, his unnamed partner swept past him and ordered Colborne out of his office and up to the front. "Get behind there with that other sonofabitch," he ordered in a bullying manner, "and get busy filling up that bag with greenbacks. You fuck with me, try stalling, and I'll blow your damn balls off!"

The bank officers shared a worried look but made no reply. They redoubled their efforts, scooped up the last of the visible cash, and handed it over the counter. Motioning them to raise their hands and back up, Broughten took the bag and started for the front door. It was then that Braxton's toady, an amused sparkle in his eye, waved the barrel of the Starr toward the rear exit of the bank. "That way," was all he said.

Broughten stared at the man and silently cursed himself once more that he'd adhered to that damned threat from Seibert to see him jailed if he was carrying a loaded gun. His compliance, given that the marshals wouldn't expect this alteration, was going to get him killed. Once out the back, this bastard was going to steer him away and shoot him or do it instantly if no one was present. Charlie would be fit to be tied when he discovered he'd once again been double-crossed.

At the rear door, Jeff glanced over his shoulder. The man was aiming the Starr at his back, and he was too far away to try wresting it from him. He turned the knob, stepped down to the ground, and the bore of the pistol dug in between his shoulder blades, propelling him forward. An instant later, Sheriff Parslow stepped from the corner of the building, gun drawn.

The lawman's unexpected appearance shocked Broughten, yet it offered him a sliver of hope. Perhaps he'd escape being killed. "Going somewhere?" the sheriff asked.

If Parslow presumed the man with Broughten would surrender, he was very mistaken. Parslow'd never been in a gunfight and hadn't even aimed a pistol at anyone. His challenge, delivered in a croaking voice, revealed his trepidation, and he was ashamed by it. The holdup man shoved Broughten aside, swinging his pistol upward as he did so. At a distance of ten feet, he took aim at the sheriff and fired.

A blossom of flame erupted from the barrel of the Starr, and a long flare of grayish-white smoke followed it. The bullet screamed by Parslow's head and whined quarrelsomely as it ricocheted off the bricks. Turning sideways, an instinctive movement to make himself a smaller target, the sheriff snapped off a shot of his own that likewise missed its target, the lead ball speeding away to an unknown fate. His opponent fired again, and a hole appeared in the hem of Parslow's linen duster. Although both men were ducking and weaving like heavyweight prize fighters, his foe was finding the range.

Parslow squeezed the trigger once more, cursing in exasperation as the man, who was moving away from the building, failed to fall. He took a slight stumble, but the sheriff's attention was diverted by the sight of Broughten diving through the open rear door of the bank and kicking it closed behind him. In that instant, the gunman shot again, and this time, he found his mark.

The bullet tore through the calf of the sheriff's left leg, causing him to stagger and fall. Pain, almost like being scored with a red-hot branding iron, coursed through him, and it was all he could do to keep from dropping his weapon. Grimacing in agony, he lurched forward on his elbow and glimpsed his antagonist, now having advanced to point-blank range, preparing to finish him with a final shot. He saw the man's eyes blaze in triumph, saw his thumb bend back the trigger of the double action revolver, and as he leveled it, Parslow fired.

The bullet struck the man in the temple, his skull exploding in a welter of blood, bone fragments, and brain matter. Propelled backward, he lurched two steps, fell sideways, and collapsed in a heap. Before his final death spasms ceased, the sheriff, feeling he was soon to lapse into unconsciousness, feebly cried out for help.

When the first shot echoed from behind the bank, Seibert watched as Braxton sprang from the bench and strode into the street, his pistol at the ready. The man riveted his attention on the bank's front door, and Tom stepped from the building, Ward right behind him. Despite the volley of gunfire, the outlaw never chanced a quick glance behind to see if the commotion might draw the attention of the curious or concerned.

Wilkinson stole a quick glance behind them to see if any other strangers were lurking in the street, yet only saw a few startled faces who were peering from the corner of adjacent buildings. As the marshals closed the distance, they moved away from each other. Seibert scuttled to the left, his legs moving in a crablike fashion, until he positioned himself at an angle to Braxton's left side. If the bandit whirled in his direction, he'd not be able to view Ward right away, and the sun, now nearing its highest position, wouldn't shine directly in his face. He was calm and mentally prepared for any move Braxton would make.

Wilkinson sidled to the right, his rifle up and ready. When there was a twenty-foot gap between himself and Tom, with the outlaw's back to his front, he bent his left knee, dropped it in the dirt, and made challenge. "Federal marshals," came the shout, "drop that gun and get your hands in the air!"

It was clear, they later agreed, that Charlie Braxton intended to get the bank's money or die trying. Whirling about, his face flushed with fury and disbelief, he brought his pistol up and thrust it forward as fast as he could. "You sonsofbitches . . ." he screamed, and he might have said more if he'd had time. Broughten had warned him, yet he hadn't heeded it. Seibert, especially with his weapon already drawn and ready, was way too fast.

Tom squeezed the trigger of the Colt in one smooth motion, a touch so light it mimicked a lover's caress. The big revolver bucked in his grip, spitting flame, and before Braxton could get his weapon leveled, a piece of red-hot lead slammed through his shoulder, and the report of the weapon boomed along the closely built storefronts. As he fell to the ground, he pulled the trigger of his pistol, but the shot whizzed harmlessly between the lawmen. The outlaw attempted to rise, and Wilkinson, centering his aim at the man's midsection, triggered the Spenser. The .56-caliber slug struck Braxton in the chest, sprawling him flat on his back. Still, he refused to submit.

To the amazement of both men, Braxton, the front of his coat now covered in crimson, fired again, an act which was followed by a gasp and then a wail of pain by someone behind them. They responded with a last volley that tore through his body, leaving him shot to ribbons, motionless and dead in the street.

Seibert, his Colt at the ready, rushed forward and stomped on Braxton's wrist, forcing the gun to fall from his fist into the dirt. As Tom reached down to grab the weapon, he spotted a man cowering behind the corner of the post office. "Fetch Doctor Demarest," Seibert yelled to the man. "There's someone hurt out here, possibly more inside."

Wilkinson was at the front of the bank, and Seibert joined him a moment later. They exchanged nonverbal signals, then Ward stepped aside as Tom kicked in the door. Inside, Colborne, Gordon, and Broughten lay on the floor. The banker and his teller looked shaken, yet the former robber appeared little perturbed. "The fellow Charlie hired figured to keep all the loot for himself," he declared. "Herded me out back, where I expect he was going to shoot me in the back and take off. Sheriff found us, and they shot it out. Both of them are still out there; I'm not sure what happened. Couldn't help the sheriff," he said in accusation, "because your deputy threatened me if I brought a loaded gun. I didn't."

Broughten tossed his empty gun to Seibert, who checked it and contemptuously pitched it back. Going back out the front, the marshals maneuvered between the buildings, peered around the corner, and found both men on the ground. The mysterious outlaw was clearly dead. However, to their relief, the sheriff's wound, while serious, wasn't likely to be fatal. "I'll go around and get the doctor back here," Tom said. "Thankfully, this looks like a through and through."

* * *

The gunpowder haze was dissipating by the time Seibert returned to the street, but the cordite smell and the pungent odor of shed blood assaulted his nostrils. From everywhere, it seemed, the citizenry was converging. Some of them were simply curious, he thought, yet others betrayed a ghoulish desire to witness a victim of violent death. In the minute he'd been absent, souvenir hunters had emptied the cartridge loops on Braxton's gun belt. His spurs were gone, and someone desperate for a memento had taken the man's battered hat, spilling his greasy hair into the dust. Tom was thankful he'd taken a moment to pick up the outlaw's pistol, as it would have surely disappeared as well. Given how fast people were arriving, he made a mental note to apply this observation to the likely reaction from these same folk when Ted Harper was killed. A lot of those they'd spoken to were lying about what they'd done that day, especially given what he was witnessing in the aftermath of this shooting.

Demarest was wrapping the upper arm of a young girl sitting on the boardwalk in front of the post office, and Seibert approached and spoke to him. "Doctor," he said, "if you can do so, the sheriff is lying behind the bank and urgently needs your attention. He's taken a bullet through the calf of his left leg, a through and through wound. He's lost a fair amount of blood."

The physician ignored the request until he finished wrapping the arm of the frightened child. "There, there, young lady," he said with a kindly smile, "just a splinter from one of these awning supports, most likely. You can take her home," he told her mother. "I'll be around later this afternoon to make certain she's alright." The woman thanked him, put her arm around the shoulder of her now crying daughter, then leveled a furious glare at the marshal. His hard, uncompromising stare took her aback, and without a word, she hurried away.

Demarest hastened between the buildings to the rear of the bank. Seibert returned to the body of Charlie Braxton. He'd never enjoyed shooting people and had promised himself if he ever began to, he'd hang up his guns for good. One thing, though—a matter of substantial import—had changed; he no longer felt the slightest pity for them. Every time he'd given them an opportunity to surrender, and his actions were always in defense of his own life or that of others. Still, as he looked at the dead man, whose open mouth and sightless, staring eyes were being invaded by a horde of black flies, something within him relented, and he called to Larry Everhart, the hardware store owner, whom he noticed standing nearby. "How about getting a tarp or something and cover this man until the undertaker arrives. There's another in the same condition out behind the bank."

Everhart shook his head in disagreement. "Why should I ruin some of my inventory for a sonofabitch like that?" he snarled. "If he'd got away from here with the bank's money, there's no telling what might happen to this town. If Colborne didn't have enough insurance, it would have closed, followed by a lot of the businesses around here. The hell with that bastard!"

"For Christ's sake, Everhart," Tom exploded, "I'm not asking you to wrap him in silk. I don't give a damn if it's used burlap. Just cover his face with something so the children that are in this crowd won't be looking at those damn flies that are laying eggs on him."

The store owner voiced another objection, and Seibert cut him off. He was weary of this town and the people who lived in it. "Mr. Everhart," he said in exasperation, "the government of Tennessee will reimburse you for any expense you incur. Just do what I tell you."

* * *

Behind the bank, Dr. Demarest greeted Wilkinson with a reproachful look. "Are you finished throwing railroad iron at each other?"

Ward started to tell him it was lead they'd been firing but thought better of it. "I've tried to staunch his wounds and used my belt for a tourniquet. It seems to have slowed the bleeding."

The physician examined the sheriff and nodded approvingly at Ward's efforts. "From the looks of this, I'd say you've had prior experience. Were these handkerchiefs you shoved in his wounds clean?"

"Freshly laundered and not employed."

"That's a blessing. Well, young fellow," he said to Parslow, "thanks to this man, I believe you're going to be fine." Turning to Wilkinson, he asked the marshal to go down to his office and bring a stretcher. "Once I've cleaned up these bullet holes and sewed you up," he continued, "you'll be a guest of the hotel for a while."

Wilkinson charged up between the buildings. When he emerged, he saw Seibert supervising the covering of Braxton's corpse. "Stand by," he called, "I'm getting a stretcher from Demarest's office. I'll need you to help me carry the sheriff over there." Tom waved in acknowledgment, then pointed Everhart, his features creased with dislike, down the same path Ward had used.

When Wilkinson returned, Parslow, his color somewhat improved, had propped himself on his right elbow, a dead cigar clamped between his teeth. The marshals, taking great care, rolled him onto the stretcher, and a minute later, they arrived at Demarest's office. His wife, a most efficient nurse, had his tools, bandages, and solvents already laid out for use. "You can have your belt back now," the physician stated, loosening the strap around the sheriff's leg. "It's a damn good thing, too; your trousers are about to fall down."

They all laughed at the quip. Telling Parslow they'd make arrangements for him to be cared for at the hotel, Ward and Tom started for the door. "Marshal Wilkinson," the sheriff called, "before you go, I have a couple of things to tell you. First, thank you for taking care of me out there; I was worried I was going to bleed to death. Second, I had the man who covered up the robber I killed pull down his mask for a moment so I could see his face. He's a ne'er-do-well named Jim Spence, who's also known around Shelbyville as a barfly, loafer, and petty thief. It's no wonder that Braxton fellow is dead," he concluded with a wince as Doctor Demarest began tending his wound. "He sure knew how to pick them: Ted Harper, Jeff Broughten, and Spence."

Chapter 36

WILKINSON, USING A term he learned from a British colonel, a fellow observer during the Franco-Prussian War, summed up the rest of the day as a "royal cock up." By the time Mr. Crump, the undertaker, came and carried away the bodies and the lawmen had dispersed the crowds of curious oglers, it was well past noon. Ward had the briefest moment to ask the lean, austere man, his beard glistening with some sort of scented oil, if he'd embalmed Ted Harper. "I did," he replied, "although it was a day later than it ought to have been. His being on ice helped, but the corpse will deteriorate quicker because of the delay." When asked if he'd removed the bullets, the answer was no. "I sewed up the holes," he said. "If they're needed, exhume him right away. The one that struck his testicles isn't in his body. It's likely buried in the alley where he fell."

Broughten, having obediently hung around, was told to go back to the Harper farm and stay there. "Deputy Seibert and I will be out there tomorrow afternoon," Wilkinson informed him. "And that grave better be open and down to where the casket can be raised when the physician arrives to perform the autopsy," he warned. "If you have to, do the digging yourself."

Delbert Flynn attempted to intercede, and Ward turned on him as well. "I told you, sir, that if you didn't want the federal government involved in this matter, you should have kept quiet. I'll tell you right now that we're prepared to head home the moment the Tennessee Attorney General informs Judge Morton that he wants this investigation retired. Until then, though, if you interfere with us or advise Broughten or your sister not to cooperate, I'll recommend to His Honor that you be indicted for obstruction of justice or contempt of a federal judge." The legislator spluttered in indignation but said nothing. Turning on his heel, he stalked away, kicking clods of dirt as he stomped along.

The marshals made a quick stop at the telegraph office to wire news of the robbery to Parslow's deputy, Simon Garrett, then headed back to the hotel to request a room for the sheriff. When Wilbur Cochran heard that, he snapped at McCormick to get cracking and have storage space on the first floor cleared and made up for the convalescing lawman. Wilkinson thanked him, and with neither he nor Seibert having any appetite, they went down to the south square shops and tried to interview a few owners. Once again, their efforts were in vain.

The windows along the street all sported the same sign: *Closed.* "You can tell it's more exciting to go gawk at dead bodies than sell your wares," Tom sniped. "Could be," Ward agreed in disgust. "Then again, maybe there weren't any customers. Gardner's and Stafford's restaurants look open, but they'll be busy now. Let's go back, get a little lunch, and we'll try again with these people in a couple of hours."

They had their lunch, during which Dr. Demarest had Sheriff Parslow brought over. Cochran ensconced him in a comfortable if not spacious room next to his office. Finding him well cared for, the lawmen decided to call on the schoolteacher, Jordan Delaney, a witness to the gunfight between Ted Harper and Fred Reichert. "There's no class today," Wilkinson declared. "Maybe we can find him at home."

* * *

Delaney lived in a small frame house, which the marshals learned the town provided. Tall, fiftyish, with lank graying hair, he was thin, austere, and long-faced. He peered at them with an uncertain gaze through his gold-rimmed spectacles, which had a precarious perch on a nose that would have better graced a bird of prey, Ward thought in bemusement. "I'm afraid you've caught me in the middle of packing up, gentlemen," he said wearily, gesturing to boxes that were lining the walls. "I'll be leaving when the term ends later this month."

"We won't keep you long," Wilkinson replied. "Were you present when Mr. Harper shot Reichert last year?"

The schoolmaster's reply was bitter and regretful. "Yes, I was there. Reichert believes I saw the whole thing, sided with Harper, took a payoff from him, or that he intimidated me from testifying. It's undermined my authority here; the children no longer respect me. It's time I was moving on."

"What did you see?"

"Hear. Hear is the operative word. I never saw the shooting."

"Very well," Ward said tolerantly, "what did you hear?"

Delaney grimaced at the memory, and his lips compressed into near invisibility. "I'd gone down there to see about having my horse shod, only to find the two of them arguing. Harper was claiming Reichert's work was poor and that he would not stand for it. The smith condemned that statement as a lie and demanded he pay up for the services rendered. One word led to another, each more heated than the last, and I realized I would not get one in edgewise anytime soon. I'd turned away, had my back to them, and was heading out the door when I heard the shot. The Reverend Hoffberger was the person who witnessed the act," he ended with considerable resentment. "Yet he said he couldn't determine who drew first. I'd have been better off if I'd have done the same."

"Ted's pernicious behavior continues to corrupt even beyond the grave," Seibert opined in an unpleasant tone once they were outside. "Now that we have a second witness to the Reverend Hoffberger's presence, do we go visit him?"

"I don't believe so," Wilkinson rejoined, though he chewed thoughtfully at his lower lip. "Going to see him, I reckon, will be about as useless as talking with the mayor. Hoffberger will repeat what he said earlier, and he might be telling the truth. I doubt the good reverend ever witnessed a gunfight prior to that day, and supposing the two men grabbed for their pistols at anything like the same moment . . . well, you get the idea. Since he's made that statement to the sheriff, nothing he would add now would stand up in court. Let's go back and talk to Gardner and Stafford. Their lunch crowd should have slowed by now."

* * *

Bill Gardner's restaurant was a small place, two buildings in from the corner of Chapel Street and flanked on each side by grocery stores. When the marshals entered the establishment, they found the hardworking owner, a large, rather rotund man, busily mopping the floor. He extended a sweaty paw, motioned them to a table, wiped his streaming face with a towel, and asked them what they wanted to know. When Wilkinson told him, the man was cooperative, if not especially informative. "Yes, I knew Ted Harper," he harrumphed. "He brought his wife here for dinner twice. Thought he was a big wheel, but shit won't roll. Did he try to shake me down for money? The answer to that question," he said quietly, yet firmly, "is no."

"Why do you think that was?" Tom asked. "We're aware of several business owners around the square from whom he was extorting money."

Gardner's face set in determination. "A few years ago, a tramp, someone who was riding in a boxcar, got put off the train here. In order to get some money, he held me up right before closing. He came at me with a knife and was lucky I didn't shove it up his ass. As it was, I took it off him, grasped him in a bearhug, and just about squeezed the life out of him. By the time I dropped him to the floor, he'd stopped screaming; man was unconscious. Dr. Demarest later told me I'd broken several of his ribs."

"I gather Harper was afraid of you."

"Being in the war as I was has led me to have terrible dreams that never go away. When that tramp attacked me, it was like being on the battlefield again. I can't say that Harper feared me, but it's likely he figured there were far easier marks to be had than me. That was better for both of us, Marshal. Given how I reacted when that drifter attacked me, I might have killed him."

"Did anyone ever try to get you to join in a conspiracy to murder Harper?" Ward inquired.

The restauranteur smiled wistfully. "There was long-winded talk for more than a year about eliminating him, but I didn't consider any of it serious. When mentioned, I said that I'd deal with him myself if he ever bothered me. I can tell you he was around the square from time to time, often enough to suggest to me he was doing more than legitimate business."

"Anyone you have in mind?"

"You'll recognize them when you meet them. I'm very sure that my competitor down the street, Mr. Stafford, isn't one."

* * *

Leroy Stafford, the marshals noted, wasn't as industrious as Gardner, even though he needed to be. Tracked-in dirt lay on the floor, along with dropped food. Seibert noted ants infesting part of a biscuit along a wall side table, and his mouth twisted in disapproval. An enveloping odor fouled the interior, which seemed to emanate from the kitchen. Both men found it loathsome.

It surprised neither man when Stafford appeared in an apron that was far from clean. "Didn't hear you come in," he said, rubbing his eyes and attempting to smooth out the flattened hair on the left side of his head. It was clear he'd been asleep. "We won't be open again until six o'clock."

Wilkinson, recalling that Denise Harper had termed the man the deadliest person in town, thought she might be right. "We're not here to eat, Mr. Stafford. We're US marshals from Nashville, investigating the murder of Ted Harper. Mind talking with us for a few minutes?"

Stafford, who smelled like his kitchen, scratched at his greasy scalp and waved them toward the back, but Ward told him it wouldn't take that long, suggesting that the conversation remain out front. "Your neighbor, Mr. Gardner, tells us you aren't likely to be a person Ted Harper was stealing from. Is that so?"

Stafford blew a gust of air through his mouth, revealing decaying teeth. "If he'd taken money off me, I'd have had to close. It's no secret I'm struggling here," he admitted with a shrug. "Probably will have to shut down by summer. Gardner runs a better restaurant than me, and travelers to town eat at the hotel, especially if they're on company business. That doesn't leave many customers for me. I'm being squeezed out. Harper realized that and left me in peace."

"Were you approached about joining a conspiracy to kill Harper?" Seibert asked, eager to end the conversation.

"I got a handwritten note that was shoved under the door one night. I ignored it."

"Do you still have it?"

Stafford blinked, not expecting such a question, then responded with a slow nod. "I believe I have it back in my office. Don't know why I kept it, but would you like to see it?" Both lawmen replied affirmatively, and he disappeared down a hallway off the kitchen, where they heard him muttering and shuffling papers for a couple of minutes. Then, there was a cry of triumph, and he returned, waving the paper above his head. Wilkinson took it from his hand, suppressed his excitement as he read it, and then handed it to Seibert.

Tom recognized the importance and asked Stafford if he'd mind if they hung on to it for a while. "Not at all," he replied. "The next time I saw it, the thing was going into the stove."

The marshals thanked Leroy and returned to the street. "That gives us another example of Faye Sillinger's handwriting," Wilkinson said with satisfaction. "We deserve some compensation for enduring that odor."

"He must be broiling a skunk in there," Tom grumbled in disgusted agreement.

Wilkinson, seeing the lengthening shadows, consulted his watch and proclaimed an end to the workday. "I'm beyond tired," he told Seibert, "and there's nothing more to do here this afternoon. Let's go down and have one of Guthrie's lagers, then head back to the hotel for supper. We can look in on the sheriff as well. Once that's done, I'd like us to do a quick review of what we've learned today, followed by whatever each of us chooses. I'm going to write a letter to Charlotte, read a little, and pray for uninterrupted sleep."

Tom grunted in agreement. "It'll be about worth Broughten's damn life if he wakes me up in the morning before I'm ready. I figure Flynn knows better."

Chapter 37

THE BEER WAS pleasant to their parched throats, yet the lawmen would have gladly forgone the salvos of "Hip, Hip, Hooray" they received when they stepped through the batwing doors. The cheers echoed off the walls. Everyone in the saloon wanted to buy them a drink, told them their money wasn't any good, and made a pest of themselves asking questions about the holdup. Wilkinson decided a single drink didn't constitute a conflict of interest, accepted with good grace, then politely declined refills, saying he and Tom still had work to complete. Upon leaving the watering hole, Seibert observed that, for the moment, they were as popular in town as those who'd pulled the trigger on Ted Harper.

As the marshals neared the hotel veranda, Tom spoke out of the corner of his mouth, "Speaking of skunks . . ."

Ward studied the figure sitting on the porch and grated, "Ah, shit! I don't have any intention of obliging that sonofabitch this evening. Do you think we can get away with shooting him?"

Timothy Billings, the Shelbyville newspaperman, showed the effects of the dozen-mile ride he'd made. The telltale dust of the roadbed covered his clothing despite his attempts to brush away the grime. Sweat mixed with the dirt to streak his ruddy face with brown rivulets, and his thick sideburns looked like cobwebs had infested them. "Marshal Wilkinson, Marshal Wilkinson!" he called in anxious excitement. "The county is buzzing over the attempted bank robbery this morning. When I left Shelbyville, it was all people there were talking about. I've got around while I was waiting for you. Talked with the banker, Dr. Demarest, and the sheriff, poor man. But I need your perspective and that of your deputy to complete what will be the biggest headline story the paper has had in years!"

"Well, however big a story it may be," Ward said, the weariness in his voice unmistakable, "it will have to be without us. We have no comment on the matter."

"What do you mean, no comment, Marshal?" Billings blustered. "It was you two men who foiled the robbery, killed that nefarious outlaw, Charlie Braxton, and would have done away with that derelict, Jim Spence, if the sheriff hadn't done it first. Why the false modesty?"

"There's no modesty of any kind, Mr. Billings, false or otherwise. What I'm telling you is that we have no intention of speaking about this matter. It was happenstance, not related to our purpose here. I'll remind you of what I said when I first encountered you the other day, concerning what I promised and what I threatened, depending on how discreetly you keep our names and knowledge of our presence out of the paper. Those terms still stand."

"You're gagging the press's freedom, sir. People have a right to know."

"Yes, Mr. Billings," Wilkinson replied, a wintry tone entering his voice. "They have a right to know whatever you report to them, and that news does not include us. We're not suppressing a damn thing you want to print. We decline to supply any information toward it. You can tell your readers what you wish; however, if I discover that you've put words in my mouth or that of my deputy, I'll see you prosecuted for libel. Good day, sir."

The lawmen disappeared into the hotel, leaving the frustrated editor in their wake. McCormick was behind the front desk, and the sly expression on his face told Ward that the weasel of a clerk had been gossiping to Billings. "Don't get too excited about seeing your name in the paper," he told the man, his voice no less severe. "I have a strong feeling the story he prints won't be mentioning our names, either. Come on, Tom," he said, "let's eat. I'm as hungry as a Montana wolf in January."

* * *

The meal was a fine beefsteak, and Wilkinson dipped into his pocket for a bottle of claret to go with it. Afterward, the marshals visited Sheriff Parslow for a few minutes, exiting when the man began yawning. They forewent a cigar, returned to their room, pulled out the map, and made some new notations. "Faye Sillinger," Seibert declared, "has to be involved in this up to her ears. We know she has motive, and what documentary evidence we possess points to her."

"Whatever she was doing out that morning, she deliberately lied about it," Ward agreed. "That makes it important, but why that is, I still can't fathom."

"Could she have been going to notify the shooters of his arrival? He'd pass right by her shop."

"Maybe," Ward said after a deliberative moment, "but I doubt it. Harper wasn't trying to hide from anyone, and everything we know shows he was keeping an appointment at a particular time and place. You'd think those who were ready to kill him that day would be on high alert for his appearance."

"But why so public? And if he was going to receive a payoff that way, why handle it so each of those being extorted would have a guaranteed witness?"

"I thought about that after you were asleep last night; we didn't have time to discuss it today. I wonder if Harper expected to see one of them elsewhere and was a bit surprised when both showed up. It's doubtful he was afraid, and he didn't expect an ambush until it was too late. Might be that his vanity had reached such a level that he didn't give a shit whether anyone observed."

"Do you figure Faye was taking the shooters their guns?"

"Now, there's a right astute question if I ever heard one. Even more interesting would be if she was out to carry the weapons away after the fact. If so," Ward gloomed, "by now, they're buried in a trackless thicket of woods or at the bottom of a pond, weighted down by rocks."

"Not necessarily. Think about it. About the last person one would expect to be carrying a weapon would be Miss Sillinger. So, let's say she heads out before the appointed time, gets there after the killing, puts the guns in the pockets of her dress or coat, and takes a roundabout route back home. I'll grant you she might have agreed to dispose of those pistols, but if she hasn't, they're up there at her house right now."

"Or she and the rest of them got in the wagon we saw tracks for out back of the saloon, got out later, and then walked home. I can see why she might have kept them now that you've brought up the possibility. She's tormented by what Harper did to her. In her mind, having a gun around might ensure it doesn't happen again."

"Do we search her place tomorrow?"

"No, I don't believe so. If she's ever had them and intended to dispose of them, they're long gone. Her house, though, will be the first one that gets combed through. Who else do we have?"

"Stuart Redmond. I have him marked down as a shooter. He has motive and opportunity by being close by. I did notice that he wasn't at Guthrie's this evening."

"Yes, and neither was his pissant lookout, Ezra White. He must show up there only when he can bum a nickel off Redmond for sitting on his ass and spying for him. Did you notice anybody new when we were in there this evening?"

"One or two. We haven't talked to him, but I think one was the Whipple fellow who owns the general store."

"The one with the formidable wife?"

"That's the one. I've sort of put them at the tail end of the list, considering the reputation of Mrs. Whipple. From what we've heard, she'd have cut off Ted's nutmegs with a dull, rust-coated knife if he'd tried his bullshit on her."

They enveloped the room in laughter, and neither man attempted to quell his guffaws. "I'd have paid good money to witness that event," Ward chuckled with great mirth. "Anything more?"

"One thing," Tom replied. "This afternoon, Bill Gardner told us, 'You'll recognize them when you meet them' when we asked him if he knew anyone who was paying off Ted. I feel he knows who the other shooter is, and that person is located very close to his place of business."

"That would make it one of the three grocers and dry goods storekeepers that adjoin the restaurants," Ward stated after consulting his map. "To change the subject," he continued, "Obadiah will arrive tomorrow evening. In the morning, I propose we go to Reverend Hoffberger's services; I'd like to see who attends. After our meal, we'll get the horses and ride out to the Harper place and see if Broughten took my warning to heart. We'll be back here in plenty of time to meet the train. For now, though, I want to write a letter to Charlotte."

Wilkinson pulled out a sheet of writing paper and was delighted to see Tom doing the same. Like many men, he thought Tom was prone to demonstrate his love by doing things for Frances and his children rather than verbalizing the fact. Even though it hadn't succeeded with his first wife, he felt women needed and wanted to hear their husbands tell them they loved them. He dipped his pen into a small well of ink and began to write.

My Darling Charlotte:

How I regret it is necessary for me to be here in this place and not at your side. The investigation proceeds slowly, and the citizenry impedes us at almost every turn. Still, Tom and I are making progress, far more than the county sheriff managed. Hopefully, by this time next week, I will be home, my love, and can resume taking care of you as I should.

In the next couple of days, you will no doubt learn that we thwarted a bank robbery this morning. The outlaws resisted, and there was a brief gun battle. What I don't expect you'll learn from the press accounts is that we received a tip, caught them by surprise, and were never in any real danger. Neither of us were hurt.

Oh, my darling, my eyes weep for the sight of your countenance; I miss you intensely. Keep yourself well and let Miss Wadsworth do most of the work. It is hard for me to suppress my impatience to return to your loving embrace, and I adore you more than my mere power of words can ever express.

With love, your husband,

Ward

Chapter 38

WILKINSON AND SEIBERT eased into the church just moments before the service was to begin. They had no desire to be noticed, and they timed their entrance, to the distaste of the greeter, to the split second. Finding the rearmost pew empty, it gratified them to see that the only people near them were a young couple who seemed to have scant interest in the proceedings and lost themselves in each other's gaze. Nobody paid them the slightest mind, and when the congregation stood for the final hymn, the marshals exited the way they'd come.

"Interesting scripture," Tom remarked drily as they walked back to the hotel. "I'm still trying to determine what the Reverend meant."

Ward emitted a bark of cynical laughter. "So am I. Joshua, the second chapter. If I've ever heard the story of Rahab the harlot and her secreting the spies of Israel within her Jericho home being employed as the basis for the weekly sermon, I don't recall it. Its use here today is quite ironic, don't you think?"

"Convenient, too. You could make the interpretation that outsiders such as us ought to be well treated, protected even, despite our intent to bring to justice well-respected members of the community. In another way, it's a warning to keep inviolate the secrets of those who committed the murders and not betray them to the authorities. Reverend Hoffberger gets to play it straight down the middle, not taking a stand on either side."

"Brilliant," Ward agreed. "The savviest politician doesn't have a thing on him. Let's get dinner and then take a ride out to Harper's."

Ninety minutes later, after a filling meal of chicken and dumplings, they were on the road to the Harper farm. "Now that we're away from eavesdroppers," Wilkinson said, "did you recognize any of the parishioners?"

"Mayor Wiley and his wife were there, and so were the Colborne's and Fred Reichert's wife. There were a couple of others, but I didn't see very many I knew. There are more churches in town. Did you see any others?"

"Mr. Black, the druggist; David Franklin, the furniture man; Bunting, the clothing store owner; and Finchum, the barber. A couple of those men had Harper's claws in them. Most interesting was Larry Everhart."

"I don't know how I missed him. Was there a woman with him?"

"He was alone. However, if you studied who was sitting near him, within his line of sight was Jeanne Clarke. She looked his way more than once."

"The millinery woman? Well, I'll be damned. I thought she was a spinster instead of a widow."

"Perhaps he didn't want us running around trying to figure out what single woman he was fooling around with. It's a wonder to me that Harper wasn't squeezing her the same way he was Larry."

"Maybe he was. Perhaps Miss Clarke couldn't afford to be too persnickety about her choice of clients and endured Mrs. Harper. Could be she decided she wasn't responsible for her husband or wasn't aware. Regardless, she goes on the list of those with a motive."

* * *

Main Street lay deserted as the marshals trotted their mounts along the thoroughfare. Overnight, there had been a light shower—an ideal rain, Ward thought, that settled the omnipresent dust without creating a mire. Here and there, families were sitting on their porches, but no one smiled, waved, or called. By now, everyone knew who the lawmen were, and no one wanted to be seen talking to them if they could help it.

At the entrance to the farm, Ward and Tom glimpsed a large tent standing at the rear of the house. Tying the horses at the hitching rail, the lawmen avoided the residence and headed for the canvas pavilion, where they could hear the snick of metal cutting into earth. A glance through the flap, which was open at both ends to promote ventilation, revealed Broughten and one of the ranch hands stripped to the waist, their torsos gleaming with perspiration. "Looks like you're making good progress," Wilkinson observed, his tone as neutral as he could manage without gloating.

The sweating men leaned on their shovels and tried to recapture their wind. Broughten, his glare withering, said, "Like we had a choice. If you come looking for Mrs. Harper, you're out of luck. She took off to Pulaski with her brother, said she'd be too upset to be here while Ted's body was being violated."

"It's good that we don't need to see her," Ward riposted in a bright tone. "You can get back to your digging. Around nine tomorrow morning, the Davidson County coroner will be here to perform the autopsy. Be sure you have everything ready for him. Good afternoon, gentlemen."

They strolled back to their mounts, and the sound of the shovels striking earth recommenced. Seibert, ever wary, kept his hand near his gun; trust in Jeff Broughten remained absent. "Ward, he won't wait around for us to notify jurisdictions about his presence here; he's going to make a run for it. My guess is he's waiting to see if that sleazy pettifogger, Flynn, can work out some sort of pardon for him."

Wilkinson erupted in malicious laughter. "That little sonofabitch won't make a run for it tonight. He'll be tuckered out."

Chapter 39

AT FIVE-THIRTY, Obadiah Howell stepped from his train, and seconds later, he spotted Ward and Tom advancing to greet him. His features relaxed in a mischievous grin, and he called out to them. "Two inmates here to welcome me to the asylum." After the chuckles subsided, he continued, "This is a rather pretty little town from what I could see from the window. Can't believe I've never been here before."

Obadiah's eyes searched the platform, and once satisfied there were no eavesdroppers, he spoke in a quiet murmur. "First things first, Charlotte is fine," he told Ward. "I saw her this morning before going to the depot. Also, I've arranged for her to stay at a resort hotel at Monteagle from mid-July until the baby arrives. Your job, once you get home, is to convince her to go. Your wife is a stubborn, headstrong woman; do you know that?" Thinking about their past conversations on the subject, Wilkinson produced a rueful grin.

"Where is your luggage?" Tom asked. "All I see is your medical bag."

"I'm having it taken to the hotel. Anywhere fit to eat around town?"

"Gardner's, we're told, is pretty good," Seibert replied, "but we've had all our meals at the hotel. The food is excellent. Over there," he continued, pointing at Stafford's, "is the deadliest man in town, according to one resident. Another says the food is a surefire cure for constipation."

"A ptomaine palace," Howell harrumphed. "That's ptomaine with a P."

"What?" Ward inquired with a curious look.

"Food poisoning. Only a damned idiot would eat there. The water he's using probably isn't the best, either. Dysentery and diarrhea aren't very good advertising."

"You ought to smell the place. Any appetite you have will evaporate in an instant."

"An ideal place for the corpulent, then. About odor, there's something I need to talk to you about. It will wait until after supper, though. It's a matter that could spoil your desire for food. For now, let's go to the hotel so I can check in. The snacks Helen packed for me ran out long ago; I'm ready to eat."

The evening meal was by Wilkinson and Seibert's expectations mediocre. There were more of the chicken and dumplings, a dish that Obadiah enjoyed, yet the rest of the menu was sandwiches and soups that were composed of leftovers from previous meals. There were other dishes, such as stewed plums, that none of them found appealing. "As you can see," the waiter apologized, "we rarely have much clientele on Sunday nights. You'll be better pleased by tomorrow's menu."

Later, they walked off the meal with a nighttime stroll through the station square. Wilkinson pointed out the various businesses, noted the alley by the saloon where Ted Harper met his end, and mentioned the people he and Tom suspicioned. At last, they ended up in front of the stockyard scales. "None of these creatures will reveal our conversation," Howell observed, his sarcastic wit on display. "I've got a question about what is going to happen tomorrow."

"Oh," Ward uttered in surprise, "what do you want to know?"

"Do you know if the undertaker embalmed Harper before burial?"

"I found out yesterday. I doubt you've heard, but we prevented a robbery at the bank on the north side of the square yesterday morning. The two robbers resorted to gunplay and came up short; we killed one of them, the county sheriff got the other. During the aftermath, I asked the undertaker about Harper. He told me he had embalmed him but stated that he performed the procedure a day or so later than was ideal."

Howell exhaled a long breath of air. "That's a relief. The level of talent of the undertaker, the airtightness of the coffin, and what state the body was in prior to it being embalmed will have a lot to do with how difficult the examination becomes. Without conservation, the body's state would be the consistency of sludge after this amount of time.

Might have had to sift him like some miners do for gold."

"Are you expecting problems, regardless?"

"It's possible. Being embalmed doesn't mean decay doesn't occur. All it does is delay it. Instead of having the body turning to liquid, it might still have enough integrity for me to search for the bullets with little difficulty. All that depends on the variables I just mentioned. There's going to be an odor when we open the casket, and it's going to be a lot worse than the stench coming from that ptomaine parlor."

"Won't you need help with him?" Seibert asked. "He'll have to be turned hither and yon, won't he?"

"Would make things a lot easier. Still, I know what to expect; you do not. The smell that awaits when that lid's opened will most likely be beyond anything you've encountered. If the embalming, which is done with an arsenic liquid, by the way, hasn't held up, the decomposition odor's going to be a combination of very rotten meat and spoiled milk. Those not used to it are going to gag and probably vomit. It gets into your clothes, your hair, even the pores of your skin. Once you've smelled it, you'll never forget it."

Ward and Tom looked at each other, their expressions revealing their unease. Then, gathering himself, Seibert looked Obadiah in the eye and declared, "I'll assist you. Ward, while we're doing what needs to be done with Harper, why don't you ride over and talk to Perry Jessup. He's right next door."

"Sounds like a good idea," Wilkinson agreed. "What do you wear when you do one of these, Obadiah? It would be nice to rustle up some old clothes for Tom to put on while you're doing that. Afterward, we can burn them, or at least boil the stink out of them."

"I wear a long leather apron and have a spare that Tom can use. Can't help you with the clothes. Might be, if it's not too cold, you could strip to the waist and wear gloves. The apron will protect your trousers as well as they can be. Be sure to bring a bandana to put over your face; you'll need it."

* * *

At eight the next morning, Ward and Tom walked their horses up the south side of the square, flanking on both sides the rented buckboard Dr. Howell was driving. Shopkeepers, most of whom were yet to speak with the marshals, looked on with a mixture of curiosity and worry. Who was this new stranger, another lawman? Where were they going that required a wheeled vehicle, and for what? They followed the trio of men with their eyes as they crossed the dual tracks and headed up to the hotel, then looked at each other with puzzlement as the men wrestled a trunk into the bed of the buckboard. The new week, most of them decided, was beginning as badly as the previous one had ended.

The tent was still in place, its flaps stirring in the gentle breeze, when the men pulled rein at the house. Inside the canvas, Wilkinson glimpsed the dark silhouette of the coffin sitting atop the ground and pointed it out to his companions. He stepped from the saddle and looked about for Broughten or one of the ranch hands and, seeing no one, motioned to Tom that he was going to the bunkhouse. "That lazy prick knew we were going to be here early this morning," he snapped in anger, "and he will not lay in there and assume there's nothing for him to do."

Ward's fist pounded on the door, and an irritable voice that wasn't Broughten's answered the thudding blows. "Where's your foreman?" Ward demanded when the sleepy-eyed hand, a man he'd not seen yesterday, came to the door. "He knows damn well we're serving a warrant here this morning."

The man gave Wilkinson a fierce scowl and struggled to maintain his temper. "He left before dawn, headed for Shelbyville. Said he was supposed to catch the train to Nashville and meet Mrs. Harper's brother. Didn't tell me what they were going to do there. He told me and Johnny, who you also just woke up, that we could sleep a couple of extra hours because we'd spent part of our day off digging up Mr. Harper's casket. From what he said, you're a bit early," he announced in an accusatory tone, "but I don't reckon he gave a shit when you got here since he would not be."

"Alright, mister. I believe you. Do you have a key to the house?"

"Mrs. Harper would never trust us with that. What do you want in there?"

"I was going to leave a copy of the warrant on the table, but I reckon I can slip it under the door. You and Johnny take your time this morning but do me a favor and stay close by the house. If Mr. Broughten doesn't like it, you tell him to see me. My associates will need you to help them close the casket when they're done, and, of course, we'll need help getting it lowered again. Then, you can close up the grave."

"You mean we can take it easy until then?"

"That you can."

The man shrugged, displaying a sly grin as he did so. "Give us a few minutes," he said, "and we'll be right out."

Furious at himself, Ward headed back to the tent. "Tom," he called, "once more, you're at the head of the class, and I'm over in the corner with the dunce cap on my head!"

"How so?"

"Broughten, according to one of the hands, has hightailed on a train for Nashville at this moment. Said Jeff told him he was going to meet Flynn there. My guess is that you were right. They're going to use his 'good citizen' act in revealing the plan to rob the bank as a poker chip to get a statewide amnesty from the attorney general."

"Good citizen, my ass!" was Seibert's caustic reply. "That little cocksucker's never done a selfless act in his life. The only reason he informed us was that he harbors hopes of getting into Denise Harper's petticoat and that he wasn't sure he could outdraw Braxton."

With his friend having voiced his indignation for Broughten, Wilkinson turned philosophical. "All of that is undoubtedly correct. For now, though, let's get on with the present tasks. Obadiah, do you need my help in opening that coffin?"

"I doubt it, but before you go to your appointment, it wouldn't hurt to have you standing by. This is a fancy casket, hinged top instead of being nailed down. Here, Tom," he said, "take this bandana and wet it down with some of this."

Seibert took the neckerchief, then held up the small bottle that followed and sniffed the mouth. "What is this, lavender?"

"I've got a half pint of bourbon here if you'd prefer that. Whichever you choose, it will smell a hell of a lot better than what's likely to come out of there when we open it. Ward, you stay well back unless we need you."

Wilkinson nodded and stepped away while Tom and Obadiah donned their lavender-perfumed masks. Both men were wearing ragged shirts that the hotel was planning to use for cleaning rags and long leather aprons that they slipped over their heads. When they were ready, Howell stepped forward to the casket and gave a firm tug on the handle. At first, there was resistance, but after a couple of more pulls, it gave way. The hinges relaxed, and the lid popped open.

There was a brief rush of trapped air that had a faint smell, Ward thought, like garlic. Howell peered down into the recesses of the dirt-encrusted walnut coffin and nodded in approval. "This is as good as we could expect," he announced in a muffled tone. "There's some deterioration, but not enough to be too much trouble. You can go ahead on if you wish, we may be awhile."

Ward strode back to the bunkhouse where the still sleepy-eyed ranch hands were lounging on the steps. "If those men need a hand, I'd be obliged if you'd help them out. While they're performing this autopsy, I have to go see Perry Jessup. Do you know how to get over to his place?"

"Sure," Johnny replied. "Go back out to the road, go left, and keep on until you get to the next lane. It'll take you right up to the house."

"Thanks. You boys continue to take care of my friends today, and I'll see you get Sunday dinner at the hotel in town, on me. See you after a while."

Chapter 40

WILKINSON MOUNTED AND trotted his horse out the drive. He was relieved to see that Tom wasn't displaying any pallor or, worse, nausea. Swinging onto the road, Ward rode less than five minutes before a path intersected and a dried-out signboard proclaimed "*JESSUP FARM.*" He headed up the rutted track and soon beheld a house and outbuildings. No one stirred in the farmyard, but there was telltale smoke curling from the chimney.

The property gave every sign of being well tended: mowed lawn, tilled fields, sturdy fences, and healthy cattle. Still, the place had a weather-beaten appearance that revealed times were hard. The modest white frame house needed painting, its coat blistering and peeling. On the barn roof was a gaping hole, and if not repaired, it would only get worse as time passed. The chicken coop and corn crib both needed carpentry work. Jessup looked like a man who was short of money, short of friends, or both.

Ward got down, tied his horse to the rail, and, removing his hat, knocked at the door. A middle-aged woman with prematurely graying hair and deep lines about the corners of her eyes and mouth answered it. Her dress, covered by a threadbare apron, showed signs of wear, with frayed cuffs and shiny spots from many cleanings. She'd once been an attractive woman, he gathered, but unremitting work and worry had aged her before her time. Not comprehending the marshal's badge on his coat, she spoke in a wary tone, "Can I help you, sir?"

"Are you Mrs. Jessup?" Ward inquired. She replied she was, and he introduced himself. "I'm the United States Marshal from Nashville. Me and my deputy are investigating the murder of Ted Harper. I'm here to speak with your husband."

Mrs. Jessup studied Ward's face with nervous apprehension, then stood aside to let him enter. "He's back in the kitchen. Follow me, please." They passed through a parlor and a cramped dining room and made their way to the back, to the kitchen, where Perry Jessup sat at a small table drinking coffee. Along the way, Ward further noted the straightened circumstances of the family. The carpet in the parlor was ancient, faded and stained by endless days of sunlight and untold steps of tramping feet. Almost all the furniture appeared handmade, presumably by the owner. Ward felt sorry for them, thinking how Ted Harper must have increased their burdens.

Jessup was a wiry, grizzled man, who displayed the same visible signs of overwork and exhaustion as his wife. His hair was iron gray, thinning away to wisps on top, and his unshaven cheeks were hollow. The dark eyes were lusterless, narrowed with fatigue. He made no effort to arise from his chair. "Pardon me if I don't get up, Marshal," he said in a tired voice, "it's been a long morning. Take a chair and have some coffee."

Wilkinson thanked him and pulled up a chair while Mrs. Jessup poured the visitor a cup and set it before him. "I'm here to talk with you about Ted Harper," Ward began after taking a sip. "Several people have stated he attempted to make trouble for you. As a result, I have some questions about that."

Jessup stared at him, his worn-out look almost palpable. "What do you want to know? I doubt there's anything I can tell you that would be of great interest."

"Did you have trouble with Ted Harper?"

"He wanted as much of my farm as he could lay his hands on and thought two old people would be easy pickings."

Wilkinson's insatiable curiosity overwhelmed him, and he asked a question he soon regretted. "Didn't you have any family around to help defend you against his antics?"

The question brought a grimace to the older man's face, as if a festering wound had burst. "Our daughter, she's our youngest, lives two counties over. Her husband's a blacksmith. They live far enough away that we don't see them and their children as often as we'd like. Still, they're the joy of our life and the reason we keep going." Jessup paused, and his gaze rested on the window as if he was searching for or hoping to see something in the distance. "With our sons," he continued in a halting voice, "that's another matter. The war was the undoing of them both."

Ward had heard such stories more times than he could remember, and the marshal cursed himself inwardly for raising the awkward subject. He knew that Mrs. Jessup, unable to tolerate the recitation that was to come, had fled the room and that they were alone. Now would come the remembrances of a stalwart young man, with his whole life ahead, who likely lay buried in an unmarked grave or had a disfiguring wound. *Well, Ward*, he thought bitterly, *you brought this on yourself.*

"Our oldest son," Perry began, his voice tinged with grief, "died in battle at a place called Ezra Church, down in Georgia. The absurdity of such a thing knocked what religion I had out of me, and I've never darkened the door of a house of worship since. What's happened to Junior has hurt the worst.

"Our second son," he continued, almost in a monotone, "survived the war, yet was never the same. He couldn't adjust when he came back, like some things he'd seen or had to do wouldn't quit bothering him. The only time he seemed calm was when he'd go in that back meadow of ours, down to an enormous oak tree, and just sit there for hours by himself. After he left, I spent some time down there to see what he liked about it, and except for the humming of insects and the smell of cow dung, there wasn't a sound of any kind. It was the only place he could find peace.

"Anyway, like I said, he was restless, couldn't settle himself down. Two years after he come home, he announced one evening that he was going west, and he up and left the next morning. We haven't laid eyes on him since."

"I gather you have heard from him?"

Jessup gave a sad nod. "Every year or so we get a letter, always from a different location, and no forwarding address. It seems he drifts from place to place and has seen a lot of the west country. In his letters, he claims to have been a buffalo hunter, gold and silver miner, stagecoach shotgun messenger, ranch hand, and perhaps some other things he wasn't proud of for all I know. Said he's fought Indians, claim jumpers, and road agents. Every time I go get our mail, my wife wills me to bring home a letter from him, and every night, she gets on her knees and prays to her God that he'll walk through the door the next morning. We don't know if he's alive, and I suspect we'll never find out when he isn't."

The abrupt end of the man's lament found Wilkinson struggling for words. Embarrassed, he told Jessup he was sorry to have brought up a painful topic and made the clumsy suggestion they return to discussing Ted Harper. "What did he try to do to you?" he asked.

"In trying to take my land, pretty much anything you could imagine. First, he offered to buy it. I wasn't interested; my grandfather started this farm, and Harper's ridiculously low offer made it easy to refuse. He tried sweetening it a bit from time to time, but considering what we have invested in years, toil, and commitment, it was never tempting. When that didn't work, he started pressuring us."

"In what manner?"

"My fences started being damaged, and my cows would end up over on his pasture. He always claimed I wasn't maintaining them properly, yet I knew that wasn't so. Funny thing is, wherever my fence line didn't abut his land, like where mine and Del Orange's property coincide, there was never a problem. He began talking about taking by adverse possession any of my herd that got over on his property. When he found he couldn't make that work, he really got tricky and nasty."

Wilkinson arched an eyebrow, and Jessup plunged ahead. "First, he tried to isolate me by buying up the land of the man who lived behind me, probably flimflammed him in some fashion. Then, he wanted an easement across my property to drive his cattle to a large pond over there. That lying bastard of a brother-in-law of his presented me a document that purported to pay me for the privilege, but a lawyer I hired said there was a clause he dropped into it, which was written in a language that only a Philadelphia attorney could understand, that actually gave him an option to buy me out after five years. I wouldn't agree to terms on the easement, and they took me to court.

"They hauled me over to the county court in Shelbyville. After my attorney was done, the judge dismissed their argument and warned them not to come back with that type of nonsense again. Harper had to pay all the court costs, but that didn't help with my lawyer's fees. In that way, he bled us dry."

Wilkinson listened with sympathy, no longer shocked or astounded by the cynical workings of Ted Harper's mind. "And after that?"

"It wasn't too long before he got caught up in that shooting scrape with Fred Reichert, a thing that was totally unnecessary. I was there getting my horse new shoes and witnessed the whole thing. Harper had no call to talk to him like he did, even if he thought the work he received was unsatisfactory. There's no question in my mind that he made the first move for a gun."

"Why didn't you appear before the grand jury and tell them that?"

Jessup reddened, and for some moments, he wouldn't meet Wilkinson's eyes. "Heard about that, too, have you? Well, the truth is that Harper came to me and made me a proposal I couldn't ignore. He must have figured what I'd tell the grand jury and told me he'd quit pestering about my farm if I'd not appear. We were in such circumstances that I couldn't fight another battle with him, and I accepted with the understanding that if he ever reneged on that promise, I'd go to the county judge and confess that he'd offered me a bribe. Until his death, he kept that promise."

"Didn't you ever hear from the court?"

"I expected to, yet never did. I figured the sheriff—the old one, not this new fellow—would come out here with a warrant and haul me over to town, but I never saw his face. There was some rumor he was in cahoots with Harper or was afraid of him—could be both were true. After a while, the case against Harper collapsed, and I sort of forgot about it until you mentioned it."

"Where were you on the day he was killed?"

"Where I most always am, right here. With only my wife to help me, there's always something to do, and I'm not as quick and spry as I used to be. Can't say it overcame me with any sorrow when I heard the news."

Ward nodded in acknowledgment. "Reckon I can understand that, given the way you've said he treated you. Might be the worst neighbor I've ever heard of. You mentioned this Del Orange fellow; we've heard his name a few times. What kind of man is he?"

Jessup emitted a sardonic chuckle. "He's a lot like my younger son in some ways. Del was in the war, too, and he isn't quite right. He doesn't much like people. Stays away from them unless he can't avoid it. We speak once or twice a year on average. His spread is over on my right. If you were to ride over there now, I'd expect you'd find him unless he's off hunting or fishing. There's no wife or kids, and I've never heard of him having a lady friend. He's a loner and prefers it like that. He's a first-rate farmer, though—one of the best in the county—and has never caused me to lose sleep."

"Did Harper ever bother him?"

"He was after him to sell, but he was mighty careful about how he did it. Like I said, Del doesn't like people much, doesn't like to be fretted, and would have shot Harper if he'd tried some of the tricks he did on me. Whatever happened between them, he didn't get any of Del's land."

Wilkinson stood to go, and Jessup rose with him. "I need to be getting on, sir," Ward said, extending his hand. "I know you have more chores to do, and I've delayed them long enough. Thank Mrs. Jessup for me for her hospitality."

Perry followed Ward out and waved in farewell as he rode out the lane toward the primary thoroughfare. As the marshal receded from view, he thought of the bit of information he hadn't provided. It was little enough to do for a good neighbor.

Chapter 41

THE SUN WAS nearing its zenith when Wilkinson returned to the Harper farm. Howell and Seibert were still in the tent, their search incomplete. "Having any luck?" he called as he drew rein before the house.

"We've got two," came Tom's reply. "The third one seems to have shifted. Obadiah thinks that resulted from the embalming."

Wilkinson started in their direction, but Seibert waved him back. "Don't come over here, Ward, unless we ask you to help. Some things are better not seen if it isn't necessary."

"Or smelled," Obadiah added. "If you want to be useful, go to the well and get us some water. Those two hands have disappeared, and we haven't time to go hunting them. If you see them, find out if there's a bathtub on the property; me and Tom are going to need to wash."

Wilkinson got his canteen, poured the stale contents into the horse trough, and brought up a fresh bucket from the well. When full, he took it to within twenty feet of the tent flap and placed it on the ground. Even there, he could detect an unpleasant odor that was a sour mixture of old milk and something that was vague, unfamiliar. "What is that stink?" he questioned, his nose wrinkling in distaste.

"You're smelling the arsenic," Obadiah responded, stepping away to sprinkle some additional lavender water on his bandana. "It's leached out a bit as I've looked for these slugs. The first is a .45, from a Winchester rifle perhaps; it was lodged in his lungs. The other is smaller, appears to be a .32."

"That'll be a pistol. Any idea about the distance when fired and what posture Harper was in when they struck him?"

"The undertaker did a fine job sewing closed the holes that were made in him. He was upright or crouched when the .45 hit him, and it came from behind. None of his wounds were through and through. I'd say the shooter was at least twenty or thirty feet away, perhaps from the rear of that saloon you showed me. The second bullet splintered the humerus of his left arm and remained in the bone. It's badly deformed yet still recognizable. From the way the undertaker sewed the hole, Harper was likely on his side or back when this shot struck him. The third one, wherever it is, entered his chest just below his ribs. I'll find it soon enough."

"Any theory on the coup de grâce?"

"The testicles were shot away, and the angle was straight down. Beyond that, I can't tell you much other than, given that the damage wasn't total, it was a small-caliber weapon. If I had to go out on a limb, I'd say it might be a derringer."

"A woman's gun, or a gambler's," Ward replied, and he thought of Faye Sillinger. "I'll let you have your water break while I see if I can get these two lazy pricks to find a tub and get some water heated."

"We've had to disarrange old Ted a great deal," Seibert said, his voice showing no sympathy for his plight. "It's a good thing this casket won't need to be opened again. All his fancy clothes are cut up and shoved into the bottom corner, and he's no longer neat and tidy. Obadiah says in a few years, he'd have got this way regardless, not that I care a tinker's damn."

"If he hadn't been a sonofabitch all his life," Ward said brutally, thinking of his treatment of the Jessups, "he wouldn't be dead. Even if he was, with the slightest spark of human decency, his remains wouldn't be in this condition."

In an even fouler mood, Ward stalked away to search for the farmhands. He came upon them stretched out asleep under the eaves of the main house, where the rays of the sun hadn't yet reached. "Get up, you do less sonsofbitches," was on his lips, but with an effort, he controlled his fury. "Johnny," he roared in his best parade ground voice, "on your feet."

The men jumped as if a bee had stung them. To the second man,

Wilkinson said, "You failed to tell me your name when we spoke earlier. What is it?"

The marshal's anger was ill-concealed, and both men shared an uneasy look. "Al," he replied, "but most folks call me Slim."

"Well, Slim, I thought I told you and Johnny to make yourselves available to my friends, not to sleep away the whole damn morning. Hopefully you enjoyed it because the rest of the day is going to be work. Do you have a bathtub around here?"

"There's one out in the barn. Why do you want to know that?"

"Because working around a dead body, even one that is preserved, is an unpleasant, smelly business. They're going to need to wash once they're done. I want you to get that thing out and get a fire going to heat some water. When they're finished, I expect it to be ready."

The men headed off, Johnny grumbling about taking orders from anyone other than Mrs. Harper or Jeff Broughten. "Shut up," Al admonished, "and don't make trouble. If he takes a notion, he can have us in the county jail before we can fart. Keep bitching, and you can say goodbye to that Sunday dinner he promised."

The tub, filled with a half inch of dust and coated with cobwebs, had sat idle, Wilkinson thought, since Methuselah walked the earth. He supervised the cleaning and remained close to the reluctant hands until the tub was spotless. When a fire was heating a cauldron of water, he felt satisfied with the progress and headed back to the tent.

As Ward rounded the corner of the house, he heard a cheer of triumph. "We've got it," Dr. Howell exclaimed when he saw Ward approaching. "That damn thing was harder to find than a disease-free whore in Nashville during the summer of '63."

"Where did it migrate?"

"Down into his abdominal cavity. It looks very similar to the other one we found. Could have been from the same gun."

"Might also mean those who carried the handguns weren't familiar with firearms and didn't feel comfortable handling a Colt. Do you need any help to close up the casket?"

"No, but we'll need some help to lower it again," Tom replied. "Go get those two loafers, and we'll get that done."

When Ward returned with the two farmhands, the casket was closed. The cloying smell still hung in the air; both men blanched at the aroma. “Takes some getting used to, doesn’t it?” Dr. Howell proclaimed with a smirk. “Pull your kerchiefs over your nose and doctor the fabric with a little of this whiskey. Once you’re ready, we’ll lower Mr. Harper back into his grave, and you can fill it in at your leisure.”

The bourbon was cheap rotgut, among the category of what Ward had heard a liquor drummer refer to as something better poured back into the horse. Obadiah, a connoisseur of good whiskey, would not waste it on an exercise of this type. At least it was good at quelling some of the pungent odor. With the doctor and Tom on one side and the hands on the other, they took up the ropes and eased the vault back into its earthen tomb. “Give it a few hours for the air to clear,” Obadiah advised Al and Johnny, “then it should be alright. Once you’ve got a good coating of dirt on top, you can uncover your faces.”

The hands nodded, and Wilkinson herded them back around the house to check on the cauldron. Finding it bubbling, he returned for a moment to tell Seibert and Howell that the bath would soon be ready, then started drawing buckets of cold water from the well to temper the heat. “You go ahead, Tom,” Obadiah said, “I’ve got to pack up this trunk. Toss your apron down here; I’ve got an airtight bag to wrap it in. Also, tell those hands to burn the hand-me-downs you’ve got on, and here, take a cake of this soap. I use it every time I have one of these.”

Chapter 42

AN HOUR LATER, Dr. Howell heaved himself onto the seat of the buckboard, grasped the reins, released the brake, and turned the team—a matched pair of black horses—down the farm lane and back to town. After a few minutes, Wilkinson signaled he should pull into an unoccupied turnout, then sidled along the wagon to confer. "When are you planning to return to Nashville?" he asked his friend while his eyes swept the road.

The question caught Obadiah off guard. "I'm on the nine o'clock train tomorrow morning," he said in a surprised tone, "provided that's alright with you. There's nothing more I can do for you as far as I can see. I'm eager to get back to my patients, your wife among them."

"It's fine," Ward replied. "I wish you were already there. Once you do get back, I've got a message I want you to deliver for me to Judge Morton. Soon, Tom and I are going to need help here, three or four men at least. We're going to be serving multiple search warrants, and when we conduct the searches, I want to do as many of them as possible all at once. That way, some of our suspects won't receive warning and try to conceal or destroy evidence. While I don't expect violent resistance, that's always possible."

"Will you want them sent here?"

"No, that would alert our suspects. Have them meet up in Shelbyville and report to the Deputy Sheriff there, a man named Simon Garrett. He's the man in charge while the sheriff heals up. I'll coordinate with him to send us a coded message when they arrive, plus another to dispatch them. When they come, we'll meet them at this precise location."

"How soon?"

"Four days at the most. Tom and I have had enough of this place. We've got another full day of interviews, which we'll do tomorrow, then a day to determine our targets and get ready. I want to conduct these searches on Thursday if the men can assemble. If not, then Friday at the latest. I'll write a letter for you to take to the judge."

"Anything more?

"Yes, there is. In going through the papers at Ted Harper's house, we found a ledger book that contains a list of coded names, the dates of payments, and the amounts of money he was extorting from people. It's a primary evidence document because it would tell us who had the greatest motive to kill him, but we can't figure it out. None of the letters used in the code names match the initials of the town's shopkeepers and business owners."

Howell's eyes lit up in anticipation. "A puzzle! You know I'm intrigued by such things. I'd be delighted to have a look at it, provided we have something to eat first."

"How about we head down to Guthrie's. You haven't tried the exceptional lager he sells, and I'm certain he'll have something around to go along with it."

"Sounds good to me. First, let me drop my trunk at the train depot to be stored for tomorrow's trip and then return this rig to the livery owner. He wasn't very friendly, a rather cantankerous old fart, to be plain about it. What's his gripe with you and Tom?"

"Reichert's real problem was Ted Harper," Seibert answered. "They got into an argument last year over the quality of some farrier work, and gunplay ensued. Reichert took a bullet, yet Ted wriggled out of an attempted murder charge. Based on what we've heard, Ward and I believe this was the ultimate act that pushed people over the edge. Soon after, they hatched a plot to kill him."

"As a result," Ward continued, "he isn't keen on us being here to investigate Harper's murder. Also, though he doesn't know it, we eavesdropped on a clandestine meeting at his stable on the first night we were here. He was a participant. The day clerk at the hotel, McCormick, who is a spy that carries news of strangers to contacts at the saloon, a man named Stuart Redmond, who we think is one of the shooters, a fourth man who is the unquestioned leader of the group, and one or more others that said a single word or didn't speak at all. These people comprise all or part of the group that planned or were involved in the killing."

Obadiah whistled through his teeth. "No wonder he got that expression on his face when we arrived. I expect he figures you're going to arrest him whenever you appear."

"No doubt," Tom confirmed with a mirthless chuckle. "He tried to kick us out of his stable and deny us service until we told him there was a cell in Shelbyville for him to be held as a material witness. That changed his tune in a hurry. He's as happy about that as we are being here."

* * *

It was midafternoon by the time they completed the tasks, each requiring mundane paperwork. Dr. Howell, after a quick scan of his watch, stated that it would be better to go back to the hotel and get to work on the ledger book. "It's only a couple of hours to supper, and I don't wish to spoil that. If you wish, we can try the saloon for a nightcap after we eat, my treat. Do you know if he has any decent whiskey?"

Back in the room, Ward pulled out the ledger book, and Tom used straight pins to attach the fire insurance map to the wall. It was stuffy in the chamber, the day turning off humid, and there was a threat of rain in the air. Finding the window had a screen, Obadiah raised it to provide some ventilation, pulled the single chair over by it, and then sat and lit his pipe. As he did so, the marshals, having assigned each business and shop owner a number, made notations on a sheet of paper about each one, especially those who would be the subject of search warrants.

For the next half-hour, the room was silent except for the muffled conversation between Ward and Tom. Obadiah sat facing the window, puffing on his pipe, filling the room with aromatic smoke. Occasionally, he produced the odd grunt or contemplative noise, yet like his friends, he seemed stymied by the code. Finally, he stood, placed the sheet of names on the chair, and wandered over to where the marshals were still at work. "What is that you've got there?" he asked. "Isn't that a fire insurance map?"

"It is," Ward replied. "We needed a map of the town, and this was the only thing we could get our hands on. Found it hanging in the post office. Local photographer made a print of it for us. Are you familiar with these things?"

"A little. At the bank, our loan committee sometimes uses them in determining whether to extend credit, or how much credit at particular locations. An area that's prone to fires isn't an ideal risk."

Howell peered at the map, closely studying the notes Ward and Tom had prepared. "Looks like you're down to a few people to talk with," he remarked, "all in this row of shops south of the square?" Ward murmured an agreement, and the physician's eyes roamed across the drawing a second time. Frown lines materialized on his brow, and he returned to the window to retrieve the list of coded names. For a couple of minutes, as his friends watched in eager anticipation, he glanced from the map to the list and back again. "I'll be a sonofabitch. Your answer's been here the whole time," he announced, "you just didn't see it."

Obadiah, enjoying his ability to extend the suspense, grinned. "Look at these ledger entries, then check the abbreviations on the map. See BL there, that's short for Blacksmith; CN, that's short for confectioner. All the others are on there as well. Harper wasn't identifying these people by their names; he was using their occupations. It's fortunate you had this map out, or I'd never have solved it."

Wilkinson, holding the coded list next to the map, called off the names to Seibert in a muted whisper. There had been a dozen people being squeezed for cash or goods by Harper. "We had some of these identified," he told Obadiah, "but not all. We'll be able to finish our interviews tomorrow. We might go back and see a few of these people again. The dining room will be open in thirty minutes," he said in a buoyant tone, "let's go down and see if they'll open early for us."

The men put away the working papers, took the map down from the wall, and stowed all of it in the valise that Ward kept with him everywhere. Downstairs, Mr. Cochran told the waiter to seat them early. Soon, they were tucking into pork roast, sweet potatoes, stewed apples, and fresh bread. "When we get home, Frances will have me on bread and water," Tom joked.

As they'd had nothing since breakfast, the men ate with relish. There was pie and coffee for dessert, and they wolfed it down as well. "We've reached our limit," Wilkinson said when the waiter reappeared with the coffee pot. "I believe we'll go walk this off for a spell before calling it a night. This was the best supper yet."

They went out to the lobby, where the lugubrious clerk, McCormick, stood behind the desk, pulling a long face. As prearranged, Ward began a casual conversation with Obadiah. "Tell our wives we'll be home in a few days," he said. "Tom and I have to stay here to make it look good, but we're far from making an arrest. Let's take a walk, then head on down to Guthrie's."

Chapter 43

ONCE AWAY FROM the hotel veranda, the three friends veered to the right, disappearing in the growing twilight. They made for the far corner of the passenger depot, ascended the platform, then walked down the boardwalk to mix with a few travelers who were departing a newly arrived train. Soon after, McCormick came into view, scurrying toward the saloon. With no sentry posted out front, Wilkinson planned to join the man once he'd gone through the batwing doors and discover who he was hurrying to see.

Without warning, though, as if he had a sixth sense, the desk clerk halted, pirouetted about, and focused his gaze on the spot where they'd flattened against the wall of the terminal. The man gasped in astonishment, stumbled on, stopped and stared back, reversed course, then gave up. Turning his back to the men, he ran back to the hotel in a panic-stricken flight.

Irritated, Ward was about to tell them to come along when he noticed the suppressed amusement on Obadiah's features. The physician's goatee was twitching, the ends of his mustache gyrating back and forth. He soon lost the battle with his facial muscles, and the loud guffaws he produced echoed along the platform. "The way he was twisting and sashaying around," the doctor chortled, "would make you think he tried to fart and shit himself instead."

The three men erupted in hilarious laughter, drawing the scornful glare of a middle-aged woman who found their gaiety unseemly.

"From the look she displayed," Tom noted, "perhaps McCormick did have an accident." This brought another roar of merriment.

"Let's go," Ward said as their amusement subsided, "before the man he was going to tip off gets away."

* * *

It was a slow evening at Guthrie's, too early for many people. Besides the proprietor, there were two sales agents at a table; they'd been in the hotel dining room, Wilkinson recalled. A laborer in rough work clothes was finishing up his beer at the bar, and after a last massive swig, he wiped the foam from his lips and left the establishment. In the far corner, a fourth man, someone who wasn't familiar, sat alone, his face set in a pensive mask. There was something about his appearance that struck Ward as odd. Then, he realized what it was. There was a thin coating of dust on the sleeves of the man's shirt and along his trousers from his knees to the cuffs. In between, his clothes were clean, as if he'd been wearing an apron.

Ward walked up to the bar where Obadiah was ordering a glass of lager and a shot of the saloon's best whiskey for them. "That fellow in the corner," he murmured to Guthrie, "is he from around here?"

"Yeah. That's Harry Henderson. He owns one of the small grocery stores up the way."

"A regular?"

"Not really. Comes in here a couple of nights a week after he closes. Gets a sarsaparilla and sets in the corner over there. He doesn't drink, except for that stuff. Kind of a fish out of water in a place like this if you want my opinion, but he's never any problem and puts money in the till."

There was a familiar thread in the saloonkeeper's answer. A few of his customers were newcomers, people that prior to the killing of Ted Harper had rarely crossed the threshold. Now, they made regular appearances a couple of times a week while not attempting to make friends or seeming to have a particular reason for coming by. They just showed up, nursed a drink or two for a couple of hours, then headed for home. One of the entries in the coded ledger book was a grocer on this block.

"This Henderson fellow ever in here at the same time as Stuart Redmond?"

"Not that I can recollect. Harry's here at the beginning of the week. Stuart's around at the end. What are you getting at, anyway?"

"A theory, nothing more. Anyone else along this block that only comes in on certain days?"

"Old Man Whipple comes in on Wednesday and Thursday afternoons, now that you mention it. Surprises me he undoes his wife's apron strings that often."

"Seen anymore of Ezra White?"

"He shows up just like horseshit on the road. Hasn't been around since you collared him the other night, though. That threat to put him in state prison and put him to continual hard labor must have put the fear of God in him. Can't say I miss the twenty-five cents a week he spends here."

Wilkinson thanked Guthrie, then headed for the table where Tom and Obadiah were waiting. Harry Henderson was gone. "Based on what I heard from Guthrie," Ward related, "I'm of the opinion that the man who left out of here a minute ago is the third shooter. He's a grocer up the street who has found the saloon a place to be a couple of nights a week."

"Sounds like Stuart Redmond," Tom observed.

"It does. He, Ronald Whipple, and the third man, Harry Henderson, all have businesses along here, and all started coming to this saloon after Ted's murder. Further, they come at the same time of day but never come on the same nights."

"This is where your conspirators meet McCormick," Obadiah said. "It's convenient, and it's a place where men go without having the wife along. From here, the recipients of his news pass it on to someone you haven't identified as yet. Stands to reason it's the man with the commanding voice you overheard in the stable."

"I think I know who that is," Ward observed. When he bent forward to whisper it, Tom nodded in agreement. "From what we've discovered, almost has to be."

* * *

It was fully dark when they returned to the hotel. The night clerk was on duty. McCormick had gone home sick, the new clerk informed the marshals. "Must have eaten at Stafford's," Obadiah said in a facetious tone.

Back in the room, Wilkinson wrote his letter to Judge Morton while Seibert and Obadiah Howell smoked by the window. Tom, Ward noted as he organized his thoughts, was talking to the doctor about his daughter. His friend seemed troubled, but the concentration on his task caused him to lose the gist of their conversation. When he was done, he looked up from his portable desk to find they were discussing a different subject. "Here it is, Obadiah," Ward said, wearily stuffing the communication in an envelope. "Let's get some sleep, and we'll see you in the morning."

Slumber arrived readily to the exhausted friends, but to those they were pursuing, its oblivion would not come. Along the row of businesses south of the tracks, people spent the day speculating where the marshals had gone and who was the older man with them. Rumor was they'd gone out to the Harper farm, which caused one person to posit they were digging up Ted's corpse. Others dismissed the idea and told him to stop being silly. What they all agreed on was that those who hadn't yet faced questioning from the marshals would soon do so.

Businesspeople involved in the conspiracy stared at their ceilings. Those already visited by Wilkinson and Seibert dreaded the men would return. Already, they had accused several of being victims of Harper's greed; proof of the fact might lead to arrest for conspiracy to kill. Those who'd bluffed their way through the questioning wondered if their bravado would hold.

Harry Henderson, certain he was now in the sights of the lawmen, twisted and turned so much that his wife banished him to the parlor. Where the hell had McCormick been this afternoon? What good was the lazy bastard if he couldn't give timely warning?

Edna Whipple, having witnessed the gun battle between the marshals and Charlie Braxton, feared for her husband. She had no illusions about their ruthlessness or their marksmanship. She fretted anew over what he'd done in the plot to kill Ted Harper and what would happen if they found him out. Beside her, he lay snoring like a steam boiler, a fact she found aggravating.

Stuart Redmond's insomnia resulted from being unable to decide: should he stay put, as the plot's leader was demanding, or take off in the middle of the night? A friend was advising him not to do anything rash. Rash! Wasn't taking part in a murder as rash an act as one could imagine?

Faye Sillinger hadn't such qualms. She regretted nothing she'd done, and any loss of sleep she suffered was from the latent effect of the abuse she'd endured from Ted Harper. If the rest of them would just hold tight, she told herself, then all would be well. Unhappily, she thought, most men were weak or no account.

Chapter 44

MILES AWAY, IN THE quiet of a rural night, the man who'd planned and carried out the plot sat alone on his front porch rocker, calmly smoking his pipe. They were getting close, these marshals. He'd warned the others something of the kind could happen, yet he doubted they believed him when they made the agreement to stop Ted Harper. It had surprised him as well, expecting it to be investigated as a local matter. Still, the news hadn't disturbed him much. Long experience taught one to expect continuous change, much of it having negative consequences.

His earliest memories of growing up on the farm were the solitary, carefree times of his life. At nine, his mother died, leaving his father to raise him, his brother—two years his junior—and a sister who was four. Since he was already an excellent shot, his dad gave him the job of hunting meat for the table while he tended the fields. "I got little ammunition, and he relied on me to bring back that many pieces of game," he said to himself. "We were always short on powder and ball."

Five years later, worn down by overwork and lingering grief, his father collapsed during the spring plowing. This left the fourteen-year-old boy to support the family alone. By herculean efforts, aided by his siblings, they maintained the farm only by the narrowest of margins. On two occasions, he found it necessary to run off unscrupulous types who thought they could gain the land through enticement, trickery, or threats. During a particularly hostile conversation, he found that marksmanship was also useful when contending with humans.

An agent for a long-forgotten land company became irate at his repeated refusals to sell, him being a then seventeen-year-old youth. The agent mounted his horse and made several belligerent remarks about arson, poisoning of wells, and destruction of fences. He was wearing a pistol, and in his agitation, whether or not intended, he dropped his hand to its butt. That movement earned the man a bullet.

"I was holding a shotgun," he remembered, "and had Pop's pistol in my waistband. Thought he was going to shoot me and just reacted on instinct. Good thing I pulled the pistol, otherwise I'd have blown him in half."

The revolver, an old .36-caliber powder and ball Navy Colt, had a slight pull. The bullet, aimed at the visitor's head, took off the lobe of the man's left ear instead. Bleeding profusely and in shock from the pain, he wobbled forward in the leather, grasping the saddle horn to keep from falling. After being told that if he ever came back, he'd lose what remained, the man galloped away, never to return. Word got around, and people left the siblings alone.

Then came the war. He'd determined to remain on the farm and was stunned when his younger brother, excited by the prospect of escaping the drudgery for what he was certain would be a short, glorious war, announced he was going to enlist in a local company. After much fruitless argument, the older brother arranged for an overseer—an older man who was incapable of military service—to manage the place and look after his sister. Then, for the purpose of looking after his sibling, he joined up as well.

The plan's success was short-lived. A few months after their company merged into an infantry regiment, an order plucked him from the unit and placed him in a special group of sharpshooters, men singled out by their superiors for exceptional marksmanship. His attempts to decline were of no avail, and a few weeks later, with no warning at all, the brigade his brother was still a part of packed up and marched away. They were never to meet again.

The following May, while stationed in Chattanooga, he learned his brother was dead. After being seriously wounded at the Battle of Shiloh, his brother had succumbed to typhoid fever at Corinth, Mississippi. Assigned to the newly christened Confederate Army of Tennessee, he assuaged his thirst for vengeance by killing as many Yankees as possible: artillerymen, skirmishers, forward observers, officers, and enemy snipers. He especially wanted to kill them, as they were the ones most likely to kill him.

Fueled by hatred, his kills were personal, but the manner of them, frequently conducted at distances of over three hundred yards, was not. For a long time, he recorded them in a tiny tally book, the number of them rising into the dozens, then over a hundred. In the fall of 1863, during the siege of Chattanooga, after felling a blue-coated officer who was studying the Confederate lines through field glasses, he didn't retrieve his ledger after returning to camp. The rage was spent.

While the killing was now mundane, the method was becoming more lethal. He now carried an English Whitworth, a .45-caliber rifle with a hexagonal barrel that was accurate at tremendous distances. It had a sliding blade sight with an adjustment for windage and could be graduated up to twelve hundred yards. Despite its heavy recoil, he fell in love with the weapon.

He was now known to the enemy. "The Gray Reaper," they called him. One tale said that General Sherman had put a $500 bounty on his head. The bluecoats began using their own snipers to eliminate him, often employing two-man teams. One of them employed a spyglass, the other a rifle. To counter that, he began eliminating the spotter, then moving before his partner could find him again.

The experience brought him infinite patience and attention to detail. He selected his nests with care, disguised them with camouflage, and decorated his clothing and hat with sprigs of foliage. He learned to remain motionless for hours, waiting for his target to appear, watching for hiding places of opposing snipers, letting them be the first to break cover, and shooting them down before they could see him. As the Whitworth left a powder flare, his first rule was to determine a route by which he could escape. Those were the meticulous habits that kept him alive.

As indifferent as he'd become to killing, it was an incident during the Atlanta campaign that determined the direction of his post-war life. One day, a member of the regiment he was supporting fell wounded between the lines, the bullet smashing his pelvis and lodging in his bowels. Some of his comrades attempted to retrieve him, only to be driven back by deadly fire from the Union lines. Screaming in agony, he yelled for them to shoot him and put him out of his misery. The company commander called for him and asked him to do so.

At first, he'd declined. To kill enemy soldiers from far away was one thing, but it was quite another to take the life of a wounded comrade who was nearby. The request became a direct order, and with feelings of revulsion, he'd done as he was bade. It hadn't helped when members of the man's mess thanked him. The act made him feel dirty, like someone selected to execute a deserter.

Afterward, down to the very moment, he came to realize he no longer possessed empathy—none for himself or anyone else. Regardless of the misfortune witnessed, and he'd seen plenty, it wasn't meaningful to him. There'd always been trouble in the world, and there always would be; everybody was going to experience some. How they dealt with it was up to them.

With the end of the war, he returned home to find much of the farm in need of repair, yet not as despoiled as he'd feared. His sister, now nineteen, was eager to marry her beau, a former Confederate cavalryman, and head to his Alabama home. Since she'd gone, there had been solitude: no wife, no children, no demands, no noise—just peace, until Ted Harper came along.

For a considerable time, Harper's return to the county was of no concern. His father owned the family farm, and although he was a tiresome old fart, he caused no problems. On his occasional forays into town, he heard people nattering about the outrages and excesses of the son, how he swindled the unwary and worse. It meant nothing to him until he began having problems with the man himself.

On Harper's first visit, he bluntly asked what it would cost to buy the farm, a question which was answered with equal bluntness; the property wasn't for sale, nor would it ever be. A month later, he was back. He'd told Harper his answer hadn't changed and ordered him not to return. Not to be deterred, Ted showed up a third time. This visit stirred emotions he hadn't felt since 1865.

"Harper," he'd said, his voice deadly calm, "the last time someone came here uninvited, pestering me to sell this property, was twenty-five years ago. He left most of his left ear on the ground about fifty feet behind where you're standing now. I'm giving you fair warning that if I see you on my land again, that's what will happen to you, at the very least."

Harper had taken his promise to heart and stayed away, yet he was aware that Ted was putting the arm on his good neighbor, Perry Jessup. If Harper wrested away those acres, he might try to limit the access he had across Jessup's land to the main road. That would make for a long, unnecessary detour when he was bringing in stock or moving it out to market.

Fred Reichert's shooting, followed by Harper's escape from any punishment via the legal system, sealed the matter for him; something had to be done. If it wasn't, he figured that someday soon, while doing one of his endless chores, he'd get a bullet in the back. He didn't intend for that to happen.

One day in town, while he was in the rear of a store, he overheard the now recovered Reichert talking with a dry goods merchant about getting rid of Ted Harper. After ascertaining he was the only other person in the place, he approached them, asking if they were serious. At first, it appalled them that their conversation wasn't private, but once they realized he was determined, they welcomed him with open arms. Neither of them had had any experience in killing. He, however, had all that the human mind could contemplate.

Over the succeeding weeks, the two of them recruited several members, although he'd hoped for more volunteers. During that time, he learned of Harper's extortionate activities and came to loathe the man. It was significant that these were his first emotional feelings in years. When the group was complete, he started planning Harper's demise with the same infinite care he'd employed to eliminate Yankee soldiers.

He started by spending many hours walking through town in search of locations to carry out an ambush. There had to be cover, a place Harper wouldn't suspect trouble, an avenue for escape if things turned wrong, and a route where few would notice the shooters leaving should they succeed. It wasn't likely that anyone would inform on them, yet it was best not to take chances.

The next thing required was to entice Ted to a meeting. All things coalesced when two shop owners on the south square consented to be the cheese in the trap. They would independently contact Harper, beg the need to be at their businesses all day on a particular Saturday, and ask if he would meet them in the alley beside Guthrie's saloon to receive his next pound of flesh. To bolster their confidence, he told them he would be the third gunman.

It had come off without a hitch. Harper died in a hail of bullets, without injury to any of the conspirators. All of them slipped away unnoticed. The county sheriff, an inexperienced man, wasn't able to find anyone who admitted seeing or knowing anything about the matter, and at last, the lawman returned to Shelbyville in defeat. Many of the group, feeling the danger was past, breathed a sigh of relief. He, however, along with a few others, remained alert.

Stuart Redmond had come up with the plan to get news from the hotel about any suspicious strangers in town. He'd agreed to it with reluctance but did so despite his lack of trust in McCormick. The desk clerk never stopped to think, and in his wartime experience, men like him ended up dead.

When news came to the saloon, Redmond soon reported it to him. Occasionally, a meeting would follow, although he discouraged them because they were dangerous to their security. Also, they disturbed his tranquility.

The meeting at Reichert's barn on the evening the marshals came to town would, if he had anything to do with it, be the last. The less the conspirators were together, especially in such clandestine circumstances, the better. Nothing was required other than sticking to their stories and remaining calm. Reckless talk of killing the marshals, as some of them were contemplating, was the height of foolishness. That would bring more marshals, maybe Pinkerton agents, and they wouldn't hesitate to twist arms, perhaps break one or two if need be. Once they had suspects, someone would die—by a bullet or a noose but die they would. Vengeance, he knew, would demand multiple sacrifices.

He sighed and tapped out the ash from his pipe. It was getting late. Earlier that day, using a spyglass, he'd watched the activities under the tent at Harper's farm. They had to be searching for the bullets in Ted's body, he reasoned, since nothing else would be of value. Given the pace of their investigation, they would be around to see him soon. He had a plan for that unless they tried to murder him. If they did so, all bets were off, but he doubted that was their intent. Del Orange headed inside and went to bed.

Chapter 45

THE NEXT MORNING, Wilkinson was up before dawn. Simon Garrett, Sheriff Parslow's deputy, was due to return to Shelbyville, and it was imperative that he talk to him. Washed and dressed, he left Tom undisturbed, went downstairs, and then proceeded to the temporary room where the sheriff was still convalescing. The young lawman was awake, the aggravation of his wound overcoming his desire for sleep, and he nodded that Ward should enter. For a few minutes, the two men talked in hushed tones, but they halted when they heard footfalls and a jingle of spurs in the hallway. Garrett thrust his head into the room where Ward, his finger to his lips, motioned him inside.

Garrett gave Wilkinson an inquiring look, which drew an encouraging grin from the marshal. "Was McCormick out there?" Ward asked.

The deputy shook his head. "The night clerk's still here. He's half asleep."

"Good. Listen carefully. Marshal Seibert and I are going to need help when we serve these search warrants. I'm sending a request for help. If it's granted, there will be several lawmen, federal marshals, that will arrive in Shelbyville in a few days. They're to contact you. When that happens, send me a wire saying, 'I have a package for you.'"

"What then?"

"When I'm ready, I'll send you a return message: 'Deliver it.' The following morning, after you hear from me, we'll meet them at that turnaround just outside town on the way to Shelbyville. Do you know the one I'm talking about?"

"Yes. Two miles from here."

"That's the one. Have a pleasant journey, deputy. Looks like we're going to have rain." He shook the young man's hand and went back to his room.

* * *

An hour later, with Seibert and Obadiah Howell in tow, Wilkinson returned to the first floor for breakfast. McCormick, a morose scowl plastered on his phiz, was now behind the desk. Seeing his sour expression, the doctor added to his discomfiture. "Well, good morning, sir," he said in the most expansive, jovial manner. "It's a great day to be alive, isn't it? I'm returning to Nashville today and wanted to let you know my tab goes on the account of my colleague, Marshal Wilkinson. He's the one with the State of Tennessee expense account. That's a great thing to have, don't you agree?"

"Is that right, Marshal?" McCormick rasped, his voice sounding as if he needed a dose of magnesia.

"Of course it is, Mr. McCormick," Ward affirmed. "Doctor Howell is here at the behest of the attorney general, as are we all. His stay will be a part of my bill."

The desk clerk, his expression reflecting that someone was operating on his hemorrhoids with a dull scalpel, was still swearing under his breath when Ward, Tom, and Obadiah entered the dining room. The waiters once again stifled their amusement as best they could. After the meal of eggs, bacon, creamy grits, flaky biscuits with honey in the comb, and a pot of coffee, they strolled down to the passenger depot. While Ward and Tom waited on the platform, Obadiah checked to make certain that his trunk was ready to put aboard, then came out and announced the train was on time. The friends had an amiable chat for thirty minutes until a locomotive, its stack billowing smoke, chugged into the station in a welter of hissing steam and squealing wheels.

The men rose to their feet, walked down to Obadiah's car, and bade him goodbye. "Ward, Tom," he said, his voice carrying to anyone within thirty feet, "I'll see you in a few days. I'll let your wives know that you're staying out of trouble most of the time."

This drew a jolly, good-natured snort, which was followed by the bellow of "All Aboard!" from the conductor. The doctor went up the steps, and a moment later, the train pulled away.

When the caboose passed by the lawmen, Wilkinson turned to Seibert, all the lightheartedness gone from his voice. "The stores are open," he said, his voice evidencing a hard edge, "let's go talk to Harry Henderson."

The marshals exited the platform, stepped across the tracks, came out around the corner of the freight depot, and headed to the small store at the far end of the shops that framed the south side of railroad square. Early shoppers, concerned about being seen as an informer or fearful that more gunfire might break out near them, gave them a wide berth. "We're as popular this morning as a long piss in a circular wind," Tom remarked in a chipper spirit.

The sally brought a smile from Wilkinson, yet there was no warmth in it. "The pressure on those that murdered Harper is ratcheting up every minute. We've been here almost a week. There isn't anyone in town between the age of six and senility that doesn't know why we're here. Even with the smoke screen we've laid down, I'm sure the guilty, at least some of them, think our foot will soon be on their neck. From now on, because of the possibility some of them might decide we need gotten rid of, we'll have to be more careful."

Ward stopped for a moment, took out a small book from his vest pocket, and studied the list of coded names found in Harper's records. One of them was 83ST5$. "Store, five dollars a month," he muttered. "Harry was eating sixty dollars a year to advance Ted's bottom line, with no end in sight; no wonder he shot the sonofabitch."

"If he didn't," Tom replied, "it was that other one, down the street, Jerry Wilson."

Harry Henderson was putting up a display of fresh produce when the marshals entered his store: onions, carrots, and other tuberous root vegetables. Thinking it was a customer, he turned with a broad, welcoming smile, then shrank back as if the lawmen were among the horsemen of the apocalypse. The color drained from his face. His mouth contorted into a gaping oval, yet try as he might, he could not speak.

"You know why we've come, sir," Wilkinson said to the frightened man. "We're here to hear you tell us about your one-sided business arrangement with Ted Harper."

Henderson's head swiveled around, looking for an avenue of escape, but there was none. The marshal's deputy, wearing a tied-down gun, was standing in the doorway, his thumbs casually thrust into his pockets. He seemed at ease, but his eyes missed nothing. His colleague, the man who'd spoken, retrieved a stool from beneath the counter and motioned for Henderson to sit. Unnerved, he did the only thing he could: obey.

The grocer sat yet did not speak. "It's no use denying or pretending you don't know what we're talking about, Mr. Henderson," Ward informed him. "We found evidence in Harper's own records that you were paying him five dollars every month. It wasn't a unique circumstance, either. He was stealing from at least a dozen others around here. Was that why you entered into a conspiracy against him, then put a bullet in him?"

The accusation of murder seemed to course terror through the grocer. If the marshal knew about all of Harper's victims and about his role in the plot to eliminate the man, how much more did he know? Still, he had no intention of confessing. "You got no proof I shot Harper or anyone else," he grated, his voice clotted with emotion. "I've never owned a gun in my life."

"Not having owned a gun doesn't mean you've never used one. You ought to ponder your situation, Henderson. In our experience in these matters, someone will lose their bravado and talk to keep from hanging; might as well be you."

"*Hanging?!*" The word leached from the man's lips in a horrified yelp, almost as if he could feel the hemp stretched across his throat. Again, his features paled, and again, he lapsed into silence.

"Harper died by violence, didn't he?" Wilkinson responded, his expression without guile. "I'm surprised that you're surprised that execution might be the penalty for the guilty. Me and my deputy are certain you're one of them."

Henderson's mind was working in furious desperation. Had the marshals figured out McCormick's role in surveilling strangers and coerced the truth from him? Was that why he'd failed to get his lazy ass down to Guthrie's and warn him? Were they running a bluff and hoping he'd panic? Remembering the advice of Mr. Orange, he steeled himself and shook his head. "I don't know a damn thing about what you're accusing me of doing. Unless it's your intention to arrest me, I'm going to have to ask you to get out of my place and let me get back to work."

"Where were you at the time of the shooting, Mr. Henderson?" Tom demanded, ignoring the man's dismissal. "Right here," he replied, "where I always am on workdays. You don't make any money being closed."

"Did you know Harper?"

"I knew him to be a sonofabitch, if that's what you're asking. Webster's dictionary, providing it defines such a word, will have his picture right beside it."

The marshals had obtained all it was possible to get. Wilkinson rose to his feet. "Don't think for a moment, Mr. Henderson, that we're buying the tales you've told. We're certain you're one of the shooters of Ted Harper. Also, we're aware of your sudden desire to spend time in the saloon. Ironically, some other owners along the row here have likewise discovered that craving. When we get enough proof, which we will, we'll return for the arrest you mentioned."

Back on the boardwalk, Seibert swore in annoyance. "Damnation! We learned nothing tangible from that interview. We know he's lying, that he's guilty, but none of that is presentable to a jury. The defense would tear us to shreds."

"I'm not sure I agree, Tom," Ward said with a small smile. "I'll tell you why when we get back to the hotel, which ought to be now; there's the smell of rain in the air."

They stepped under the eaves of the veranda right when the skies opened. Sheets of rain lashed the windows, and there was a momentary patter of pea-sized hail on the roof. Prior to going in, Ward bent forward and whispered in Tom's ear. "The one truth I believe Henderson told is that he's never owned a gun. I also believe our mastermind provided them, and Miss Sillinger is maintaining them. Things are coming into focus, although not fully as yet."

Retrieving their slickers, the marshals lingered in the lobby, coaxed a cup of coffee from the restaurant, then headed out when the storm slackened. The streets, now empty, were slippery with mud.

* * *

The next stop was the grocery and dry goods store of Ronald and Edna Whipple. Neither of the lawmen had met the couple. The only information they possessed was the scurrilous, unfounded gossip that the lady of the house lorded over her husband. Even if that was true, Ward considered, that didn't make either of them murderers. It was significant that Ted Harper's code book didn't include them.

Mrs. Whipple was at the counter when they entered. Seeing them, she willed herself to remain impassive, displaying no trepidation at their presence. "What can I do for you, gentlemen?" she said tonelessly.

The stars on their coats were visible, and her neutral greeting did not fool Wilkinson. "We want to talk to you and your husband about the killing of Ted Harper," he said. "Is he here this morning?"

Edna, her hair drawn back in a severe bun, was wearing a plain cotton dress of a light blue color. Without preamble, she turned her head to the back room and called in a commanding voice, "Ronald, those US Marshals from Nashville are here to talk to us about Ted Harper. Come out here and meet them."

Ronald Whipple was a tall, slender man with severe male pattern baldness. Most of his remaining hair was a pair of bushy eyebrows and a thick mustache. He had a long, horsey face, a protruding nose, and watery brown eyes that blinked at them through a pair of gold-framed spectacles. Unlike his wife, who appeared unaffected, he displayed some anxiety, rubbing invisible streaks from the lenses of his glasses. It took both marshals aback when he opened his mouth. His was the remaining unidentified voice from the meeting in Reichert's livery stable.

Wilkinson started to ask him what he was doing meeting with several other men to discuss the marshals' arrival in town and how to impede their investigation, then restrained himself. This was still a secret, one of his and Tom's hole cards. Rather than reveal what they knew, he determined it was better to see if the man would lie. "Did either of you know the Harpers?"

"His wife came by once in a while," Ronald answered. "Given Ted's reputation, we were glad he let her do their shopping."

"Did you know he was stealing from merchants in town? We have documentation that shows he was extorting money from at least a dozen."

"That's terrible," Edna Whipple interjected. "We heard rumors about that man, but I believed most of them to be exaggerated. How was he doing it?"

"Threats, intimidation. In at least one instance, he learned a man's secret and used it against him. Those are the kind of acts that got him killed. Did he try to get money out of you?"

"He most certainly did not!" Edna asserted. "I'd have run his no-good hide out of here on the prongs of a pitchfork."

Seibert, who kept his gaze focused on the street, exhibited the slightest smile at the statement. "Were you aware there was a plot hatched to kill Harper prior to him being shot?"

Edna shook her head, then cast a brief, inquiring look at her husband. That act showed she wasn't sure what her husband knew or that they'd never discussed the matter between them. When he likewise answered no, he revealed to the marshals he was telling a falsehood. That prompted the next question, which asked if they knew who'd shot Harper. That also drew a negative reply.

"Were you here when the shooting occurred?" Ward resumed.

"Yes, Marshal," Edna confirmed. "We were doing inventory when the shooting began. Business was slow that day." Pointing to the back room, she continued, "We hunkered down back there until we were sure it was over. By the time we came out front, people were heading down the boardwalk to see what happened. We figured there were enough folks to handle whatever had gone on and went back to the job."

Ward and Tom exited, then headed to Wilson's store. When they were out of sight, Edna Whipple looked at her husband and frowned. She hadn't lied about them being in the store; Ronald had called to her precisely at noon. What she hadn't told the marshals about was seeing Harry Henderson going down the boardwalk a minute or two earlier.

Chapter 46

THE RAIN, HAVING resumed while the marshals were in Whipple's, was continuing unabated. Water streamed off the awnings before splashing in gathering puddles along the boardwalk. There was a dank smell in the air, and the dark clouds gave a dismal aspect to the day. As they stood on the planks, a dray wagon trundled by, the large draft animals splattering the gluey mud of the street around the lawmen's feet with their ponderous hooves. The driver added to the filth by spitting a long stream of tobacco juice in the same direction.

"Fuck you, too, mister," Tom called, modulating his voice so that only the man on the wagon seat could hear. The driver rewarded him with a sudden stiffening of his shoulders and a flick of the reins that urged his team to greater speed. "I'm telling you, Ward," Tom said, slipping the leather thong off the trigger of his pistol, "these people have had about a bellyful of us. We need to be on our guard in case a few of them decide to throw something other than a cud of tobacco." Wilkinson took a long look about the square and nodded in bleak agreement.

Wilson's store was like the Whipples', so much so that it bemused both men. There were the same barrels and the same shelves, all containing the same products. "How many in this town, Ward, six?" Tom muttered softly.

"At least," the unseen owner answered. He appeared from the back, momentarily dumbfounding both men. Jerry Wilson, they were to agree, was one of a kind.

The man was diminutive at five feet tall with a slight frame. Despite appearing wiry and strong, he weighed little more than a hundred pounds. His smallish head, covered with a mop of dark hair, overlooked a thin face, smooth cheeks, and an upper lip that sported whiskers so sparse they appeared to be more likely found on a cat or even a rat. His dark, beady eyes darted back and forth from one lawman to the other, yet there wasn't a trace of anxiousness. Unmistakably, though, Wilkinson thought, was that he was the type of person Harper had exploited.

"What can I do for you?" Wilson asked, his orbs never resting.

"We'd like to know your relationship with Ted Harper," Ward responded. "During our investigation, Marshal Seibert and I found evidence that he was extorting money from you, among others."

The man shrugged, yet unlike most of the others they'd confronted, he neither looked away nor dropped his gaze. "Yes, he was stealing from me. I didn't think it was that well kept a secret."

"Were you aware there was a plot to kill him?"

"Oh, yes, but don't expect me to reveal anything. It was like a holiday when he got shot. I once contemplated ending his existence myself, then decided it was too dangerous to attempt. I always figured if I was patient, someone would do the job for me. As my pappy once said, 'he tried to take in too much territory.' Hope you won't think badly of me if I exult over his downfall."

Seibert, who was keeping an eye on the street, could not stifle a grin. "Ah, Marshal," the eccentric merchant observed with a chortle, "I can see you're no fan of Mr. Harper or at least understand why I celebrated his death with great satisfaction. He was lower than the scum on a whorehouse pisspot, especially in view of the way he ill-used and abused certain women in this town."

"So we're reliably informed," Wilkinson commented. "Are you telling us you know who killed him?"

"I wasn't there to see it if that's what you're asking," Wilson replied with a smile that generated fury or endearment, depending on one's point of view. "While I have a pretty good idea, the fact is, I wasn't in town. Figured it might be a slow day business-wise and traveled to Shelbyville to meet with a supplier."

Ward realized that no useful information was going to be extracted from this man. He was clever, and there was little more that he could think of to ask him. All his questions produced answers that didn't advance the inquiry. As it ever had been, there wasn't enough documentary evidence. Unable to think of anything more original, he asked, "Why did you pay him?"

"Similar reasons to why the others did, I'd imagine. Harper was intimidating, and he was good at infecting his victims' imaginations with what would happen if they failed to meet his demands. No one wants to be beaten or, worse, have their business destroyed. The sheriff, being hours away and afraid of Ted as well, would not be of any help, and people here figured the new man wouldn't be any different. That may have been a false belief. Down here, we became hopeless and isolated, with no way out that we could see. You will get no one to tattle on those who found one."

Wilkinson started to speak, but Wilson, his wispy mustache hairs twitching, had more to say. "The funny part about how Harper met his end is that they used his own tactics against him. For myself and many others, he set upon us when we were closing, when no one was around to hear or help. That he never saw it coming until it was too late is the height of hilarity," he concluded with a vengeful laugh.

"I can see how you might feel that way. It's been an interesting conversation, Mr. Wilson, thank you. During our discussion, you've confirmed much of what we know and may have unintentionally given us an additional lead. Let's go, Tom."

The marshals stepped outside, passed the unappetizing aromas of Stafford's restaurant, and then headed straight for Guthrie's. "What lead did we get back there?" Tom asked.

"None," Ward replied with a chuckle. "I just wanted to wind up Mr. Wilson a tad. He's the most peculiar man we've met since we got here."

They shared a moment of quiet laughter, then came to the saloon just as "Lige" Guthrie was opening the tall doors behind the batwings. "Well, gentlemen," he boomed in greeting, "my first customers of the day. What can I get you?"

"Two glasses of lager," Ward said in a friendly tone. He rather liked the saloonkeeper. "Would you have anything to eat?"

"I could rustle up some bread and cheese, maybe an apple if you'd like."

"That sounds fine. Sometimes, the noon meal takes a little longer than we'd like, and there's much to do."

Ward and Tom took chairs at the rear table, being careful to keep their backs against the wall and their faces to the door. Two minutes later, Guthrie returned with a plate of food, then walked to the bar and pulled their beers. Bringing them over, he pulled up his own chair and sat with them. "Everything's shipshape for the moment," he related. "Got to take moments of leisure when you can."

The beer was good, the bread chewy and delicious, and the cheese creamy. Guthrie informed them it was goat cheese, supplied by a local farmer. Both men, despite their surprise, gave it fulsome praise. "Does Jerry Wilson ever come in here?" Wilkinson asked between swallows of beer.

"Sometimes. Nothing regular, though. He's an odd duck. Brandy drinker when he comes around. I have little call for that, except for an occasional traveler and him. Always keep a couple of bottles on hand."

"Ever have anyone join him?"

"Not that I recall. Wait a minute, one time, Del Orange was in here to buy a bottle. He doesn't spend time in here given his dislike for people. He went over and spoke to Jerry for a minute or two. I could hardly believe it."

"When was that?"

"During the winter. It was still cold weather, but I don't remember when."

"That's very interesting," Wilkinson said with an approving nod. "I believe we'll have another of your lagers, and I'll buy you one if you've got time to sit a little longer."

* * *

At one o'clock, Wilkinson paid their tab, and he and Tom returned to the boardwalk. The rain was past, with brief breaks in the clouds giving a glimpse of blue sky. To their right was a vacant lot, an abandoned building, a narrow strip of open space, a bedspring factory, and the confectioner's shop of Stuart Redmond, with the last structure distant from the others: John Ferguson's print shop. "About thirty to forty yards of nothing," Ward mused. "If we're correct, and two shooters came from the opposite ends of the boardwalk, the one from down here came a damn long way with no one seeing him. We may have to ask up at the mills if anyone saw someone going that way at noon."

Tom looked up at the sprawling Baldwin & Simon's Mills—a combination sawmill, forge, and corn grinding operation—with a scowl. "We discussed this earlier. My view is it would be a total waste of time. If Ted had tried anything there, he'd have ended up on the sharp end of one of their saws. As a business, they have good reasons to know nothing, and no employee is going to volunteer anything that would cause him to end up on the witness stand."

"Probably so," Ward agreed, "but if need be, we'll try. Let's go on down to this bedspring place."

"We going to visit Redmond?"

"No. He's a waste of time, given how he acted when we caught him trying to escape from Guthrie's. We'll save him for the search warrant."

The factory, which constructed metal bedsprings for beds, a recent improvement from wool strips or ropes to support mattresses, was a hive of activity. Ward and Charlotte had them for their bed, which provided superior comfort but emitted annoying squeaks. Not willing to halt work for even a second, the manager, Douglas Miller, came to the front of the building and irascibly demanded to know what they wanted.

"You know exactly why we're here, sir," Ward replied in an equally irritable tone. "It's what we've been asking everyone. I'll give you three guesses, and the first two don't count."

The flippant reply seemed to aggravate Miller even more. "Yes, yes, Ted Harper. Who gives a shit about what happened to him? Not me, I can tell you, and not any of my employees."

"Were you open the day he was shot?"

"Hell, yes, we were open! We work twelve hours, six days a week. I don't tolerate shirkers, malingerers, or the lackadaisical. Nobody was lollygagging out front when he was shot. If they had been, they wouldn't be here today. No one left to see what happened after the shots rang out, either.

"I'll tell you another thing," Miller said vituperatively, "just so you won't have any more half-assed, time-wasting questions for me. I don't know who killed him, and I don't give a damn. The only thing better than him dying would have been if he'd died a lot harder. He was a worthless sack of shit who was too lazy to work at a proper occupation and made a living leaching off others. Now, if there's nothing more, there are more sets to get done before the end of the day, and I don't pay overtime."

"What do we do about him?" Tom asked upon leaving.

"Nothing," Ward replied. "At the rate he's going, he'll drop dead by the time he's forty-five. Either he's so driven he can't relax, or he's got a boss somewhere that's pressing him for more production. If he's doing this to support a wife and children, I feel rather sorry for the poor bastard."

* * *

The last shop on the row was the print shop run by a Scotsman, John Ferguson. The round-faced man, his features wreathed by a thick, dark beard, was genial enough but provided nothing that aided their inquiry. "I knew Ted Harper, at least by reputation," he admitted, "but never had reason to do any business with him. He was an ass, if rumors are true, and it wasn't any surprise when he got himself killed. I was here when the shooting broke out, was running a rush job. Had no interest in going up there to see what happened."

"Did he ever try to extort money from you?" Wilkinson asked.

"No," Ferguson replied with a harsh laugh. "Might be that he was afraid of what I'd do."

"Such as?"

"Print up a sheet of his threats and demands, nail them up all over town. He wouldn't have liked that. He wanted to operate in the shadows as much as possible."

"Did you see anyone out and about that day?"

"The customer I was doing the rush job for was here. Saw little of anyone else. Come to think of it, I stepped out for a cigarette—can't remember when—and saw Stuart Redmond pass by. He's the confectioner up the way."

"Do you have a feeling for when you saw him?"

"Eleven-thirty, maybe. I don't know where he'd been. Figured he was going back to his shop. He didn't speak or even wave as he passed by."

"Coming from the south?"

"He was, yes."

Ward and Tom thanked him and stepped back out into the street. "He was the last one," Tom stated, "and he gave us a very interesting piece of information."

"Definitely. Redmond was out to pick up the pistol he used on Harper. That suggests that Faye Sillinger may have been out that morning to deliver the weapons at predetermined spots, or it might have been the leader who did that. We still don't know. Let's go back to the room and get our interview notes in order. Once that's done, we'll go to dinner."

It took some time to catch up. Dr. Howell's being with them the previous day had left little time available for routine tasks. The list of Ted Harper's victims and their code numbers occupied an entire page of Wilkinson's summary. The amount of damage he'd done to the local economy was significant.

83MI3$ - Faye Sillinger, Seamstress
83BA3$ - James Finchum, Barber
83TA3$ - Peter Taylor, Tailor
83DR4$ - Lou Johnson, Dry Goods Merchant
83CO3$ - Stuart Redmond, Confectioner
83MY3$ - Jeanne Clarke, Milliner
83CB3$ - Will Sharp, Cobbler
83DB5$ - Kenneth Paul, Dry Goods Merchant
83GR5$ - Harry Henderson, Grocer
83DG4$ - Jerry Wilson, Dry Goods Merchant
83HW9$ - Larry Everhart, Hardware Merchant
83BS4$ - Fred Reichert, Blacksmith/Livery Owner

"There's no code number for Frank Bunting," Ward remarked to Tom. "He was forking over at least $50 a year to keep Denise Harper in nice clothes. Out of this group will be most of the search warrants. They were paying Ted and had prime motives for murder."

"What about Jessup and Orange?"

"Jessup, no. I don't believe he was involved any more than a lot of folks. He just didn't tell all he knew. Orange, though, we'll search his place, but that won't be until the very end. Is there anything interesting in your notes?"

"One thing. You remember Obadiah saying the bullet that tore Harper's nuts off wasn't in his body? His view was that the gun used was a derringer. That bullet is likely in the alley next to the saloon. Do you want to go see if we can find it?"

"It would be worth a try. Let's go to Everhart's and get ourselves a shovel. By then, the dining room will be ready to open. Once we've eaten, provided the ground has dried a little, we'll go down and see if we can turn up anything."

Only a few minutes were required to get the shovel. Wilkinson wanted to tell the store owner he'd be wise to make an honest woman out of Jeanne Clarke as quickly as he could but kept his own counsel. To reveal what he knew would jeopardize their plans. "We won't have need of this for more than an hour, sir," he said to Everhart. "Think of it as a loan. When we return it, I'll give you consideration for the time."

The five o'clock hour arrived when Ward and Tom entered the hotel lobby, and McCormick was more than intrigued when he saw the digging implement in Seibert's hands. Tom stowed it in the room while Ward, keeping the nosy desk clerk pinned in place, remained in the lobby. When he returned, they entered the dining room, both men hungry for the pot roast that was featured on the menu. After fifteen minutes for the meal to set a little, Tom retrieved the shovel, and they walked down to the saloon.

Chapter 47

AT THE SAME HOUR, a weary Obadiah Howell trudged up Spring Street in Nashville to his brick and timber home. There, he sank into the loving embrace of his wife, Helen. He'd found the train trip tedious, with nothing to see from the windows but leaden skies, sodden fields, ditches filled with muddy water, and cattle huddling under trees to escape the frequent downpours. He was glad to be back.

When the doctor's train had arrived, the storm was slackening. He hired a dray driver to deliver his trunk to the house and gave the man an extra fifty cents to take it inside and inform Helen that he had an urgent errand to perform. From there, he'd headed to the courthouse.

District Court Clerk Harvey Bryant was busy drafting orders when Howell stepped into his small office. Recognizing the Davidson County Coroner from his infrequent visits, the young man stood and spoke a cheerful welcome. "Good afternoon, Doctor, what brings you by today?"

"I've just returned from Buckland Station, where I assisted Marshal Wilkinson on the Harper murder. I have a letter from him he wanted me to deliver to the Judge as soon as I arrived."

Bryant excused himself for a moment, then returned to inform Obadiah that the magistrate would see him now. Withdrawing the envelope from his coat, Obadiah stepped through the nearby door and into the judge's chambers. The white-haired jurist was sitting in an armchair and waved him to the seat across from him. "Well, Dr. Howell, do you know the contents of this message?" he inquired.

"I haven't read it, Your Honor. But I have a good idea what's in it. Ward and Tom have run into heavy resistance down there in Buckland Station. I believe they will soon make arrests if there is no interference.

They're concerned about that, sir."

Morton opened the envelope, withdrew the letter, adjusted his spectacles, and began to read.

May 21, 1883

Judge Morton,

Despite resistance, much of it organized, Marshal Seibert and I are close to completing our investigation and making arrests. To serve our upcoming warrants, guard prisoners, and help secure our personal safety, I am requesting at least three additional officers; four would be better. We will need them in Buckland Station by Friday, the 25th, at the latest.

If available, request the officers meet in Shelbyville. I have made arrangements with Bedford County Deputy Sheriff Simon Garrett to coordinate their arrival in Buckland Station. There may be combinations too large to be overcome by Marshal Seibert and me alone.

Ward Wilkinson
United States Marshal

The implications of the last sentence saw the judge bolt to his feet, and his voice boomed down the corridor. "Mr. Bryant, come in here at once," he bellowed, "I have some wires for you to send." Sitting at his desk, he scribbled furiously on a sheet of paper: *Marshal Wilkinson needs help in Buckland Station, TN. You and your deputy go to Shelbyville on receipt. Deputy Sheriff Garrett will coordinate the next move.* "Put my name on this," he instructed the clerk, "and send it to these two men. Let me know at once if there are any return messages."

Bryant turned on his heel, and they could hear his rapid footfalls as he headed out to send the judicial orders to the US Marshals in Chattanooga, Tennessee and Huntsville, Alabama. Obadiah, his task performed, rose to leave. "Thank you, Doctor," Morton said, "for your alacrity in bringing this to my attention. I know, given that you are friends and did service together during the war, that you would have done so regardless. Nevertheless, I am extremely grateful."

"Whatever I've done, Your Honor," Obadiah said with feeling, "is minor compared to what *they're* doing. That place is a hornet's nest right now."

Chapter 48

THE SKY WAS reddening to the west as Wilkinson and Seibert began their search for the missing bullet. They asked Guthrie to come out for a moment and show them where Harper had fallen, which he did as well as he could remember. "The center of his body was about five feet back from the corner here, but it's possible," he reminded the marshals, "that it might have been in a different location by the time I saw it. Many people came by here, someone turned his pockets inside out, and blood was in the dirt in places apart from his corpse. This entire area was trampled upon, and some of his blood was smeared."

"Understood," Ward assured him. "We may be on a fool's errand. Still, we're going to try it."

Tom used the point of the shovel to trace a four-by-four-foot square, then began digging out square foot segments at a depth of three to four inches. Ward, wearing a pair of old gloves, crumbled the sod with his hands, searching for the small piece of lead. After a couple of rows, the marshals changed roles. The sun slipped below the horizon, and the hunt continued.

Now, they were searching in the pale light of a single gas lamp that stood next to Leroy Stafford's restaurant. The illumination wrought ghostly shadows on the ground—not ideal, yet enough to continue. The marshals extended the area by four feet, two in front and rear of the original square, but the slug continued to elude them. "I doubt he was up against the wall," Ward theorized as he wiped sweat from his brow. "He'd have had no room to maneuver at all. We'll go out two feet on the restaurant side of our box. If it doesn't show up, we'll call it a day."

Tom moved toward the middle of the vacant lot, traced another area, and began scraping off the upper layers of soil. On the third shovelful, as Ward disintegrated a large clod, a hard pellet remained in the palm of his hand. "Look here, Tom," he said, his voice excited. "I believe we have it."

Seibert jammed the shovel in the turned-up earth, and both men studied the small projectile as Wilkinson rubbed away its coating of mud. So focused were the lawmen on their find that they failed to detect the threat approaching from behind them until it was almost too late. A moment later, two men, each brandishing a long-bladed knife, burst from the gloom and set upon them. The marshals, startled by the sudden assault, backpedaled in hasty retreat.

Ward had just dropped the spent slug into his coat pocket when he heard the tramp of feet. Whirling about, he glimpsed the duo, clad in dark clothing, wearing masks, with hat brims pulled down to their eyebrows. He thought to reach inside his coat for his pistol but feared it would provide time for the attacker to slash his right arm to ribbons. At the moment, he sorely missed having his old cavalry saber in hand.

The only illumination, save for the gaslight, came from the distant lamps of private houses. As Wilkinson withdrew toward the nexus of the street, he could see the knife was a straight blade, similar to what one would find in a kitchen. The only thing that heartened him was a growing realization that his opponent was amateurish in using it as a weapon.

The man continued to advance into the light, and for a moment, Wilkinson thought he looked familiar. He continued to paw with the blade instead of thrusting. All Ward could do was remain alert for an abrupt change of tactics or for the man to make a mistake.

The decisive moment came when Wilkinson's attacker became fully illuminated, coming parallel with the corner of the saloon. Whether he'd planned his attack this way or just became impatient for it to be over, Wilkinson would never know. The masked man altered his grip, brought the knife to shoulder height, and took a long stride forward. Then, uttering a guttural cry, he slashed downward with all his might.

Ward saw the steel glimmer in the glare of light and jumped backward. He felt the whisper of the blade as it sliced through the heavy air, followed immediately by its cutting edge contacting his clothing. He was aware of a slight stinging sensation as the tip nicked his stomach, yet that was the extent of his wound. His belt absorbed most of the damage, and at last, the knife fell away from him. Its wielder, overbalanced, took a stumbling step forward, trying to bring his weapon level once more.

It was what Ward had been awaiting. He snatched the Colt from its shoulder holster, swung from the waist, and struck the man in the face as he attempted to right himself. There was a satisfying jolt that radiated up his arm, along with an audible thud as the heavy gun barrel connected with flesh and bone. The man cartwheeled backward, the knife flying from his grip. His head struck the packed earth with a jarring thump, and his body rolled over several times. When it stopped, he was lying on his stomach, motionless.

Seibert's concurrent bout with his assailant was likewise desperate, and even more so given that this man knew how to handle a knife. It was a wicked-looking hawkbill blade, its menacing tip wagging back and forth as he advanced. At first, Tom zigzagged in a diagonal toward the wall of the saloon, initially to prevent tripping over the shovel, and second, to hamper the tactics of his attacker, who was right-handed. One of his slashes scraped down the bricks, causing a winking spark to glow.

Retreating toward the front of the saloon, Tom thought of a strategy to combat his foe. It was an impulse, possibly even a rash one, but he was tired of being a mouse the cat played with. His pursuer was coming on, single-mindedly slashing at his arms and face or thrusting the point at his torso. When they reached the corner of the building, the man made another determined jab. Stepping aside it, Tom grasped the man's wrist and took his chance.

The man tried to pull away, but knowing it was death to lose his grip, Seibert hung on with all his strength. He grabbed hold of the man's sleeve, yanked his arm into the awning post, then smashed his knuckles against the wood. Still, he didn't drop the knife. Instead, he hit the marshal in the stomach with a clubbing punch, nearly doubling him up with a second blow. Tom knew he couldn't take a third.

Stepping away from the man's left hand, Seibert catapulted the right into the post a second time, then a third. There was a shriek of pain from the attacker's lips, and the blade clattered harmlessly as it landed on the boardwalk. He aimed a punch at Tom's face, but he slipped it and rammed his right elbow into the man's nose. There was a crunching noise as it broke, with crimson spurting and saturating the mask.

As the man reeled back, clawing at the bandana that was now strangling him, Seibert buried the toe of his boot in the man's stomach. Doubled over, blood pouring down his face, and wracked with violent retching, the attacker never saw the boot heel kick that slammed into his chin. Lights exploded in his head, his legs crumpled beneath him, and he fell to the ground in an unconscious heap.

Tom bent at the waist, placed his hands on his knees, and drew in a series of ragged breaths that radiated pain through his ribs. Ward was just reaching down to tear the bandana from his opponent's face. The man's identity wasn't a surprise, and Wilkinson swore in disgust. He walked over to his friend, wiped the gore from his gun barrel, and asked if he was alright.

"I'm ok," Seibert replied, his words dribbling out in irregular gasps. "I think the bastard might have cracked one of my ribs."

After some minutes, Tom, his breathing back to normal, straightened his posture. While his friend recuperated, Wilkinson, having identified his attacker as Stuart Redmond, was collecting the weapons and any other evidence he could find from the fallen men. As he returned to Seibert, Tom remarked, "What's the matter with your trousers, Ward? It looks like your pants are near to falling down."

"They are," Wilkinson admitted with chagrin. "When he tried to gut me, he sliced my belt almost all the way through. Maybe we can get Jerry Wilson to reopen long enough to buy me a new one."

Seibert went out back of the saloon, pumped a pail of water from a nearby well, then returned and dumped it on Redmond's damaged face. The man regained consciousness with a splutter but, in an instant, wished he were still insensible. His cheek, lacerated nearly to the bone, bore a cake of darkened blood, his nose lay flattened, and his eyes were mere slits from swelling that distorted his features into a grotesque mask.

The other man, as both marshals predicted, Ezra White, was now stirring on the ground, moaning in agony. Tom, realizing he was awake yet having his anger far from spent, strode over and kicked him in the posterior as hard as he could. "Get up, you sonofabitch!" he demanded.

Chapter 49

BY NOW, THERE WAS a knot of people, most of them spilling from the saloon, that were jostling each other for a look into the vacant lot. Two hotel guests were the first to notice the carnage when they dropped by Guthrie's for a drink. Wilkinson directed them to have the saloonkeeper come out, and almost instantly, he appeared, a coal oil lantern in his hand. "What in hell happened out here, Marshal?" he asked, taking in the battered visages of Redmond and White.

"Never mind that now," Ward replied. "Are there any of your current customers you can trust to get Dr. Demarest and bring him back here?"

"Marvin," Guthrie yelled over his shoulder, "go up to Doc's house and get him down here on the double. Tell him there's two people badly hurt and a couple of others that might need a bit of tending. You know you've got blood on your shirt?" he asked Ward.

"Yeah, courtesy of Stuart Redmond. If he'd got a little closer, it'd be a lot worse. Do you suppose any of these dry goods merchants are still in their stores? He cleaved my belt in two, and I'm having to hold up my pants."

"Do you know the size?"

"Forty ought to do."

"Clem," Guthrie said to his helper, "tell these people there's a free drink for everyone who has his ass back at the bar in the next two minutes, with a two-for-one discount on the next ones if they stay there and keep out of these men's way. I'm going up to Wilson's with the Marshal."

Ward told Tom where he was going and, along with Guthrie, set off at a brisk pace. Two minutes later, the saloonkeeper, seeing a lamp in the back of the store, was pounding a thunderous tattoo on the door, which brought the diminutive owner to the front at a brisk pace. "Hold your horses," he called in a cranky tone, "can't you read the sign? I'm closed!" He was uttering another sentence of complaint when he recognized Wilkinson. His features, almost contorted in fury, took on a curious expression. Opening the door, he said, "Well, hello again, Marshal, Mr. Guthrie. What brings you here at this hour?"

"I've had an unfortunate occurrence with my belt," Ward replied. "Mr. Guthrie said you'd be able to provide me a replacement."

Wilson, noticing the blood on Wilkinson's shirt, studied the marshal's face, expecting to hear more. When nothing was forthcoming, he displayed a sly smile, one that Ward had noticed during their earlier encounter. "I'd say you need a forty or forty-two," he suggested.

"Forty will be fine."

"I'll have it for you in just a minute. Whatever happened with your old one," Wilson continued as he headed to a back corner of the store, "might have been unfortunate, but it wasn't accidental. Would you like a fresh shirt to replace the one you're wearing? I don't believe your wife, or any laundress, will have success getting that blood out of it." Wilkinson allowed that he'd take that as well.

Wilson soon returned with the items, and Ward gratefully cinched up his trousers. "I don't suppose you're going to tell me how you ended up in this predicament," the shop owner remarked, his mustache twitching in amusement.

"Someone mistook me for a cinnamon loaf or a layer cake," came the answer.

The little man finished scribbling the receipt and handed it over. "Well," he said as the customers were exiting, his wry grin having returned, "I'd say the piece they wanted was likely a lot smaller than what they got."

* * *

Wilkinson and Wilson hustled along the boardwalk, toward the saloon. As they neared, they saw Dr. Demarest, his medical bag in hand, arriving from his house on the north side of the square. Seated on the boardwalk, outside the batwing doors, Redmond and White held their heads in their hands, each attempting to outdo the other in groaning. Tom had pulled a chair from inside and was sitting several feet away, his pistol at the ready. His expression, though stoic, was one of considerable discomfort.

The physician examined the swollen, bruised, and bleeding faces of Redmond and White with consternation. "Did you two do this?" he demanded from the lawmen.

"Yes, Doctor," Seibert countered, his teeth clenched. "They tried to murder us and damn near succeeded. They're lucky that's all they got. We're going to need your attention as well."

"What happened to you, sir?" Demarest asked, his tone considerably softened. "That one there," Tom replied, pointing to Ezra White, "slugged me in the side a couple of times while I was trying to get a knife off him. Feels like a mule has kicked me."

The doctor had Seibert pull up his shirt. He poked and prodded, asking questions as he did so. When he finished, he called to Guthrie, "You got any ice in there?"

"Back in the back, buried in sawdust."

"Go get me three or four pounds as quick as you can. These men are going to have swelling, but at least it won't be as bad. Now, Marshal Wilkinson, I see blood on your shirt. What's with that, sir?"

"A scratch, I think. The tip of a knife grazed my stomach."

Demarest had Ward remove his shirt, then grunted in relief at what he saw. Guthrie returned with the ice, chipped down into several small blocks, and he instructed the three battered men to hold the blocks against their bruises and contusions. "Bring me a bottle of whiskey," he ordered the saloonkeeper. "Doesn't have to be good quality, just contain alcohol. When he brings that, Marshal," he continued, turning again to Wilkinson, "we'll clean that up, and I'll do a little sewing. You were mighty lucky that wasn't any deeper."

The physician wetted a clean rag with some of the bourbon and wiped away the dried blood, embedded fibers of Wilkinson's shirt, and any other material he could find. The alcohol burned the raw wound, causing Ward to grimace in pain. Demarest then clipped away the body hair around the cut, threaded a needle, and sutured the wound closed. When finished, he advised, "You ought to give that a couple of days if you can. Stay in your room, rest, and expose that to the air as much as possible."

Guthrie replaced Redmond's and White's ice with a fresh block, and Demarest returned his attention to Seibert. "You've got bruised ribs, and pretty severe, too. I'm going to wrap them with a bandage. You ought to rest a few days," he said with a sigh, seeming to know Tom wouldn't heed his advice.

"I'll do that tomorrow, Doctor. Beyond that, I can't promise."

"As I always tell patients," Demarest replied with a knowing nod, "it's their funeral, not mine."

After some preliminary work to clean away blood and swath Redmond and White's heads with bandages, a wagon carried the men up to Demarest's surgery. "You'll have to come up with somewhere to put them in the morning," the physician told Wilkinson. "I don't have the space. It will be several days before the swelling goes down enough in Redmond's face for me to work on his facial fracture."

"What about Ezra White?"

"He's got a broken right hand, a bruised stomach, and possibly a fractured jaw. I won't know for certain until the swelling subsides. He's also got a severe bruise on his buttocks; wonder how that occurred?"

"Ever have anyone try to kill you, Doctor?" Ward replied. "Those two tried very hard to kill us. Sometimes, you can't turn off your aggression the instant the battle is over. I witnessed such an aftermath during the Franco-Prussian War, when French troops were overrun despite inflicting heavy losses on the enemy. For a couple of minutes, the Prussians mowed them down with rifle fire or bayoneted them, even though they had their hands raised. As far as I'm concerned, and will so state in my report, he received that injury from falling on the shovel we were using."

* * *

On arrival at Demarest's office, he had the men, now under arrest for the attempted murder of federal officers, placed on cots in a small room. Mrs. Demarest shuddered when she saw the extent of their injuries, then hurried away to prepare items for her husband's use. The doctor and Wilkinson continued to confer outside, leaving Tom alone with the prisoners. "I'm going to give you two sonsofbitches a solid piece of advice," he said, his voice hard and cold. "Do not try to escape! If in the attempt you abuse the Doctor, his good lady, or anyone else that looks after you before we reach Nashville, I'll hunt you down and kill you. Consider yourselves warned."

Seibert shackled the men to their beds and went outside. The conversation between Wilkinson and Demarest was drawing to a close. "Do you want me to stay and guard them tonight?" Tom asked.

"That won't be necessary, gentlemen," the physician replied. "In the shape they're in, neither one of them can ride. If they tried, they'd fall. As for walking, I'd say they'd be near crawling by the time they reached Redmond's shop. Go back to the hotel and get some rest; they aren't going anywhere."

By now, it was nine o'clock, but the marshals' night wasn't over. Both of them were dog tired and hurting. "Demarest says we have to get those two out of his place in the morning," Ward told Tom. "I'll be damned if I know where to put them. We can't take them to Shelbyville right now; they're too hurt to ride, maybe us as well. Also, we have to have Deputy Garrett there to meet our associates."

"There's a building out back of the hotel cookhouse that might do. I believe they keep food and other supplies in there. Mr. Cochran would probably allow us to put them there if there's room."

"That's better than any idea I've had by far. Let's go in and see if he's still up."

Chapter 50

THE FOLLOWING DAY, save for escorting their prisoners to their new quarters, the marshals spent much of the time in their room. They shackled Redmond and White to a sturdy floor-to-ceiling cabinet that covered the entire length of the rear wall. It was far too heavy to move, especially being crammed with kitchen supplies. Along with cots, the hotel provided a chamber pot and two excellent daily meals, courtesy of the state. Otherwise, there was a lot of silence for the men to contemplate the errors of their ways.

The hotel had always had a padlock on the door to prevent thefts, and that didn't change. Just to be certain, Ward took the precaution of appointing the kitchen steward, the keeper of the key, as a temporary marshal. "You don't have to do a thing other than what you're already doing," he assured the man. "The state of Tennessee will, in time, pay you two dollars a day while they're here. All you have to do is make certain that door's locked behind you each time you leave."

The prospect of two dollars a day brightened the steward's countenance, who until then had a sour expression on his face. "It'd be wise," Wilkinson continued, "for two of you to go whenever you have to be in there. I don't expect problems with them, but if there are any, let me know at once. When anyone else wants in there to take out the chamber pot, allow them to wash up, or when Dr. Demarest wants to look in on them, let me or Marshal Seibert know. One of us will go along."

After the noonday meal, one that Mr. Cochran had delivered to their room, Ward and Tom wrote up their report of the previous evening's assault. As yet, there was no message from Simon Garrett, but that concerned neither man; it was a bit too early to expect that. Wilkinson sat bare to the waist, allowing his cut to breathe. Seibert got up frequently to pace about the room. His ribs, he told Ward, seemed to stiffen up and ache when he remained for too long in one place.

On one of his circuits, Tom turned and asked, "You don't suppose that some of the conspirators will try to free them?"

Ward pondered the question for a moment, then replied, "I'm not sure if I care if they do."

"Why is that?"

"If they do, they're still in no shape to travel. Medical attention is a must, and that means we could, providing we had nothing better to do, sit outside Dr. Demarest's house and follow him wherever he went. Someone would have to harbor them, which, except for a select few, I doubt will happen. They'd be easy to find."

"Someone like Sillinger would harbor them."

"I'm sure she would. However, we're soon going to be searching her place. If they escape and turn up there, we'll be adding to the charges against them: escape for one, harboring fugitives for the other."

"There hasn't been a single request from anyone to visit them. That might put pay to the assertion of Denise Harper that Stuart Redmond and Peter Taylor are 'special friends.'"

Wilkinson snorted in derision. "I'd say that was a figment of Mrs. Harper's vindictiveness or overactive imagination. Let's go over our plan for these searches one more time."

Tom pulled out the map, then pinned it to the wall. "The two of us are going to Sillinger's first thing, right?" Ward nodded. "Depending on the number of marshals who appear, the plan might diverge from there. Let's assume we have four. That means they could split up and hit Harry Henderson and Redmond's while we're at the seamstress."

"Redmond can wait," Wilkinson said. "He's not going home. No, I think we'll have them go through Fred Reichert's place. When we're done with Faye Sillinger, I want us to go through Jeanne Clarke's house. The others can do Larry Everhart's property, somewhat to keep him busy while we're at the apple of his eye's, plus Will Sharp."

"After that?"

"Not sure if we'll need to do any others here in town. Finchum,

Taylor, Paul, and Wilson," he ticked them off quickly. "I don't see the point. Changed my mind about Bunting, too. I don't see him or Lou Johnson, either."

"Out of town is Del Orange. How about Perry Jessup?"

"Not for Mr. Jessup. I'm sure he didn't have any part in the plot. I'll grant you he had a motive, but I don't believe he acted on it. Like a lot of folks around here, his only sin was failing to mention all he knew. Say, it's after five. Let's get the names affixed to these warrants and go down to supper."

Chapter 51

SIMON GARRETT'S MESSAGE arrived the following afternoon. To the lawmen's surprise, Wilbur Cochran delivered it. "I've ordered that all messages for you come to me. This came a few minutes ago. If you like, I can take a response to the telegraph office for you."

"That's alright, Mr. Cochran," Ward replied, "thank you for bringing it. Should it need a reply, we'll take it. Tom and I are about to go mad from being in this room all the time. We'll see you for supper. That rabbit fricassee we saw on the menu ought to be amazing."

When Cochran was gone, Wilkinson tore open the message and smiled. "Here it is, Tom. Let's take a walk over there, then give Dick Reichert a heads-up that we'll be needing our mounts in the morning. I think we'll skip Guthrie's tonight; don't want to take the chance someone might see us and decide to flee. Out of sight, out of mind for now."

They walked over to the telegraph where Wilkinson sent the message, "Deliver it," to Simon Garrett. Minutes later, having asked to have their horses saddled and ready by eight o'clock, they returned to the hotel. The rich meal, accompanied by a bottle of red wine, was most satisfying—so much so that their heads drooped even before they left the supper table. "I believe it's about time to turn in," Ward yawned. "Mr. Cooper should be in for McCormick by now. I'll ask him to knock on our door at six o'clock if he hasn't seen us by then."

The wakeup wasn't necessary. Wilkinson, excited by the prospect of finishing this investigation and returning home to Charlotte, was wide awake well before the pre-light of dawn. The marshals were downstairs at five-thirty, perused a week-old Shelbyville paper, then headed to breakfast as the doors of the dining room opened. "Marshal,"

Cooper said in a conspiratorial whisper from behind the desk, "I noticed you reading the news," he confided. "That publisher, editor, whatever he is, came in right after midnight. He's down there in 106 right now."

Ward thanked him, then hastened to join Tom. "We've got to eat and get the hell out of here." Tom raised his eyes from the bill of fare with a look of alarm. "Billings is down the hall in Room 106. I don't want him to see us, start following us around, ask damn fool questions, or want to see Redmond."

"We'll have the special," Tom told the waiter, "and coffee."

"What's the special?" Ward asked.

"Something that's ready to serve and will be here in a minute. It's biscuits and gravy, I believe."

True to Seibert's word, the waiter was back in thirty seconds. "Is there a back way through the kitchen?" Wilkinson asked.

The man gestured to a door, adding, "Through there."

The marshals ate hurriedly, drinking down their coffee while it was still quite hot. "We'll be back for more coffee later on," Ward said. Then, he and Tom slipped out the back. To their relief, no one was about, save for a kitchen employee returning from the cookhouse.

They walked steadily northward. "I'm glad we don't have to run," Tom admitted to Ward. "I don't believe I could do it." Crossing Main Street, they passed in front of Reverend Hoffberger's church, turned left, traversed the length of the north square businesses, and then swung south at David Franklin's furniture store. Once there, they traversed the open ground of the north square as quickly as they could, went over the tracks, hugged the left side of the stockyard corral, and then made the last few yards to Reichert's. As well as they could determine, no one had seen them.

Passing through the feed store, they tipped their hats to Mrs. Reichert, who returned their courtesy with a chilly glare. "You'll think a lot less of us in a while," Wilkinson said in an unintelligible mutter as he and Tom went through to the livery. Being early, the mounts weren't ready, with Dick Reichert in the process of harnessing a four-horse team. The marshals told him it wasn't a problem and saddled their animals themselves.

A few minutes before seven o'clock, they climbed into the saddle, rode out of the barn, and headed down the south side of the square. They rode to the end of the shops, made a wide skirt around the hotel, then rejoined Main Street and headed out to the rendezvous point. "We'll be there in plenty of time," Ward said, after a brief consultation of his watch. He slowed his horse to a walk, a development that Tom and his sore ribs appreciated.

The turnaround was empty when they pulled rein. Stepping down, they hitched their mounts to a couple of second-growth trees that extended from the cutbank and settled down to wait. Wilkinson, knowing that in a town of early risers several residents must have seen them ride out, wondered what they were thinking. Given the falsehood they'd planted about leaving soon, that their investigation was wallowing, some could conclude they were pulling out, heading for home with their tails between their legs. That ruse wasn't valid any longer—not with the attempt on their lives by Redmond and his halfwit acolyte, Ezra White. The possibility concerning him was that one of the town conspirators, a firebrand like Faye Sillinger, might incite some others to arm themselves and ride out if they thought the marshals were heading for Del Orange's farm. That would mean gunplay, a result Ward wanted to avoid.

The hour dragged by. Ward, still deep in thought, saw Tom rise to his feet, then realized both horses were producing soft nickers. Indeed, Ward's own animal was tipping its ears forward to the horizon, its nostrils flared. Something or someone was approaching them from the direction of Shelbyville.

Minutes later, a group of horsemen appeared in the distance. As they grew closer, a grin spread across the face of both men. They knew the lead rider well. Striding into the road, they raised their hands in greeting, and the column came to a halt. Bob Brannigan, US Marshal from Chattanooga, looked down from his saddle and grinned in return. "Looky here, boys," he said in a bantering fashion, "it's Marshals Wilkinson and Seibert. Wonder what they've done to get themselves in such big trouble in a little place like this."

The sally drew good natured laughter from the other officers, some

Ward knew, some not. Along with Brannigan was his very accomplished deputy, Clay Moore. In the second row was Rocky Bridges, the marshal from Huntsville. The man riding beside him must be his deputy. It surprised Ward to see a fifth man, but he was glad to have him regardless of where he'd come from.

"Howdy, Ward, Tom," Brannigan said as he stepped down from the leather and extended a sweaty palm. "You know Clay and Marshal Bridges, I believe. The fellow in the fancy green vest is Rocky's deputy, Billy Foster. Our fifth man is Bernie Linsley. Bernie is the Deputy Sheriff of Hamilton County, but I've deputized him and brought him along. From the wire Rocky and I got, sounded pretty serious."

"It might be before we're done," Wilkinson said, motioning for everyone to dismount. "A couple of nights ago, a man involved in the murder Tom and I have been investigating, along with an idiot he got to help him, tried to kill us while we were searching for additional evidence at the murder site. It was a near thing; we got nicked up a mite."

"Shooting scrape?" Brannigan inquired, concern in his voice.

"No," Seibert replied, "they came at us in a vacant lot after dark. Tried to get us with knives. Ward's got a cut that's coming along alright. I took a couple of body punches while disarming the other fellow. My ribs are pretty sore."

"Going to be ok?"

"Yeah, I'm getting there. You ought to see them sonsofbitches," he said flatly. "They're a lot worse for wear."

"Gather around, men," Wilkinson called, trying to regain control in the wake of the cheers that erupted. "It's a mile and a half into town, and we have several search warrants to serve this morning. The reason Marshal Seibert and I are here comes from a request by the Tennessee Attorney General that we investigate the broad daylight, middle of town killing of a local resident named Ted Harper. You passed his farm a couple of miles back. No witnesses came forward, and none were located when the county sheriff investigated. The people here wanted Mr. Harper dead for many reasons. They have no intention of exposing his killers."

"Who was this Harper?" Bridges asked.

"Just about everything. Probable out-of-state bank and train robber back in the 70s, involved in real estate fraud, swindler, abuser of women and the weak. In recent years, he began extorting money from local business owners. Some of them were involved in his murder."

"Sounds like they were public servants."

"You could see it that way. After he got off Scot-free last year from an attempted murder charge, the locals hatched a conspiracy to get him. We believe a local farmer, a former Confederate veteran, planned the operation. But we don't have any evidence that's not circumstantial. That's what these warrants are for."

"Who are we serving them on, Ward, and what is it you want to find?"

"We'll work in three pairs this morning. Deputy Linsley, I'd like if you'd remain here until noon today. Prevent anyone coming from the direction of town from going beyond this point until that time. I don't want anyone getting word to Mr. Orange about our searches. After that, I don't care a damn if he knows. When it gets to be noon, come on in and find us."

"What if someone refuses and tries to pass?" Linsley inquired.

"Pull your gun, tell them it's on my authority, and direct them back to town. Tell them to talk to me if they don't like it. Now," Ward continued, "the warrants. We'll begin with three businesses and houses. Some of these people live above their business in the same building. We're looking for weapons that were used in the murder. One was a Winchester, which I doubt we'll find unless Del Orange has it. There are two pocket pistols, one a .32 caliber, the other is a .38. We also believe there's a derringer. Harper took bullets from all these weapons. Further, any documents that relate to Harper's abuse of these people and any letters or diaries that discuss the plot will obviously help.

"Tom and I will begin at the seamstress shop. She claims Harper physically abused her, and we know he extorted money from her. She hates him with a passion. Bob, I want you and Clay to take Harry Henderson. He's a grocer, who we suspect was a shooter. Rocky, you and Billy will have Fred Reichert; he's the man who Harper shot last year. He owns a livery stable, blacksmith shop, and a feed store. We know he was involved in the planning at the very least."

The lawmen stepped into the leather, and Wilkinson spoke again. "Despite the treatment Tom and I have received, most of the people here aren't bad folks. A bully who never seemed likely to face any consequences for his actions pushed them beyond toleration. Be firm but do the best you can not to disrupt their businesses more than necessary."

"Any likelihood of violent resistance?" Rocky Bridges asked.

"I wouldn't think so. Then again, I didn't figure on any from Stuart Redmond. The most probable is the woman we're going to serve, Faye Sillinger."

"Why so?"

Seibert joined the conversation. "She's the only person we've had anyone mention that admits they saw anyone out and about around the time Harper was shot. This is apart from their customers, who they won't identify by name. Ward has a theory, which I've slowly warmed to, that she gathered up the weapons used in the killing—the pistols at least—and carried them back to her house. After all, who would suspect a seamstress to have such things? We hope to find them there."

"Then," Wilkinson resumed, "there's the matter of the fourth gun. It wasn't until we were here that we learned Harper had his balls blown off by a bullet, which was fired while he was flat on his back. The slug we dug out of the ground where he died was .41 caliber."

"Could be a Remington 95," Brannigan mused, tugging at the corner of his long, drooping mustache. "Tell you what, Ward," he said, holding up his hand to signal the group to halt, "slight change in plan. Clay, you go handle Henderson. Take Rocky and Billy with you when you serve him. Rocky, make it clear to the sonofabitch that you'll be nearby at Reichert's if he does anything stupid. Tell him there are three more besides yourselves and that he won't survive to face a jury if anything happens to my deputy. Meanwhile, I'll go with you and Tom. From what you say, this poor woman might be ill-disposed enough to get the drop on you if she has the chance. While you search, I'll have my eyes on her."

Wilkinson met Brannigan's gaze and nodded in agreement. His friend was in his fifties now, his hair and whiskers liberally streaked with gray, yet there wasn't a man he respected more. After the war, he'd gone west, got involved in mining, and then served stints as sheriff in various towns and camps. Wells Fargo had hired him as an investigator, which led him to spend several years crisscrossing multiple states and territories in pursuit of robbers and highwaymen. Tiring of the incessant travel, he'd accepted the marshal's appointment to Chattanooga in 1880. Despite his age, he wasn't a man with whom to trifle; tougher than a woodpecker's bill, a colleague had noted.

* * *

The group of lawmen crested the ridge, glimpsed the town, then started down Main Street. At the junction of High Street, well before Hoffberger's church, Ward led the party off to the right for a wide swing around the upper part of town. He didn't wish anyone, most notably Faye Sillinger, to witness their approach. After a brief ride, they turned south, went behind Bill Martin's complex of shops, then crossed the tracks to descend on Henderson's grocery. "This is it," Wilkinson pointed. "Reichert's is the next place down. When you're done, we'll meet over there in front of the stockyard."

The three men, stars plainly visible on their lapels, got down; Wilkinson, Seibert, and Bob Brannigan clattered away. Recrossing the tracks, they trotted their mounts along the rear of the north square shops, then traversed the short distance to Sillinger's seamstress shop. She was setting outside with her coffee when they pulled rein.

Faye saw them coming, and her lips thinned. Who was this other one, the one with the hard face and smoldering eyes? No doubt he was as awful as those Nashville marshals, like most men, soulless. Rising to her feet, she stepped to the edge of the boardwalk and belligerently jutted her jaw. "What the hell do you want?" she demanded in the wintriest tone imaginable.

Wilkinson sighed. "Miss Sillinger," he said in an emotionless tenor, "this is a warrant signed by the Tennessee Attorney General to search this premises."

Faye took the proffered document, scanned it for a moment, then threw it to the boards and ground the heel of her shoe upon it. Her features were taut with anger. "This is bogus," she hissed. "An absolute outrage. Who died and made you King?"

"We're not royalty, Miss Sillinger, but by laws of this state and the federal constitution, we have the right granted by that order I gave you to enter on this property and search. If you believe the state granted the warrant in error, you'll have to hire an attorney and challenge it in the courts. However, I warn you, it's doubtful the Tennessee Supreme Court will agree. In the meantime, though, you'll have to stand aside. If you refuse, it will force us to place you under arrest."

After bristling at them for several moments, Faye relented. Still, she subjected the marshals to a withering tirade, the likes of which Bob Brannigan would later say he'd only heard from one other woman. "I was in Deadwood, Dakota Territory, and saw this rather unattractive female, dressed in buckskins, get into an altercation with a couple of men on the street. She called them everything from a cocksucker to a dirty sonofabitch. Miss Sillinger didn't go quite that far, but it was close. That lady I mentioned, if you could refer to her as such, was known as Calamity Jane."

They entered the building, the proprietor's denunciation reverberating in their ears. Ward and Tom proceeded to the back room where Sillinger kept her sewing equipment, supplies, and other articles. Once done with that, they ascended a small set of stairs to the living quarters. Seeing how upset she was, Brannigan maintained a watchful eye on her, calling her back when she followed behind the men. "I'd be obliged if you'd stay out here, miss," he said, speaking to her for the first time. "We'll finish as quick as we can without creating any more disorder than is necessary. Try to calm yourself, if possible."

Faye turned her wrath on him, forgetting for the moment Wilkinson and Seibert were continuing their search. However, as her ire subsided, she became more anxious. Apprehensive glances gave way to obsessive stares at the open doorway. When the marshals returned, her head dropped in despair. Soft sobs emerged from her throat.

Ward was carrying a cloth bag. "It was overhead," he told Brannigan, "just inside a trapdoor to the loft. If it hadn't been close, we'd have never found it. There are three handguns in here: a Remington 95 derringer, just like you predicted; a Smith & Wesson Model 2, .38 caliber; and a .32 Ivor Johnson pocket pistol. Interestingly enough," he continued, looking at Faye Sillinger, "the Remington was fired in the fairly recent past and hasn't been cleaned. There's still a cartridge in the second barrel."

"Typical of someone not experienced with firearms," Seibert observed. "The others are of a kind you'd expect someone who is inexpert to use. Either they couldn't handle a Colt or hoped they could shoot straight enough with these as long as they didn't have to shoot very far."

Wilkinson had Brannigan search the woman's business records while he and Tom kept watch on the seamstress, who seemed deflated. "Go back to 1881," Ward said. "I expect you'll find an unexplained three-dollar monthly expense, provided it's recorded at all. If it isn't, it's not of great importance. We know she was paying because of Harper's records."

Ten minutes later, Brannigan admitted defeat. "There's nothing in here," he informed Wilkinson.

"You want to tell me who was in this with you?" Ward inquired of Sillinger. The only answer was a stare of defiance. "Very well, then. Miss Sillinger, you are under arrest for conspiracy to commit the murder of Ted Harper and being an accessory after the fact. It is possible, once we get all the facts, that we may amend these charges to include murder itself. You're confined to your residence subsequent to other arrangements being made for your transfer to the Bedford County jail or another such place of the State of Tennessee's choosing. Mr. Ross, the photographer, will be along to take your photograph, and should you decide to flee, your face will adorn wanted posters in every nearby state. Good day, miss."

* * *

When the men returned to the stockyard, Rocky Bridges and the deputies were waiting for them. "Henderson wasn't any problem,"

Moore reported. "We didn't find much. There is reference to the payments he was making to this Harper fellow in his records. Anything you want us to tell him?"

"Yes. Go tell him I'm placing him under arrest on suspicion of murder and confining him to his residence. Also, like I told Miss Sillinger, the town photographer will be around to take his picture. If he bolts, his face will appear on wanted posters far and wide."

"Did you find anything at the lady's place?" Bridges queried.

"You bet," Seibert rejoined. "We've got the guns!"

Bridges chuckled when he discussed the search at Reichert's. "You didn't tell me you were having your horses boarded there. He got so mad that I thought he was going to have a stroke."

"We'll survive," Ward said. "Was there anything to find?"

"Not that Billy and I could find. I found an invoice where he did some shoeing for Harper that was never paid. I brought it with me. If they're accounting for the money he was paying, they've hidden it somehow in all the different businesses they're running. Oh, he told me to tell you not to bring your horses back to his livery."

Wilkinson laughed, but the sound was cold. "The last time he said that, I told him he'd go to the Bedford County jail. This time, I'll have another message."

Ward stomped across the square and found Reichert in his blacksmith shop. The man roared in complaint but was cut off before he could finish his first sentence. "Mr. Reichert, you're under arrest for conspiracy to commit the murder of Ted Harper and being an accessory before and after the fact. You're confined to your residence until transfer to the county jail or wherever the Attorney General designates. Further, our mounts will continue to be boarded in your livery. Mr. Ross will be by to take your picture for a nice wanted poster should you decide to take off. That's all, sir! I won't stand around debating with you."

Chapter 52

LEAVING REICHERT SPEECHLESS, Wilkinson went back to the group of lawmen. "I've tolerated all the bullshit I intend to from that man," he declared to Tom. "The first opportunity that comes along, he's going to Shelbyville jail."

"Who's next?" asked Bridges.

"There are three left. Rocky, you and Billy go see Will Sharp, the cobbler. He acted like a jackass when Tom went to interview him. Claimed he knew nothing, yet we come to find out he was paying regular to Harper. I doubt there's anything there. Still, go through his place good and proper, might learn him a lesson. The other two are Larry Everhart and Jeanne Clarke. They've been having a clandestine romance, you might say. He owns a hardware store, and she's the milliner in town. Neither is married, but Harper extorted money from both of them to keep the affair quiet. He was taking more off Everhart than anyone else. Your guess is as good as mine whether there's anything to find."

"Who do you want me and Clay to take?" Brannigan asked.

"Take Everhart. We'll search Miss Clarke's place."

The marshals made their way to the north side of the square and descended on their remaining targets. Sharp, predictably, threw a conniption fit yet did little more than fill the air with impotent swearing. Despite finding nothing, Bridges and Billy Foster gave the ill-tempered cobbler plenty to clean up. He was still howling oaths and imprecations as they rode away.

Larry Everhart was more shocked by the visitors' arrival than any anger he might have felt over being searched. More and more people were learning about him and Jeanne Clarke, a consequence he'd hoped to avoid. Pretty soon, he feared, the state would haul one or both of them before a grand jury to be questioned about what they knew. If not then, perhaps in the trials that were sure to follow for those who'd done the shooting. The thought left Larry's stomach in knots.

Not bothering to read the warrant, Everhart meekly turned aside to let the marshals search his small office and his bachelor quarters that occupied the upper floor. Considering what was occurring, he wondered if all those nights of steamy passion entwined in Jeanne's arms were worth it. If he wanted them to continue, he decided it might be a good idea if they got married.

The search of the hardware store discovered little, save that Ted Harper had been squeezing nine dollars a month out of Everhart. Bob Brannigan, once he got the gist of Larry's bookkeeping, whistled in disgust. He decided, like Tom Seibert, that the man's death wasn't the worst thing that had ever happened. He'd seen several men like that in his western wanderings; they'd gotten killed as well.

Given his opinion of Harper, it was ironic that Tom Seibert discovered the evidence they'd long been seeking. It'd been there all the time, secreted away in the private diary of Jeanne Clarke. The young woman, as pretty as any female he'd seen in town, Wilkinson thought, was stunned when the marshals appeared at her door with a warrant. The impact of her words, written during the continuous upset of many months, hadn't dawned on her. Now, they would bring down all the conspirators.

Ward found Tom sitting in front of Jeanne's mirror, studying the volume with rapt concentration. When he asked what it was, Tom's reply was astonishing. "Maybe the answer to this whole damn mess." He thumbed back a couple of pages, then looked up at his friend. "Get a load of this," he said.

"She was keeping a diary and has some interesting things to say: June 16, 1881, for example. 'Poor Larry visited me tonight in a horrid state of worry. Ted Harper, that ghastly creature that robs me blind, saw him coming to my house the other night. He's telling Larry he'll tell everybody in town about us if he doesn't start giving him money to keep quiet. I can only imagine what some of those hypocritical old biddies at the church would say if they knew.'"

Seibert scanned the page, then continued. "'Larry says Harper told him he'll inform on us even if we stop seeing each other. It sounds about like that man. I don't know what we are going to do but keep paying.'"

"Skip ahead until you find entries following the shooting of Fred Reichert," Ward said, his voice betraying his excitement. "Maybe she'll talk about the plot to kill Harper."

Tom fanned through the pages until he came to the previous winter. "This may take a while," he said, "Miss Clarke was a voluminous writer. You might want to go down and keep her company unless you just want me to bring this along and read it later."

"Let's do that. Take it back to the hotel while we go through Stuart Redmond's shop. We'll join you later for dinner."

It floored Jeanne Clarke when they told her that the only thing they wanted was her diary. She went white to the lips, remonstrating with them to reconsider. "Oh, please, gentlemen," she pleaded, "those are my private thoughts, never meant to be seen by anyone else, not even Mr. Everhart. If what I've written came to light, it would be very embarrassing for me."

"I'm sorry," Wilkinson said, "but it's evidence in a murder case. In due time, we'll return it to you."

"Will the prosecutor cite what I've written in court?"

"He could." The answer mortified Jeanne, and she brought her hand to her mouth.

Outside, Tom handed the reins of his mount to Ward and headed back to the hotel. He felt for the lady. Over the years, he'd heard many people say their parents, or others they knew, had burned their papers regularly, or at least late in life. All of a sudden, that seemed like a good idea—that and never keeping a diary. He climbed the steps, passed McCormick as if he didn't exist, and went upstairs.

Tom sat down on the bed and began to read Jeanne's entries:

October 15, 1882. We learned today that the grand jury in Shelbyville refused to indict Ted Harper for the attempted murder of poor Mr. Reichert. People in this town are in an uproar, demanding that something be done. The question is, will this agitation lead to action?

December 6, 1882. According to Larry, there is some desultory talk going around about doing away with Ted Harper. I think this is just blowhards who won't be found when it's time to actually do anything. I hope Larry isn't involved. Mr. Harper can shoot. Larry doesn't know a thing about guns.

January 1, 1883. Larry says there is planning underway to get a group of people organized to take on Ted Harper. I'll believe it when I see it. Wish he'd take less interest in such gossip and give more thought to us getting married. (That entry brought a smile from Tom.)

February 15, 1883. Larry reports that Del Orange overheard some townspeople discussing getting rid of Ted Harper. It seems he asked them if they were serious. If so, he wants to join them. I don't know if this was a while ago or if it just happened. I don't know Mr. Orange. He lives in the country, stays to himself, and seldom comes into town. I've heard he was in the war. Perhaps he will have the courage to act.

March 10, 1883. Electrifying news. Larry tells me there was a meeting with several people committed to eliminating Ted Harper. Mr. Orange will lead the effort. I, along with all the business owners, had an invitation to take part in this meeting, but I declined. I'm not up to shooting it out with Ted Harper. Still, Larry says Faye Sillinger attended. He says she's enthusiastic about the idea.

April 1, 1883. I don't know if he was supposed to say, but Larry spilled the details of this plan to kill Ted Harper while we were together tonight. According to him, Harry Henderson and Stuart

Redmond will lure him to a meeting where they'll shoot him. Mr. Orange will back them up some way so that nothing goes wrong. When the act is done, they'll ride off in some wagon. Faye Sillinger, I still can hardly believe she's involved, will take the weapons back to her place. Don't know what she's going to do with them once she has them.

Larry also says that Mr. Reichert, who could blame him, and Ronald Whipple are a part of this group. They won't be part of the shooters but will assist in other ways. I asked him how he knows this. He told me he has decided not to attend any more of these meetings, doesn't want to be a party to murder. Of this, I am very glad.

April 15, 1883. It happened at noon yesterday. Ted Harper, at long last, got what was coming to him. No more intimidation, no more payments, no more worries about being in the hole at the end of the month, or that slimy bastard reneging on his word and tattling about me and Larry. I'm giddy with excitement. Larry says Mr. Henderson and Stuart Redmond, as he'd told me earlier, walked up from their stores and pulled guns on him. Said Mr. Orange was there, too. Couldn't contain myself when he was here last night; what a celebration!

April 30, 1883. It looks like Sheriff Parslow has abandoned his efforts to find Harper's killers. Everyone is breathing a sigh of relief. Looks like we are in the clear. Maybe now things can get back to normal. Will be the first peace in this community since Ted Harper came back from whatever privy pit he was inhabiting.

May 17, 1883. Two strangers arrived in town yesterday afternoon and are guests at the hotel. Something about them, Larry says, is disturbing. They are formidable in appearance, well-mounted, and heavily armed. Just when we were beginning to relax.

May 19, 1883. One of them was here today, a US Marshal Tom Seibert, from Nashville. Not an evil man, but is here along with his superior, Marshal Ward Wilkinson, to reinvestigate the Harper killing. Larry says that man was by to see him. I fibbed about paying Harper, but the other marshal figured out Larry was one of his victims. That's disturbing.

There were subsequent entries about the bank robbery shootout, the attempt by Stuart Redmond and Ezra White to kill the marshals—an act that Larry Everhart, according to her, termed "incredibly stupid"—and the unease that followed. Tom no longer cared. All the evidence they required was in his hands.

Seibert was sitting on the veranda when Wilkinson and the other marshals returned from Redmond's. They were in good humor. "Stuart was corresponding with a friend," Ward stated, "who made reference in his last letter to him that shooting Harper had been a bad idea. It's here in my saddlebags. How did you make out?"

"Everything is in Jeanne Clarke's handwriting," Tom announced. "Either Larry Everhart was an uncontrolled blabbermouth, or she was very persuasive in getting him to talk. Redmond, Henderson, Del Orange, and Miss Sillinger are all mentioned by name. She's detailed the plot as well. With the circumstantial evidence we possess, there's enough to bring hanging charges against whomever the prosecutor can get an indictment."

As they were talking, Deputy Bernie Linsley trotted his mount up to the hotel and climbed down. "Any trouble?" Wilkinson asked.

"No trouble," Linsley replied. "Had to turn one person around; most, though, were coming this way. I just let them be."

The men entered the hotel lobby and headed for the dining room. "Mr. McCormick," Ward said as he went by, "you're under arrest for being an accessory after the fact in the murder of Ted Harper and obstruction of justice. Don't even think of trying to leave town."

As they enjoyed the hotel cuisine, Ward spoke to Tom, who was sitting next to him. "Someone needs to go down and inform Ronald Whipple he's under arrest for accessory before and after. I don't want to charge anyone else with obstruction. Hell, if we did that, half the damn town would be under arrest."

* * *

Once the noonday meal was done, Ward and Bob Brannigan paid the Whipples a brief call—long enough to tell Ronald he was under arrest for his role in the Harper killing. Hurrying back, Wilkinson told the men to mount up for the ride to Del Orange's farm. "I don't know what sort of reception we'll receive," Ward advised. "Tom and I have never met the man. The story we've heard is that he was in the war and served in an elite sharpshooter unit. He's said to still be a crack shot.

"Further, we're certain he was the planner for this assassination. It's his voice we believe we heard in Reichert's livery stable when we eavesdropped on a meeting the conspirators held on the night we hit town. If so, he's very calm, in control of his nerves, never seems to get excited. That may mean he's a cold-blooded, unfeeling killer, yet I have my doubts. He vetoed the idea of any violence against us. Some of the group clearly declined to follow that veto."

"How do you figure on handling this?" Brannigan asked in a concerned tone.

"When we get there, I'll ride up alone." Tom uttered a word of protest, but Ward continued. "If all seven of us go, he could get alarmed and start shooting. One won't be so threatening. Besides," he said, his grin unconvincing, "there won't be so many targets for him to pick from."

"What do you want *us* to do?"

"You and Clay, when we get to the lane up to his farm, circle around and come up behind the house. Not too close, but near enough to intercept him if he tries to flee. The rest, stop at the tree line. Billy, I see you're carrying a .50 Sharps. Give that to Tom if you don't mind. He's the best long-range shot I know."

Billy Foster handed over the rifle, and Seibert looked at Ward. "What I want you to do, Tom, is to find a vantage you can shoot from when we get sight of the house. If he opens fire on me, I'll make for the nearest cover. I want him alive, but we shoot to kill if he wants a fight. Let's go."

Chapter 53

THE COUNTRY LANE to Perry Jessup's farmstead extended on until it arrived at the Orange farm. The two men had a friendly agreement to share the thoroughfare. About a quarter of a mile past the house, the lane bent to the right, then the ground sloped upward. The track skirted a mound, then curled through a belt of trees that flanked both sides of a small stream that meandered at right angles to the route. A narrow wooden bridge, well maintained, bisected the rivulet, and the lawmen clattered over it to find a bare, unobstructed plain all the way to the farmhouse, which stood five hundred yards distant.

There would be no cover—nowhere to hide if lead began flying. Behind him, Wilkinson heard Rocky Bridges swear. "Ah, shit! Ward, are you sure about this?"

"No," Wilkinson admitted, "yet I think it's the most likely way we'll all ride away from here with our lives."

Seibert, having dismounted, studied the ground for several moments, then walked up to where Ward was sitting his horse. "If I'm to protect your life, we need another plan. It's too far away for me to shoot accurately, even if I had the Whitworth. Why don't you let me ride with you and bring Rocky's shotgun along. That way, if he lets us get up close, we'll have a good chance. If he starts while we're away, at least there'll be two repeating rifles for him to worry about."

Wilkinson considered the proposal and decided Tom was right. While he was in thought, Seibert produced his spyglass and studied the terrain ahead. There was a small depression out there, three hundred yards or more away, probably where generations of cattle had wallowed over the years. That might be a place of refuge if a battle began. When he raised the scope further, he realized there was a solitary figure at the front of the house. "Do we know for sure this fellow lives alone?" Tom asked.

"Yes," Wilkinson reiterated, "he's a known loner. Do you see someone up there?"

"Sitting on the front porch as pretty as you please. I have a notion he's aware of our presence. Don't see a gun anywhere, at least not a long one."

At that revelation, Ward decided, "You've got your wish. Give Billy back his Sharps and take Rocky's scatter gun. Bob, you and Clay go back down until you're underneath that mound before circling around. We'll give you five minutes head start."

Brannigan and Foster trotted away. Wilkinson monitored his watch, and when the sweep had made its five revolutions, he signaled to Seibert. They urged their mounts forward and rode out into the open. Bridges's shotgun was in Tom's left hand, balanced against the horn of the saddle.

Neither man spoke. Both knew the risk they were taking, and both recognized the fear in the pit of their stomachs. Ward's mouth was dry; a glass of Guthrie's lager would be welcome right now, he decided. Tom harbored no such fancies. His only deliberation concerned Del Orange and how he'd respond if the man went for a gun.

The distance fell away, four hundred yards, three, then two. Details of the farmhouse and outbuildings, little more than discernable shapes when Ward and Tom began their ride, were now in sharper focus. The dwelling place had a fresh coat of paint, its whiteboards gleaming in the early afternoon sun. There were a few chickens roaming over the yard, the only things in motion. Orange, if it was him, continued to sit. At fifty yards, when no hail came from the porch, Wilkinson pulled rein. "Mr. Orange," he called, "is that you, sir? Mind if we come up?"

"I'm Orange," came the reply. "Ride on up. Coffee's on if you're of a mind to light and sit a spell."

The marshals continued, Tom concentrating on Del Orange's hands. So far, they held nothing but a tin cup. There were no weapons in sight. "I thank you for the offer of hospitality," Wilkinson said as they neared the porch. "Unfortunately, this isn't a social call. We're US

Marshals assigned here to investigate the murder of your neighbor, Ted Harper. We're here to arrest you for his killing."

"Figured as much," Orange said with unconcern. "You could have had all these men ride up with you, wouldn't have made any never mind to me. If I'd wanted a fight, you'd have been laying out there in the field long before now."

The confident voice was the same one they'd heard in Reichert's barn. "You don't seem anxious," Wilkinson observed. "Most people find a murder charge pretty serious."

"Can't say that I am. Charging is a long way from proving."

"Well, believe it or not, we've accumulated enough evidence to put your head in the noose. Could say the same for Henderson and Redmond."

"Redmond." The farmer, his hands still encircling his coffee cup, uttered the name with faint disgust. "I warned him and the others against bothering you. Some people have little sense. Don't have the slightest sympathy for him."

"We're aware of your warning," Ward replied. "We heard you say it in Reichert's livery."

One of Orange's eyebrows tilted. "Do tell. I was right about you. Told them there would be no more meetings after that one, it wasn't safe. Reckon I made that decision a little too late."

"You'll have to come with us, you know?"

"Rather figured that as well. Already talked with Perry about feeding my stock. He can handle it until I get back. Still, if you leave me here, you'll always be able to find me. I don't go anyplace, except maybe to hunt and fish."

"What makes you believe you'll be returning?"

"When my defense attorney gets through detailing to a jury what Ted Harper was like, can you imagine what they'll think when all of them people around here that he was abusing, defrauding, stealing from, get on the stand and tell what he did to them? I doubt any group of twelve men in this county would all vote for conviction."

Thinking of the various misdeeds of the dead man, Wilkinson determined Del Orange had a point. Still, it wasn't their call to choose who was to be tried. "What happens in court, Mr. Orange, isn't for us to decide. Our only charge is getting you there. What the prosecutor can do with the evidence to persuade a jury is up to him. Shall we go?"

"Don't see why not. Let me pour out this coffee pot, and I'll get my horse."

"Do you have a rifle?" Tom asked.

"Doesn't everyone? Mine's just like the one you have in the scabbard there, a Winchester 76."

"You'd have surprised me if you'd said anything else. Is it in the house?"

"Inside the front door. You can't miss it."

Seibert retrieved the rifle, and then they walked their horses over to the barn and watched as Orange saddled his mount. By the time he finished, Bob Brannigan and Billy Foster had joined them. "On the way out," Del said, "I'd be obliged if you'd give me a moment to tell Perry that I'll be away for a little while."

"Sure," Ward replied, "but it might be longer than you think."

* * *

Back in town, Wilkinson burned up the telegraph wires. He had too many prisoners in a town with no jail. Much as he disliked it, he had no place other than the hotel supply building to confine Del Orange. "You'll have to tolerate this for a while," he told the farmer. "It's the only place available. Good news is that the dining room is first rate. Try not to kill Stuart Redmond or the idiot that's with him, Ezra White."

Ward sent two wires to Judge Morton. The first read: *Your Honor, have all principals in Harper murder under arrest. Thank you for the assistance. Request you consult the attorney general on the disposition of prisoners. No jail here. Suggest reasonable bail. All suspects are business owners and farmers. None are flight risks. Given notorious and deserved reputation of the deceased, doubt that conviction is achievable in this county regardless of evidence.*

As soon as Wilkinson finished the first, he sent a second: *Your Honor, on return will ferry two prisoners, one a Harper shooter. Both charged with attempted murder of myself and Marshal Seibert. Request bail for the other two. If possible, need an expeditious reply. Wish to release Marshals Brannigan and Bridges, along with deputies, to return to home base tomorrow.*

Now, there was nothing to do but wait.

A familiar face was waiting in the lobby when Wilkinson returned from the telegraph office. Ward wasn't happy to see Timothy Billings yet pretended to be otherwise. He was eager for the marshal to fulfill his promise of an exclusive interview after the Harper investigation was complete, and Ward, having nothing to do but wait for answers to his messages, obliged by giving him a statement that covered the murder investigation and arrest of suspects. "I caught glimpses of you around town this morning," Billings said, "but you were busy going in and out of places and didn't appear as if you had time to talk. Who are all these men with you?"

"US Marshals from Chattanooga and Huntsville, Alabama, along with their deputies. They were helping serve search warrants this morning and make arrests."

"Who did you arrest?"

Ward gave him a list of those charged, yet only talked in general terms of the plot and its execution. "Much of what we know, sir," he related, "will have to wait for grand jury testimony. We do not expect more arrests in this matter."

"It's my understanding that men assaulted you and your deputy the other evening," the newspaper editor persisted. "What was that about?"

"Stuart Redmond, a confectioner in this town, attacked Marshal Seibert and me. He's a serious suspect in Harper's shooting. He attacked us while we searched for additional physical evidence at the site of the murder, and he recruited an acquaintance, one Ezra White, to assist him. They failed in their attempt to kill us and are in custody here until we return them to Nashville to face federal charges. Afterward, Redmond can still face prosecution for Harper's killing, and White as an accessory after the fact."

"Will you incarcerate the others in Shelbyville, or will they go to Nashville?"

"Still to be determined. If the county prosecutor conducts the trials, I'd expect it will be in Shelbyville. That's not decided either, though. Not my call, regardless. Anything else?"

"Can you talk about the bank robbery?"

Wilkinson sighed; the man was indefatigable. "If you insist," he replied.

The supper hour was approaching when answers to Wilkinson's wires arrived. "I'm sorry, Mr. Billings," he said, masking his relief, "I have to get back to work. Perhaps again some other time."

Ward arose from his rocker along the hotel veranda and went inside. Judge Morton's reply stated that for the time being, the state was content with the bailment of all parties that were unlikely to flee: *Those charged with conspiracy or accessory, provided without violence, a three-hundred-dollar bond, 10 percent cash is sufficient. Shooting suspects: thousand-dollar property bond. Your attackers will receive no bail. Davidson County jail for them. You may release Marshals Brannigan and Bridges at your discretion.*

The second wire was from the county prosecutor. From its content, it was obvious he'd heard from the Attorney General: *Offer bail to all suspects who will accept it. Any that refuse or can't make the amount, transfer them to the Bedford County jail. On your way back to Nashville, come see me in Shelbyville.*

That will be soon, Wilkinson thought, a jubilant thrill coursing through him. If not tomorrow, Sunday for certain.

At supper, Ward told the marshals they could head back by noon the next day. "I thank you for everything you've done," he praised. "Your being here halted the urge anyone might have had to try something foolish. Tom and I have to bail most of these people, then we can all get out of here. Before that, though, we'll go down to Guthrie's saloon. He sells some of the best lager you'll find anywhere."

Chapter 54

AT EIGHT IN the morning, Wilkinson was at the bank to talk to Harry Colborne. "Would any of these business owners be able to withstand a three-hundred-dollar forfeiture?" he asked.

Colborne answered almost instantly. "A few of them might," he replied, "but they'd be hard-pressed. It would reduce some to near penury. I'd say that's a circumstance they'd want to avoid at all costs."

"What about a thousand?"

Colborne laughed. "Bankruptcy would result."

Wilkinson thanked him, then went back to the hotel. "We have authorization to offer all the people we've arrested, except for Redmond or White, bail. For those facing nonviolent charges, it's three hundred dollars, and 10 percent cash will be sufficient surety. Everyone make sure you issue a receipt, no checks."

"How about Orange, Harry Henderson, and Faye Sillinger?" Tom inquired.

"We'll allow Miss Sillinger to take the nonviolent bail. We don't have unimpeachable evidence that she shot Harper while he was still alive or even that she shot him at all. For the other two, however, a thousand-dollar property bond will be required. You and I will handle those."

Bob Brannigan whistled. "A thousand dollars with your property as surety; you'd just damn well better believe that I'd be wherever and whenever I was told to be."

The marshals fanned out, eager to finish their tasks and go home. Del Orange signed his paper, got his horse, and headed back to his farm. He seemed serene, Ward thought, yet anyone who was as phlegmatic as he was difficult to read. Harry Henderson agonized over the decision until being told that the option was being incarcerated in Shelbyville for an indefinite period. He signed his bond and went back to work.

The rest paid up, although some voiced their displeasure at the process. "Me and Billy got told we were Ted Harper with a badge," Rocky Bridges harrumphed.

"Who was that?" Ward asked.

"Your pal, Fred Reichert."

"Bullshit! He's got three separate businesses, all successful, and is probably among the most capable in this town of absorbing such a cost. I ought to revoke it and haul his complaining ass to Shelbyville. Was there anyone else?"

"Miss Sillinger wasn't happy," Brannigan stated. "That woman discombobulates me. If I was with her, I'd have to sleep with one eye open. She didn't gripe, just fixed us with a look that said you'd be dead if I had my way. I've been all over and haven't encountered that from a lady over two or three times."

"If you were with her, and the missus found out," Seibert teased, "you'd never rest easy. Might not be a derringer, but a frying pan or rolling pin might not be out of the question."

That brought a burst of general laughter, and the men bustled about in their preparations to leave. Wilkinson walked down the hall off the lobby and had a quick word with Sheriff Parslow, who was continuing to mend from his leg wound. He wished him well and said he'd see him at the trials. After that, he looked in Mr. Cochran's office, thanked him for his many kindnesses and accommodations during the stay, then went up to the room and grabbed his things. Tom's were already gone.

Downstairs, Ward checked them out, agreed upon the final amounts with McCormick, got all the receipts, then headed out for the last time. When the attorney general received the expense report for all the train tickets, lodging, meals, livery costs (including the rental of five horses), photography, and physician's charges, the man might well decide the results weren't worth the cost.

The desk clerk, now under arrest and smarting from forking over thirty dollars to stay out of jail, wished Ward neither a pleasant trip nor the hope he'd return. From the look on McCormick's face, Wilkinson reckoned he was hoping for a train derailment.

In the meantime, Brannigan and his deputy, Clay Moore, rousted Stuart Redmond and Ezra White from the hotel supply building and marched them down to Reichert's livery stable. "Well, ain't you a pretty sight," the marshal goaded the men, their still swollen faces wrapped in bandages. "Looks like you went a few rounds with John L. Sullivan." Then, his mood darkened. "Consider yourselves lucky. If it had been me, I'd have killed one of you to teach the other a lesson."

* * *

The livery was a blur of activity when Wilkinson arrived. Men were throwing saddles on horses while Seibert was informing Fred Reichert—"for the last damn time"—that he would meet his requisition for a wagon. "Look around," Reichert said, almost gibbering. "You see any wagons? You see any wagons anywhere?"

Tom turned from him in disgust, telling Ward that he was certain the man was secreting them. "The other day, there were two wagons down here. I saw them. My view is that we ought to rescind his bail and transport him to Shelbyville on the wagon we're going to have to get from Bill Martin."

Wilkinson considered that for a moment, then demurred. "I'll ride up there with you to get one. Mr. Reichert," he concluded, his tone withering, "at first, I felt sorry for you. But that's no longer true. You shall figure prominently in my report to the Attorney General."

Martin provided a wagon and a driver yet remained the surly, brusque individual they'd met before. "Go with these marshals and drive them damn fools over to Shelbyville," he told his employee. "When you get them there, take the wagon to the livery, change out the horses, and get back here. I'll not have you shillyshallying in town all night and expecting to be paid for Sunday."

At eleven, the cavalcade moved out, going out the north side of the square, then disappearing. Arriving at two, Brannigan, Bridges, and their deputies were in the nick of time to catch trains, hastening their goodbyes. "Good luck, Ward," Bob called from the window seat of his car as it lurched away from the platform. "Let me know when the baby comes."

* * *

The last passenger train to Nashville was gone, and it looked like Wilkinson and Seibert would stay the night. Wilkinson had the driver take the prisoners over to the sheriff's office while Seibert returned the rented horses the departing marshals had ridden. When he returned, Simon Garrett informed him that Ward was off to see the county prosecutor. "I've got your two punching bags in a cell back there," he told Tom. "While we're waiting for Marshal Wilkinson, take a load off and have some coffee."

Ward tied his mount to the courthouse hitching rail, then went up the steps. He thought he might be on a fool's errand coming here. It was Saturday afternoon, and government offices often closed by one o'clock. It surprised him when he found the door to the building unlocked and the county attorney, Aaron McKee, in his office.

The man, his tie discarded and the sleeves of his white shirt rolled up to the elbows, invited Ward inside, then produced a pair of glasses and a decanter of bourbon. "I'm pleased you could stop by, Marshal," he enthused. "I wanted to talk to you about your investigation, along with your contention that a jury willing to convict the killers of Ted Harper can't be impaneled in this county."

Wilkinson accepted the liquor and took an appreciative swallow. Over the next thirty minutes, he detailed the discovery of evidence, the identity of the suspects, and the arrests. He also enlightened McKee on the motives of the conspirators, laying bare the crimes and misdeeds of Ted Harper. "Del Orange told me he doubted any twelve men in this county, once they heard Harper's victims tell what he'd done to them, would ever agree to convict. I think that could be true, especially from the testimony of the female victims."

McKee poured a second measure, the deepening frown on his face showing that he didn't like what he'd heard. "Given what you've told me, you are doubtless correct. I'm not sure I could find one anywhere. Regardless, the state is going to prevail on me to prosecute. I will make a request for a venue change, preferably to Nashville since you're going to have Stuart Redmond in custody there. It may not make much difference, but few if anyone there will have heard of Ted Harper."

* * *

It was midafternoon when Ward returned to the jail. He was dreading a night on the hotel's lumpy mattresses and the unappetizing diner cuisine. That was one thing about Buckland Station he would miss. When he went inside, Tom arose from his chair, his voice filled with elation. "While you were gone, I went over to the freight depot and talked to the dispatcher. There's a train that will leave for Nashville at five-fifteen. It has to be replenished with wood and water, along with adding a car or two. It will arrive about a quarter to five. He says we can load our horses onto one of the cars being added and put the prisoners in the caboose so long as one of us keeps guard on them. Says we'll make home by eight-thirty."

Ward consulted his watch: three-thirty. "Let's get on over there. I'll send wires to our wives and another to Sheriff Culver. Hopefully, he can have deputies there to take Redmond and White to jail."

An hour later, the marshals were loading their mounts. Given Tom's sore ribs, Ward had him ride in the caboose with the prisoners while he stayed in the boxcar with the horses. Arriving on time, they were happy to see the sheriff, who marched the bandaged men to a waiting wagon. "What happened to these two?" he queried in a mocking tone. "Looks to me like they fell off a two-story building."

"Well, Ross," Wilkinson replied, "they tried to kill us. It didn't go so well for them."

"Could always take them up to the top floor of the jail some late night."

"Ah, better not. They're looking at ten to fifteen years, and that one in the blue shirt might be looking at a murder conviction. If so, the fall might be shorter but no less unpleasant."

Chapter 55

WILKINSON AND SEIBERT found their houses ablaze with light when they reached their doors. Their wives were joyous. Even Tom's testy daughter, Ruth, was in a good humor. "I don't want to see hide nor hair of you tomorrow," Ward told Tom as they parted, "unless the crime of the century is reported. We'll start on the Harper paperwork on Monday. If we're lucky, Judge Morton won't want to see our friends for a few days."

Charlotte met Ward at the door and melted into his arms. Her swollen stomach, he thought, seemed even more distended, and the humidity of the city, along with its odors, reminded him even more keenly that he wanted her away from Nashville when the time was near. "I'm so happy to have you home," she whispered, her breath warm against his cheek. "How was Buckland Station?"

"I think if the man whose murder we went there to investigate had never existed, it would be a lovely place. It's prosperous, well laid out, and has everything going for it since the railroad arrived. Unfortunately, it had the curse of a monster in its midst—one who took some of its residents down along with him. I'll tell you all about it tomorrow. For now, let's have a drink and go to bed; it's been some endless days."

They struggled out of bed the next morning and somehow found their way to church. Their appearance caught the Howells off guard. "Didn't know you were back, Ward," Obadiah said in greeting. "When did you get in?"

"About nine last night. We had a couple of prisoners with us. Fortunately, Sheriff Culver got my wire and was at the station to meet us. If he hadn't, it would have been ten or later getting to the house."

"Everything go alright?"

Wilkinson stifled a yawn. "Mostly. We made many arrests, all of whom made bond, except for those we brought here. They ambushed me and Tom outside Guthrie's saloon while we were searching for the bullet that didn't remain in Harper's body. It didn't work out so well for them."

"Either of you hurt?"

"Nicked up a little. I've got a cut that's healing well. Tom, though, took a couple of hard blows to his ribs. Dr. Demarest diagnosed them as bruised and said he might even have a couple cracked. He's been able to get around, even ride, but he's had a lot of pain."

"I'll be by tomorrow morning to examine him."

Helen Howell observed Charlotte's expression and realized she hadn't learned of this development before now. "Come to the house for lunch after the service," she encouraged. "We can talk more then."

Ward and Charlotte took their seats in the pew. "When were you going to tell me all this?" Charlotte asked, her voice less than cross but not happy either.

"Later today," Ward answered in a meek tone, realizing he was being chastised. "I didn't want to spoil being home with news that I couldn't improve upon no matter when I told it. Was rather hoping I could find a way to talk about it that wouldn't be upsetting. Seems I failed to manage that." His head was bent, and his eyes were fixed on the rounded top of the pew in front of them. Such was his misery that his wife's heart melted.

Charlotte thrust her arm inside Ward's and pulled him close. "Don't take on so," she whispered. "I'm not that disturbed. You can tell us all about it over lunch. I'll have something to talk about as well." At that, she turned enigmatic, saying little the rest of the hour.

* * *

The meal at the Howell's was very pleasant, after which they retired to the parlor for cake and coffee. "Before you leave," Obadiah said, "I have my report on Harper's autopsy ready. Remind me to give it to you."

"Thanks," Ward replied. "We've got to write up our findings for the attorney general tomorrow. It's going to be a large document. So too will be the expense report. By the time Tom's detailed the costs we ran up, the state may think twice before having us do something like this again."

"Let's hope so," Helen declared.

"I'm hoping," the doctor stated, his voice now serious, "that Tom's homecoming was as nice as yours. We had a long talk about Ruth the last night I was there in Buckland Station. She has a hard time coping with his absences; he says it's a longtime problem. The older she's got, the worse it is. Says Frances has tried to talk with her about the issue but has had little success."

"That may explain some of his jittery behavior while we were there," Ward replied. "He wasn't happy once he discovered what a wretched human being the deceased was. I offered to let him come home and go it alone at one point. I'm glad he didn't. Might not be here if he had."

"Regarding that, you were going to tell us about these prisoners of yours."

"You didn't meet any of them, Obadiah. One is Stuart Redmond. He is, according to evidence we obtained, one of the shooters of Ted Harper. The other is a local barfly, Jack of All Trades, master of none, acolyte of his. His name is Ezra White. He's short on brains and long on thirst. For drinking money, he sat outside the saloon on evenings when Redmond was there to see if the desk clerk at the hotel would bring any news about the shootings he'd overheard. He also gave Redmond early warning to clear out the back and go home if any strangers appeared."

Ward accepted more of Helen's excellent coffee and continued. "We figured out what they were doing and braced them with it. I'll let you read the report when I'm done. A few nights later, they ambushed us from behind the saloon while we were digging around in the dirt for that derringer slug. Just as we found it, they descended on us from the darkness and tried to knife us. Redmond came after me, White after Tom."

"What shape are they in?"

"According to Dr. Demarest, Redmond has a fractured cheek; I hit him with my pistol. White has a broken nose and possibly a fracture of his jaw. After Tom disarmed him, he kicked him in the backside as hard as I've ever seen it done. He was furious, and I can't say that I blame him. Ross Culver said the two of them looked like they'd fallen off a two-story building."

The description of the men's condition resulted in uncharitable laughter. "Better them than you," the doctor guffawed. When it subsided, Charlotte announced she had something to share.

"I know that you and Obadiah have been scheming for weeks to have me leave Nashville for the birth of our child," Charlotte told Ward. "While you were gone, I've made all the arrangements for the store to be managed while I'm away. It's still May, and I'm sweating like a pig. When do we leave?"

Chapter 56

MONDAY, MAY 28, found Wilkinson at the office by seven o'clock. There was two weeks' worth of correspondence to read and reply to, all the evidence from the Harper investigation to tag and store, plus the reports to prepare. Also, he needed to go up the street and inform Judge Morton of his return. He made coffee, sat at the battered worktable, and then made quick work of the mail. Some of it was trivial (which he condemned to the wastebasket), some was put in a "might answer someday" folder, there were a few wanted circulars, and there were a couple of items that he roundly damned for having to be answered right away. Taking out writing paper, he was scribbling away when Seibert entered the office at eight.

"Good morning, Tom," Ward greeted, his pen never faltering. "Coffee's on. I'm answering a letter from our masters in Washington. The damned fools want to decrease our budget for next year. Also, there's an inquiry here that arrived last Friday from a sheriff in Des Moines, Iowa. He's heard a rumor about Jeff Broughten."

"I wouldn't waste time with that. Send it over to the attorney general. After all, you and I are certain he's going to make some sort of accommodation with Delbert Flynn for him to be free from any out-of-state warrants."

"True, but I believe I'll approach it a different way. Since he's not wanted by us, I'll reply that his inquiry is a matter for the attorney general. By the time he gets my reply and resends it, maybe Flynn and the AG will have decided what their plan is for Broughten. Regardless, it keeps them out of our hair while we deal with this mess."

Wilkinson finished his letters, enjoyed some tasty oatmeal cookies that Tom brought fresh from Frances's oven, then headed up Broad Street to see the judge. Tom was already working away on the trip's expenses, a total, Ward thought, that would cause considerable stomach acid production when the state comptroller saw it. Minutes later, he entered the courthouse and arrived at the office of Harvey Bryant.

The young man, always in perpetual motion, was filing documents with his right hand while trying to read from another he held in his left. Hearing the marshal's bootheels on the floor, he turned and gave a quick smile. "The judge is preparing to hold a trial this morning," he revealed. "I'll see if he has a few minutes for you." A moment later, he was waving Ward forward. "It can only be four or five minutes. I'd advise getting to the point."

With a nod, Wilkinson strode forward. Going into the chambers, he spied Morton struggling into his robes. The judge motioned him to go ahead, and mindful of what Bryant had said, Ward spoke in clipped sentences. "We got back late Saturday, Your Honor. The two men who attacked us are in Sheriff Culver's jail. We are starting the reports this morning. Do you wish me to present my findings to you before I send them to the attorney general?"

The elder man's eyes flared. "Most definitely. I want to see why the state's attorney felt federal marshals needed to be requested to resolve a local matter. Further," he continued, "I'm curious. It sounds like it was an interesting case. Also, on Thursday, I want those two rapscallions that assaulted you and Marshal Seibert in this court for arraignment at ten o'clock. It's my intention to make an example of them. Tell Mr. Bryant to put that on the docket. Now," he concluded, checking himself in a mirror to see if he was tidy, "we can discuss this in more detail later. It's time for court to be in session."

* * *

Wilkinson returned to the office. Tom was continuing to go through the blizzard of receipts. He raised his head from the various piles he'd assembled and waved a single sheet on which he was adding sums. "I'm presuming all the chits are here," he called with an amused grin.

"When the AG sees this, he may have to change his drawers. I've totaled vouchers for trains, livery, hotels and meals, the photographer, Dr. Demarest's fees, Obadiah's postmortem fee, and the telegraph. Unless there's more or I've made an error, the amount is two hundred and fifty dollars."

Ward chuckled. "So may the comptroller. Those are all the receipts. Do the expense report, then tag and document the evidence. I'll start sketching out the overall document. Oh, Judge Morton wants us to have Redmond and White in his courtroom on Thursday at ten o'clock. Told me he's going to throw the book at them."

Seibert gave an affirmative grunt, then returned to his sums. Wilkinson went to his desk, took out a new sheet of paper, and pondered where to begin. Minutes later, with nothing more on the page than the facts and dates relating to being requested to investigate the murder of Ted Harper, his jaw clenched in determination. He was going to detail all of Harper's dirty laundry and be damned to those who wouldn't approve.

Ward began with the details of his interview with Sheriff Parslow. What had the man said about Harper: "threats, intimidation, cheating, and stealing." He constructed a few brief paragraphs about the dead man's early life, then referenced his reappearance in Buckland Station sometime following a train robbery that he'd taken part in with Jeff Broughten and the late, unlamented, Charlie Braxton. He also discussed the discovery of Broughten, a wanted felon but now foreman of the Harper farm, and the attempted robbery of the Buckland Station bank. This section of the report included Broughten's admission that he and Harper were involved in the Iowa robbery, that Harper ended up with most of the loot, and that Braxton's appearance was because he received none of his share.

Next was the interview with the widow, Denise Harper. Here, he examined Ted's deviously gained real estate holdings, the discovery of considerable sums of cash in the safe at his farmhouse, and the coded list that contained identification of his extortion victims, amounts paid, and when they were paid. To that he added a list of those victimized by Ted's scheme.

The succeeding paragraphs were about Faye Sillinger. Ward used her own words to illustrate how Harper had abused her, then referenced the examples of her handwriting. He listed the receipt for the baby clothes he'd artfully acquired, the note to Leroy Stafford inviting him to the meeting where the plotters planned Ted's demise, and the long-ago letter to the former Bedford County sheriff alleging the man had committed rape.

Ward followed that by examining the rest of the extorted business owners, their association with Harper, and how much he'd gouged them. He made a special note that Ted had preyed on the solitary, vulnerable, small, weak, or female. Those that were formidable, or had spouses that were, Harper had given a wide berth.

Last on the list was Fred Reichert. Wilkinson saved him until then, not out of antipathy for the man, but because his shooting by Harper was the catalyst for what came after. *The Reichert shooting*, he wrote, *resulted from a dispute between the smith and Mr. Harper over alleged dissatisfaction with farrier work performed.* He pointed out that eyewitnesses had divergent opinions on who first pulled a weapon, yet all agreed the complaint by Mr. Harper was bogus. Given that Mr. Reichert has a solid reputation as a blacksmith, that Mr. Harper was already extorting money from Mr. Reichert, and that he was also extorting goods and services from others instead of money, it could be construed that this was another instance in which Ted Harper was stealing. Further, given that he carried a pistol to Mr. Reichert's livery stable, one can surmise he went there expecting trouble or intending to cause it.

Wilkinson completed this discussion by introducing the written admission by the former sheriff. Harper had refused to be arrested, had made plain he'd draw on the officer if he attempted to take him into custody, and had only surrendered when his attorney, Delbert Flynn, agreed the time was right. With witnesses indecisive or given an incentive not to appear, the grand jury failed to return an indictment. This outcome caused certain residents of the community to decide that Harper was now so powerful that the law couldn't touch him.

To offer an illustration, Wilkinson inserted the interview with Perry Jessup and enumerated the schemes Harper had attempted to force the elderly man off his property. Jessup's statement that Ted had agreed to stop harassing him in exchange for failing to answer a grand jury subpoena was, Ward resolved, a satisfactory conclusion to this portion of his report. Only now, having laid out a scathing portrait of the deceased, did he turn to the murder.

Chapter 57

IT WAS THE growling of Wilkinson's stomach that caused him to raise his head. Where had Tom gone? He hadn't heard him say he was leaving. What time was it, anyway? He consulted his watch, and the positions of the hands on the dials left him fuming. "One-thirty. Three and half hours and barely half through this damn thing," he said aloud.

Ward spied a note on the corner of the worktable and walked over to it. It said: *Ward, I've finished the expense report and tagged all the evidence. Have gone home for lunch, may be late getting back. Ruth's been in a better mood since we've returned, and I want her to have my attention if she wishes it. Decided not to bother you when I went out. You hadn't said a word since you began writing, and I didn't want to break your concentration.*

Wilkinson stood there for a moment, groaned, stretched, and tried to decide whether to go down the street for something to eat. He was about to opt for more work when his stomach growled again, this time more irritably than before. Fetching his hat and linen duster, he was about to go out when the door opened, and Tom stepped inside. "It's alive," Tom proclaimed in a bantering fashion. "And just in time, too. Frances sent me along with a ham sandwich, some cheese, and a couple more of those oatmeal cookies you liked so well this morning. To top it off, I picked us up a couple of bottles of ale. Doubt it's as good as Guthrie's lager, but it'll hit the spot just the same."

Ward attacked the food with appreciation, reminding Tom on multiple occasions to thank his wife for her thoughtfulness. After he finished eating, they went out, walked a mile around the downtown area, then returned to the office. Refreshed, he sat back down and composed anew.

Ward began by writing about the day of the murder, April 14: *At twelve noon, outside of a saloon owned by Mr. Elijah Guthrie, Mr. Harper, while waiting to receive payoffs from his extortion scheme, was shot and killed by at least three individuals. These are Delvin Orange, Harry Henderson, and Stuart Redmond. Despite it being on Saturday, in the middle of the day, no one has ever come forward to admit seeing the act or the individuals escape. As stated in the report of Sheriff Parslow, there was an organized agreement among the planners and many townspeople not to cooperate with any inquiry.*

Here, Wilkinson referenced the autopsy report of Dr. Obadiah Howell. It was, as he expected, thorough and compact. *The deceased was Theodore Harper, a man of thirty-six years. He expired from several gunshots, principally from one that entered his back and lodged in his lungs. Death from this wound was unavoidable and would have occurred in a brief time.*

The bullet was a .45-75 caliber. Its trajectory suggests the shooter fired from a distance away. Two bullets were from handguns, one a .38 caliber, the other from a .32. These struck the deceased at a much closer range, while he was crouched or in a kneeling or sitting position. Neither of these shots would have caused the near-instantaneous demise of Mr. Harper as the first shot did.

There was evidence of a fourth shot striking Mr. Harper, but the bullet wasn't in the body. The trajectory of this shot, perhaps fired from a derringer, was straight down while the victim was lying on his back, and it was possibly inflicted after death or at least while he was unconscious. The result was massive damage to the testicles. This last bullet would have resulted in severe hemorrhaging, soon resulting in death from exsanguination.

Ward continued: *During the investigation, Marshal Seibert and I found a spent .45-75 cartridge near the right rear corner of Guthrie's saloon, to the rear of where Mr. Harper was shot, a distance of thirty to forty feet. Evidence suggests Mr. Delvin Orange, a local farmer, fired this shot. Mr. Orange, a noted sharpshooter during the Civil War, was, according to certain evidence, the principal planner in the plot to murder Mr. Harper. Mr. Orange owns a Model 76 Winchester .45-75 rifle, which is in our custody.*

Due to the discovery of certain other evidence, I executed a search warrant on Friday, May 25, 1883, at the residence of Miss Faye Sillinger of Buckland Station. Found in her possession was a .38-caliber Smith & Wesson Model 2 revolver, a .32-caliber Ivor Johnson pocket pistol, and a .41-caliber Remington derringer. These weapons are believed to be the ones employed in the shooting. It is also believed, but not certain, that Miss Sillinger fired the bullet from the derringer. These weapons are in our custody.

Wilkinson, having dealt with the circumstances of the murder, identifying the shooters, and discovery of the weapons, then focused his attention on the conspiracy. He began his chronicle with their first day in town. He wrote: *On the night of our arrival in Buckland Station, the plotters spotted and suspicioned Marshal Seibert and me. Mr. Andrew McCormick, desk clerk at the hotel, went to Guthrie's saloon as soon as we checked in to report to Mr. Ronald Whipple, a dry goods store operator and one of the planners, our arrival. Mr. Whipple, Stuart Redmond, and Harry Henderson, the latter two being among Mr. Harper's alleged killers, derived a scheme after the fact to spend part of their afternoons, two days a week, in Guthrie's saloon to receive intelligence from Mr. McCormick. Henderson was there Monday and Tuesday; Whipple, Wednesday and Thursday; Redmond on Friday and Saturday.*

Later that same evening, we followed Mr. McCormick to Mr. Reichert's livery stable. Inside, there was a clandestine meeting involving five people. These people included Del Orange, Andrew McCormick, Ronald Whipple, and Fred Reichert. The fifth man, most likely, was Stuart Redmond or Harry Henderson. Overheard were remarks that indirectly referred to the plot, speculation about who we were, and assertions by Mr. Reichert that Marshal Seibert and I were gunmen hired by Mrs. Harper and ought to be killed. Mr. Orange ordered the attendees not to harm us, advising we might be Pinkerton agents or lawmen. They did not follow this good advice.

Wilkinson then listed the remaining people he and Seibert had interviewed and noted whether they'd been cooperative. He mentioned their specific comments, usually vitriolic, about the deceased. Of particular importance, he recorded every instance where someone admitted, even obliquely, that there was a plot or that they knew some of its details. He reiterated that most knew about the plan to kill Harper. As he'd promised the man, Ward took pains to state Fred Reichert's deliberate attempts to hamstring their inquiry. He concluded with: *The only reason we succeeded where the sheriff did not was his inexperience and our long-term familiarity with criminal investigations, especially murder.*

The following paragraphs detailed the elaborate ploy crafted by the secretive confectioner, Stuart Redmond. Wilkinson wrote: *It was his goal to prevent himself and fellow conspirators from being descended upon in Guthrie's saloon by potential gunmen or lawmen.* To follow that, he discussed the attempt made on his and Seibert's lives. He introduced Ezra White, White's role as Redmond's lookout, and how he and Seibert had unraveled their subterfuge. He contended: *This discovery was key, providing tangible evidence of a conspiracy that continued after the fact of the crime.*

Continuing, Ward wrote: *On the evening of May 22, while searching for the bullet not found in the Harper autopsy, Marshal Seibert and I were suddenly and viciously attacked by Mr. Redmond and Mr. White. Despite inflicting injuries on us, we overcame them, and they are now in the Davidson County jail. They're charged with the attempted murder of federal marshals. During that search, Marshal Seibert and I found the last bullet. It was a .41-caliber slug.*

Wilkinson went on to discuss Harper's use of the town's fire insurance map to create the code names for his extortion victims and mentioned that Dr. Obadiah Howell unraveled it. Then, having dispensed with all other issues, he turned to the search warrants.

Ward had already disposed of the search of Faye Sillinger's home, and he dispensed of the rest, save for Jeanne Clarke's, in a few words. From time to time in the report, he'd employed information from her diary, mostly for chronological purposes. Yet now, he turned to the major events in the plot to kill Ted Harper. Her smitten suitor, Larry

Everhart, had furnished these events and revealed all the secrets the collaborators had sworn to protect. Clarke's late-night ministrations, Ward mused upon once again with a shake of his head, must have been something to behold.

Quoting from Jeanne's diary, Wilkinson listed those arrested for murder: Del Orange, Stuart Redmond, and Harry Henderson. All of them were free on bond except Redmond. Those charged with conspiracy or being accessories were Sillinger, Reichert, Whipple, McCormick, and Ezra White. All of them were out on bond except for White.

Despite his liking for Elijah Guthrie, Ward came close to charging the man with conspiracy. He never truly believed his assertions that he knew nothing of the shooting or that Redmond and the others were using the saloon as an intelligence drop. Larry Everhart fit the same frame, but Ward figured in the weeks and months ahead, Everhart and Miss Clarke would have enough problems. If the prosecutor wished to add to them by presenting evidence against them at the grand jury proceedings, that would be his business. Notwithstanding their surreptitious love affair, many others would finger-point, saying they were solely responsible for the arrests, and perhaps punishments, of the conspirators. He had a niggling feeling that she'd be blamed the most. That thought made him sad.

Wilkinson's summation remained, and seeing that the day was far advanced, he went about it with a will. He began: *At noon, on April 14, 1883, Mr. Theodore Harper was standing near the corner of Mr. Elijah Guthrie's saloon in Buckland Station, Tennessee. Evidence states he was there to receive illicit payments from Mr. Stuart Redmond and Mr. Harry Henderson, two local business owners from whom he was extorting money. Moments after these men arrived, they participated in the killing of Mr. Harper. Besides the aforementioned, the evidence shows that a third shooter was Mr. Delvin Orange. His participation was likely caused by Redmond and Henderson's lack of proficiency with firearms. Mr. Orange is a crack shot.*

It is probable, yet not definite, that Miss Faye Sillinger was present or nearby and fired a fourth shot into the body of Mr. Harper. As aforementioned, the slug found buried in the ground outside the saloon matches the caliber of a derringer found in her possession.

After the act, the shooters rapidly left the scene, at least according to those queried about the matter. Some person or persons, presumably the shooters, rifled Mr. Harper's trouser and coat pockets, apparently in search of a small book in which he kept track of his nefarious activities. This item, never recovered, was probably destroyed. However, the records recovered from Harper's safe are thought to mimic the contents of the book. Deceased's widow, Denise Harper, freely gave these records; no warrant was required.

Made mention of by every person questioned was the lack of shoppers on that Saturday. Most referred to lower-than-normal numbers entering their establishments and mentioned that the numbers decreased as the morning hours advanced. This suggests it was an open secret that an attempt on Mr. Harper's life was going to be made. No one wanted to be around to be struck by an errant shot, have to lie about seeing anything, or perhaps be accused by Mr. Harper of being in on the plot if he survived.

The shooters departed in a wagon that was parked behind the saloon. The person who brought it there was likely Mr. Orange. With the tail dropped and tall box boards to shield those in the bed, it was a matter of moments to climb aboard and for Mr. Orange to drive away. Wheel tracks in that location are like those of a wagon I saw at Mr. Perry Jessup's farm. Mr. Orange had the opportunity to help himself to it. While the tire tracks are similar, dray wagons make regular deliveries to Mr. Guthrie's saloon via a rear door of the building. Given that we discovered these tracks a month after the killing, this evidence is not conclusive.

It's further believed Mr. Orange drove the wagon in a southeasterly direction until he was well beyond the row of shops that line the south side of railroad square. At that point, his shooters disembarked and made their way home. Mr. Orange presumably returned to his farm. The area beyond the square is populated with a scattering of private dwellings, and it might be possible, given it was the noon hour, to move through the area unnoticed.

It was a short walk for Mr. Redmond, yet only one person observed him: Mr. John Ferguson, owner of the print shop. Mr. Henderson's route was longer, yet nobody admits having observed him outside that day. It is significant that several people observed Miss Sillinger walking in a northeasterly direction toward her shop around twelve-thirty. The belief is she was transporting the weapons used in the shooting. Also significant is her statement that she didn't venture out that day.

Having planned and executed their plot to kill Mr. Harper, those involved moved to protect themselves by presenting a united front to all inquiries about the murder. They encased themselves in the armor of interconnected lies and plausible denials about where they'd been that day, what they'd done, and what they'd seen and heard. Those who were on the fringes of the conspiracy, along with those who'd had no part in it at all, joined in, believing the action essential to further protect their community. Many feel that those who took action did so on their behalf. They view them as heroes.

Ward paused for several minutes, reflecting on what he would say in conclusion. Over the years, he and Tom had worked several cases where the perpetrators, vile as their actions might be, were capable of generating sympathy. One of the worst had been a hotel operator who'd gruesomely murdered three men he held responsible for failing to come to the aid of his sister while she was being sexually assaulted. After the woman died, he'd gone on a rampage. This situation, Ward decided, was one of them.

Wilkinson desired to convey compassion without excusing: *It is clear from the preponderance of the evidence that the deceased, Mr. Harper, was a feared and despised man in his community for a decade prior to his death. Nevertheless, this investigation uncovered nothing illegal in his transactions prior to the winter of 1881. Any instances occurring prior to that date are unknown.*

Beginning that winter, Mr. Harper, through personal threats and intimidation, extorted money, services, and property from a growing number of victims in the merchant community of Buckland Station. This culminated in a dispute with Mr. Fred Reichert, one of Mr. Harper's victims, that resulted in the serious wounding of Mr. Reichert.

The citizens of the town watched as Mr. Harper set the law at defi-

ance. He refused to be arrested, threatened violence if an attempt was made, then allegedly used bribery along with the talents of his attorney to influence the grand jury not to return an indictment against him. Only then did the citizenry band together to take action.

A group of the small merchant class, in league with a respected local farmer, banded together for the specific and illegal purpose of taking the life of Mr. Theodore Harper. They did so because they no longer believed in the lawfully appointed authorities in their county to protect them from crime. Therefore, they took matters into their hands, becoming judge, jury, and executioner. In such a guise, they meted out a rough form of frontier justice, an act they must answer for in a duly constituted court.

Ward finished with: *In the town of Buckland Station and even Bedford County at large, law enforcement, punishment of crime, and the administration of justice failed during the past several years. It's possible that it could occur again.*

Epilogue

WHEN DELBERT FLYNN read Wilkinson's investigation report, his rage was titanic. The state comptroller's wrath when he discovered the cost of the inquiry was even more prodigious. Enlisting the aid of the attorney general, the legislator garnered an audience with Judge Morton and demanded he order the marshal to excise most of the first half of his report. He was angered beyond reason when the venerable jurist refused.

"Just because you gentlemen disagree with the conclusions of this report doesn't mean they aren't valid," Morton told them. "I won't require Marshal Wilkinson to delete a single word. Mayhap in the future, you'll think carefully before requesting federal officers' assistance and handle the work with your own resources. Further, if I learn that you've quashed the evidence he and Marshal Seibert discovered about Mr. Harper in the trials of his alleged murderers, I'll make it my business to see it introduced during the attempted murder trials of Mr. Redmond and Mr. White."

On the way down Broad, their meeting ended, Flynn fulminated about having the judge impeached. "Did you hear him imply he was going to invite Timothy Billings to the proceedings? That dirty sonofabitch!"

The attorney general, well acquainted with Morton, told the man to save his breath. "Spewing verbal diarrhea about the street, boasting that you'll have him removed, is an exercise in futility. You can't threaten him, and he knows it. I'd advise you to coordinate with the Bedford County prosecuting attorney to determine how you want to manipulate these trials."

Aaron McKee resented Delbert Flynn's interference. Despite that, owing to his own political ambitions, he found it necessary to humor him. To a few trusted friends, he referred to the legislator as a "meddlesome asshole" behind his back. Most of June was taken up with parliamentary sparring between the young prosecutor and a capable Nashville attorney, who was hired by the merchants of Buckland Station. Sensing that sentiment for Ted Harper was lower than a well bottom, he campaigned for the trials to be conducted in Shelbyville. This put McKee in the awkward stance of having to petition the State Supreme Court for a change of venue.

By the time the court rendered its decision, Wilkinson and Seibert were in Muscle Shoals, Alabama, investigating fraudulent military contracting and murder. Charlotte, finding the blazing heat of Nashville intolerable as her pregnancy neared its conclusion, was enjoying the cool breezes of Monteagle. The judicial panel ordered the trials to take place in the capital city.

McKee had artfully obtained indictments against the conspirators without revealing any of Harper's dark history, yet that would soon change. The preliminary hearing was as mundane as could be until McKee made motions to suppress testimony from Faye Sillinger, Jeanne Clarke, and several others. The result was a full-blown argument that ended with the courtroom cleared and a conference in the judge's chambers. Although he agreed to take the motions under advisement, he soon rejected them as unfair to the defendants.

In August, their Alabama assignment concluded, Ward rushed from the Tennessee River to Monteagle for the birth of his child, a girl he and Charlotte named Agnes. Back at home, Tom found his daughter, Ruth, sulky again and his wife, Frances, worried. Word came that the early trials would begin on September 3rd.

It soon became apparent to Aaron McKee, and especially Delbert Flynn, that Faye Sillinger's testimony would be a disaster. Her deposition, despite whatever else it included, detailed her molestation by Ted Harper. Also, the prosecutor realized he'd be unable to shake her from her statements. When he met her, she fixed him with a stare of loathing so fervent that it staggered him.

The defense attorney was preparing to add the testimony of Fred Reichert and intended to buttress it with Perry Jessup's assertion that Harper had bribed him to prevent his appearance before the Bedford County grand jury. In addition, he was going to call Jeff Broughten to the stand and interrogate him about his knowledge of Ted's bank and train robbing days. He also stated that if McKee introduced Jeanne Clarke's diary into evidence, he'd call her to the stand and acquaint the jury with how Harper had extorted money from her and Larry Everhart. He had a hunch there might be a man on the jury who was in an extramarital relationship or had a relative or friend who was.

Finding themselves wrongfooted, McKee and Flynn backpedaled. Asking for a delay in the major trials, they approached the defense and offered to drop the accessory charges and then allow the rest of the defendants to plead to a simple charge of obstruction of justice with a minimum sentence. All, except for Faye Sillinger, agreed.

On September 10, the judge accepted the plea deals, sentenced the defendants to a year in prison, then stunned the prosecution by suspending the sentences. With that result, McKee threw up his hands and let Sillinger walk.

All that remained was the ticklish problem of what to do about Orange, Redmond, and Henderson. Denise Harper, taking a shrewd, pragmatic view of the matter, told her brother to get out of the mess as quietly and cheaply as he could. So long as there wasn't a public record of her husband's disreputable actions, she didn't give a damn what people said behind her back. She had his real estate, his labor contracts, and Jeff Broughten, who'd received an amnesty from the attorney general, eating out of her hand. She'd make out alright.

The judge agreed to a best interest motion to drop the charges against the men for lack of evidence, but not before clearing the courtroom and subjecting McKee to one of the most humiliating denunciations ever administered in a Tennessee court. He called the prosecutor a "dunderhead, an incompetent idiot from a mudsill backwoods county, and the finest example ever that proved future lawyers ought to be the product of a professional education." At the end of his diatribe, the judge advised: "The next time you find yourself immersed in a matter such as this, young sir, either recuse yourself or decide that you'll not yield to political influence. Now, compose yourself," he said kindlier, "the court is going to reconvene."

Wilkinson and Seibert were in the courtroom when Del Orange's prosecution and that of his co-conspirators ended with a whimper. The farmer and former sharpshooter met the marshals' gaze and gave them a placid "I told you so" look. His view that no court would condemn anyone for terminating the life of a man with a perverted legacy like Ted Harper's carried the day. Harry Henderson just looked relieved. Stuart Redmond, awaiting trial in the attempted murder of Ward and Tom, was in handcuffs. He exited the building and went back to jail.

In the end, it fell to Redmond and Ezra White to take the fall for the rest. In October, a jury convicted both men. Redmond, doubtless the instigator of the attack, received fifteen years' imprisonment. White received twelve, which Judge Morton later told Ward was "leniency in the presence of stupidity."

During a noonday meal, it greatly amused Tom when Ward told him Judge Morton's reasoning. "Well, Ezra has got none smarter, that's for certain," Tom declared. "When I kicked his ass, it affected what little brains he possessed. It will afflict him for life."

"I can't say I'm sad this case ended this way," Wilkinson declared once he'd ceased laughing.

"Neither am I," Seibert agreed. "I'll always be of the opinion that Ted got what he deserved. Let's get back to the office. There's a half-day of paperwork to do, and Sheriff Culver came by while you were at Judge Morton's. He wants us to look into a suspicious death over in Edgefield."

From the Publisher

Thank You from the Publisher

Van Rye Publishing, LLC ("VRP") sincerely thanks you for your interest in and purchase of this book.

VRP hopes you will please consider taking a moment to help other readers like you by leaving a rating or review of this book at your favorite online book retailer. You can do so by visiting the book's product page and locating the button for leaving a rating or review.

Thank you!

Resources from the Publisher

Van Rye Publishing, LLC ("VRP") offers the following resources to readers and to writers.

For *readers* who enjoyed this book or found it useful, please consider receiving updates from VRP about new and discounted books like this one. You can do so by following VRP on Facebook (at www.facebook.com/vanryepub), Twitter (at www.twitter.com/vanryepub), or Instagram (at www.instagram.com/vanryepub).

For *writers* who enjoyed this book or found it useful, please consider having VRP edit, format, or fully publish your own book manuscript. You can find out more and submit your manuscript at VRP's website (at www.vanryepublishing.com).

Thank you again!

About the Author

JAMES T. SIBURT attended Virginia Polytechnic Institute & State University and Vanderbilt University, where he earned post graduate degrees in History and in Library & Information Science. His previous written works, published in various magazines and journals, are on Tennessee history and Civil War military topics, and he contributed two articles to the 1996 *Tennessee Encyclopedia of History & Culture*. His fiction writing includes several volumes of historical mysteries and police procedurals, most of them set in late nineteenth-century Tennessee. Retired from a thirty-year career as librarian for the US Army Corps of Engineers—Nashville District, he currently resides in Hendersonville, Tennessee. In addition to writing, his interests include travel, golf, and the National Hockey League's Nashville Predators.

Made in the USA
Middletown, DE
29 November 2025

23526369R00175